The Mapmaker and the Pope

A NOVEL BY

RON MESSIER

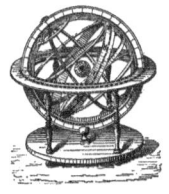

The Mapmaker and the Pope

A NOVEL BY

RON MESSIER

TWIN
OAKS
PRESS

ISBN-13: 978-1-937937-27-0

First Paperback Edition
January 2021

Printed in The United States of America

Twin Oaks Press
twinoakspress@gmail.com
www.twinoakspress.com

Design
Art Growden

Cover Illustration
Kevin Faulkner

*To all my professors who have guided me and inspired me,
and to my students who continue to journey near and far
in their search for knowledge.*

TABLE OF CONTENTS

Author's Note 1

Prologue 4

Part I, Chapter One 9

Chapter Two 18

Chapter Three 32

Chapter Four...41

Chapter Five..50

Chapter Six 58

Part II, Chapter Seven 64

Chapter Eight..79

Chapter Nine 93

Chapter Ten 103

Chapter Eleven..114

Part III, Chapter Twelve 124

Chapter Thirteen...133

Chapter Fourteen 140

Chapter Fifteen 150

Chapter Sixteen...157

Chapter Seventeen...166

Chapter Eighteen 177

Part IV, Chapter Nineteen 193

Chapter Twenty...205

Chapter Twenty-One..214

Chapter Twenty-Two..221

Chapter Twenty-Three...227

Epilogue..232

Acknowledgements..239

For Further Reading...243

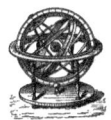

AUTHOR'S NOTE

In 1970, I spent the winter in Cairo, Egypt, looking at the works of medieval Arab geographers. I bought a copy of *Kitab Surat al-Ard* (The book of the picture of the earth), written by Mohammad Abū'l-Qāsim Ibn Hawqal. It is a detailed description of the many places that Ibn Hawqal saw on his travels from one end of the Islamic world to the other. It is accompanied by a series of maps that he drew: a map of the world and a series of regional maps. It is his regional map of the Mediterranean world that especially struck me. It looks more like a map as we know maps than does any other of that period. The general shape of the Mediterranean is quite recognizable, the Iberian Peninsula, Italy, Greece, the Bosphorus, the east coast of the Mediterranean, the Nile River, the North African coast all the way to Morocco on the Atlantic Ocean, the Atlas Mountains, the Strait of Gibraltar, and back to Iberia. Although the map is clearly not to scale, the place-names that we know, especially along the coastline, are roughly in the correct locations relative to each other and relative to recognizable physical features such as rivers and mountains.

We know very little of Ibn Hawqal's personal life. We know where he was born, but not the year. We know where he went and where he was at a few specific points in time because he tells us that. From descriptions of what he observed, we can form some judgements about what interested him. Other than that, we know very little of his personal thoughts and feelings. We sense, perhaps, his ideological sympathy for and loyalty to the Fatimid dynasty ruling first from its capital in modern-day Tunisia and then from Egypt. I was intrigued by the suggestion by some scholars that he might have been a *da'i*, an Ismaili Shiite propagandist, or even an intelligence agent—a spy. What an interesting combination: an intelligence agent whose mind was sharp enough to figure out how to produce visual images of the landscape for which he had to prepare intelligence reports to his employers, who were testing the waters as to where they would expand their state, westward into Morocco or eastward toward Egypt. Whether he really was an intelligence agent or not, we can only speculate. Based on the medieval sources, we cannot prove it conclusively one way or the other.

Since we know so little about Ibn Hawqal, yet speculate so much, I have named the mapmaker in this story Hakeem Ibn al-Harith al-Nusaybini. He is not Ibn Hawqal, but a man who, from what we know and what we can imagine, is *like* Ibn Hawqal. The mapmaker does interact with real historical characters: The Fatimid caliph in Mahdiya; Jawhar, the commander of the Fatimid army; the rival caliphs in Baghdad and Córdoba; the emir of Sijilmasa. Many of the minor characters in the story are simply invented but remain, I hope, in the realm of what is plausible.

The pope, the other principal character in this story, is Gerbert d'Aurillac, who later became Pope Sylvester II. He grabbed my attention when I spent time in Fez, Morocco, in the mid-1980s. There is a very strong tradition in Fez that Gerbert, as a young man, spent time there at the Qarawayeen University, one of the oldest universities in the world. That idea was recently endorsed by Professor Eamonn Gearon in his lecture "Qairouan University" in the Great Courses series "Turning Points in Middle East History." It is further confirmed by Gerbert's earliest biographers and, perhaps more reliably, by the *Oxford Dictionary of National Biography*. We know that he studied in the diocese of Vic in northern Spain, just beyond the frontier of the Islamic caliphate of Córdoba. There is strong speculation that he also spent time in Córdoba, arguably the most important intellectual center in the western Islamic world.

Although we know far more of Gerbert's life, we do not know exactly when he was born either. He was a full generation younger than Ibn Hawqal, perhaps twenty or thirty years younger. Given that Gerbert was a brilliant scholar of mathematics and astronomy as it was taught in the Islamic world, plus the fact that he eventually constructed an armillary sphere to illustrate the positions of the heavenly bodies as they orbited around the earth, it seems highly plausible that he would have gone to Córdoba and on to Fez. He could well have been there when Ibn Hawqal was there. It is not beyond the realm of imagination that he could have met the mapmaker, that the mapmaker could have served, if only briefly, as one of Gerbert's mentors.

Gerbert, toward the end of his life, was chosen to be pope of the Catholic Church. He was invested as pope in April 999—the eve of Y1K, the first millennium! There is some debate among scholars as to how much angst the end of the millennium produced in Europe. It seems logical that many, if not most, people were barely aware of the significance of the event, or even aware of the event itself. On the other hand, there is some evidence that many people took the "scare" very seriously. Those who remember Y2K not so long ago can easily relate to this. Gerbert's reaction to Y1K is quite revealing.

Elizabeth Hickey, in her author's note at the end of her novel *The Painted Kiss*, the story of the relationship between Viennese painter Gustav Klimt and his model/mistress, says, "The act of writing historical fiction is inherently a compromise. The literal truth, as opposed to the artistic truth, of characters' lives rarely (if ever) allows for the successful plotting of a novel." At the end of her brief note, she concludes, "The aim of historical fiction is not to render the past exactly as it happened—an impossible task—but to imagine it as it might have been."

The Mapmaker and the Pope is the story of how these two individuals, brilliant in their own right, became the men they were, how they acquired the knowledge and the skills to do the work they did. My task as an author and yours as readers is to imagine the challenge of learning how to draw a map of the world, let alone of the world in an age when maps as we know them did not exist; to experience the challenge of learning how to use an astrolabe, perhaps even of building one. Descriptions of these processes may seem quite daunting. But they reflect how I imagine the mapmaker and the pope, each in his own world, struggled with them. If you find these sections difficult to follow, slow down, proceed step by step. You can vicariously experience some of their frustration, some of their struggle to understand.

Each of these men was drawn away from his love of learning into the realm of politics and intrigue. Yet in so many ways, they were very much alike. When they finally came together, they were able to share their respective worldviews and innermost beliefs.

A word on non-English-language names and numbers. I have attempted to render non-English words and names as simply a possible. Where Anglicized versions exist, I used them. When I felt compelled to use Arabic words, I rendered them in a simplified form without diacritical marks, providing a translation where the narrative allowed. Although I refer to the adoption of Hindu and Arabic numerals, I use westernized versions of "Arabic" numerals to enable readers in English to understand them. Rather than rendering place-names in Arabic script as they appear on maps that I reproduced, I use Latin or Roman script.

THE MAPMAKER AND THE POPE

PROLOGUE

rother Anthony set down his red quill, blotted the ink on the letter his patron had asked him to write, and wiped the nervous sweat from his brow. He signed and sealed the letter: *Written by the hand of Anthony, Notary and Secretary of the Holy Roman Church.* The heading of the letter read: *Rome. December 31, 999. Sylvester II to Erkanbald, Abbot of Fulda.*

Brother Anthony was a cleric of the Canons of the Basilica of Saint John Lateran. He was honored to be the pope's personal secretary and humble servant. He was a small man, thin, befitting his ascetic lifestyle. His head was close-shaven, his dark beard cut rather short, neat, giving his sunken cheeks a shadowed look. His eyes, bright and wide open, revealed his curious nature. He had attended the cathedral school and learned to read and write. In fact, he had read much of Holy Scripture and even a few books that he had managed to borrow from the pope's personal library. He was learned enough to know that according to the Julian calendar, this was the last day of the year.

In spite of his perspiration, or maybe because of it, Anthony felt chilled. As he always did in winter, he was wearing the simple habit of a monk, made of heavy, undyed wool. He lifted the pointed hood of his habit from his shoulders and covered his head. He read the letter again. He was not anxious about the letter for what it said. It was a straightforward missive confirming Erkanbald as abbot and exempting the monastery from all control except that of the Holy See. Rather, it was what the letter did not say: no mention, not the slightest hint, of this day, the last day of the millennium, the day he believed the world would come to an end.

As Brother Anthony sat there staring at the letter he had just finished, His Holy Father the pope seemed to recognize his secretary's anxiety.

"Brother Anthony, I know that you are particularly anxious today and I know why. But it is time for us to leave for Saint Peter's to celebrate the Vigil of the Circumcision of our Lord. When the mass is over, after midnight, we shall return home, get a full night's sleep, and start anew the new millennium. Trust me, everything will be fine."

Anthony saw in the pope's full, round face the same seriousness and calm, thoughtful gaze that the pope always seemed to have. He wondered if that look was just a mask the pope wore to hide the deep concerns that his office surely presented.

"How can you be so sure, Holy Father? You know what people are saying about the end of the world. Preachers have described omens in the heavens—a fiery meteor streaking across the sky. Another told of a giant torch falling through an opening in the roof of the celestial globe, and when the gap closed a giant dragon appeared. In Aquitaine they say that it rained blood, staining people's clothing. French nuns report seeing fiery armies in the sky."

"Brother Anthony, you know that these are just stories told to frighten us."

"Yes, Holy Father," Brother Anthony was now talking more quickly, "but what of the rash of great fires that ravished many of the great cities in France and Italy? Even here in Rome, flames scorched the huge beams supporting our own Saint Peter's."

"Yes, but thanks be to God," the pope was quick to respond, "the cities averted widespread destruction. And as you recall in our own near disaster, the prayers of the faithful directed to Saint Peter himself caused the flames to retreat."

"But the famines brought on by droughts, floods, and feudal wars—"

"Are these any worse than they have been in decades past? They may seem so only because they happen to be upon us now."

"You know what they are saying about the Day of Judgement, Holy Father. You know what they are saying about…" Anthony hesitated. "About you, Your Holiness."

"Just what are they saying about me, Brother Anthony?" The pope wrinkled his forehead, even though he must have already known the answer to the question.

"They say that you are a magician, that you are a sorcerer, that you studied among the Saracens in Spain and in Africa, that you sold your soul to the devil in exchange for knowledge. Some say that your crosier is the iron scepter of the anti-Christ foretold in the book of Revelation—a sure sign that the world is coming to an end."

"And do you believe what they say, my son, about me?"

"Well…no, Holy Father. But I do not understand why you are so calm about our possible impending doom! I wish you would explain that to me."

"Of course, my son, but we must go. We can talk on the way to Saint Peter's."

The Holy Father, Pope Sylvester II, vicar of Christ here on earth, and his devoted servant Brother Anthony wrapped themselves in heavy cloaks and stepped out into the cold December night. The pope's carriage awaited them in the inner courtyard of the Papal Palace adjacent to the Church of Saint John Lateran. It was a closed carriage with heavy curtains covering the window openings. The carriage exited the courtyard through the tall gate between the two towers at the west end of the palace. It continued on a western route toward the great Basilica of Saint Peter. Perhaps to ease his nervousness, every few minutes Brother Anthony pushed aside the curtain over the window next to him to gauge their progress through the streets of Rome. They soon passed the Colosseum, the venue of such spectacles as gladiator combat and the martyrdom of saints now a little more than a half millennium ago. He could only imagine the clamor of the cheering crowds, replaced now only by the howling wind. The Colosseum stood in eerie silhouette against the moonlit sky, no longer a symbol of Rome's ancient glory. In fact, it stood in semi-ruin, a quarry for urban construction elsewhere in the city and for the aristocratic estates in the surrounding countryside.

Rome in this era of the Ottonian emperors was a far cry from the Rome of the caesars. The city's population had exceeded one million inhabitants in the second century after Caesar Augustus. In the era of Emperor Otto III and Pope Sylvester II, less than twenty thousand people remained. Vast empty spaces hollowed out the center of the former great city, now reduced to several small settlements centered around the sixty or so churches. Was not such a drastic retrenchment of the once great city in itself a sign of the imminent end-times?

They rode in silence these first several minutes. Perhaps the pope was mentally rehearsing his sermon for the eve of the Feast of Christ's Circumcision, the eve of the new millennium. Or maybe he was trying to decide just how much of his own story he was willing to share with his secretary.

"It is true, my son, some of what they say," the pope began. "I have traveled into the world of Islam, and I have studied with Muslim scholars in Córdoba and very briefly in the city of Fez."

Brother Anthony was not startled by this admission. It confirmed some of what he had heard in the rumors. But he was surprised by His Holiness's forthrightness.

The pope continued, "By far the most interesting of them all was a man called Hakeem Ibn al-Harith al-Nusaybini.

The carriage had reached the ancient Roman Forum, another witness to the bygone glory of the empire. But Brother Anthony's attention was now focused entirely on what the pope was saying.

"We only spent a few months together. I have never admitted this to anyone else, but he had a greater influence on me than any other teacher I have had. During his lifetime, he traveled to the ends of the earth. And he drew pictures of his routes to better report his findings to an ambitious rival to the caliph of Baghdad. We call these pictures 'maps.' He understood both the heavens and the earth better than anyone else I have ever met. He often found himself skirting the border between the world of Christendom and the house of Islam. He taught me how to negotiate those borderlands."

"If your Muslim teachers were as learned as you say, were they not concerned about the end of the world at the end of the millennium?"

"They were not," the pope replied. "And I will tell you why. For them, it is not the end of the millennium. According to their calendar, today's date is the twentieth day of the month of Muharram in the year 390. The Muslim calendar begins with the Prophet Mohammed's migration from Mecca to Medina in the year 622 of our calendar. They are a long way from the end of their millennium."

The carriage passed the Church of Sancta Maria in Capitolio as they circled around the northern edge of the Capitoline hill. The Church of San Marco was already in sight on the right-hand side of the Via Sacra. There was an open stretch of road as the Via Sacra turned to the north toward the Ponte San Pietro across the Tiber River, past the Castel Sant'Angelo, and finally to Saint Peter's Basilica. They pulled around the south side of the basilica, all the way to the door just to the south of the apse on the west end. Anthony helped His Holy Father out of the carriage, and the two entered the sacristy, where the pope would vest for the sacred mass. By now the pope and Anthony were surrounded by other attendants. There would be no more talk of the pope's early life and his time among the Saracens.

Brother Anthony assisted the pope in the elaborate vesting procedure. He handed his patron each item in the prescribed order and assisted him in dressing as the Holy Father softly recited the prayer associated with each vestment. Sylvester had been pontiff for only a little over eight months. He could not have been used to quite this much official decorum. His face revealed no emotion, except perhaps discomfort.

As Anthony handed the Holy Father his golden, jeweled crosier, he whispered in the pope's ear, "I want to learn more about Córdoba and Fez and especially about your teacher, the mapmaker."

"Yes, Brother Anthony. But first the mass. I will tell you all about the mapmaker, as well as my own humble story from the very beginning— tomorrow."

PART I

CHAPTER ONE

Upper Mesopotamia, 924

As he began to feel that he was getting old, al-Harith had one regret in life. He did not have a son to follow in his footsteps. He was from a rural family, a family of plowmen for many generations. But he had not followed in the footsteps of his father and grandfather. Rather, he learned to recite the Quran. More than that, he learned to read and write Arabic with ease. He was called hafiz—"wise"—someone who could recite the entire Quran from memory, and likewise he knew most of the hadith of the Prophet Mohammed. As a young man, he became an imam in a neighborhood masjid in a modest-sized merchant-class quarter in the town of Nusaybin in south-central Anatolia. In his own mind, al-Harith was neither Shiite nor Sunni. He saw the distinction between the two sects of Islam as merely political. For him, being a Muslim was a matter of his personal relationship with God. The simple message that he preached to his congregation was to be a pious Muslim, a good citizen, and a loyal friend.

Al-Harith was now in his late forties. He was not a tall man, and his girth was now considerably wider around the waist than when he was twenty years younger. His hair and beard were prematurely white. As a sign of his status as imam, he almost always dressed in white and wore a full white turban. He had married later in life than most men in Nusaybin. Samira, his wife, was in her mid-thirties, much older than the average marrying age for women. She was not beautiful, and her family could not offer much of a dowry. Al-Harith had met her when he had visited her family to comfort them at the time of her father's death. He had found it hard to believe that no one had yet sought her hand in marriage. More than any other unmarried woman he knew, he thought of her as *a good woman.*

Al-Harith and Samira had been married for three years before their daughter Mariam was born. Two years later, Samira gave birth to a second daughter, Yasmine. Both births had been very difficult. After Yasmine was born, Doctor Hamid said that Samira should not become pregnant again. Another two years went by after the birth of the second daughter. Al-Harith approached Samira with a proposition.

"Habibi," al-Harith said, addressing his wife with a term of endearment, "there is a matter of some importance that I wish us to discuss. You know that our marriage was not just a marriage of convenience arranged by our families. You also know that I love you very much and that I will always love you. But we have now been married for several years and we do not yet have a son."

Samira, lowering her eyes as she turned to face him, could already anticipate what was coming next.

Al-Harith continued, hesitatingly, even slightly stuttering, "You are well aware that our religion allows a man to take a second, third, and even a fourth wife. Uh…what do you think about *me* taking another wife?"

What al-Harith said was true. Islam allowed polygamy—under certain circumstances. But the truth of the matter was that very few men took more than one wife. For one thing, a man needed the permission of his first wife. It was only natural for a woman to object to such an arrangement. That was why al-Harith had been reluctant to approach Samira with his proposition.

She now looked him straight in the eye. "My dearest husband, I do appreciate your asking my permission. Some men would pass right over that requirement."

She is going to say no, al-Harith thought. But he was surprised at Samira's reaction.

"I do believe you when you say that you love me," Samira said. "You have been the kindest, gentlest, most honest and generous husband any woman could ever hope for. Since you have no brothers, I know how much it means to your family and to you personally to have a son to extend your family's patrimony to the next generation. Like you, I wished for a son who would carry on your important work here in Nusaybin as imam. And, alas, it seems to be true what Doctor Hamid said, that I cannot conceive again after the birth of Yasmine. So yes, I grant my permission for you to take a second wife."

The grateful husband put his arms around his wife and held her tight. "Thank you, Samira—for your understanding and for your love."

Samira said, smiling and only half-joking, "But remember the second condition our Holy Book places on you—to treat each wife exactly alike. That means that even though I am getting old, you will take me to your bed from time to time. And what's more, I will appreciate the help that a younger woman will bring to the household chores of cleaning, cooking, and washing your clothes."

"Yes, of course, my dear," al-Harith said, also smiling.

Within a month, with the permission of Samira, al-Harith married another, much younger, woman named Aisha, the same name as the youngest wife of the Prophet Mohammed. The older woman welcomed this addition to the family. The younger wife was pleasant enough and a very hard worker. She would be of considerable help in caring for the children and doing the other household chores.

Within less than a year, Aisha gave birth to a baby boy. From the very first moment that al-Harith looked into his infant son's eyes, he saw a bright sparkle that led him to give his son the name Hakeem—the wise one. From that time on, al-Harith became known as Abu Hakeem. His son's full name was Hakeem Ibn al-Harith al-Nusaybini.

Nusaybin, seven years later

From a very young age, he was a dreamer. Hakeem's main responsibility as a child was to care for the few goats that his family owned. Shortly after breakfast each morning, he would take the animals to the rolling hills of lush, green pastureland outside of town. In the first few years of his life, Hakeem never went more than a few miles from home. Yet from his favorite hilltop, he could look around in any direction and wonder what was beyond the distant horizon.

He was supposed to bring the animals home in the early afternoon in time for dinner. But far too often, his father would have to come looking for him. He would find the little boy lying in the grass, gazing up at the clear blue sky as his mind wandered who knew where. The flock wandered too. Sometimes they were in sight. Frequently, they were not. On those occasions, the father rebuked his son, as he felt obliged to do, but in truth the rebuke was rather mild. Abu Hakeem had learned that on this matter, his son was simply incorrigible. He would waken the boy from the dreamlike trance, and they would gather up the goats together.

Dinner was the main meal of the day, shortly after the midday prayer—unless father and son had to round up the animals first, in which case dinner was served late. In most households, male members ate first as mothers and daughters served. Women would eat later, in the kitchen. But in Hakeem's family, they all ate together. After all, there were only two male members of the family. But it wasn't that. Abu Hakeem took the Quranic notion of equality of all people in the eyes of God quite literally.

Almost every day after dinner, Abu Hakeem would spend about an hour teaching his son to recite the Quran. He started from the very beginning, with the chapter appropriately titled "The Opening."

The father would recite,

"In the name of God, the most Gracious, the most merciful…"

And the son would repeat the verse. When Abu Hakeem was satisfied that Hakeem's pronunciation and intonation were correct, he would add another:

"Praise be to God, Lord of the two Worlds…"

Once the lad mastered the ten or so verses for the day, he was assigned as homework, using his father's copy of the Quran as the model, the task of imitating what he saw, letter by letter, word for word, verse after verse. As the weeks and months went by, Hakeem became more adept at reading and writing and reciting by memory. It took nearly three years for him to complete the entire Quran.

The boy might have learned the Quran more quickly had he not been so curious. Every evening he pestered his father to tell him stories, stories that were beginning to become popular and would soon be gathered in a collation called *A Thousand Stories*. Abu Hakeem worried about his son's apparent lack of discipline, but he indulged his son's curiosity nonetheless.

When Hakeem was approaching his eighteenth year, Abu Hakeem could see that his son was becoming increasingly restless. He had grown into quite a handsome young man. He still had the same bright sparkle in his eyes that had so impressed his father when he was a toddler. His long curly hair was light brown, much lighter than was typical of boys in this region. Even when he wore his favorite skullcap, his long curly locks bounced over his forehead, causing his sisters to call him affectionately "Curly-Locks." He was small in stature, smaller than most boys his age, but extremely athletic. He was not accustomed to doing hard manual labor like most of his friends, but he excelled in playing the sports that were popular in his neighborhood, especially gameball. That involved each of two teams trying to kick a "ball"—a stuffed animal bladder—through two markers at either end of a playing field that was nearly a mile long. The game required tremendous speed and endurance. Hakeem was among the very best players.

It had been some time since Hakeem had to take the livestock to pasture every day. The family had hired a neighbor's child to do that. Abu Hakeem was relieved that *he* no longer had to round them up in the afternoon. Hakeem continued to read the Quran and to study *tafsir*, Quranic commentaries, in the few books that were in the small library in the town's large congregational mosque.

He also became adept at writing and using Arabic numerals that had recently been adapted from Hindu numerals. That particular skill set him apart from most people in town, even many of the merchants who dealt in long-distance trade and thus needed to quantify their inventory, income, and expenses with some degree of accuracy. Hakeem was able to hire out his services to keep the books of some of these merchants, bringing some income to the family and providing some spending money of his own.

The day came that Abu Hakeem had expected and feared the most. His son came to him in a manner so similar to when he had approached his wife for permission to marry a second time.

"Abi, you know that I respect you and love you so very much," Hakeem said. "I am eternally grateful to you for raising me to be the man that I now am. Please, Abi, I would like to go to Baghdad. They have a great academy there, masters of knowledge, men who have traveled to the edges of the world, men who have described far-off places to the minutest detail and who have drawn pictures of the face of the earth."

Hakeem had heard stories of this academy from merchants who traveled the Silk Road and passed through Nusaybin en route to Constantinople, from as far away as Bukhara and Samarkand, through Baghdad and Damascus. Most people considered the stories to be nothing other than rumors. But young Hakeem could not help but think that there was truth to what they said, that there was a vast world beyond the upper reaches of the Tigris and Euphrates Rivers. And the key to this knowledge was in the minds of the masters and in the books in the library in Baghdad, in the Bayt al-Hikma, the

House of Wisdom.

The House of Wisdom was one of the most important intellectual center in the entire Islamic world. Many learned scholars traveled there, mostly Muslims but also Jews and Christians. The library contained hundreds of books, many in duplicate copies—books written in Arabic, but also foreign books in their original languages, most of which were translated into Arabic from Greek, Chinese, Sanskrit, Persian, and Syriac: books on medicine, mathematics, and astronomy, on alchemy, geography, and philosophy.

Abu Hakeem was of course disappointed when his son informed him of his desire to leave Nusaybin. But he loved his son beyond measure and knew that the boy's happiness could never be fulfilled here in his hometown.

He put his hands on his son's shoulders. "Hakeem, you are indeed your father's son. Just as I left my family's farm to follow my calling to become an imam, I know that you too must follow your dream. I will do whatever I can to help you."

The next several weeks went by quickly. With an uneasy mixture of sadness and joy, the family came together to help Hakeem prepare for the journey of his life.

Hakeem's mother spent most of her time, even to the neglect of some of her normal responsibilities, preparing his clothing. Um Hakeem had decided that he should have two complete outfits in good repair: loose-fitting trousers with baggy legs called *serwal*, tunics, waistbands, robes, turbans. These should all be carefully color coordinated, shades of off-white, tan, and brown, so that different components could be matched in such a way as to create a number of different ensembles. No son of hers would be seen in the capital city looking like an indigent.

Hakeem's older sisters were now in their twenties and, like their mother, had not been quick to marry. Both were very attractive young women who nevertheless still lived at home. Being from such a fine family, either one would have been an excellent catch for any eligible young man in Nusaybin. But Abu Hakeem was not about to marry off either of his daughters if not by her own choice, and neither had yet found someone to her liking. Both girls loved their little brother and doted on him like mother hens. They now showed their affection by teasing him ceaselessly about his impending departure.

"Before you came along"—Yasmine poked him in the shoulder—"I had a room all to myself. Thanks to you, I had to move in with Mariam. I can hardly wait to have my own room back again."

Mariam added, "Not to mention that we will finally have some peace and quiet around here, rather than having to listen to your endless chatter of distant places that you hear about from your merchants, places that are clearly only names, places *you* will never see in your lifetime."

Hakeem taunted back, "Yes, I know you suffered *sooo* much as you begged me after supper to repeat the stories I heard."

Nonetheless, the two girls worked hard together to produce a brand-new heavy, brown woolen overcoat, tightly woven in alternating strips of geometric patterns. They said in the same teasing tone, "It will protect you from the cold nights, so you can depart for Baghdad in late winter rather than waiting until early spring as you plan." In spite of the teasing, it was clear that the two girls would miss their little brother, who was not so little anymore.

Abu Hakeem, trying very hard with only limited success to control his emotions, was determined to do all in his power to ensure his son's success in pursuit of his dream. He provided his son with the better of his two horses. He purchased for him a new pair of leather riding boots, well-oiled to make them supple and waterproof. At great sacrifice, he converted most of his modest savings into twenty gold dinars, with which he hoped to guarantee that his son would arrive in the capital city able to support himself for the first year of the adventure of his life. Most important, and as a testimony of his fatherly love, he gave his son his own copy of the Quran.

Abu Hakeem's Quran did not come without paternal advice. "Travel is inherently dangerous, my son. You should never be on the open road alone. You should contract to travel under the protection of an organized caravan."

A bit annoyed at what he was beginning to think was excessive fatherly worry, Hakeem said, "Is it not true that the Abbasid authorities have managed to keep the routes relatively safe as long as one stays on the main roads?"

"Yes, that's true," Abu Hakeem said, "yet we still hear stories of bandits along the way. Just the other day, I heard such a story as I was playing backgammon with a group of friends."

Now he had his son's attention. Even his two daughters came closer to hear their father's tale.

Abu Hakeem continued, "This caravan, hoping to save time, chose a route passing near the center of the great Syrian Desert, a route where wells are few and far between. After a march of several days, they approached a well, desperately needing to replenish their water supply. They caught a thief who had climbed down into the well and cut the ropes on the water buckets. The thief's plan was to hide in the well until the caravaneers died of thirst. He would then climb out of the well and claim all the merchandise—"

"This sounds like such an ill-conceived plan," Hakeem interjected. "Did it work?"

Abu Hakeem hesitated. "Well…"

Hakeem cut him off. "I know, two guardsmen climbed down into the well and killed the thief. I heard this same story a few days ago in Abdelhady's shop when I was bringing his books up to date."

Detecting a note of cynicism in his son's voice, Abu Hakeem said, "It may well be just a folktale. But the truth of it is there is danger along the route. You must always be careful. You must be extremely vigilant of your possessions, especially your purse. Keep it close to your body, preferably concealed under your shirt.

"Yes, father," Hakeem said a bit impatiently. "I promise I will be careful."

"What's more, Abu Hakeem added, "Whenever possible, you should stay in a reputable, well-frequented *funduq*." The inns had been established specifically for travelers needing one or two nights of lodging as they traveled over long distances. *Funduq*s mostly attracted merchants but also increasingly students.

Samira, always in the role of the matriarch of the entire family, loved her husband's son as if he were her own blood. She too had advice for the soon-to-be traveler. "You must stay clear of *funduqiya*s."

Hakeem looked at her quizzically. "*Funduqiya*s…?"

You heard me," she snapped. "Young girls, often slaves, always sensuous and seductive, whose company is offered to clients of a *funduq*—for a price."

Hakeem could only wonder how he might react if he met such a *funduqiya*. Gender segregation was deeply ingrained in the culture he had grown up with. The Holy Quran required modesty of women. Whenever they went out in public, they were to cover the hair on their head and to cover their bodies from the neck down to their wrists and ankles. All of the grown women whom Hakeem had ever met, females who had reached puberty, complied with this requirement.

The custom was relaxed in the home. Hakeem saw his mother's and sisters' hair and arms. Only once had he seen his older sister Yasmine naked, when he accidentally walked into the room where she was taking a bath. The family usually bathed in the public hammam, but Yasmine was taking a bath at home on that particular day. She had just stepped out of the wooden tub when Hakeem entered the room. Her back was turned toward her brother. As she turned to reach for a towel, Hakeem could see the full length of her body, droplets of water rolling down her smooth, olive-colored skin, from her long auburn hair, over her firm breasts and belly, down to the dark triangle between her legs.

Yasmine screamed and Hakeem ran out of the room. He was every bit as embarrassed as his sister. Nonetheless, a sexual feeling rose within him that he had never felt before. That was the first time he had ever seen a naked female body.

Hakeem set off in early spring. His friend Abdelhady helped him plan his route and contract escort with a caravan going to the capital city. Hakeem was told that the journey would take approximately one month. The weather was still quite cool. Hakeem wrapped himself in the new woolen overcoat his sisters had made for him. With all his worldly possessions packed in two large saddlebags, and with a head full of dreams and tears in his eyes, Hakeem bid his family goodbye, not knowing when he would see them again. He would head east toward the city of Mosul, and from there he would follow the Tigris River south all the way to Baghdad.

CHAPTER TWO

Baghdad, 943

At midafternoon on the last day of the journey, the caravan approached Baghdad from the northwest. Impatient to arrive, Hakeem rode at the front of the line. From his vantage point at the top of a hill, he could see the walled city at a distance and was amazed.

Is it perfectly round? he asked himself. It seemed that it was, and it must have been designed that way from the very beginning.

He saw that the city was surrounded by an outer wall and then a much higher inner wall. Four gates led into the inner city, each covered by a gold dome. Each dome seemed to be equidistant from the others, and each gate was connected to one on the opposite side of the city by a wide diametric street that crossed the entire urban space.

Hakeem entered Baghdad through the Damascus Gate, first through the outer wall and then under the domed gate of the inner wall. He paid the leader of the caravan, handing the man one of the gold coins his father had given him, having removed that one coin from his hidden purse earlier in the morning. The caravan master gave him four silver coins in change. "Thank you for your service, sir," Hakeem said. "I sincerely appreciate the safety and the comfort that you provided me on this journey."

"Come now, young man, what comfort? Overland travel is never comfortable," the well-seasoned caravaneer said.

"All right, then—relative comfort," Hakeem replied with a half smile.

Hakeem started to ride along the main thoroughfare leading to the city's center and the imperial palace. A continuous row of buildings lined each side of the street, each structure attached to the next, forming what resembled a solid wall. As in every other town he had traveled through, including his own town of Nusaybin, all of the buildings looked the same: very plain, with solid walls and doors opening onto the street but no windows. Hakeem guessed that the doors opened into courtyards or small gardens rather than directly into the house itself. In fact, he could not tell from the outside what the function of the space behind each door was. At irregular intervals, archways opened onto side streets, darker and narrower than the main thoroughfare.

As he rode toward the city center, he encountered another wall and another gate—this one with its heavy wooden doors shut tight and two burly guards posted on either side. This was as far as he could go. He dismounted and approached the guards.

"What business do you have at the imperial palace?" one of the guards asked, looking rather stoic and very official.

"I was told that the House of Wisdom lies beyond this gate," Hakeem said.

"Indeed it does, but you will need special authorization to gain access to this area." The guard looked Hakeem over, his stoicism apparently giving way to curiosity. It was perhaps unusual for such a young man to ride right up to the entrance to this restricted area without prior authorization. "In addition to the palace, there is the royal mosque and a number of other government buildings, including the House of Wisdom. You will need authorization."

"How can I get such an authorization?" asked Hakeem.

"Why do you ask?" said the guard. "And who is asking?"

Full of enthusiasm, Hakeem answered in a rapid staccato, "I am Hakeem Ibn al-Harith, and I seek to study at the House of Wisdom." He drew himself up straight, shoulders back and chest puffed out just a bit, hoping he didn't appear as naïve and rustic to this city guard as he felt.

"Quite determined aren't you?" the guard observed. He shook his head, but a smile tugged at the corners of his lips. "I suppose there is something different about you…" He seemed to come to a decision. "The Wizarat'l-Ulum administers the House of Wisdom, including the library, all of the books therein, and all that the scholars do. There is an office of that ministry near the large congregational mosque on the east side of town between the Khurasan Gate and the Basra Gate. It is closed now, but you can go there tomorrow morning to seek your authorization."

Hakeem resigned himself to the fact that he would have to wait for the morrow to reach his ultimate destination. He suddenly realized that he was exhausted. All he wanted now was a hot bowl of red bean and lentil soup and a warm bed. "Where can I find the nearest inn that charges modest prices?"

"Retrace your steps for one city block and turn right. There is a students' hostel on the right side of the street called Funduq At-Tulaabi. The innkeeper provides clean, safe housing at a price students can afford, at least for a short-term stay. Tell the innkeeper that Omar al-Kiyami sent you. He will treat you fairly." As an afterthought, the guard added, "By the way, the innkeeper does not allow *funduqiya*."

Hakeem nodded, remembering his stepmother's advice. He thanked the guard, whose replacement had just arrived, and leading his horse, he began to retrace his steps to the first intersection. The now off-duty soldier caught up with him at the first intersection. Hakeem turned right as he was instructed. The soldier turned left and accelerated his pace as if he were on a mission.

A young stranger in a new town could not be too cautious, but Hakeem felt reassured by the plain but well-swept appearance of the hostel's courtyard.

As it turned out, Omar al-Kiyami's advice was sound. The innkeeper was very accommodating, and Hakeem booked the last available room, telling the innkeeper he would stay for only a short time until he could find a permanent place to live. The innkeeper told Hakeem where he could stable the horse that his father had so generously given him.

Hakeem was not inclined to believe in destiny. Luck perhaps, but not destiny. Later that evening, as he was eating his soup at the inn, sitting alone at one of the long common tables, a man somewhat older than himself but still young walked over carrying his own supper and sat down next to him. He was neatly dressed, his black, curly hair neatly wrapped in a colorful turban that matched his cloak. His furrowed forehead and piercing eyes suggested a man in a permanently serious state of mind.

After they exchanged polite greetings, the stranger initiated conversation. "I have never seen you before. Are you newly arrived here in Baghdad?"

"Yes," Hakeem replied, wondering just how much information he should share with a stranger. He continued to eat his soup.

"Where are you from?" the man asked, sizing up the newcomer.

"From Nusaybin." Another short answer. "Who wants to know?" Hakeem ripped off a piece of bread and dunked it into his bowl.

"My name is Suhrab."

Hakeem hesitated but said, "I am Hakeem Ibn al-Harith. Have you lived in Baghdad long?"

"Almost ten years. I rent a small room in a house around the corner. I have most of my meals here at the inn."

"You must know Baghdad very well. Is the city really perfectly round, as it looks when seen from the hilltop on the north side?

"So you noticed that. Yes, it is indeed, but it was not always so. The original city crumbled long ago. But when the Abbasid caliph came to power, now over a century and a half ago, the new ruler, al-Mansur, decided to make an ideological statement. New regime, new capital city."

"But why round?" Hakeem asked.

"A circle is a perfect shape. It symbolizes completeness."

"How do you know all of this?"

"That is what I do here," Suhrab said. "I am a student at the House of Wisdom."

"What a coincidence," Hakeem exclaimed, hardly believing his good fortune. "I have come here all the way from Nusaybin to do exactly that— to be a student at the House of Wisdom. Is it difficult to be admitted as a student?"

"There is no such thing as coincidence," Suhrab said thoughtfully. "The will of God, perhaps, but not coincidence. As for the House of Wisdom, a person is accepted only if one of the masters agrees to take him on as a student. And the criteria for that are straightforward. The candidate must have potential, a creative and inquiring mind, an insatiable curiosity, and a willingness to work very hard. Do you have those qualities?"

"Yes." A one-word answer, but said eagerly and emphatically.

"In the morning, then, I will take you to the ministry office for authorization to enter the inner city. Then you can present yourself to one of the masters at the House of Wisdom. I would recommend my teacher, a man called Abu'l-Hasan Ali al-Mas`udi. An old man but very wise. He is kind and has traveled the world. He has devoted his life to learning how to describe that world. I think you will like him."

But will he like me? Hakeem wondered.

He could not fall asleep that night as he contemplated how he might convince Sheikh Abu'l-Hasan that he had the potential that Suhrab described.

"So, you want to study at the House of Wisdom!" Abu'l-Hasan's question was more statement than question.

"Y—yes," Hakeem replied, feeling his usual boldness desert him in the company of this learned man.

Abu'l-Hasan had received Hakeem in his studio, a relatively spacious paneled room, the panels giving way to niches filled with books and scrolls.

The professor was seated cross-legged on an elevated platform, or "chair," with a few opened books at his side. The senior scholars at the House of Wisdom were said to "hold a chair" at the academy. Abu'l-Hasan was impeccably dressed in a white silk tunic elegantly embroidered with tiny silver stars and a white cloak with baggy sleeves bordered in the same silver thread. A tightly wrapped white turban covered his head. His high, shiny forehead and visibly bare temples suggested that perhaps his head was shaven. A short, neatly trimmed beard garnished his face. Hakeem had never met a professor before, but this one looked exactly how he had imagined a scholar of this stature would look.

The professor motioned the aspiring student to sit on the floor in front of him. He continued to speak as he looked above Hakeem rather than directly at him. "You are one among so many young upstarts with exactly that same ambition. Of the many who come, we admit very few. Of those, only the very best stay for as long as one year. Most find the task of mastering the contents of a lecture, having heard it a single time, to be too difficult. They find it even harder to read a book and absorb its contents with a single reading. We have many books but usually only one copy, sometimes two, so students have very limited access." The great master lowered his gaze to Hakeem and stared straight into his eyes. "What makes you think that you are up to these tasks?"

"Sheikh Abu'l-Hasan," Hakeem said, addressing him with a title of respect for his great knowledge, "I think that I have the determination and the stamina to succeed." *I must sound more confident*, Hakeem thought. "I will do all that you ask of me. I will not disappoint you, by the will of God, I promise."

"Suhrab speaks highly of you. He knows my standards; he knows that I take on very few of those who come. How did you convince him to bring you here?"

Hakeem considered his reply before answering. It seemed that Suhrab had visited the sheikh last night after he and Hakeem parted ways. "I do not know, sheikh. Perhaps he saw my travel-weary face and dusty clothes and the stiffness in my body from hours of riding. He saw that I had come a considerable distance, that I had endured discomfort along the way, that I was willing to hurt in order to learn. And here I am."

"I see. Perhaps you have convinced Suhrab, but you have yet to convince me."

Several seconds of silence passed. Hakeem couldn't read the professor's expression.

Finally, the sheikh said, "Very well, young Hakeem. You have one month to prove yourself worthy of admission. We will start tomorrow morning, two hours after morning prayer."

The following morning, Hakeem did not wait to hear the first call to prayer just before dawn. He had performed the ritual washing before prayer, as well as prayer itself, so many times over the years that it had become routine. But he did not want it to be routine *this* morning—what could well be the most important morning of his life. He sat impatiently on his mat holding two pieces of thread, one white and one black. He remembered his father teaching him that there were two dawns, a false dawn and a true dawn. In the Quran, God himself taught how to distinguish between the two. Hakeem quoted God's words from the second chapter: "The true dawn is when the white thread that is the light of dawn appears to you distinct from the black thread that is the darkness of night."

As soon as he could see that one thread was white and the other was black, he knew that it was time to pray. He poured clean water into the basin on the table near his bed and began the ritual washing. Today, he articulated each step silently in his mind. He cleansed his body so that his mind would be cleansed for prayer as he said, "Bismillah"—in the name of God. He washed his hands to the wrists—*three times*, exactly as it is prescribed. He rinsed his mouth and cleansed his nostrils, then he washed the whole of his face—*three times*. Then he cleansed the right arm to his elbow and the left—*three times*. *Why three times?* he wondered. But he remembered his father saying that it was the will of God, and that was reason enough. With a wet hand, he wiped each ear—*three times*. Finally, he washed each foot to the ankle—*three times*, beginning with his right foot. He unrolled the small prayer rug that his father had given him. He was now ready to pray.

Standing straight, facing south toward Mecca, hands raised, he said, "Allahu Akbar." *God is great!*

Then prostrating and touching his forehead to the floor, he said, "Subhana rabiyya a'ala." *Glory be to my Lord the Most High.*

He rose to a sitting position and said once again, "Allahu Akbar," and prostrated a second time.

Then he stood and said a third time, "Allahu Akbar." This concluded one prayer unit. He repeated the unit a second time, as is prescribed for morning prayer, then finished by turning to the right and then to the left, reciting in each direction, "Assalumu alaikum wa rahmatullah." *Peace be upon you, and God's blessing.*

One is so conditioned to offer an expression of peace to those praying on either side that the gesture is made even when praying alone.

Hakeem added a special intention in his prayer this morning: for God to bless the endeavor upon which he was about to embark at the famous House of Wisdom in the court of the powerful caliph of Baghdad.

Hakeem's first session with Sheikh Abu'l-Hasan was very short. The sheikh started with a simple question.

"Do you know the verses in the Quran that contain the phrase 'the heavens and the earth'?"

There are many places where that phrase appears in the Quran. And many of them were now suddenly flashing through Hakeem's straining memory. He could not settle upon a single one. "My father would know them all. He is hafiz. But I am not hafiz. I could recite some but surely not all."

"Then your first assignment, young man, is to find the verses. When you have read and contemplated them all, then you may return and we will talk." With that, the master dismissed his new student.

As Hakeem walked back to the *funduq*, he felt disappointed. Beginning his studies with phrases from the Quran was not what he had expected. He had hoped to acquire new wisdom from the great master, to learn everything there was to know about the world around him. Instead, the sheikh told him to consider scattered verses in the Quran that he more or less already knew from his studies with his father, verses he heard recited every year during the month of Ramadan.

One verse came to mind as he walked, and it seemed to speak to what had brought him to Baghdad in the first place. It was in the sura called "Al-Hajj," the pilgrimage:

> Do they not travel through the land so that their hearts and minds and their ears may thus learn to hear? Truly it is not their eyes that are blind, but their hearts which are in their breasts.

Hakeem had traveled here to acquire wisdom. He was already finding out that learning was not a passive process. It was a process of discovery. Nor was it just a work of the mind. He would have to put all of his heart and soul into it. He was eager to begin. He was ready to "travel through the land" in search of knowledge.

But first he would go to the library to read the Quran. Of course, he had his own copy of the Quran, the one his father had given him—a precious gift indeed. Books were not as expensive as they had been years ago when they were written on parchment. Now they were written on paper. And the number of skilled copyists was much greater than in years past. Hakeem treasured his Quran. He thought of his father every time he read from it. No, he did not need to go to the library every day to complete his assignment, but that was where he liked to read. That was where he liked to be.

It took Hakeem several days to complete his task. He came to the library every day, an hour or so after morning prayer, and stayed until *salat al-asr*, the late-afternoon prayer. He wrote down the verses with the phrase assigned by his teacher and committed them to memory—but not only to memory. He contemplated the verses and summarized them in his mind. It had quickly become obvious why Sheikh Abu'l-Hasan gave him this first assignment. He would be ready to report to the sheikh at the time of his next lesson.

When he awoke the next morning, Hakeem could hear gentle rain falling on the pavement outside the window of his room. He looked outside to see that the street was quite wet. It must have rained most of the night. As he did every morning of his life as far back as he could remember, he praised God and asked his blessing for the day ahead. He ate a simple breakfast of bread, baked fresh that very morning at the bakery around the corner. He dipped it in olive oil that, according to the innkeeper, was produced at his uncle's farm outside the city. He drank a bowl of warm goat's milk, allegedly from the same farm. The innkeeper made such a point of emphasizing the origin of the produce that Hakeem wondered if it was really true.

It was still drizzling when Hakeem left the *funduq*, and there was a chill in the air. He wore the heavy coat his sisters had so lovingly made for him, the hood pulled up. He was also wearing his riding boots so as not to get his feet wet. He walked slowly through the streets, head lowered, avoiding the puddles positioned intermittently along the way. What would he say to Sheikh Abu'l-Hasan in what would be only his second encounter with the great teacher?

"Good morning, young man. Come and sit. Tell me what thoughts about 'the heavens and the earth' you bring from your journey through the noble Quran."

No small talk from this man, Hakeem thought. *He is getting right to the point.* "Most of the verses," the student began, "tell me that all of the earth, and all of the celestial bodies beyond, all of these belong to God. He is the creator and master of all that is in the heavens *and* the earth."

"Does any verse stand out above the others?"

"The verse that resonated most with me is in the sura 'Al-Jathiya.'" Hakeem recited from the chapter on kneeling: "Verily, in the heavens and the earth are signs for those who believe."

"And how does that speak to you, Hakeem?"

The young student was pleased that his teacher called him by his personal name. "It seems to be saying that the whole world, all that we see here on earth as well as what we see in the sky, is meant to bring us closer to God."

A look of satisfaction came over Sheikh Abu'l-Hasan's face. Hakeem hoped that any initial suspicions the sheikh might be having that Hakeem would be a good student were moving a step closer to being confirmed. "Excellent! Here is another verse upon which you should meditate. It is found in the sura 'Al-nur,' the chapter of light." It was now the teacher's turn to recite:

> "God is the light of the heavens and the earth. The parable of his light is as if there were a niche, and within it a lamp. The lamp is enclosed in glass. The glass, as it were, a brilliant star, lit from a blessed tree, an olive tree, neither of the East nor the West, whose oil is well-nigh luminous, though fire scarce touched it: light upon light! God doth guide whom He will to His light: God doth set forth parables for men: and God doth know all things."

"That is a beautiful verse," Hakeem exclaimed. "'Neither of the East nor the West.' I like the inclusiveness of that thought. I think that is what my father liked about it too. He repeated it often."

The master proceeded to explain his own interpretation of the verse. "It is a paradox. To know God is to know the heavens and the earth, and to know the heavens and the earth is to know God. Traveling horizontally across the surface of the earth, and then vertically up to the heavens, that is the path to God. But…" a long pause, "since the earth is much closer to us than the heavens, that is where you must start, my son. You must embark on your own journey, first horizontally, then vertically."

"How and where do I begin?"

"You will start by studying the ancients. The scholars here at the House of Wisdom owe a very large debt to the ancient Greek intellectuals. First, you will read Ptolemy. He was a great mathematician, astronomer, and geographer—even somewhat of a poet. He wrote two important works of which we have copies in Greek. Do you read Greek?"

That was a rhetorical question. Hakeem was quite certain that Sheikh Abu'l-Hasan knew he did not read Greek.

"Not to worry," the professor said. "We have Arabic translations here in the library, translated nearly a half century ago by one of our own scholars, Ibn Ishaq al-Kindi." Sheikh Abu'l-Hasan pronounced the translator's name with precision and reverence. "Al-Kindi was a philosopher, born in the city of Basra. He was of the Kinda tribe, hence his *nisba*, al-Kindi. He was educated right here in Baghdad. He did much more than translate Greek works into Arabic. He wrote treatises on a wide range of subjects—ethics, logic, psychology, medicine, mathematics, astronomy, pharmacology, astrology, optics, and even a work on musicology."

Very impressive credentials, Hakeem thought.

Sheikh Abu'l-Hasan continued his discourse on Ptolemy. "His first work, the *Almagest*, describes the motions of the sun, moon, planets, and fixed stars. He models the positions of these heavenly bodies by creating combinations of circular motions. He then computes the positions of the heavenly bodies and other celestial phenomena using tables based on those models."

"I'm not sure I understand, sir."

"I am not surprised. We will return to the matter later. The other book is *al-Geographia*. The name describes its content. It depicts the earth and explains, at least theoretically, how to produce such a depiction. That is where you will start. I assume you do not have a copy of that?" Another rhetorical question. "You will have to come daily to the library."

"Of course, master. I will be here every day after morning prayer."

"Very good. I am giving a lecture in the mosque after midday prayer and Friday sermon at the end of this week. I expect you to be there. We will then meet again on *yaum al-ahad* of next week. By Monday you shall read book one of *al-Geographia*."

"Yes, *ustadh*—and thank you."

On Friday, Hakeem arrived at the prayer hall of the House of Wisdom just as the midday prayer was about to begin. It was already crowded. The first men to arrive stood in the front line closest to the qibla wall, the wall facing Mecca—in Baghdad, the wall on the south side. The line filled up from the left to the right, each man standing with feet slightly spread apart. Each new person to join the line placed his left foot against the right foot of the person to his left. When the line was complete, a second line began. Being one of the last to enter, Hakeem was in the last row of men. Some women came to the mosque for Friday noon prayer. By choice, they formed lines behind the rows of men. The idea of fully prostrating, kneeling, and touching one's forehead to the ground with one's rear end high in the air in front of a row of men was not appealing to most women.

Today, there was nothing out of the ordinary with the prayer. It was precisely this—the regularity of it, establishing a steady and predictable rhythm to everyday life—that Hakeem appreciated most about praying. Almost always he found prayer to be moving, a time to feel close to God. At prayer's end, as is the custom, Hakeem rubbed his hands over his face, turned to his right, and said to the person next to him, "Peace be upon you," and likewise to the person on his left, "Peace be upon you."

The khutbah, the Friday sermon, was fine. The topic that the imam addressed this day was the importance of being a good citizen. It was not the first time Hakeem had heard this idea. His father had preached on the subject often enough. But somehow it had a greater impact on Hakeem today, here in Baghdad, the capital city of the *mamlakat'l-Islam*. Before arriving in Baghdad, Hakeem had never heard this term, *mamlakat'l-Islam*, had never thought of the realm of Islam as being united under the same rule of law. But he was soon to find out that it was only ideally so. There were threatening political fissures within this realm.

When the sermon was over, most of the people began to exit the prayer hall. Only the students who had come to hear the master teacher Sheikh Abu'l-Hasan remained. The young man who had prayed immediately to Hakeem's right, whose left foot had touched his own right, was one of those students. He was a heavyset man, at least a head taller than Hakeem and solidly built, perhaps a little older than Hakeem. He had a round and jovial face, covered only with a shadow of a beard, shaven, it appeared, two or three days earlier.

The young man introduced himself. "My name is Musa al-Maghrebi. I am from the imamate of Fez in the far west. You are new here?"

It was unclear if he was asking a question or making a statement. "Yes," Hakeem said. "I have been here only a few weeks. I have come to learn about the far reaches of the world and everything in between. I am a student of Sheikh Abu'l-Hasan. Or, to be more precise, I am *provisionally* accepted as a student. My name is Hakeem Ibn al-Harith. You should just call me Hakeem."

"I too am one of his students," said Musa. "I have nearly completed my second year of study here. I have a small room on the top floor of a house just outside the Bab Khurasan. Let us have dinner together with my host family after Sheikh Abu'l-Hasan's lecture is over."

Hakeem was somewhat taken aback by this stranger's abrupt kindness. "I…I think I would like that very much. But…don't you have to ask your host before you invite someone to break bread with his family? Especially someone you just met?"

"In most households, yes. But my patron is a wealthy merchant. He has a large family. He lives with his wife and his mother and his five children. His mother does most of the cooking, and there is always more than enough, even more left over than the servants can consume. Besides, we have developed a very close relationship over the past year. They treat me as one of the family. They are pleased when I bring a…a *friend* to eat with us."

"Very well then. I accept. You can tell me what it's like to be a student of Abu'l-Hasan."

"I can tell you this, Hakeem. Sheikh Abu'l-Hasan is an excellent teacher. His style of teaching is to plunge his students into a difficult text and watch them struggle with it for a while. He will then help them sort out that which still confuses them." Musa reached out and put his hand on Hakeem's shoulder. "Trust me. That approach is very effective. You will learn—if you persevere."

Just then Sheikh Abu'l-Hasan returned to the prayer hall. He sat in his chair along the far wall to the left of the qibla, and his students, eleven of them, sat on the floor in a semicircle in front of him, their attention focused on the great master as he began to speak.

"Today, I want to talk with you about the cosmos, which is Pure Being, and the ultimate, absolute, and infinite reality that stands *beyond* being. The cosmos is, at the same time, continuous and discontinuous with respect to its origin."

The eyes of every student focused on the sheikh and their ears hung on every word.

This is not going to be easy, Hakeem thought. *Hopefully Musa will be able to explain this to me later.*

Sheikh Abu'l-Hasan then recited verses from the Quran: "Glory to God who did take his servant for a journey by night from the Sacred Mosque to the Farthest Mosque, whose precincts he did bless, in order that he might show him some of his signs: for he is the one who hears and sees all things."

The sheikh explained that these verses described the first stage of the journey of the Prophet Mohammed, the horizontal plane from Mecca where the Prophet lived to the city of Jerusalem.

The sheikh continued, "The hadith compiled by Anas Ibn Malik provides more details. It all started when Mohammed was in the Sacred Mosque in Mecca. The angel Jibra'il brought Buraq, the heavenly steed that carried Mohammed to the Farthest Mosque in Jerusalem. Mohammed tethered Buraq to a bronze ring embedded in the corner of the wall of the Temple Mount and prayed. The second part of the journey, the horizontal ascent, is described in the Quran's sura 'An-Najm.'" Sheikh Abu'l-Hasan recited from the chapter of the star:

While he was in the highest part of the horizon, then he approached and came closer, and was at a distance of but two bow-lengths or even nearer; so did God convey the inspiration to his servant what he meant to convey. The Prophet's mind and heart in no way falsified that which he saw. For indeed he saw him at a second descent, near the lotus-tree beyond which none may pass: Near it is the Garden of Abode. Behold, the lotus-tree was shrouded in unspeakable mystery! His sight never swerved, nor did it go wrong! For truly did he see the signs of his Lord, the Greatest!

Sheikh Abu'l-Hasan then commented on the recitation. "Prophet Mohammed, may peace be upon him, ascended a ladder through the seven spheres of heaven. That was the vertical part of the journey, all of which occurred outside of the realm of ordinary time. Hadith tell us that despite the long distance between Mecca and Jerusalem, let alone the distance between the earth and the celestial planets, beyond which the Prophet traveled, he is said to have made the journey and returned in a single night."

"That is impossible," exclaimed Hakeem. Too late—he realized with embarrassment that he had drawn attention to himself. *I must discipline myself to listen respectfully*, he thought.

"According to some," the sheikh continued, barely skipping a beat yet casting a severe look in Hakeem's direction, "the door of his house through which he passed when he left Mecca was still swinging on its hinges when he returned."

"But in the meantime," the sheikh said, "the Prophet had stood before God himself, the Origin or Source of all Being. This Origin is also substance, a series of accidents, the essence of which all cosmic forms are but reflections and theophanies. The various cosmological schemes are means of depicting this relationship in a space that transcends purely physical space and a time that is beyond profane time."

"How does that relate to us, *ya ustadh*?" asked another student.

He must be one of Sheikh Abu'l-Hasan's advanced students, Hakeem thought.

The sheikh answered, "Our cosmology provides a vision of the cosmos that enables us to pierce through the visible world to the higher states of existence, and creates a science of the cosmic domain that acts as a ladder to allow man to mount to the roof of the cosmos."

After the lecture most of the students left, but Hakeem, Musa, and two others remained to chat with their teacher. Hakeem was hungry for knowledge, but he knew that his confusion must show on his face. Even though he had heard the story of the Prophet's Night Journey before, he had not understood much of what the sheikh had explained.

Seeming to realize this, the sheikh said, "Don't worry, my son. What I have just described is the destination of your intellectual quest. You will understand it when you arrive. I will see you on *yaum al-ahad*."

CHAPTER THREE

Hakeem and Musa left the mosque and headed straight for the house where Musa lived. It should have taken no more than ten minutes to walk the distance, but their walk was interrupted as soon as they turned off the main street into one of the narrow side streets. As they approached an alley off to the left, they heard scuffling accompanied by a muffled scream for help.

"Someone is in trouble," Musa exclaimed.

They hesitated only for a second, then rushed into the alley. The alley was dark but still light enough for them to see a man being brutally beaten by two ruffians. A heavyset man stood behind the victim, holding him upright by the arms. The other assailant, taller and stouter even than the first, shouted, "Take this, you sinner!" as he pounded the captive's face with his fists, swinging both arms as if he enjoyed it.

A blood-soaked sack covered the victim's head.

The two thugs, startled by the sudden appearance of Musa and Hakeem, let their victim fall to the ground and ran out of the alley, knocking the two students against the wall.

Musa rushed over and removed the sack that covered the victim's face. Despite blood smeared around the man's nose and mouth, Hakeem recognized him as one of the students who had left Sheikh Abu'l-Hasan's lecture shortly before the two of them.

Musa gently supported the student's head. "Nuri, my friend! Are you alright?"

The injured man opened his eyes slightly, nodded, and said in an almost inaudible voice, "I think so."

"Can you tell us what happened?" Musa asked.

"They jumped me from behind and dragged me into this alley. Luckily, they did not have time to inflict much harm before you came along. Thank God you two arrived when you did."

Musa and Hakeem helped Nuri to his feet.

"They put that sack on my head," Nuri said. "Were you able to see who attacked me?"

"Not a close look at them both," said Musa, "but I know at least one of them. The taller one was Haytham al-Khariji. I caught a glimpse of that jagged scar on the side of his face. I don't know who the other one was."

Nuri seemed to recognize the name. "So it was Haytham. He and his companion overtook me by surprise. Haytham is such a coward. He would never fight one on one."

"When we arrived, he fled like a coward as if his life depended on it." Musa turned to Hakeem. "Haytham al-Khariji was a student at the House of Wisdom until about a year ago. He was expelled."

"Why?" Hakeem asked. "Was he a poor student?"

"Not at all," said Musa. "He was actually quite a good student. He is called al-Khariji because he is a follower of the Kharijite sect. Actually, more than just a follower. He is an extremist—you might even say a terrorist."

"An extremist? In what way?"

"Just as the earliest Kharijites back in the first century of Islam supported neither Ali as caliph nor his cousin Mu'awiya who overthrew him," Musa said, "Kharijites today continue to oppose the caliph. They support neither the Abbasid caliph here in Baghdad nor either of the two rival caliphs in Andalusia or Ifriqiya."

"Then whom do they support?" asked Hakeem.

"Theologically, they claim that leaders should be chosen on the basis of personal, moral merit. There is a Kharijite challenger mounting a rebellion these days in North Africa."

"With what justification?" Hakeem was puzzled by the idea that anyone could challenge the authority of the caliph in Baghdad.

"Kharijites have a rather narrow view of what is meritorious," said Musa. "They accept as moral *only* what *they* define as moral. Anything else is sinful. The most extreme of their type believe sinners cannot be brought back into the fold—indeed, that they should be killed. Haytham al-Khariji is at the far end of the scale of extreme. He was expelled from the House of Wisdom for being overtly outspoken against the Abbasid caliph. Worse than that, as we have just seen, he lashes out with violence against those he considers to be sinners."

Musa returned his attention to Nuri, using his own cloak to wipe the blood from his friend's face. "I expect, Nuri, that had we not come along just when we did, you would have been seriously injured…" *If not dead*, was the unspoken implication.

"Really, I am fine," said Nuri. "Just a few cuts and bruises. And I am very dirty."

"We are going to my house around the corner," Musa said. "Come with us and get cleaned up and have some dinner."

After this rather unpleasant delay, the three students arrived at the house where Musa lived. This would be the first home that Hakeem had been in since he left his own home several weeks earlier. The house looked very plain from the outside. Musa knocked at the heavy door, and soon a servant came to open the smaller door within the larger one. They walked through a narrow corridor into a very large garden. Hakeem was surprised at the size of it. This was a large house indeed. He never would have guessed that from the outside.

Musa beckoned one of the servants. "Take Nuri to my room. Bring him a basin of clean, warm water, and fetch him one of my clean tunics to wear. Then have him join us for dinner."

It was already later than usual for dinner, since they had stayed after Friday prayer for the lecture. They proceeded directly to the dining room, where the male members of the family were waiting.

Musa introduced his new friend to the master of the house, al-Sayyid Husayn, a man in his early fifties, very richly dressed in a white linen tunic with white embroidered accents around the collar, along the buttoned front, and on the cuffs. His turban was of the same pure white linen.

"It is so nice to have you with us, Hakeem. Musa has told me a lot about you."

When was that? Hakeem wondered. He had only just met Musa that day at the mosque. Musa had extended his invitation just before Sheikh Abu'l-Hasan's lecture and had not been home since.

"These are my two sons, Mustapha and Said," al-Sayyed Husayn said. "And this is a close friend, Yusuf al-Nasafi, who is also joining us for dinner. "

The master's wife and three daughters would eat later in another room.

The low wooden table was already laid out: six places, each with a white napkin and thin, round flatbreads at each place. The six of them sat around the table on cushions. As custom dictated, the head of the household went person to person with a kettle of warm water, a basin, and a towel to wash the hands of each of his guests.

Hakeem was puzzled. The master of the house had not been warned that Musa was bringing a guest. Yet there was already an extra place set for him, almost as if they had been planning on his presence all along. Another place was quickly set for Nuri, who soon joined them at the table. They began with an appetizer of green and black olives marinated in oil with thyme.

Conversation consisted of small talk on a variety of subjects, interrupted by the arrival of the next course, which the host proudly described. "This is fattened capon in a sauce of vinegar and oil and a special paste called *murri* made with small salted fish and sweetmeat.

The older son, Mustapha, added, "This is a special dish we often have on Fridays."

"I don't like it very much," the younger child, Said, complained, scrunching his nose and turning it upward.

"Shush!" his father said.

Hakeem was surprised that there was no mention at all of the unpleasant incident in the alleyway. He was still quite shaken, making it hard to think of anything else. Still, he did not bring it up. Being the newcomer to this group, he did not want to take the lead in conversation.

Yusuf al-Nasafi talked about his tailor shop in the bazaar. "You cannot imagine the increase in counterfeit designer fabrics that is flooding the market these days," he grumbled. "Just yesterday, one of my suppliers delivered several bolts of 'Tabari' fabric that was clearly not really woven in Tabaristan."

"How could you tell?" Musa asked.

"The average person cannot tell if the counterfeit fabric is well done. But for someone whose profession is to buy and sell fine fabric, the difference is obvious. Fabric from Tabaristan is woven so tightly that the finest geometric patterns are measurably sharper."

"So what did you do?" Hakeem asked, sensing that it would be good to be a participant in the conversation if not the leader.

"I bought the counterfeit fabric anyway—at a lower cost, mind you. It is actually almost as good as the real thing. I will clearly distinguish for my customers the difference between this fake 'Tabari' fabric and that which actually comes from Tabaristan. If the customer still wants it, I will sell the imitation for a lower price."

Yusuf asked Hakeem several questions about where he was from, how long he had been in Baghdad, how long he had known Musa. Aside from the discussion of his tailoring business, he offered very little information about himself. Hakeem guessed that the man was middle aged, about the same age as his own father. He was rather richly dressed, also in a fine linen tunic with silk embroidery, leading Hakeem to think that he was quite successful at his business.

Musa, Nuri, and Hakeem lingered for at least an hour after the meal. Before they parted, Musa informed his new friend of the etiquette of being a student at the House of Wisdom.

"Always come well prepared to your meetings with your teacher, having read what he has asked you to read. Never be late. Answer his questions as fully as you can. Listen carefully to his comments. Ask questions, be inquisitive but never disrespectful. Remember who is the master and who is the apprentice. The master has much wisdom to share. Your task is to absorb it like a sponge absorbs water."

On the morning of *yaum al-ahad*, Hakeem awoke well before morning prayer. He had read his assigned lesson, although there was much in it that he did not understand. He was even more nervous about this session with the great master than he had been about his first two. Wanting to make sure that he would not be late, he went to the prayer hall at the House of Wisdom for morning prayer rather than saying his prayers at home. He took some bread and dates to eat his breakfast afterward while waiting for his appointment with Sheikh Abu'l-Hasan.

He entered the master's studio and approached his teacher, who was seated on his raised platform. Sheikh Abu'l-Hasan motioned Hakeem to sit in front of him. He immediately asked, "Are you all right, Hakeem?"

"Why yes, *ustadh*." In truth, Hakeem was still a bit shaken by the event in the alley on Friday afternoon, but he was eager to begin his lesson.

The master opened with a direct question. "So, you have read book one of Ptolemy's *Geography*. What, in your mind, is the single most important concept that Ptolemy wants his reader to know in this first chapter?"

"Master, there are so many."

"Yes, but the *most* important one—in your mind?"

"Well, I was surprised that Ptolemy makes a distinction between making a picture, or 'map,' as he calls it, of the whole known world versus a drawing of just one region—that the difference between them involves two very different processes."

"Go on," said the master, nodding with approval.

"First of all," Hakeem said, "his reference to the whole *known* world implies that there are parts of the world still unknown to us."

"Yes, Ptolemy was well aware that he knew only a quarter of the globe," said the sheikh.

Hakeem paused for a moment to gather his thoughts. "That seems perfectly conceivable to me, but I had never thought of it before. A picture of the entire world he likens to drawing a picture of a man's head. Whereas, making a map of just one region is like drawing a picture of an ear or an eye."

"Very good," said Sheikh Abu'l-Hasan.

"World cartography," continued Hakeem, his confidence rising, "deals more with quantities than qualities, since it gives consideration to the proportionality of distances between *all* places. Regional cartography, on the other hand, deals more with the qualities of things. It sets out the individual localities, each one independently and by itself, registering practically everything down to the least thing therein: harbors, towns, districts, branches of principal rivers, and so on. All of that said, if we are talking about drawing a human head, I can see where drawing the whole head would be more interesting than drawing just an ear…but…"

"Very interesting, Hakeem," the teacher said. "You do not have to choose between the two. Ptolemy is right…and you are right. We are talking about two quite different disciplines and means of achieving results. In both cases, the mapmaker begins by systematically assembling the maximum of data from the reports of people with scientific training who have actually traveled to the individual countries."

"What kind of data, *ustadh*?"

"You must know the absolute distance between two locations and the direction of the interval between them. But in the case of world cartography, an astronomical component is necessary. One gathers astronomical data with an instrument called an astrolabe, an instrument that can calculate apparent motions for the sun, moon, planets and fixed stars.

"These calculations are then recorded in tables that allow us to compute the instantaneous positions of the heavenly bodies and other celestial phenomena. Knowing the exact positions of these, observed from a particular place on earth, allows us to establish that location on earth from where the observation is being made relative to the stars and planets, and relative to other places on earth where the same celestial phenomena are also observed. Does this make sense to you, Hakeem?"

"Yes, *ustadh*. If I read Ptolemy correctly, it is a question of triangulation. If one knows the position of two points, one can determine the location of a third point by measuring the angles of the trajectories of the first point to the third, and then the second to the third."

"Basically, yes," the sheikh said. "But it's a little more complicated than that. It involves the relative positions of several points on earth *and* in the heavens, as well as sophisticated mathematical computations called trigonometry, which you will have to study in due time."

"My impression is that Ptolemy is much more interested in the astronomical approach than in direct observation from one's own travels on the ground." Hakeem hesitated before saying, "With all due respect, sir, I think my own preference is the exact opposite." He waited to see how the professor might react to this bold statement.

"You are correct in assessing Ptolemy's preference. He believes that measuring the astronomical phenomena is less subject to error than surveying what is on the ground. The latter requires physically traveling the distances between one place and the next—or relying on the reports of those who have already traveled to places around the known world. Of course, both approaches are necessary. One complements the other. Ptolemy sees that the heavens and the earth are intricately connected. The stars in the sky are fixed on the outer surface of the cosmos, which turns on an axis around the earth."

"What is your preference, master?"

"I do not speak for Ptolemy now. The heavens are closer to God, who controls the movement of celestial bodies. That movement is not subject to error and can be measured by man using sighting and shadow-casting instruments. The earth, on the other hand, is closer to us. Measuring both distance and direction between locations is, unfortunately, more subject to error."

With a slight smile on his face, Sheikh Abu'l-Hasan continued, "So, as for your own preference for studying the configuration of the earth, it is too early to tell, my son. You still have much to learn before you are ready to do either. Spend some more time with Ptolemy. Come back in two weeks' time. The next time we meet, we will talk about the difference between distance and direction, latitude and longitude, about Ptolemy's catalogue of coordinates, and about spherical maps versus planimetric maps. Enjoy the journey. I will see you in two weeks."

"Thank you, Sheikh Abu'l-Hasan. In two weeks then."

As Hakeem was leaving, he spotted Musa at the far end of the hall outside of Sheikh Abu'l-Hasan's studio. Musa was talking with two other men, whom Hakeem recognized—Suhrab, whom he had not seen since his first encounter with him shortly after he had arrived in Baghdad, and Yusuf al-Nasafi, the other guest at dinner with Musa and his adoptive family. As Hakeem approached them, the two men with Musa quickly said goodbye and left. That seemed odd to Hakeem, but perhaps they were in a hurry to attend to some other business.

"Are you next in line to see the master?" Hakeem asked.

"Yes, but I will not be long. Would you join me this afternoon for something to drink after afternoon prayer?"

"I would like that very much. I plan to read here in the library until prayer time. I will be very tired by then and will need a break. Where shall we meet?"

"At the small restaurant called Matami Farid," Musa said. "It's just outside the palace gate heading toward Bab Khurasan, second alleyway on the left off the main road."

"Until this afternoon then. *Ma'a salaama.*"

Matami Farid was indeed small: one cozy, somewhat cramped room with a long table and benches on either side. Musa sat on a stool at a smaller table back in one corner. Hakeem could see the kitchen through a doorway beyond.

Musa beckoned his friend over to occupy the table's other stool.

"Have you been waiting long?" Hakeem asked.

"I just arrived a few minutes ago. Would you like something to drink? I highly recommend some warm cider."

"That would be wonderful. Thank you."

Musa hailed the waiter and requested two ciders before turning back to Hakeem. "How was your lesson today with Sheikh Abu'l-Hasan?"

Hakeem summarized the experience, adding, "I'm happy to be his student, but frankly, I am a bit intimidated in the presence of such a great mind."

"There is more to that great mind than you can first imagine. The master is a brilliant man, to be sure—extremely well read, especially in philosophy and history. He has not only read our great Islamic scholars such as al-Khwarizmi and al-Kindi but also the ancients—Aristotle, even some Plato. I know very little about Plato myself, but he has been of much interest among the teachers at the House of Wisdom. Sheikh Abu'l-Hasan firmly believes that one must trace knowledge back to its roots, however far back that might be."

"The sheikh mentioned this al-Kindi at our second meeting. I used al-Kindi's translation of Ptolemy. The other names I do not recognize."

"If you continue as a student of Sheikh Abu'l-Hasan, you will learn of these men. And many more. But you will have to be aggressive in acquiring this knowledge, both through your own reading and through your lessons with our master. I hear that he will be leaving Baghdad soon. He is going to Egypt."

"I am surprised he would want to leave this place," said Hakeem. "Is not

Baghdad the center of intellectual pursuit in all of the Islamic world?"

"Of course, but local rulers in other parts of the world of Islam are trying to establish centers of learning of their own. They are aggressive in getting the best teachers."

"And the Abbasid caliph allows that?"

Musa lowered his voice a bit. "There is not much the caliph can do about it." He shook his head. "The caliphate is not what it used to be. The caliph's political power is considerably diminished in the last few years."

"But is he not still the *amir al-mu'minin*?"

"He is still Commander of the Faithful, yes, but no longer a political and military leader. That power has been reduced by the military might of the Buwayhids and the three brothers who lead them. These warriors swept out of the mountains of Daylam on the southern shores of the Caspian Sea to conquer the central heartland of the Islamic empire."

"If the caliph is still the Commander of the Faithful, how do the three brothers justify their authority?"

"It is not a question of authority; it is a matter of power. The father of these three was a fisherman and a Zoroastrian by faith, but he converted to Shiite Islam. The Buwayhid brothers belong to the Shiite sect called 'Twelvers' since their founder was the twelfth imam after Imam Ali, nephew of the Prophet and the first Shiite imam. But it is said that they began as Zaidi Shiites."

"Why would they change from one sect to another?"

"Zaidi Shiite doctrine insists on hereditary succession and would require them to install an imam from Ali's family. The Buwayhids are not direct descendants of Ali. The Twelver sect, with its occulted imam, was more politically attractive to them. Mind you, the Buwayhids are less interested in controlling the faith of Muslims; they are perfectly comfortable allowing the Abbasid caliph to retain that privilege and the title *amir al-mu'minin*. In all other matters, the Buwayhids rule."

CHAPTER FOUR

Hakeem spent the next two weeks deeply ensconced in the remainder of Ptolemy's *Geography*. Musa had helped him find an inexpensive place to live just around the corner from Matami Farid. There was a small neighborhood masjid just up the street where he could pray on those occasions when he preferred not to pray alone. His room was on the top floor of a private house owned by a friend of al-Sayyid Husayn, Musa's landlord. The room was modestly furnished with a sleeping mat and a small table on which rested a pitcher and a basin for ablutions. The only other furnishings were a stool in the corner and a chamber pot. With one very tiny window, the room was rather dark. It was not a good place to study, but it was only a few minutes' walk to the House of Wisdom. Hakeem preferred studying in the library there anyway.

Musa also advised Hakeem to sell the horse that he had been keeping at the same stable since arriving in Baghdad. "Baghdad is a large city, but you can walk just about anywhere in less than an hour. The stable owner can find you a good buyer."

Even though he loved the horse, Hakeem reluctantly agreed. "I will miss riding him, as I used to do every day at home. You know, we even won the annual derby in Nusaybin two years in a row." But he had to plan for how he would support himself once the money his father had given him ran out. His father had promised to send him money from time to time, but Hakeem was old enough to feel that he should make his own way. He would try to find some regular employment that would bring him at least a small income.

There were only a dozen or so students who came regularly to meet with their professors or to use the library. Hakeem had met them all and knew them at least by sight. Hakeem saw Musa almost every day at the library. They met from time to time at Matami Farid late in the afternoon for small talk and warm cider. Hakeem wondered why he did not see Suhrab anymore at the academy.

When the two weeks that he had been given to complete his assignment were up, Hakeem felt ready for his next lesson with the great master. As usual, Sheikh Abu'l-Hasan began by asking a question, this time about the different ways to measure distance that Ptolemy had used.

"The most important of these units is the stade," Hakeem said, "the standard unit of terrestrial distance among the ancient Greeks. One stade is approximately 185 meters. Stades could be converted into degrees according to the assumed equivalence of 500 stades being equal to one degree."

"You describe the units of measurement," Sheikh Abu'l Hasan said, "but how are these units actually measured?"

"It involves calculating movement along a straight line or in a specific direction for a certain length of time—"

"But there is a problem with measuring distance as the space traveled over time," the master interjected. "As you can imagine, there are many variables beyond our control that affect the speed at which we travel from one place to another, obstacles in our path such as mountains and rivers. Even upon the sea, the wind affects the speed at which we travel. Not to mention that we have yet to come up with a way to measure time with minute accuracy. So much for distance," said the teacher. "Now, how about direction?"

Well, I fell short on distance, Hakeem thought, hoping he would do better on the second part of the question. "Ptolemy alludes to three ways of describing direction: one, based on points on the horizon where the sun rises and sets; two, based on following certain stars in the sky; and three, based on conventional names of the winds that blow from various directions."

"Very good," said Sheikh Abu'l-Hasan.

Well, that went a little better, thought Hakeem.

"Let us turn to latitude and longitude," said Abu'l-Hasan.

As in his earlier meetings with the master, Hakeem gained confidence as the lesson went on. "Latitude and longitude are ways to locate a specific place in the world, be it a city, a river, a mountain. What I did not understand is how he determined the latitude and longitude of a specific location. Nor did I understand how he establishes where to put that on a map."

"You are correct to say that latitude and longitude form the very basis for a map of the world," Sheikh Abu'l-Hasan said. "They constitute a grid upon which places can be inserted in a way that records where they are in relation to other places. They form a skeleton, if you wish. Let us start with latitude. It is the easier of the two to establish with some degree of accuracy. A parallel of latitude is a circle on the terrestrial sphere that runs parallel to the equator, the center circle dividing the earth into two equal parts along an east-west axis.

"Places on a particular latitude have their own unique characteristics, such as the ratio of the length of an upright stick to that of its shadow on the longest and shortest days of the year, as well as on the equinoxes. Another is the amount by which the longest day of the year exceeds the equinoctial day or, equivalently, the ratio of the longest day of the year to the shortest, or simply the length of the longest day, measured in uniform time units. Other unique variables of a particular latitudinal parallel include which stars are always visible, which stars rise and set, and which stars can be seen directly overhead. Did you follow all of that, Hakeem?"

"Er…ah…yes, *ustadh*."

Continuing his lecture at the same pace, Sheikh Abu'l-Hasan now turned his attention to longitude. He proceeded to draw lines of longitude on his slate.

"I see that the lines of longitude get closer together as they approach the poles," Hakeem observed.

"That is an important observation, young man," said the teacher. "For that reason, measuring longitude is not a matter of measuring distance, but rather of measuring time. We know that the sun travels completely around the earth, three hundred and sixty degrees, in twenty-four hours, or fifteen degrees each hour. Ptolemy envisioned each interval to be one-third of an equinoctial hour, or five degrees. In this way, he created a net that is fundamentally one of time."

Hakeem was quick to interject, "And the more accurately one can measure time, the more accurate the net will be?"

"Exactly! But as you discovered yourself, measuring time is not as precise as one would need or like. But theoretically, if the coordinates listed in Ptolemy's tables were accurate, one could refer to those coordinates of latitudes and longitudes and know exactly where one is on the face of the earth in relation to all other places on this same earth."

"And using those same coordinates on a smaller scale, one should be able to produce a map," said Hakeem.

"Right again. Still, there is the problem of visually or graphically recording this on a flat paper or parchment. Our Arab geographers have made significant strides in figuring out how to do this. So, to that you must turn next."

Now a fully accepted student at the House of Wisdom, Hakeem spent the next several months reading books in the library. He started with translations of some of the ancient Greek classics. He read that Aristotle demonstrated that the earth was spherical by observing eclipses, or shadows, of the earth and moon, and that the closer one got to the equator, the warmer became the temperature. This latter idea was confirmed by Hakeem's reading of Hippocrates and Galen, and in the much more recent medical treatises of al-Kindi, whose translation of Ptolemy Hakeem was now so familiar with. Hakeem wondered why the temperature was warmer here in Baghdad than back home in the hills of Nusaybin. His father had always said that the differences between one place and another, and between one group of people and another, were the will of God, as he quoted from the Quran: "And among His signs is the creation of the heavens and the earth, and the variations of your languages and your colors." *Okay, so the will of God*, Hakeem thought, *but it is nice to know how God accomplished that.*

During these months, Hakeem did not have any formal sessions with his teacher, although he did see him from time to time at Friday prayer, where they would exchange greetings. The teacher would ask, "What are you reading these days?"

The obedient student would answer, "I am doing as you instructed. I am reading the works of the early scholars who were here at the House of Wisdom, some more than a century ago. This week I am reading…" Hakeem would name the scholar he was reading at that time.

One day it was Mohammed Ibn Musa al-Khwarizmi.

"Do you have time to come to my study?" The sheikh asked.

The two of them walked to the master's studio, and Hakeem summarized what he had read. "In his book *On the Calculation with Hindu Numerals* he introduced symbols representing the integers one through nine."

"And what about the concept of *sifr*?" asked the teacher.

"That is literally 'nothing'—zero. He used a dot or a circle as a placeholder in columns where no integer appeared."

Sheikh Abu'l-Hasan showed his approval with a slight smile. "Did you look at his *Compendious Book on Calculation by Completion and Balancing*?"

"I did," answered Hakeem, feeling rather pleased that he could answer in the affirmative.

"Excellent! Tell me then, what is the basic operation called *al-jabr*?"

Hakeem frowned. "Does it refer to performing the same function to both sides of an equation to balance the two sides?"

The master stroked his beard with his right hand. "Answering the question with a question suggests that you are uncertain of your answer. Perhaps you can show me what you mean." He picked up a slate and a piece of chalk, and using the Hindu symbols that al-Khwarizmi introduced, he wrote the equation $x^2 = 40x - 4x^2$. He then handed the chalk to Hakeem. "Can you tell me the value of x?"

Hakeem looked at the slate for several moments. It felt like an eternity. Finally, he said, "If I add $4x^2$ to both sides, I can get rid of the negative term to simplify the equation." He wrote: $5x^2 = 40x$. "Then I can divide each side by five and get…" He wrote: $x^2 = 8x$. "Then if I divide each side by x, I learn that x equals eight."

Sheikh Abu'l-Hasan seemed truly amazed—and quite proud of his student. "You seem remarkably at home using these new symbols to represent numbers."

"Memorizing what each symbol represented was the easy part."

"As you have found, it's much more than symbols representing numbers on a one-to-one basis," the sheikh said. "Al-Khwarizmi showed how these symbols can be used to constitute an abstract language called mathematics, a language that transcends spoken language and is equally understood by mathematicians regardless of what their spoken language is.

"There are other important books by al-Khwarizmi that you must study: his *Book of the Description of the Earth*, which is a major reworking of Ptolemy's *Geography*, and his book on trigonometry. This latter book describes how to determine the angles and sides of triangles—very useful in triangulation, a process by which we can determine distances between one place and another or find the direction of Mecca. This knowledge will be especially interesting to you as you begin to envision drawing your 'pictures of the world,' as you put it. We'll talk more about al-Khwarizmi the next time you come to see me."

Hakeem felt exhausted after this short but rather intense session of learning with his teacher. But he had a broad smile on his face as he walked home that evening.

The money that Hakeem had when he first arrived in Baghdad had almost completely run out. He had taken Musa's advice and sold his horse, but that money was also spent. He was two months behind in paying his rent when his father sent him a small amount of money by means of a note of transfer to a local banker in Baghdad. Hakeem realized that such generosity was really beyond his father's means. For weeks he had been trying to find some form of employment. He was good with numbers, so he thought he might be able to find work keeping the account books for a merchant, like he did back home in Nusaybin. Students at the House of Wisdom were not permitted to seek employment outside of their studies. He would have to be discreet in his search. He checked with dozens of merchants but was turned down time and time again. They either tended their books themselves or already had an accountant.

Finally, in desperation, he decided to confide in Musa. Musa was not only his most trusted friend. He was also resourceful. No one knew the ins and outs of surviving as a student in Baghdad quite as well as Musa.

Sure enough, Musa had a suggestion. "As you know, the small mosque in the neighborhood near where you live has a Quran school for young children every Friday that begins at midmorning and goes until noon. It so happens that the teacher has suddenly had to leave. He had to return to his village to tend to an ailing parent. You should go as soon as possible, today even, to inquire. I'm sure that the imam would be thrilled to have a student from the House of Wisdom teach the class every Friday."

Hakeem took his advice and went to see the imam that very day. The imam was overjoyed to offer the job to Hakeem. Was this just good luck, a coincidence, or a blessing from God? Whatever it was, Musa had come through yet again.

Hakeem began teaching his class the very next Friday morning and continued each Friday thereafter. Just as his father had done with him, for each session he would choose a particular verse or series of verses from the Quran. He would recite the passage in short phrases, asking the students to repeat each one after him until they memorized it. He would then carefully write the passage on a black slate with a piece of white lime chalk and instruct the students to copy his writing in black ink on their own wooden tablets. In a single session, the students would be able to do only a few phrases. It could take several sessions to do a complete passage in the Quran.

One Friday afternoon early in the fall, Sheikh Abu'l-Hasan said to Hakeem, "I think it is time that you come to my studio to report on your work. Come tomorrow at midmorning."

Hakeem felt relieved. He had begun to wonder if his teacher had lost interest in teaching him. He had done his work diligently. He felt that he had learned a great deal, but he had many questions to ask the great master.

It was the master who asked the first question. "Hakeem, can you imagine what it was like here at the House of Wisdom in the early days, in the time of Caliph al-Ma'mun?"

"I can only imagine based on the writings of the scholars who were here. Clearly, they were happy here. They must have been intellectually challenged. They learned from each other. And they seem to have had considerable support for their work from the administration."

"Yes, what you read between the lines of the scholars' work is correct. If the story is to be believed, Caliph al-Ma'mun met the great ancient scholar Aristotle in a dream. The caliph asked Aristotle to define 'that which is good.' The philosopher said that reason and revelation—that is, science and religion—are both good."

"Is that why the caliph founded the House of Wisdom?"

"Not only founded it. Al-Ma'mun was personally involved in the daily life of the academy and in the lives of the scholars. He visited the halls of learning regularly, engaged with the scholars, participated in academic discussions, and from time to time arbitrated academic debates."

"Was it the caliph's idea to commission the Ma'munic map?"

"Yes, a remarkable achievement, a representation of the world with its spheres, stars, lands, and seas, the inhabited and uninhabited regions, settlements of peoples, cities, and so on. The various sections, called climates, were represented in different colors. The map was based on a confirmation of data from Ptolemy's work and a remeasurement of the real size of the earth. The new map was also based on a series of corrections of the longitudes listed in Ptolemy's tables."

"But Ptolemy himself admitted that he had difficulty measuring longitude," said Hakeem. "How did Ma'mun's scholars do that?"

"The corrections were actually made by Indian astronomers and described in a series of treatises called the *Surya Siddhanta*. Since methods of measuring time are no further advanced than they were in ancient Greek times, the corrections were made using principles of geometry.

"The Hindu astronomers determined the celestial longitude of a number of heavenly bodies, including the sun and the moon, by first calculating the mean longitude of each—that is, the longitude that it would have if it were moving around the celestial sphere at a uniform speed. Then a correction is calculated based on the assumption that the body is sometimes ahead and sometimes behind the mean longitude. With this, they were able to more accurately measure the distance between the sun and the moon, as well as the distance between the earth and each of those celestial bodies."

"You mentioned the other day that it became a matter of triangulation."

"Good! You remember. It was when we were talking about al-Khwarizmi.

His *Book of the Description of the Earth* is really a model of a new genre of geographic writing that juxtaposes mathematical data of applied astronomy and the science of climates. These climates are parallel zones successively progressing from the equator toward the poles of the earth. Traditionally among the ancient Greeks, as well as among our own scholars until rather recently, the number of climates was seven."

"And now?"

"One of our own scholars at the House of Wisdom changed how we think about these *iqlim*. His name is Abu Zayd Ahmed al-Balkhi. He was Persian, greatly influenced by earlier Persian geographers and their concept of regions called *keshwar*, also seven in number. They were circular regions, not reflecting different climates as such but rather politico-ethnic divisions: Rum, India, China, and so forth. Al-Balkhi divided his world into twenty *iqlim*, reflecting territorial entities in the world of Islam—that is, political or administrative divisions. We might think of them as regions or provinces."

"But how does one get from the tables of coordinates of latitude and longitude to visually and accurately drawing out the space on paper?"

"Ahhh! That is the mystery, my son. Actually, one of our own students, Suhrab—you know him, I think..."

"Yes, he was one of the first people I met here."

"Well, he worked on this problem. He wrote out instructions for making a rectangular world map having horizontal and vertical scales for use in plotting the coordinates."

Hakeem was quite surprised. "And what became of it?"

"Good question. Suhrab seems to have completely lost interest in the project. He tore up his notes. In fact, now that I think of it, that was shortly before he left the academy."

Hakeem waited, but Sheikh Abu'l-Hasan did not seem inclined to elaborate on the circumstances of Suhrab's departure. Hakeem let the matter drop and returned to the Ma'munic map. "Isn't the Ma'munic map more accurate than the maps of the ancients?"

"Of course," Sheikh Abu'l-Hasan said. "And another of its innovations is the inscription of toponyms that reflect the Arab Muslim names. Between these toponyms that we are familiar with and the corrections in measurement, the Ma'munic map is far superior to any map Ptolemy could have produced."

"I have never seen Ptolemy's map," said Hakeem. "Nor, for that matter, the Ma'munic map."

"No copies of Ptolemy's map have survived. We can only try to reproduce one based on the data in his writing. As for the Ma'munic map, I have seen a copy, the only one ever produced..." There was a long pause. Sheikh

Abu'l-Hasan turned away and spoke slowly. "The copy has mysteriously disappeared."

"Disappeared! How could that be?"

"We do not know when, nor how, nor why. It was about two years ago that I saw it. Whoever removed it from the library must be either a scholar or a student here. No one else is permitted to enter. We suspect that the thief is someone hostile to the idea of a united Islamic empire under the rule of the Abbasids—someone who challenges the idea of a single, unified caliphate."

Hakeem hesitated, trying to decide if he should say anything at all. "Musa told me that the Abbasid caliph is in fact losing control these days."

"I'm afraid Musa is correct," said Sheikh Abu'l-Hasan, "although I don't think for a moment that Musa was involved in the theft of the map. He is not the only one here who feels that the caliphate is in decline. Most of us are aware of that."

"Can the map be reproduced?" asked Hakeem.

"There is a brilliant young scholar who left the academy before you came. His name is Ibrahim al-Istakhri. Some of his drawings are available here. You should have a look at them. You should also try to meet him as soon as you can."

CHAPTER FIVE

As Hakeem left the session, he thought about Sheikh Abu'l-Hasan's encouragement. It seemed that the great master was finally endorsing him as a scholar of the House of Wisdom. He had been in Baghdad only a year and still had much to learn, but he was finally one of them.

At the same time, Hakeem was disturbed to think that someone—whoever stole the Ma'munic map—would betray the trust that the academy placed in both the scholars and the students who were admitted to the elite institution of higher learning.

This was the last session that Hakeem had with the great master. Abu'l-Hasan al-Mas`udi left the House of Wisdom for Egypt within the week. There were others with whom Hakeem could consult from time to time, but for the most part he was now on his own to study and to work on his own projects without a personal mentor.

Later that afternoon, Hakeem met Musa at the restaurant Matam al-Sheikh. Musa seemed uncharacteristically agitated.

"Is something wrong?" Hakeem asked.

"No." Musa looked away. There was a long pause. "Listen, tonight there is a gathering just after evening prayer in the masjid up the street from where you live. I think you should attend."

"What is the gathering about?"

"You will have to come to find out. I am sure you will find it interesting."

Hakeem had not been to the mosque before. It was quite small and had no minaret. No muezzin announced the call to prayer from this mosque, but that was not a problem, since one heard the call from the many other mosques within earshot. Attendance at the tiny mosque was sparse, only twenty or so men, almost all of them young. Hakeem recognized four or five of them as students at the House of Wisdom.

Before prayer began, one of the attendees locked the door from the inside. Hakeem had never seen such secretiveness in a mosque.

The imam was Yusuf al-Nasafi, the tailor friend of Musa's host, whom Hakeem had met at Musa's house many months earlier. Imam al-Nasafi led the gathering in prayer but nothing more. When the prayer was over and each person had expressed a greeting of peace to the attendees on either side of him, another man, one of the last to arrive for prayer, came from the back of the room to address the gathering.

It was Suhrab. Hakeem had last seen the other student almost a year ago when he saw Suhrab speaking with Musa and Yusuf al-Nasafi outside Sheikh Abu'l-Hasan's studio. Hakeem leaned over and whispered in Musa's ear, "Did you know he was going to be here?"

"Shhhh!" Musa whispered back.

Suhrab began to speak. "I have just returned from Raqqad in Ifriqiya. I am sad to report that the Fatimid caliphate is in crisis."

Hakeem was all ears. He knew that there were challengers to the Abbasid caliph, but he knew few of the details.

"As some of you may know, there is no longer one single caliph in the Islamic world," Suhrab said. "In addition to the Abbasid caliph, there are two rival caliphs. The Umayyad caliphs, who once ruled all of the Muslim world from Damascus, were defeated by the Abbasids and fled to Andalusia in the far west. About twenty years ago, an Umayyad pretender tried to reestablish his authority in the city of Córdoba. The other challenger is the Fatimid caliph in Ifriqiya. He is a descendant of the Mahdi who reestablished the *true* caliphate in Ifriqiya almost a half century ago."

A young man in the front row interrupted, "Why do you say 'the *true* caliph'?"

"The Fatimids are Shiites, and like all Shiites they believe that the first true imam was Ali, Prophet Mohammed's cousin and son-in-law. All subsequent legitimate imams were direct descendants of Ali and the Prophet's daughter Fatimah."

"What is the crisis you speak of?" another man shouted.

"A rebellion has broken out against the Fatimid caliph. Kharijite Muslims in Ifriqiya have staged an uprising."

Still another man asked, "Who are these Kharijites of whom you speak?"

"That is a fair question," Suhrab said. "Their origin goes back to the very first civil war in Islam, when Ali was caliph. Ali's cousin Mu'awiya challenged him for his position as caliph. The conflict came to a head at a place called Siffin on the bank of the River Euphrates. Ali's army was outnumbered, but by the grace of God Ali found himself on the verge of victory, until Mu'awiya put forth a ruse that turned the tide. His forces bound copies of the Quran atop their lances and petitioned that the conflict be resolved by negotiation. Ali felt he had no choice but to accept. He could not argue with the word of God. But many of his followers saw his willingness to arbitrate as a sign of weakness, and they walked out on him—abandoned him." The word *kharaja* meant "to walk out," hence the name of the Kharijite movement.

"These Kharijites stress the moral integrity of each individual," Suhrab continued, "especially their leaders. They preach the right to reject, indeed to oppose, even violently, a tyrannical government—a principle that can easily be turned against any government with which they disagree. They vehemently oppose the Abbasid caliphate, which they see as having illegally usurped power. But, alas, they also oppose the Fatimid government seated in Mahdiya. The crisis of which I speak is the beginning of a Kharijite rebellion."

Following the speech, several of the young men listening seemed ready to sign up to fight against the Kharijites. Yet others were ready to join them.

"I am not here as a recruiter," Suhrab said. "I'm here only to inform you of what is going on. You must know that it is only a matter of time before the true caliph, the Mahdi, rules throughout the Muslim world."

Suhrab spoke with such passion that it was clear his sympathy lay totally with the Fatimid regime in Mahdiya. *Does this mean that Suhrab opposes the Abbasid caliph right here in Baghdad?* Hakeem wondered. Was that why he had left the academy so suddenly?

When the meeting was over, Hakeem waited until everyone was gone except for Suhrab and himself. He approached Suhrab, who was relocking the door. "Are you among the anti-Abbasid rebels? Is that why you left without saying goodbye?"

Suhrab was only slightly apologetic. "I'm sorry I left so suddenly. There simply wasn't time. If you ask, am I a supporter of the Fatimid caliph, the one true imam, the answer is yes."

"Why are you convinced that the Fatimid ruler is the true imam?" Hakeem asked.

"I believe that Ali, the cousin of the Prophet and the husband of the Prophet's daughter, was chosen by God. The Prophet himself announced him to be his successor."

"Did the Prophet ever clearly say that? Most Muslims believe he did not.

They say that he intended his successor to be chosen by a consensus of the prominent leaders of the community."

"I know that is the common belief. But think for a moment. Is it logical that God would leave such an important decision to chance, opening the possibility for open conflict within the community, such as we have seen during the civil war and what we are beginning to see again right here? No. The Prophet *did* make a statement."

"When and where?" Hakeem leaned forward in anticipation.

"It was at a place called Khum. The Prophet was standing high on a rock talking to the crowd in front of him. When he finished his speech, he extended his hand to Ali, who was standing in the front row, inviting Ali to join him on the platform. The Prophet said to the crowd, 'This is Ali. He is my *wali*, my friend, my soul mate; he should be your *wali* too.' From this time on, starting with Ali, imams were divinely chosen from among the household of the Prophet. Ali and his descendants alone are true imams, the sole rightful heads of the Islamic community. The caliphate belongs to them by God's choice. We will take from the Abbasids what the Abbasids have taken from the Umayyads."

All of a sudden, there was a loud pounding at the door, followed by a rattling of the lock. Someone was breaking in.

"We must leave at once," Suhrab said. "Quickly, through the imam's door to the left of the mihrab. For your sake, you should not be seen with me. When we leave, you go to the left and I will go right. Meet me in one hour in the neighborhood southeast of the Kufa Gate. There is a safe house there on the alleyway called al-Qaiyiga. You will recognize it by the single candle burning by the entrance. Be sure that you are not followed. Now, go quickly!"

The two of them fled through the imam's door, and Suhrab locked it and took off running to the right as he said he would.

It was all happening too quickly. Hakeem stood there for a moment in the street behind the mosque. He could hear the last call to prayer, the one that comes at the fall of darkness. There was no moon at all, and the alleyway was dark. He was not sure what to do. A sound behind him told him that whoever had broken into the mosque was now trying to force the imam's door open. He needed to run, as Suhrab had instructed him.

Would he meet Suhrab in an hour? He did not know what Suhrab meant by a safe house. The Kufa Gate was on the opposite side of the city. At this time of night, the central administrative part of the city was closed. He would have to go all the way around. If he was to find the right alleyway with a house with one candle at the entrance, he would need to hurry.

He took off at a run and heard the imam's door crash open behind him. "You go right and we'll go left," a voice shouted. That meant that at least several men had broken into the mosque, and at least two were now chasing him. There were probably two or more chasing Suhrab.

Hakeem was in better than average physical condition, but he had no idea what shape his pursuers were in. Could he outrun them? He did not know exactly where he was going, but the darkness, combined with his speed, was his ally. The sound of footsteps faded. He was pulling away, and he finally lost them at one of the many turns he took as he raced through the narrow streets, hopefully in the general direction of the Kufa Gate.

He ducked into a very narrow, very dark alleyway—so dark that he could barely see his hand in front of his eyes. He waited there—he was not sure how long—to make sure he was no longer being followed. When he felt reasonably confident that he had eluded his pursuers, he left his hiding place and tried to get a sense of where he was. He proceeded with great caution for a few blocks. He had just crossed a main road when he recognized it as the one leading toward the Basra Gate. He had run halfway toward his destination. He proceeded in the same direction for another twenty minutes or so and began searching for the alleyway called al-Qaiyiga. How would he recognize it? There was no one out at this time of night whom he could ask. And if there were someone out, would he be able to trust him?

Hakeem was quite sure that more than an hour had passed since he had parted ways with Suhrab. He was wandering through the narrow streets of the quarter when he suddenly saw the flicker of a candle in a small niche next to the doorway of a house. Could this be the safe house? Should he knock at the door? He decided to wait to see what would happen. If Suhrab was already inside, he might soon come out to see if Hakeem was in the alley.

More time passed, but Suhrab did not appear. Hakeem knocked on the door. Nothing. He knocked again and waited, seemingly forever. Finally, a young man opened the door. Hakeem recognized him as one of the small group who had been at the meeting at the mosque.

"I have come to meet with Suhrab as he instructed me to do," Hakeem whispered.

"He is not here," the young man said. "He never showed up. We are very worried that something has happened to him."

Suhrab's pursuers must have been faster than the ones who chased me, Hakeem thought. *Suhrab must have been caught.*

It was the afternoon of the next day before Hakeem was able to find

Musa. It was, after all, Musa who had invited him to the meeting in the first place. Surely Musa would be able to help him assess what had happened the night before. Hopefully, he would know what had happened to Suhrab. They agreed to meet at Matami Farid.

As soon as Hakeem saw Musa, he knew that something was dreadfully wrong. It was written all over Musa's face. "Suhrab is dead!" Musa said. "He was killed last night."

Hakeem drew his hands to cover his ears as if to block out this horrible news. "Killed! By whom?"

"Almost certainly by people who are opposed to the caliphate."

"Which caliphate?" Hakeem asked.

"The Fatimids. There are many reasons why they sought to apprehend Suhrab. It is possible that it could be Haytham al-Khariji and his thugs. Or it could be agents in collaboration with some of the palace guards. Some suspect that it was Suhrab who was responsible for the disappearance of Caliph al-Ma'mun's precious map."

"Why would Suhrab steal the map?"

"Because it represented an Islamic world united and ruled by the caliph of Baghdad, an idea vehemently rejected by the Fatimids of Ifriqiya." Musa, head down, turned away from Hakeem. "Suhrab was a *da'i*, an agent of the Fatimid caliph, who continues to mount a force to oppose the Abbasid dominance of the world." He now raised his head to meet Hakeem's gaze. "I too am a *da'i*. There is a small group of us here in Baghdad, as there are small cells in most of the cities throughout *mamlakat'l-Islam*. We do what we can to promote the ideals of Ismaili Shiism, which involves first and foremost allegiance to the unity—that is, the oneness—of God and to the unity of the Islamic empire under the one true imam, the caliph in Mahdiya."

"Is that why Suhrab was killed, because he believed in the unity of the Islamic world under the Fatimids?"

"I should think that is cause enough for the supporters of the Abbasid caliph here in Baghdad. The Abbasids are growing less and less secure. They have accepted that the Shiite Buwayhids have taken political control of the Baghdad caliphate, leaving the Abbasids to enjoy the religious leadership and titular privileges of the caliphate. But the two rival caliphs in Mahdiya and Córdoba are a different story. They present a real threat to the religious and cultural unity of Islam itself. And of the two, the Fatimids are the biggest threat, if for no other reason than that the Fatimid imam is the one true imam—the rightful caliph, the successor to the Prophet Mohammed, may peace be upon him. That is what we believe, and what many believe. As we speak, the Fatimids are developing a strategy to expand their jurisdiction westward to the Maghrib and eastward to Egypt and beyond. Then it's just a matter of time before they are on our very doorstep."

"Won't the Abbasids try to stop them?"

"They will try. The Abbasids still have many supporters. Apparently a group of them ran Suhrab down last night and beat him to death."

"I think there were at least four of them. Two of them chased me, and some went after Suhrab. I was fast enough to get away, but it seems that Suhrab was not so fortunate."

"Did they see you well enough to identity you?"

"I don't know. I don't think so. It was dark. What about you? Aren't you worried they might know your identity?"

"I have been careful to avoid being seen with anyone who is known to be a *da'i*. We purposely keep the cells very small. We are never seen together. We meet in obscure settings and only after dark."

Something had been troubling Hakeem since Musa's invitation to the meeting, and even as far back as his invitation to dinner so many months ago. "Why me? Why did you invite me to the meeting last night? I am no rebel. How do you even know you can trust me?"

"It was no coincidence that I stood next to you to pray that first day we met. I deliberately followed you into the mosque on the instruction of Yusuf al-Nasafi."

Hakeem was shocked. "But I don't know him. I had never even met him before that dinner at your host's home."

"Nevertheless, he knows you. He is an excellent judge of character," said Musa. "Yusuf al-Nasafi is the leader of the Fatimid cell in Baghdad. By the way, that is not his real name. He deliberately keeps a low profile in whatever circle he is in. From the first day that Suhrab met you, Suhrab sensed you would be sympathetic to the Fatimid cause. He reported that to Yusuf, who asked me to bring you to my host family's home so he could himself assess your potential as a member of our group."

"You tricked me! I thought you were my friend."

"No, Hakeem, I did not trick you. I *am* your friend. If I were not your friend, I would never have thought of getting you involved. And even as my friend, I am not sorry that I have now put you at risk. Yes, there is risk involved in being a *da'i*. But there is reward in knowing that you are doing the right thing—the right thing for God and the right thing for the one true imam." Musa placed his hand on Hakeem's shoulder. "I fear you are already somewhat at risk here in Baghdad. You had best be careful. It would be best if you and I are not seen together for a while. We can talk about our work at the House of Wisdom, but we should avoid seeing each other outside the academy."

Hakeem took a few steps toward the door but hesitated, a sudden thought striking him. "What about our teacher, Sheikh Abu'l-Hasan al-Mas`udi? Is he a member of the movement?"

"Not directly. But he is definitely sympathetic to what we believe in. He became increasingly disillusioned by the decline of the power of the Abbasid caliph. He is committed to the unity of all Muslims under the one true imam. It is possible that is why he felt that he had to leave Baghdad."

Hakeem stepped out onto the street, his mind spinning with new information. He was shocked by Suhrab's murder. He had not seen Suhrab very often, certainly not often enough. But Suhrab had been someone he really liked. Suhrab had been so kind to him those first few days after Hakeem arrived in the bustling city. He must have believed strongly in the cause that had gotten him killed. Hakeem wondered what it would be like to give one's life for a great cause. He began to realize that he was feeling sympathy for the cause that had moved Suhrab's actions and led to his death.

With his mentor gone and being unable to see his friend Musa outside of the academy, Hakeem felt alone—and overwhelmed. There were so many books yet to read in the library, so much work to do before he could be considered a geographer. He decided that he would keep a low profile. He would read and study on his own. Sheikh Abu'l-Hasan al-Mas`udi had taught him to read with a critical, discerning mind. He was confident that with the base of knowledge of the scholars who had come before him at the House of Wisdom, he could move toward his goal of producing an accurate picture of the world.

CHAPTER SIX

Baghdad, 946

Hakeem found himself particularly fond of a book called *Kitab al-Buldan*, the *Book of Countries*. Its author, Amr Ibn Bahr al-Jahiz, came from Basra, southeast of Baghdad. He lived and wrote in the early decades after the Abbasids became rulers of the Muslim world and moved their capital to Baghdad. His work, though not especially scientific in terms of geography in its strictest sense, had a very strong sense of patriotism and loyalty to the Abbasids. Hakeem committed some of his words to memory: "If it were not incumbent on us to put first what God put first and to put last what he put last, the majority would mention the homelands first, because of the place they occupy in the human heart." Hakeem was getting homesick.

Hakeem closely examined the works of two other authors. He started with the work of Ibn Khurdadhbih, a Persian by birth, born over one hundred years earlier. Khurdadhbih wrote books on Persian genealogy, world history, food and drink, and music and musical instruments. Hakeem looked at all of them, but the one he focused on the most was a kind of geography book: *Kitab al-Masalik wa'l-Mamalik*, the *Book of Routes and Kingdoms*. This was a work that Khurdadhbih wrote in his capacity as an official in the Abbasid administration. He had served as *sahib al-barid wa'l-khabar*, the director of postal and intelligence services, in the province of Jibal, a vital region northeast of Baghdad. His work listed distances between the cities controlled by the Abbasid caliph. It could be described as a form of administrative geography, listing vital information about specific places with specific details about the resources therein. Certainly, information that would be useful for any ruler in his attempt to govern—or acquire—territory.

A Muslim first and foremost, Ibn Khurdadhbih opened with a division of the world centered around the Qaaba in Mecca, the epicenter of the *mamlakat'l-Islam*. An image in Khurdadhbih's book that reinforced this idea was his circular qibla chart, so important in assisting faithful Muslims in their obligation to face Mecca when they prayed. Khurdadhbih's chart divided the world into eight parts that radiated out from Mecca at its center. This was a conceptual icon for the *mamlakat'l-Islam*. But his work quickly shifted to the region of Sawad, where the headquarters of the Abbasid caliph were located, right where Hakeem found himself reading Ibn Khurdadhbih's book.

As he read this work, Hakeem found himself becoming more and more comfortable with the term and the concept of *mamlakat*. Combined with the term *al-Islam*, it was pregnant with meaning. It somehow set apart that portion of the known world that was under the jurisdiction of the caliph of Baghdad. Although Hakeem's father had never used the term *mamlakat'l-Islam*, the unity of this realm of Islam was certainly a concept he believed in and preached in his local mosque. The shariah of Islam guaranteed the rights of Muslims and other People of the Book—Jews, Christians, and Zoroastrians. But just how unified was the realm of the caliph in reality? In view of everything that Hakeem had learned, he was beginning to question how unified it was.

The passage of months transformed into years—three whole years since Hakeem Ibn al-Harith had first set eyes on the circular walls of Baghdad. He was ever conscious that he now lived in the capital of the Abbasid caliphate, the very epicenter of the Islamic world—the unity of which he had also learned was in decline. As he reflected back on those three years, he felt a confident sense that he had accomplished what he had come here to do. He had read many of the books in the library at the House of Wisdom. He understood the concepts of latitude and longitude, distance and direction, how to measure them, and how the interrelationships between them could help him produce pictures of the world. He understood the difference between administrative geography on the one hand—a geography that reported on those aspects of the land that would be useful to rulers wanting to maintain law and order and collect taxes—and a more thorough human geography on the other—one that observed, recorded, and analyzed a people's complex existence and culture.

As fulfilling as his time in Baghdad had been, Hakeem felt increasingly alone. He sorely missed his great teacher, Sheikh Abu'l-Hasan al-Mas`udi, who had left Baghdad two years earlier. He missed his shrewd guidance in the choice of what books to read, his clear analysis of complex concepts that seemed so simple after he explained them, and, most of all, his insightful comments about the ultimate relationship between what we, so small here in our own little space on earth, can fathom about the greater world and what lies beyond.

Even years later, Hakeem had not gotten over the shock of the murder of his first friend, Suhrab. Although he had spent much time thinking about it, there was much that Hakeem still did not understand about the events of that fateful night.

Hakeem had followed his friend Musa's advice not to spend time together outside of the House of Wisdom. Nor did they engage in lengthy conversations inside the academy—only brief exchanges about their studies, as they did from time to time with other students.

But now Musa was gone too—Hakeem knew not where. He had not seen him in over a month. Could Musa's disappearance be related to the fact that he was, as Suhrab once was, an agent for the alleged Fatimid rebels in Ifriqiya?

One afternoon, after he spent his usual time in the library, Hakeem went to the house where Musa lived. He swung the heavy bronze knocker against the solid wooden door. Several seconds passed, although it seemed much longer. Hakeem was about to knock again when the doorman opened the door barely wide enough to see who was knocking. He seemed to recognize Hakeem and opened the door slightly wider, only enough to inquire what Hakeem wanted.

"Is Musa here?" Hakeem asked.

"No," the man answered curtly. "He has not been home in nearly a month. We don't know where he is. Most of his belongings are still here, but he is gone. He did not tell us he was leaving. Nor did he leave a note. I can tell you nothing more."

Hakeem thought he sensed fear in the man's voice, which left him unsurprised at this cold reception—but he was disappointed, even frustrated. He had not been back to the small neighborhood mosque where he last saw Suhrab the night he was murdered. Even though Musa had warned him against it, Hakeem decided to go now. Perhaps he could find out something about Musa's current whereabouts.

The mosque was shut tight. The door was locked. Hakeem went around to the back, to the imam's door from which he and Suhrab had fled on that dreadful night. It too was locked. At a small shop around the corner, Hakeem inquired where he might find the imam of the mosque. The shopkeeper said that the mosque had been closed for several weeks and not a single soul had been there—not the imam, not a caretaker, no one.

As Hakeem walked back toward his own house, he felt a growing sense that someone was watching him, but he could not be sure. Rather than going directly home, he decided to go to Matami Farid. He ordered a bowl of hot cider and sat quietly sipping his cider for quite some time, watching to see if anyone had followed him there, but no one appeared.

He did not go directly home from the restaurant. He went to evening prayer at his neighborhood mosque and then went back to the restaurant for a light supper. Finally, he went home.

When he arrived, his landlord handed him a sealed note. Hakeem unsealed the note and read, *You are in danger! You are suspected of being part of a subversive group of agents loyal to the Fatimid pretender to the throne, a group working to undermine the authority of the one true caliph. It is no longer safe for you in Baghdad. You should leave at once.*

This is preposterous, Hakeem thought. He had been to one meeting where Suhrab had spoken in support of the Fatimids, and he had been chased from the meeting—but nothing more. *I, Hakeem Ibn al-Harith, am certainly not a Fatimid agent!*

His first impulse was to defy the warning. *Who does this person think he is? Who is anyone to tell me I must leave Baghdad?* But he soon began to reconsider. Whether he was a Fatimid agent or not, the mere fact that he was perceived to be one was enough to put him in danger. Besides, his teacher was gone. And although there were many books in the library that he had not yet read, he had a good sense of what he needed to know about mapmaking. It was not as if there were no libraries, even great libraries, in other parts of the Islamic world—in Fez, for example, where his friend Musa was from.

Yes, that's another thing, Hakeem thought. *My best friend is missing.* Had Musa left suddenly because he'd felt he was in imminent danger? Was there any other kind?

Hakeem decided he would leave Baghdad as soon as possible. He rationalized his decision by reminding himself of his long-term goal—to travel the world in search of knowledge, to record his findings in a book accompanied by pictures of the world that he would draw himself.

It was time to go.

But where? He decided that his second venture to a new place would be in the footsteps of his teacher, Sheikh Abu'l-Hasan. He would go to Egypt.

He had been rather frugal over the three years he had lived in Baghdad, so he had not accumulated many possessions. He packed the few changes of clothes that he had and one rather thick folio with the notes he had taken during his studies at the House of Wisdom.

From what he had read in the notes of earlier scholars at the academy, he knew he would have to follow the setting sun to go to Damascus. From there, he would turn south toward Jerusalem and on toward Egypt. His book knowledge, useful as it was, was insufficient to prepare him for the journey. He needed to know more.

He went to the large merchants' *funduq* on the west side of town outside the Kufa Gate. Not wanting to announce that he was desperate to leave town, he began a casual conversation with a caravan master who had recently arrived from Damascus.

"How large is your caravan?" Hakeem asked.

"Not so large," the man said. "Only sixty camels, ten lines with six camels in each."

Hakeem knew that some of the caravans that arrived in Baghdad had as many as a hundred and fifty camels, sometimes even more. "Why so few?"

"I usually take more. I arrived here in Baghdad a week ago with a hundred camels. But I have fewer clients for the return voyage."

"You mean you are not going on to China?"

"No, I am not. I constitute one link along the Silk Road. It is safer than traveling the whole distance in that long-distance trade. I am from Damascus and I earn my living running caravans only to Baghdad and back. I know the route well, and I don't have to be gone from home so long. I am returning to Damascus as soon as I can."

"Who are your customers?" And more important, would the man be willing to take one more?

"Whoever has cargo to ship. Merchants hire me to carry their goods, but rarely do they travel with the caravan. They have agents in certain caravanserais such as this one who receive the cargo from me. They will either sell it here in Baghdad or contract to ship it on to another destination."

"Surely you are not traveling alone," Hakeem said.

"I have ten camel pullers, one for each line. I usually have up to ten camels in a line, but I do not take camels unless they are carrying cargo. Since I have less cargo for this trip, I sold some of my camels here, and I will replace them in Damascus. That is cheaper than taking a camel without a load."

Hakeem tried to inject a casual tone in his next question. "Can a person be cargo for one of your camels?"

"Rarely do I take travelers as paying clients. They can be much more trouble than cargo. Besides, they have to be fed."

Still trying to conceal his sense of urgency, Hakeem asked, "What about a healthy young student…uh…who could pay a fair price—would you take him?"

"Is that not a contradiction—a student who can pay a fair price?"

"Fair enough," Hakeem said, "but this student doesn't eat very much, has worked hard at his studies, and has saved money from his employment as a teacher. Would you take him?'"

The caravan master surveyed Hakeem with a piercing look. Even though Hakeem had feigned a casual tone, the man did not seem fooled for an instant. "If that student be you, then I might consider it."

The very next morning, Hakeem was off to Damascus.

PART II

CHAPTER SEVEN

Palmyra, 946

The great Syrian Desert separated Damascus from Baghdad, some four hundred miles as the crow flies—if it flew through the desert's center, which is almost impenetrable. Hakeem's caravan skirted the northern edge, where it gives way to more fertile plains of grass. After eighteen days of hard, steady march, the caravan reached the ancient trade city of Tadmor, also known as Palmyra. Since very ancient times, Palmyra was a principal caravan city, one of the most important links in the long-distance trade along the Silk Road between China and the Mediterranean. All caravans coming from the East stopped there.

The leader of the caravan announced that they would remain in Palmyra for two nights. They would spend a day to rest and obtain provisions for the rest of the journey to Damascus.

As a paying client, Hakeem did not need to obtain provisions for his own upkeep. That was included in what he had paid up front for his passage. Nonetheless, he decided to wander through the souk. It was smaller than the market in Baghdad, but interesting nonetheless. Its main reason for being was to cater to the long-distance trade along the Silk Road. When two or three large caravans were here at the same time, there was an abundant supply of new products coming from both East and West. And the market today was very crowded, with people walking shoulder to shoulder, often having to push their way through a human traffic jam.

Shortly after dusk, Hakeem thought that he should retire to the *funduq*, a rather large caravanserai where his caravan had booked lodging for their two-night stay. But first he would attend evening prayer at the mosque from which he could hear the melodious chant of the muezzin calling the faithful to prayer.

It was just then that Hakeem realized he was being followed. He accelerated his pace. Two men some distance behind him seemed to be picking up their pace as well. He could not imagine why anyone would be following him in this town where he had only just arrived and that he had never visited before. Perhaps the men were thieves who preyed on the traveling merchants. *But it is obvious that I am by no means a wealthy merchant*, Hakeem thought.

He did have all of the money that he had saved from his tutoring, the equivalent of about two month's earnings, in a small leather pouch hanging around his neck under his woolen shirt. *Still, there are far better prospects here for a potential thief than me.*

Hakeem turned at the next corner, even though that had not been his original intention. He pushed his way through the mass of pedestrians, hoping he might lose the pursuers here.

He paused at the end of the street to look back. The two men were also pushing their way through the crowd. Hakeem recognized the taller of the pair. The man stood head and shoulders above everyone else in the street. Hakeem remembered his height and heavyset appearance, and he recognized what Musa had described as a scar on the side of his face. It was Haytham al-Khariji, the man who had beaten Nuri. What was he doing there? *Why is he following me?* And how had he known that Hakeem would be leaving Baghdad so suddenly? Unless it was someone in Haytham's organization who had sent the warning note…

This was not the time to find answers to his questions. It was time to run. Hakeem began to run as fast as he could around the corner. He ran the full length of the street and around the next corner. He could see the mosque and headed straight for the entrance, where several men were already filing in for evening prayer. Entering in their company, Hakeem knew that he would be safe inside, at least until the prayer was over and it was time to leave.

Hakeem did not see his pursuers again that night. Perhaps they hadn't seen him enter the mosque. *Or maybe they were not chasing me after all. They just happened to be here.*

After a troubled night's rest, Hakeem awoke early the next morning to join the caravan for the second half of the journey to Damascus.

Damascus was the oldest city Hakeem had ever seen. The former capital of the Umayyad empire, now defunct, its history went back at least two thousand years. Traces of the city's long history were still visible. Hakeem marveled at them and everything else he saw. His caravan arrived late in the afternoon, just as the call to prayer resonated out from the minaret of the Grand Mosque. The caravan was not so large that it could not seek lodging within the city itself. It entered Damascus through the Bab Sharqi, the Eastern Gate, also known as the Roman Gate of the Sun. Like other monumental gates, it had a large central arch for horse-drawn vehicles and two smaller arches on either side for pedestrians. The travelers proceeded west on the Street Called Straight until they reached a modest *funduq* on the left-hand side of the street.

Hakeem was anxious to tour the famous city. He quickly deposited his small sack of belongings in his assigned spot in one of the rooms on the upper floor of the *funduq*.

Accompanied by one of the camel-runners, who was a native of Damascus, Hakeem set out to walk along the Street Called Straight. They stopped in front of a tiny structure called the Sheikh Nabhan Mosque. It had a small balcony on the front in the form of a pulpit that served in lieu of a minaret, providing space for the muezzin to sing out his call to prayer. Hakeem's guide began to tell him about the place.

"The mosque was built over a very ancient church built centuries ago to mark the place of the House of Judas."

"What is special about the House of Judas?" Hakeem asked.

"You have not read the Gospels of the Christians, my friend?"

Hakeem shook his head. He had read many books over the last three years, but he had not read the Christian Gospels.

"Never mind," said the camel-runner. "It is the house where Paul of Tarsus remained for three days without eating or drinking and, perhaps, was baptized by Ananias and was made to see. Paul of Tarsus was a disciple of Jesus the Christ. Some say he was the second founder of the Christian faith."

Hakeem's city tour was cut short by a muezzin's call to prayer. "Excuse me, dear friend," Hakeem said, "where is the famous Umayyad mosque?"

"You are very close," his guide said. "Walk along the Street Called Straight to the next corner. Turn right. Just beyond the market of the goldsmiths is the mosque. No need to hurry. You have at least twenty minutes before prayer will begin. By the way, if you are curious about the mosque, you will find to the side of the entrance an old blind man with his cupped hand outstretched to accept backsheesh. For a coin or two, he'll tell you more than you want to know."

"Will you not join me?" Hakeem asked.

"Thank you for offering, sir. But as you might have guessed, I am Christian."

"Of course," Hakeem said, feeling a bit embarrassed that he had not made that connection himself.

When evening prayer was over and each person present had offered a gesture of peace to the person to his right and left, Hakeem sought out the blind man to learn more about this holy place of worship.

The blind man was more than happy to oblige. His eyes were wide open but colorless, only pure white. His voice was soft and slow but quite steady. "Long ago in ancient times," he began, "this was the place of worship of the Sabians. Then Greeks took over the place for the practice of their own cult. Still later it became the property of the Jews. It was during that time that John the Baptist, the son of Zacharias, was killed and his head was displayed above the door called Bab Djairun. It was then that the Christians converted the building into a church where they celebrated their faith—that is, until the arrival of Islam, when it was converted to a mosque. In the same place where John's head was displayed, so was the head of Husain Ibn Ali, may peace be upon them both..." The blind man went on and on for some time and would have continued on longer, but Hakeem was ready to leave.

Hakeem gave the man a few coins. He then sat on the beautifully carpeted floor for a few more minutes, took a sheet of paper and pen and ink from his bag, and began to make detailed notes of what he saw and what he had learned from the blind man.

Later that night, when he was settled in at the *funduq*, after the evening meal and all of the other merchants and travelers had retired to their sleeping mats, Hakeem remained at the dining table. By the light of a single flickering candle, he began to transcribe his notes and to describe what he had seen:

> Here in Damascus is a mosque that surpasses in beauty any mosque in all of the Islamic world.

Hakeem paused a moment as he called to mind the story of the first

Muslim martyr—no, both martyrs.

> John and Husain were so much alike, he thought. He continued to write, The Umayyad caliph Walid Ibn Abd al-Malik restored the building to make it the spectacular mosque that it is today. The floor paving, wall panels, and columns are all in marble. The capitals atop the columns and the vaults are gold. The mihrab is covered with gold leaf and encrusted with semiprecious stones. The friezes around the tops of the walls are gilded and covered with Quranic inscriptions.

Hakeem set his pen down and contemplated what he had written. He recalled the verse in the Holy Quran:

> Lo! Those who believe, and those who are Jews, and Christians, and Sabians—whoever believes in God and the Last Day and does right—surely their reward is with their Lord, and no fear shall come upon them, neither shall they grieve.

Then he made a decision that would impact the rest of his life. He would describe anything he thought to be noteworthy—everything he saw in his travels and learned from the people he met. He would compile a book that was not so much a diary but rather a detailed description of the world that was just beginning to open up before his eyes. He would draw a verbal picture of the world. He would begin right here, right now, in Damascus.

Hakeem was now a man on a mission. He would go to Egypt to find his teacher, Sheikh Abu'l-Hasan al-Mas`udi. En route he would pass through Palestine, the smallest region of all of greater Syria, about two days march from north to south.

As the now travelogue writer approached Jerusalem from the north, he noted in his journal:

> There is a place in the city called the Mihrab of the Prophet David. It is a stone structure close to fifty cubits high. This is the very first thing one sees of the city, high on the plateau in the center. Inside the mosque are niches for the prophet Abraham and his sons, Isaac and Ishmael, and for David and Solomon, Jesus, and of course Mohammed.

Hakeem had learned as a child from his father that Islam venerated all of the prophets of the Bible, including Jesus.

Still outside the city walls, Hakeem passed the small Church of Saint Stephen—the martyr who he had learned was the first martyr of the Christian faith. For a brief moment he was tempted to enter, but the draw of the holy city itself was too strong. As he approached Jerusalem, he felt an almost irrepressible urge to go directly to the Haram al-Sharif, the Noble Sanctuary, marking the very spot from where Mohammed ascended to heaven and met face to face with God. This was one of the most holy sites for all Muslims, second only to the shrine in Mecca.

Before Hakeem realized it, he was actually beginning to run. He could hardly wait to get there.

He entered the ancient city through the Gate of the Column. It was late in the afternoon, almost time for evening prayer. As he entered the gate complex, he saw what one would see at almost any city gate: a dozen or so men, almost all of them sporting thick white beards, sitting on the long stone bench just inside the entrance, looking like elder statesmen discussing the weighty issues of the day.

Addressing them, Hakeem asked, "Can any of you kind sirs point me to the Haram al-Sharif? I would like to get there before prayer time." He wondered why the men were not heading toward the mosque themselves, but then it dawned on him: they were probably not Muslim. He knew that there were many Jews and Christians in Jerusalem.

"You are very close," one of the men said. "Just ahead, you will come to a fork in the road. If you continue along the main street to the right, the ancient Cardo Maximus, you will reach the Mosque of Omar. But if instead you veer to the left and walk another thirty yards or so, you will see an intersection. Turn left, and the entrance to your Noble Sanctuary is straight ahead."

Hakeem turned as directed at the first intersection. The street was crowded, but within just a few steps he could see the wall of the sanctuary ahead of him. He continued along the western wall.

He passed a section where several men wearing Jewish prayer shawls faced the wall, bowing their heads back and forth in a rocking motion. They were praying.

One of the men had just finished his prayers and was now walking in the same direction as Hakeem. "Is there an entrance into the Haram al-Sharif farther down this road?" Hakeem asked.

"There are several," the man said. "Just ahead is David's Gate, and a little farther, the Gate of Remission. Are you Muslim?"

"Yes, my friend. Will that make a difference?"

"You might prefer to walk all the way to the corner of the enclosure. That is where, according to your tradition, the angel Gabriel tethered Prophet Mohammed's horse, Buraq. Just around the corner is the gate through which the Prophet himself entered the Temple Mount."

"The Temple Mount?"

"This is what my people call it. The area is at least as important to us Jews as it is to Muslims. It is the site of the ancient temple built by Solomon, son of David, then rebuilt by King Herod the Great. It is not certain exactly where the Holy of Holies is located, forbidden to all but the high priests. For that reason, many Jews will not enter the enclosure at all."

"Have you ever been inside?" Hakeem asked.

"Yes. I am not as strict as some. I wanted to see the rock that lies under the dome built by your caliph Abd al-Malik. It is the sacred place where the prophet Abraham prepared to sacrifice his son Isaac—"

"Begging your pardon," Hakeem interrupted, "but it was not Isaac! Abraham was to sacrifice his son Ishmael."

"I beg to differ, sir. Our scripture is very clear on this point. 'The Lord said to Abraham: Take your son, your only son, whom you love—Isaac.'"

Having studied both Jewish and Muslim scripture, Hakeem was quite familiar with this argument. "Our scripture also says, 'Your only son,' but Isaac was never the only son. Ishmael was born first. He was the only son until Isaac was born. From that moment on, Abraham had two sons."

Both men recognized that they would not resolve this discrepancy there and then. Each had come to his own conclusion as to the identity of Abraham's intended sacrificial offering. For each, it was the product of tradition that transcended generation after generation. They agreed to part as friends.

Hakeem continued on his way to the corner of the enclosure. There was nothing distinctive to visually mark the spot where Buraq had been tethered. But there was no reason to doubt the oral tradition identifying that this was the spot. He was deeply moved. Likewise, he felt moved as he entered through the Gate of the Prophet.

Here he was in the second-holiest of all Muslim places. There were no traces of the ancient Jewish temple to be seen. In its place stood two great monuments of the Muslim faith. The Masjid al-Aqsa was the largest mosque Hakeem had ever seen, even larger than the Umayyad mosque in Damascus. He had heard it was the largest in the whole world.

Not far from the mosque was a much smaller, octagon-shaped building supporting a circular, gilded dome. *So this is the famous Dome of the Rock,* he thought. Though smaller than the Masjid al-Aqsa, it was more majestic in its uniqueness. Hakeem entered and could hardly believe his eyes. The lower section of the walls was covered with beautifully patterned stone slabs, similar to what he had seen in Damascus. Beginning at about eye level were intricate mosaics on a gold background representing a heavenly garden—trees of acanthus leaves bearing a variety of stylized fruits.

The interior space was not really a mosque: it had no prayer niche and no large space for prayer. It was more like a shrine or a reliquary. At its center, under the dome, was a large rock that Hakeem described as follows in his journal:

> The height of the rock is about the height of a man's chest. Its length and width are about the same, approximately ten cubits. Below the rock is a cave that one can enter by descending a flight of stairs behind a door. The cave is very small, barely higher than a man standing upright.

Hakeem approached the rock and noticed a depression, roughly the shape of a footprint—allegedly Mohammed's footprint. *This is the very spot*, he thought. This was where the Prophet Mohammed ascended to heaven and found himself in the very presence of God.

Hakeem began to read the inscriptions above the inner octagonal arcade. On the south side, the inscription read,

> In the name of God, the Merciful, the Compassionate. There is no god but God. He is One. He has no associate. On the east side: The Messiah, Jesus son of Mary, was only a Messenger of God, His Word that He conveyed unto Mary. So, believe in God and His messengers, and say not 'Three.'

This, Hakeem realized, was a refutation of the Christian doctrine of the Trinity.

It did not take long for Hakeem to notice that here in Jerusalem he was among the minority. Most of the population was Christian, yet the rulers were Muslim. And the Dome of the Rock, looming high on the site of the ancient Jewish temple, stood as a dramatic statement that Islam was here to stay.

Six miles from Jerusalem was the little town called Bethlehem. In the place where the prophet Jesus was born, Hakeem recorded:

> In a small church in the village there is a branch, it is said, of a date tree from which the virgin Mary ate.

Hakeem was quite familiar with the story in the Quran about Jesus speaking as an infant when he was presented by his mother to the public. The story was not recorded in Christian scripture. Yet the relic, the date palm, attested to a Christian oral tradition that held that shortly after Jesus was born, the Holy Family fled to Egypt to escape the persecution of King Herod. En route they passed through a palm grove, and Mary asked for some dates. It was the newborn baby Jesus who commanded the palm tree to lower its branch so that Mary could have some dates.

A little farther down the road from Bethlehem was the town of Hebron, the burial site of the prophet Abraham. Hebrew scripture records that when Abraham died, his two sons Ishmael and Isaac buried him in a tomb that Abraham had purchased for himself and his family. According to Muslim tradition, after the burial, Ishmael returned to Arabia, but Abraham's wife, Sarah; his son Isaac and his wife Rebecca; and his grandson Jacob and his wife, Leah, were all buried in this same place. Just being there, Hakeem felt a strong sense of kinship with Abraham's descendants. *We are all sons of Abraham*, he thought.

Hakeem's next journal entry described some of his impressions of Egypt:

> I cannot imagine how to produce a map of Egypt on one single page. It will take at least two pages, one for Upper Egypt, which extends from Awsan to Fustat, and a second for Lower Egypt, from where the Nile divides to the shores of Alexandria. The name for all of this is "Misr," which means "a civilized place."

Like so many visitors both before him and since, Hakeem was truly amazed at the sight of the Great Pyramids at Giza, impressed by both their size and their shape. He would later write,

> We have seen nothing comparable to them anywhere on the surface of the earth, not in the world of Islam, nor in the land of the infidels. We Muslims have never built, nor will we ever build, anything like them.

Hakeem headed straight for the city of Fustat, the capital of Egypt, located on the east bank of the River Nile. The city was known for its prosperity, with shaded streets, gardens, and markets. It contained very tall residential buildings, some seven stories tall, which could reportedly accommodate hundreds of people. To Hakeem, they looked a bit like minarets.

He wasted no time. His immediate objective was to find his mentor, Sheikh Abu'l-Hasan al-Mas'udi. He had learned that the great master usually sat in the Grand Mosque of Amr Ibn al-As with his students. On his first afternoon in town, Hakeem went to the Grand Mosque. His mentor was not there. Nor was he there the next day, nor the day after that. But on the fourth day, there he was, surrounded by his protégés, who were eagerly listening to his every word. He was telling a story about a conversation between a Sufi mystic and the caliph al-Ma'mun.

"The Sufi began, 'Greetings, oh Commander of the Faithful, may the mercy of God and his blessings be upon you.'

"The caliph returned his salutation and bid the Sufi to approach and be seated.

"The Sufi continued, 'May I speak openly?'

"'Speak of whatever you wish,' replied the caliph.

"'Very well. Do you owe this throne upon which you sit to the unanimous agreement and full consent of the Muslims, or do you owe it to the violence you have used against them, abusing your strength and power?'

"The caliph paused for a moment before answering. 'I owe it to neither their consent, nor to the use of violence. Rather, I owe it to a Muslim ruler who came before me, who handed to me the exercise of this authority after his death. At that time, I believed that if I had left the Muslims to their own devices, the rope of Islam would unravel, and disorder would prevail in the midst of civil war. Almighty God's laws would lose their strength. Access to the Holy Qaaba would become impossible, and the war against the unbelievers would be abandoned, since my subjects would no longer be united under one authority to direct them. Lastly, brigands would infest the roads, and the weak would be handed over, defenseless to the oppressor.'"

Sheikh Abu'l-Hasan noticed Hakeem sitting among the listeners. He looked at him only briefly, perhaps not wanting to show him special attention. He continued his story.

"The caliph concluded, 'I have therefore taken power in order to protect the Muslims, fight their enemies, and ensure the safety of the highways, and so I will lead the Muslims by the hand until they choose, by their unanimous will, a leader who pleases them, and I can relinquish my authority into his hands and become a simple subject, like any other Muslim.'"

Then Sheikh Abu'l-Hasan simply said, "And the Sufi went away." He paused. "And we will do the same. We will discuss the implications of this next time."

As the students departed, the master approached Hakeem, whom he had not seen in over two years.

"Let's go for a walk, Hakeem," said Abu'l-Hasan.

Teacher and student, side by side, left the mosque and walked toward the Nile. They passed a large domed structure with a cross on the top. "This is the Coptic Church of Saint George," explained Abu'l-Hasan. "Coptic is the oldest denomination of the Christian church. Copts claim that the language they speak, also called Coptic, is closest to the ancient Egyptian language of the pharaohs."

Hakeem was surprised to learn that there were different denominations of Christianity.

"Not at all unlike us Muslims," Sheikh Abu'l-Hasan pointed out.

A little farther along the road, they could see the southern tip of the Island of Rhoda in the middle of the Nile. Across the other side, the Great Pyramids were in full view.

"I visited the pyramids a few days ago," Hakeem said with some degree of excitement. "I have never seen anything like them!"

"Of course not, nor will you, wherever your travels may take you. You know…an Abbasid caliph claims to have written on one of those monuments, 'It is I who built these. Whosoever pretends to have the power to destroy them should know that destroying is much easier than building.'"

"That seems like good advice for a head of state," Hakeem said.

"There are so many lessons to be learned from the ancient history of this great land," replied the teacher. The sheikh pointed out a cone-shaped building on the southern tip of Rhoda Island. "This contains a nilometer, an instrument that measures the height of the River Nile as it seasonally rises and falls."

"How does it work?" asked Hakeem. "Can we go inside?"

As they approached and entered the building, Abu'l-Hasan explained that the chamber was called a stilling well. It descended to a depth below the level of the river. The octagon-shaped column in the center was graded and divided into nineteen cubits. An ideal flood filled the nilometer to the sixteen-cubit mark; less could mean drought or famine, and more could mean a catastrophic flood.

"I can imagine how important it is to know these data in order to predict the needs of the coming year," said Hakeem.

"Indeed. The annual floods are important to the government and the general population. During the summer months, the nilometer is used to regulate the distribution of water, as well as to compute the levy of taxes to be paid to the caliph in Baghdad." The sheikh paused for just a moment. "Although very few taxes actually flow to Baghdad anymore. Egypt under the Ikhshidid ruler is virtually independent as the Abbasid caliphate becomes increasingly decentralized and weak."

Sheikh Abu'l-Hasan seemed to sense that Hakeem was becoming tense as their conversation turned to politics. "Do not worry, my son. We can talk freely here. No one else can hear us. Even if we were not alone, the sound of the water flowing into the stilling well would drown out the sound of our conversation."

"Why have you come to Egypt, master?" There, he had asked it—the question that had weighed heavily on him for two years.

"I finished my work at the House of Wisdom. There was nothing more for me to do there."

"But I wonder, *ustadh*…had it become dangerous for you there?"

"In a way, yes. I was not an open critic of the Abbasid regime, but at the same time, I no longer felt free to say all that was on my mind."

"Were you a Fatimid agent?" Hakeem asked.

Abu'l-Hasan said nothing. His gaze seemed to pass straight through Hakeem without stopping. Hakeem was not surprised. If he were an agent, he would not admit it. Perhaps the nonanswer was an answer after all.

"Are you content here in Egypt?" Hakeem asked instead.

"As great an institution as was the House of Wisdom in the last century, the truly great universities in the Islamic world are now farther west, in Fez and in Córdoba. I would go there, but I am old and travel is not easy, even under the best of conditions."

"And now?" asked Hakeem.

"Let's just say that the route across North Africa is especially dangerous these days." The sheikh's eyes lowered, and he paused again. Then he looked up and said, "There is a small community of scholars here, and it is growing. Someday, hopefully before I die, there will be a great university here in Egypt as well. Now, you tell me—what has gone on in your life since we were last together? What brings you to Egypt?"

Hakeem told his master of the dramatic turn that his life had taken shortly after the sheikh left Baghdad. He recounted the meeting at the mosque with Musa and Suhrab. "Suhrab said that the Abbasid regime was sliding quickly into weakness, decline, and even corruption."

Sheikh Abu'l-Hasan nodded, as if to acknowledge his agreement with what Suhrab had said.

Hakeem continued, "He said that the Fatimid caliph in Ifriqiya would be the salvation of us all."

Again, Abu'l-Hasan nodded in assent, but in a way that suggested he was surprised Suhrab had gone that far.

Hakeem then recounted what had happened after the meeting, and the terrible murder of Suhrab.

The sheikh again nodded. "Bad news has a way of finding its way to my ears. I heard that Suhrab was killed by a group of extremists led by Haytham al-Khariji."

Hakeem was surprised that Sheikh Abu'l-Hasan already knew so much. "A few weeks ago, when I was in Palmyra, I think I saw Haytham. For a moment, I actually thought that he was following me."

"I doubt that he was after you, specifically…unless he suspects you of being a Fatimid *da'i*. More likely he is en route to Ifriqiya to join the rebellion of the Man on the Donkey. He may be passing through here soon, if he has not already. So, tell me—are you a Fatimid *da'i*?"

"No!—I mean, I did attend that meeting and listened as Suhrab spoke so passionately about the movement. And…I must admit that I was deeply impressed by what he said. But no, I did not join anything."

"Hakeem, there are no official members of the Fatimid *da`wa*. There are only sympathizers. Your presence at that meeting, and your passion for what Suhrab said, might be enough to put you in danger from the Kharijite opposition."

"But how can I be in danger? I hardly understand the mission of this movement."

"You know that the Fatimids believe in the need for a divinely guided imam who would act as the authoritative spiritual guide of all Muslims—a spiritual guide in the broadest sense, to include what we might call 'good government.'"

"I believe in those ideals," Hakeem admitted.

"Well, there you are. It is clear that the caliph in Baghdad no longer fulfills that role—indeed, if he ever did. When the Abbasids came to power two hundred years ago, they professed a rather idealistic ideology: a universal rule of law for all Muslims based on the Quran as professed by Prophet Mohammed."

"And after the Prophet died?"

"That is precisely the problem. Then leadership should pass, according to the Fatimids, to an appropriate member of the family of the Prophet. Of course, all Shiites believe that the divinely guided, sinless, and infallible imam must be a member of Ahl al-Bayt—a direct descendant of the Prophet. Fatimids take that to mean a direct descendant of Mohammed's daughter Fatimah and her husband, Ali, who was actually a cousin of Mohammed.

"Surely it is more than just a matter of succession to power."

"They also promised revenge for the martyrs of Islam, who happen to be the sons of Ali, the first Shiite imam. Needless to say, the Shiites were sorely disappointed when an Abbasid was chosen over a member of the Prophet's direct descendants."

Hakeem nodded in agreement. He knew that Shiites revered the sons of Ali. "Yet the Abbasids became quite powerful."

"And quite professional." The sheikh seemed pleased that his student was well informed, but he continued to play the role of the professor. "They established a number of professional ministries: a ministry of defense, a department of state, and an internal revenue service—and, yes, even a postal service, although that is reserved for use only by the government."

Hakeem was surprised to hear this. "When I was in Baghdad, we just took these ministries for granted. You mean there are states that don't have them?"

"Absolutely. They are Abbasid innovations. There have always been ulama, religious scholars, but now they have an official government function as the state's judiciary. As time went on, the primary function of all these ministries became the preservation of their own bureaucracy; they lost sight of their original ideological platform."

"You mean…the sole purpose of the people in power is to stay in power?"

"Exactly!"

"And the Fatimids?"

"The Fatimids…" Sheikh Abu'l-Hasan stopped as two people entered the nilometer. He motioned to Hakeem to step down several more stairs to a lower level to be out of earshot of the newcomers. The stairs were wet and a little slippery. "Be careful," the sheikh cautioned. He continued where he had left off. "The Fatimids believe that Imam al-Mahdi resumed the position as the authoritative teacher and guide in all matters nearly a half century ago. Not only was he a Shiite imam, but he claimed to be a direct descendant of Imam Ali and his wife, Fatimah." Looking straight into Hakeem's eyes, the sheikh said, "that is a dangerous political view to hold in this Abbasid-controlled world."

Hakeem wondered if that was not intended to be a warning aimed at him. "So, what did al-Mahdi do?"

"Imam al-Mahdi was forced to flee his home in Syria. He fled to North Africa, the frontier on the farthest western edge of Islam—to the city of Sijilmasa. But the story doesn't end there. After remaining in hiding for about a year, he traveled east halfway across the continent to Ifriqiya, where he established his permanent base and declared a caliphate rivaling the one in Baghdad."

Hakeem pressed his teacher even further. "Suhrab, in his lecture, said that there was considerable opposition to the Fatimid imam in Ifriqiya."

"That is true. Most of the native Berber population in North Africa are Kharijite Muslims, even though their understanding of Kharijism might be quite superficial. Fatimid missionaries worked very hard to teach them the Shiite doctrine. They organized special lectures."

"Is that like Suhrab's lecture that I attended in Baghdad?"

"Exactly—and, as it apparently turns out, at great risk to yourself. These missionaries were especially successful among the Kutama Berber tribes in North Africa, who became the initial base of support for the Fatimids. But they were not so successful among hard-core Kharijites. The latter fiercely adhere to their own independence. They reject any form of central government. They reject the Abbasid caliphate, as well as the two rival Caliphates—the one in Mahdiya and the one in Córdoba."

"In his speech, Suhrab mentioned that a crisis was about to erupt."

There was a pause before Abu'l-Hasan responded. "He was right." Worry crossed his face and crept into his voice. "North Africa is about to explode. The Man on the Donkey has succeeded in mounting a revolution."

"The Man on the Donkey?" asked Hakeem.

"His name is Abu Yazid. He began as a simple schoolteacher. When he went to study in Tahert, at that time the capital of the Kharijite imam, he was indoctrinated in the revolutionary theology of the Kharijites. He looked harmless enough—an old man on a donkey, clad in a simple robe of white wool with holes at the shoulders instead of sleeves, a high white cap on his head. He was a model of asceticism and modesty."

"But it seems that he presents a threat."

"Yes. For the last two or three years, not only has he spoken out against the Fatimids, he is actually forming a militant force and threatening to stir up opposition wherever he can. His goal is to force the Fatimid caliph to surrender his claim to authority."

"Will he succeed?"

"Ah, Hakeem, only God knows." With that, Sheikh Abu'l-Hasan said, "It's getting late. We must go."

As teacher and student walked back across the Nile, Hakeem wondered what his next move would be. "What should I do, master? If you were me, what would you do?"

"That I cannot answer, my son. You must go where your soul takes you." Another long pause. "But if it were me, if I could travel, I would go to Córdoba."

CHAPTER EIGHT

Two weeks later, Hakeem was in the port city of Alexandria booking passage on a sailing vessel bound for Tunis. That would bring him halfway to Córdoba. On the morning that he was scheduled to leave, as he came up to the gangplank to board the ship, a man approached him. The man was middle-aged, nicely dressed, and carried a folded parchment secured with a large red wax seal.

"Excuse me, sir," the man said. "My name is Suleyman Ben Yusuf. I wonder if you would be so kind as to deliver this letter to my brother, Ibrahim Ben Yusuf, who lives in Tunis. I will pay you, of course."

Hakeem was not surprised. He had received several letters from his father during his stay in Baghdad and had sent letters to him in return. Since the Abbasid postal system was only available for official correspondence, people used impromptu private carriers.

"His name is clearly written on the exterior of the letter," the man said. "You can find him on Shariah al-Lawazeen, the street of the sweetmeat sellers, as it says here below his name. It is important that you give the letter to him personally."

Hakeem noticed that below the address was also written, *The bearer of this letter is a Jew.* "But I am not Jewish," Hakeem said.

"No matter," the man said. "Ibrahim is not Jewish either, nor am I. It is a code informing Ibrahim that you should be trusted. He will let you into his house."

"But why Jewish?" Hakeem asked.

"You will be in Fatimid territory. The Fatimids are tolerant toward all religious denominations, including Jews."

"And how do you know that you can trust me?"

The man paused before he answered. "I just know."

Hmmm, Hakeem thought. He took the letter and the two copper coins and boarded the ship.

Hakeem had no trouble finding the street of the sweetmeat sellers in Tunis. He was impressed at the whiteness of the exterior walls of the houses abutting one against the other, lining both sides of the street. Each house had a stall at street level filled with a colorful array of sweetmeats for sale, assorted candied fruit, sugar-covered nuts, bonbons, and sticks of candy. Each merchant assured prospective customers that his merchandise was the best to be had along the entire lane—and, of course, for the best price. Between the stalls, heavy wooden doors, most of them painted sky blue, led to apartments behind and above the stalls. Hakeem had no trouble locating the house of Ibrahim Ben Yusuf. A simple inquiry led him to the door. He swung the heavy bronze door knocker, announcing his presence. Within just a few moments, a doorman appeared.

Hakeem showed the man the document. "Good day, sir. My name is Hakeem Ibn al-Harith. I have a letter for Ibrahim Ben Yusuf."

The doorman looked at the letter. "Very well, I will see that he gets it."

"I was told to give it to him in person," Hakeem said.

"In that case, please come in. I will see if my master is available."

It was difficult to tell what a house was like from the outside. Once inside, Hakeem was struck by how modest the house of Ibrahim Ben Yusuf was. He was escorted to a small reception room off the entrance corridor. A thick straw mat covered the floor, and sofas lined three of the room's four walls. There were no windows onto the courtyard, so it would have been dark had it not been for the lanterns hanging on the walls. Hakeem knew nothing about the man he was about to meet, but for some reason he had expected him to be a man of some importance, or at least of some wealth.

When the master appeared, Hakeem was surprised at how young he was. For some reason he had imagined that he would be at least middle-aged. This man was perhaps no more than thirty years old. He wore a simple long-sleeve green tunic with a plain leather belt around his waist. He had the short stubble of a beard and a clean-shaven head. If Hakeem were to guess what his profession was, he would have said he was a student like himself, perhaps a little more advanced.

"I…am Ibrahim Ben Yusuf. I…understand you have a message for me?" The man spoke slowly and somewhat cautiously. His forehead was furrowed, and his eyes looked straight into Hakeem's, as if he was trying to assess Hakeem's identity. Hakeem handed him the letter. Ibrahim appeared to become much more at ease when he examined the parchment and read the line *The bearer of this letter is a Jew.* "You must be Hakeem Ibn al-Harith," the man said.

Somewhat shocked, Hakeem exclaimed, "How do you know my name?"

"I knew that you were coming. It is not important how I knew. The letter you carry is not the message. You are."

Now Hakeem was really startled. "What do you mean?"

"Our organization has been observing you for some time. We know that you are a person who is fundamentally sympathetic to our cause—or, at least, sympathetic to its underlying goals and principles."

"And that cause is...?"

"The restoration of truth, justice, and equality, the one true caliphate throughout the world of Islam."

"Just what do you know about me?" Hakeem asked.

"Please, sit down." Ibrahim placed his hand on Hakeem's shoulder and gestured toward the end of the sofa in the right-hand corner of the room. He sat on a corner of the sofa closest to Hakeem so that they were almost facing each other.

"We know that you have been among the most promising students at the House of Wisdom; that you have a broad base of book knowledge; that you have an exceptionally well-tuned sense of observation. We even know that before you went to university, you were the champion horseman in your hometown. Need I continue?"

Outside of Nusaybin, Musa was the only person Hakeem had told about his riding. *He has to be somehow connected to this*, Hakeem thought. *And I wonder if Sheikh Abu'l-Hasan al-Mas`udi is also involved.*

Ibrahim continued, "We think that you can be of great service to our cause, and more importantly, that you will want to do just that."

Hakeem looked puzzled. "*If* I agree to help you, just what is it that you would have me do?"

"For a start, we now know that we can rely on you to deliver a message exactly as instructed. It is important that we get a message through as soon as possible to the war council of the Fatimid caliph al-Qa'im that is convening in Mahdiya. The revolt that is being mounted by the Man on the Donkey is picking up momentum west of here."

Hakeem nodded, knowing something of what Ibrahim was talking about. "In Egypt, Sheikh Abu'l-Hasan, my teacher, told me about this Man on the Donkey...but I know none of the details of his current status."

"I am not surprised. The news would not have had time to reach Egypt. Abu Yazid and his forces are moving in this direction as we speak. He began with only two hundred horsemen. They took the fortress of Baghaya and a few of the small neighboring fortresses, avoiding the towns that might have offered resistance. With these successes, his numbers grew. When he laid siege to the town of Tibessa, the population surrendered in exchange for clemency. In the high-lying town of Thugga, the forces of Abu Yazid entered without resistance, as betrayal opened the city's gates. From there, he went on to capture the town of Sabiba, where the Fatimid governor was taken prisoner. It is only a matter of days before he is on the doorstep of the Fatimid capital."

"So, you want me to take a message to the caliph? A message that says what, exactly?"

"We expect that Abu Yazid will march next toward Qayrawan, the spiritual center of Islam in North Africa—some people say that seven trips to Qayrawan are like one pilgrimage to Mecca. The caliph must send reinforcements immediately."

"But why me? Can't one of your regular messengers carry this warning?"

"Our messengers are under surveillance by our enemy's counterintelligence. We need a new face. And not just anyone. We need someone with your qualities, as well as someone we can trust to get the message through—no matter what it takes." Ibrahim became increasingly agitated as he spoke. His lips began to quiver, and tears were almost forming in his eyes. "I assure you, the situation is critical. People are dying!"

Hakeem felt conflicted. He readily identified with the ideals that Ibrahim attributed to the Fatimid cause, and he was distressed that Muslims were warring against Muslims, that people were suffering and dying—but it was more than he could absorb all at once.

After a long pause, he said reluctantly, "All right…if I do this *one* mission, that's it. No more after that. Do you understand? How do I get to Mahdiya?"

"You will go directly south as the crow flies toward Qayrawan, then east until you reach the port of Mahdiya. But you must be careful. There are Kharijite sympathizers everywhere. We know that you can ride a fast mount. We have arranged a swift steed. Way stations at approximately one-hour intervals will provide replacements—spirited horses bred for speed and endurance. Give your horse his head and he will take you to the next village, where you will change mounts. Time is of the utmost importance. You should leave immediately."

There was no time for Hakeem to ponder the pros and cons of what was being asked of him. He knew he had to go. There was really no reason to doubt that Ibrahim was telling the truth, that he was not exaggerating the gravity of the pending crisis. On the other hand, Hakeem had no reason to trust Ibrahim; after all, he had just met him. But he did trust his friend Musa and his teacher Sheikh Abu'l-Hasan, who almost certainly had set him up for this. He was shaking with fright, but he knew that there was only one action to take. Everything that his father had taught him about duty, about doing what was right—everything that he believed in the inner core of his being—told him he had to go.

"I will take your message to Mahdiya, God willing."

Hakeem rode hard for seven hours, stopping only to change mounts. When he was still an hour out, stopping to exchange horses for the last leg of the journey, the owner of the stable cautioned him, "The Kharijite forces have already all but surrounded Qayrawan. They have taken the suburb of Raqadda. It is virtually impossible to get through."

"I am bound by my word to try," Hakeem said.

"If you insist on going, your only chance on getting through is to circle around the city and approach from the southeast. You might just make it if you ride under the cover of darkness. I suggest you wait here an hour. Better to arrive a little later than to not arrive at all."

When the walls of Qayrawan were in sight, perhaps a mile away, Hakeem began to circle around the east side of the city as he had been told. He continued to ride as fast as his mount would run. When he was within a few hundred yards of the Bab al-Koukha, he saw a small contingent of six or seven heavily armed men forming a blockade. He approached with caution as the men formed a line across the road, their forms appearing as silhouettes in front of lanterns atop of poles. When he was within earshot, one of them shouted, "Stop where you are. State your name and purpose."

Hakeem stopped but said nothing. He nudged his horse forward at a slow walking pace as he tried to decide what to do. *I might be able to bluff my way through, but what if I fail?* The men were armed with spears and swords and shields. It was dark, so he couldn't be sure, but it looked as if they did not have bows and arrows that could take him down at a distance.

He decided he would take a chance. He spurred his horse to a full gallop toward the checkpoint. When he noticed a gap between the two men on the far side of the road, he steered his horse straight toward the gap. The man on the right drew his sword, and the man on the left leveled his spear to the height of Hakeem's chest.

I'm going to be killed! Instinctively and instantly, Hakeem changed direction and swerved toward the center of the line, literally bowling over those men-at-arms who had not yet drawn their weapons. Before he even realized it, he had made it through the blockade.

The soldiers mounted their horses and were in hot pursuit. Within seconds, Hakeem noticed that the road ahead forked. To the right, he could see the entrance to the city. To the left was the road to Mahdiya. That was where he needed to go.

He had to make another quick decision. He knew that his horse had been running hard for almost an hour and could not maintain the pace much longer. The riders that were chasing him would overtake him in a matter of minutes if he turned toward Mahdiya. He opted to head for the city gate.

The soldiers on the city wall recognized that the lone rider was being pursued by the forces that had placed the city under siege. They opened the gate just long enough to let Hakeem through.

"I must see the commander of the garrison at once," Hakeem shouted in a staccato voice. He was out of breath and shaking with more fear than the night that he and Suhrab had fled from the mosque in Baghdad.

Khalil al-Tamimi looked like a soldier's soldier, a middle-aged man, tall, solidly built, with a broad, square-shaped face under a dark, well-trimmed beard. But Hakeem had never seen a man in such distress. His face was covered in perspiration in spite of the cool evening breeze, and tension seemed to impose a harsh rigidity on his entire body.

"If you have come to warn me that we are soon to be attacked by the Man on the Donkey, you are too late!" the garrison commander said, stating the obvious.

"I was actually on my way to Mahdiya to warn the caliph's war council that the enemy is heading this way," said Hakeem.

"It's too late for that as well. There is no way you could get through the lines between here and Mahdiya."

That was obvious, given Hakeem's hazardous approach through enemy lines to get here. Making matters worse, as he had walked the two hundred yards from the southern gate to the governor's palace adjacent to the Grand Mosque, he observed even through his militarily untrained eyes that the city was poorly protected.

Tamimi confirmed this lack of preparedness. "I tried to send for reinforcements myself when we learned that Abu Yazid was fast approaching. But, alas, the carrier pigeons that have never failed to relay messages to Mahdiya before for some reason refused to fly. I have less than four hundred soldiers, whom I have quartered in inns and private houses; they are hardly enough to man the walls around the central part of the city."

Hakeem had to concede that he, like all other inhabitants of Qayrawan, was sealed off within the city's walls and at the mercy of the Man on the Donkey.

Much of the population pressured the city officials to submit to the besiegers rather than suffer an extended blockade that would inevitably end in starvation and defeat. Two days later, Tamimi surrendered the city to Abu Yazid, pleading for clemency. The city officials turned themselves in. They were taken, along with thirty other prisoners, to Abu Yazid's camp outside the city. Abu Yazid wanted to spare Tamimi himself, thinking that the commander could provide useful information about the territory still held by the Fatimids. But his blind mentor reproached him, quoting a famous folktale. "An enemy who is feared should be put to death." The following morning, Tamimi was condemned to die.

While all of this was happening, Hakeem discreetly faded into the background, blending in with the neutral population of Qayrawan. He stood in the crowd as Tamimi was paraded from the governor's palace to the open square where he was to be executed. He watched as the man who had begged for clemency for his troops placed his own head on the block. Hakeem grimaced and turned away as the heavy axe came down on Tamimi's neck and cleanly severed his head, which fell into a straw basket.

What are they going to do with that? Hakeem wondered as he watched the executioner carry the basket away. He was relieved that it was not his own head in the basket, but at the same time, he felt guilty that he had not been able to do anything to prevent the bloodshed.

In the days that followed the execution, Hakeem was appalled to see Abu Yazid's fighters roaming the streets of Qayrawan looting at will. He saw men smashing the heads of other men. What was worse, he could not tell whose side either the perpetrators or the victims were on. He heard that a number of the city's notables had gone to the camp of Abu Yazid to plead for clemency and protection. The rumor was that the Man on the Donkey had simply replied coldly, "And so you ask for mercy…even when Mecca and Jerusalem have been destroyed."

On Friday, shortly before the hour of prayer, before the Gate of the Blacksmiths at the Grand Mosque, seven banners of different colors were planted, on which the names of the caliphs Umar and Uthman were written along with the profession of faith and the phrase from the Quran, *Fight against the imams of unbelief.* A fiery preacher called for jihad against the Fatimids. Abu Yazid did not personally enter the city of Qayrawan. It was rumored that he was already leading the bulk of his army along the old Roman road toward Sousse. From there he would march on toward the Fatimid capital of Mahdiya.

Hakeem was dismayed at these displays of hatred and violence, Muslim against Muslim. It seemed that the only way he could cope with the suffering he witnessed was to become numb to it. It was almost as if he had become intoxicated. He no longer understood his own feelings. But he still felt compelled to go to Mahdiya.

As he rode along the Roman road toward the town of Sousse, he encountered an almost continuous caravan of refugees going in the opposite direction, some on horseback, some on donkeys, some in carts, many of them on foot, all of them looking as if they had been through hell itself, fleeing the terror inflicted by the warriors of Abu Yazid. One after another in the cavalcade said to him, "You had best turn around. You are heading straight to hell if you continue on this road. Ad-daffal and his unruly hoard have looted the city."

Ad-daffal was a character from Arabic folklore, an eschatological figure like the devil himself, now being attributed to the Man on the Donkey—corrupted by immense booty, having replaced his tattered tunic with silk and brocade and his donkey with a spirited thoroughbred horse.

Heeding these warnings, Hakeem veered off the Roman road and circled southward, bypassing Sousse altogether and heading straight toward Mahdiya.

When he arrived, he was relieved to find that Mahdiya seemed better prepared to resist the onslaught of Abu Yazid. The caliph had ordered the fortification of the suburb of Zawila with a wall and two towers, one at each end, and a ditch dug deep in front of the whole length of the wall. One of the towers was defended by Kutama Berbers loyal to the caliph, the other by a detachment of Arab slaves. Yet it seemed that the caliph's vision of a Fatimid empire was limited to within these walls that enclosed his capital city.

The blockade of Mahdiya began with the onset of winter. The forces of Abu Yazid controlled all of the land routes to the city, which was relatively easy to do since Mahdiya was a long, narrow peninsula jutting out into the Mediterranean Sea. Mahdiya's residents relied on the sea to maintain their supplies. But even that faltered when ships from Sicily and Tripoli were hurled onto the coast by winter storms and fell into the hands of the rebels. By late winter, the granaries were depleted, and starvation became the enemy. The starving population found it necessary to slaughter some of their beasts of burden in order to survive. Although the blockade effectively cut off supplies from getting through, Abu Yazid allowed people to leave, and many of the city's residents did just that.

Hakeem decided to stay. He found himself more and more in sympathy with the Fatimid caliph. In large part, he was influenced by the very ideals expressed by the Mahdi and his successors, ideals that called for unity and equality among all believers. But it also had to do with the momentum of circumstances in which he had found himself over the last few weeks. An event that greatly affected him was the Friday sermon delivered by the caliph himself—as it turned out, the last sermon the caliph would deliver.

"My people!" the caliph said. "Truly this accursed, so-called Man on a Donkey has exacerbated his evilness, and it has infested the land. He is in league with the devil, and he thinks he is invincible. Clearly, he is wrong. Know that you are the party of God; they are the party of Satan. Your dead are in paradise; theirs are in hell!"

Later that day, in a feeble attempt to ease the pangs of hunger, Hakeem partook in smoking some hashish in an inn not far from the Grand Mosque, an inn well known by locals and visitors alike for everything it had to offer. He was with two other men, neither of whom he had ever met before. Despite the hashish, Hakeem exercised a bit of cautious restraint and said nothing about himself to the other men.

The man who called himself Mustapha, on the other hand, said that he was a soldier. After smoking too much of the hashish, being foolishly honest, he admitted that he was an officer in the Arab *jund* fighting in support of the Man on the Donkey—fighting for the enemy. The other man, Omar, said nothing much besides his name, perhaps because he had smoked less than either Mustapha or Hakeem. In any case, he got up from the table rather abruptly and hurried out of the inn.

"The Man on the Donkey and his Kharijite supporters claim to be egalitarians," Mustapha said in a loud, complaining voice. "Yet the Berbers in Abu Yazid's army treat us Arabs as nothing more than mercenaries. Can you imagine? We are Arab. If anyone is a true Muslim, it is us Arabs!"

"Then why do you fight for Abu Yazid?" Hakeem asked.

"At first, we were supporters of the caliph in Baghdad," said Mustapha. "We considered the Fatimids as usurpers, so we joined Abu Yazid's revolution against them."

"And now?"

"And now it is clear that Abu Yazid is even worse than the Fatimids. He is the devil himself. Compared to the Man on the Donkey, the Fatimid caliph is a better alternative. The truth be known, I am here in Mahdiya specifically to make contact with someone in al-Qa'im's war council to offer the support of the Arab *jund*."

Hakeem quickly reached out and placed his hand over Mustapha's mouth. "Say no more. In these troubled times, you cannot be too careful about what you say."

At that moment, four men-at-arms stormed into the inn and came right to the table where Hakeem and Mustapha were still smoking their pipes. "You two are under arrest!" one of the men barked in a sharp tone of authority.

"What for?" Mustapha protested.

Hakeem was still alert enough to think, *These days, arrests are so arbitrary. The soldiers are just following orders. They will tell us nothing.* He said to Mustapha, "We had best just do what they say."

The captives were shackled, led out of the inn, and shoved into an enclosed cart in which they were transported to the Bab Bahr, a fortification on the very tip of the peninsula. They were locked in a small, dark cell, where they waited.

Through the night, the two prisoners remained incarcerated—no food, no water for nearly twenty-four hours. There was one small window high up near the ceiling, too high to see through. It was just large enough to let in frigid winter air. There were no furnishings of any kind, not even a piss pot. The two men spent the night on the cold stone floor.

"Do you have any idea why we were arrested?" Mustapha asked.

"None whatsoever," Hakeem answered, but he suspected that it had something to do with Mustapha's position as an officer in the Arab *jund*.

It was not until late the next day before anyone opened the door to the cell. Two men-at-arms entered, different from the ones who had made the arrest the night before. They escorted the prisoners to a room in another part of the fortress. They opened the door and motioned Hakeem and Mustapha to enter. The soldiers remained outside.

This was not an interrogation room, Hakeem guessed. That would have looked more like a torture chamber. This room was actually inviting. A table held two glasses, a pitcher of water, and another of orange juice. Of the three chairs, Omar was sitting in one. He gestured for the other men to sit.

"I'm sure you want to know why you were arrested," said Omar. He looked straight at Mustapha. "We had information that you were an officer of the Arab *jund* fighting on the side of the Kharijite Abu Yazid. As an intelligence agent, I was assigned to follow you. That is why I was with you in the inn. When you admitted to being a part of the Arab *jund*, that was all I needed to hear. I left to set in motion the steps leading to your arrest."

Hakeem could not help but interject. "Why did you arrest me?"

"Guilt by association," Omar curtly responded.

"You left too early," said Hakeem. "Had you remained with us just a few more moments, you would have heard this man express his intention to serve as a double agent, to bring the Arab *jund* over to the side of the caliph."

Omar scoffed. "You underestimate the ability of our intelligence gathering, young man. We are at least one step ahead of you. We are well aware that Mustapha intends to be a double agent. What Mustapha had not yet figured out was how to make contact with us. By arresting him, we made that part easy."

"And me?" Hakeem asked.

"An amazing coincidence," Omar said. "We have been watching you as well. We know that you served, at least temporarily, as an envoy for the man who goes by the name Ibrahim Ben Yusuf in Tunis. We were just waiting for the right moment to make contact. Fortunately for us, you took care of that by being with Mustapha last night at the inn."

"Then why leave us incarcerated in that hellhole all night if you wanted us to come over to your side?" Hakeem asked.

Even though Hakeem was clearly angry, Omar seemed only minimally apologetic. "I'm sorry about that. We too are always being watched, perhaps even by one or more of those soldiers who arrested you. We could not risk anyone suspecting you to be in league with us."

Omar returned his attention to the Arab *jund*. "The caliph has ordered the launching of a sortie to challenge the forces of Abu Yazid. We are not sure exactly when that will happen, but certainly before the end of summer. When that happens, a signal will trigger the Arab *jund* to change sides. On the morning of the sortie, instead of raising the white flag of the Fatimids on the minaret of the Grand Mosque, we will display the green flag of Islam. The minaret is higher than the walls, so it should be visible from where the *jund* is camped."

Mustapha agreed to the plan and the signal.

"So, am I free to go?" asked Hakeem.

"For now," said Omar. "But when this crisis is over—and the end is in sight—my superiors will summon you to the caliph's residence. They have in mind a very specific task for you."

Throughout the summer, the *jund* watched patiently, waiting to see the green flag. One morning, when summer was almost over, the flag appeared. Fluttering easily in the mild wind, the green flag stood in bright contrast to the orange glow in the sky as the early morning sun began to rise over the sea. As it turned out, the situation began to resolve itself. The sortie that Omar and Mustapha had agreed upon was carried out as planned. What's more, many of the Berbers who had initially supported Abu Yazid began to defect once they finished looting the countryside. They were, after all, predominantly peasant farmers. Needing to bring in the late-summer harvest, they now returned home to work in the fields in their own villages.

Abandoned by so many of his supporters, Abu Yazid had to withdraw to Qayrawan. Perhaps too late, his blind teacher, Abu Ammar, said to him, "Forgive me, *sidi*, but you have lost sight of the very truths that you yourself have preached. It was not so long ago that you were a simple ascetic advocating unity and equality among all Muslims."

Abu Yazid had always followed the advice of his mentor. And so it was again. He ruefully set aside the silk and brocade that he had begun to enjoy. He dressed in his tattered tunic of white wool and once again mounted his donkey. But it was all for naught. The Sunni population of Qayrawan, who had initially supported him as their best chance of ridding themselves of the Fatimid regime, now saw him in a new light, as the worse of two evils. They forced him to withdraw to his home in the Aures Mountains. There, the rebellion of the Man on the Donkey that had swelled like a summer storm steadily dissipated over the next many months, not to be heard of again, if not for the writings of the chroniclers.

As promised, Hakeem was summoned to the caliphal palace for his next assignment. He was shocked to meet the caliph himself. He was also surprised that the caliph was so young, and that he was introduced by name as al-Mansur Billah.

"Yes, you should be surprised," the caliph said. "The caliph al-Qa'im is dead. He died during the blockade. We thought it best not to announce a transition in power while we were in the midst of a crisis that threatened the very existence of our regime. Praise be to God, that is behind us now. We are now ready to move on with our plans to secure the one true caliphate."

"And those plans somehow include me?" Hakeem asked.

"Yes," the caliph answered. "Please sit."

The two of them sat on large cushions on opposite sides of a round brass tray that rested on an olive wood stand.

"Would you like some tea?" the caliph asked.

The tea was already on the tray, and the caliph had started to pour it himself, raising the silver teapot as high as he could above the glasses, displaying his expertise at the tea ceremony.

Hakeem was not really in the mood for tea—his only interest was to know what the caliph had planned for him—but he accepted anyway. He thought it best to be a gracious recipient of hospitality. "Will I be returning to Egypt?" he asked.

"Not at first. As you may know, when the Umayyads were expelled from Damascus, they fled to the far west of Islam, to the area known as al-Andalus. Some twenty years ago now, they set up a rival caliphate in the city of Córdoba."

Córdoba! Hakeem's ears perked up and his eyes opened wide. *Exactly where I had set off to go before I got caught up in all of this.*

"We need to know more about their strengths and weaknesses," the caliph said. "You will gather intelligence that will be helpful to us in deciding how we shall deal with them."

"What kind of information do you seek?"

"Everything! We need to know how to first secure and then to effectively govern that land. We will want to know the distances between points of interest, the itineraries followed by knowledgeable travelers, the location of hostels along the way, whether they are fortified and provisioned or not. We will want an assessment of the agricultural and mining resources. What are the water resources from rain? From irrigation? What is the climate like? What is the moral disposition of the population? What religious sects are practiced? What taxes are assessed and how much is actually collected?"

"Is that *all*, sir?" Hakeem asked, with just a hint of sarcasm.

The caliph chose to ignore the sarcasm. "Yes, that is all. The taxes are particularly important, as that is the best index of the real power of the regime. You will take careful notes and present them to my advisors in written form. If you can illustrate them with drawings of what you see, so much the better."

Perfect, Hakeem thought. *Exactly what I had set out to do to begin with—but now with an official mandate.*

"I have a letter for you to carry to a man in Córdoba." The caliph handed Hakeem a parchment neatly folded and sealed shut with the caliph's own seal. The name written on the outside was Mokhtar Ibn Abd al-Karim. There was no address or note of assurance like on the first letter Hakeem had delivered.

Hakeem reached out to take the letter. "How will I find this Mokhtar?"

"You will find him in the Grand Mosque sitting among a circle of students listening to the famous visiting scholar Abu Ja'far Mohammed. Every Friday after midday prayer, that teacher sits in his chair just beyond the Door of Saint Vincent. His students sit in a semicircle at his feet. Mokhtar will be easy enough to recognize. He wears a triangular-shaped patch over his left eye."

"An eye patch? Is that a disguise, or is it real?"

"He was blinded in hand-to-hand combat. He was once a warrior as tough as they come."

Hakeem did not find this to be particularly reassuring. "How will he know to trust me?"

"Mokhtar is not his real name. When you address him that way, he will know that you come on behalf of the Fatimid caliph in Mahdiya. You are not to give him your real name either. The security of Fatimid agents in Andalusia depends on anonymity, even within the various cells."

"And once we have made contact?"

"His instructions in the letter are to help you get settled in Córdoba. He will be your main contact with us." The caliph ended the meeting with, "Go in peace and with God's blessing, my son."

The next two days passed very quickly as Hakeem prepared once again to cross the Mediterranean. He boarded a ship in the port of Mahdiya destined for Almería at the western end of the sea.

CHAPTER NINE

I t was as if Hakeem had landed in a new world when he disembarked in the bustling port of Almería. He was immediately struck by a degree of wealth and beauty such that he had not seen before. Not in Damascus, nor in Jerusalem, nor in Fustat—not even back in the round city of Baghdad that was built as a symbol of a new beginning by the Abbasids when they came to power. The wealth was evident in the architecture of the buildings and in the overall population as a whole—artisans and laborers as well as merchants.

Everyone here is fat and prosperous, he thought. His assignment, at least in part, was to assess this prosperity and discern the source of it. *But not today. I must be off straightaway to Córdoba.*

As he traveled through the countryside, the beauty of the landscape revealed itself in the appearance and fragrance of the lush flora and groves of olive and citrus trees in such abundance that he had never imagined. It took seven days to travel from Almería to Córdoba. Hakeem made note of the length of the journey in his journal. Itineraries from point to point everywhere he went were to make up an important component of his report to the caliph in Mahdiya.

Hakeem arrived in Córdoba on a Thursday evening. On Friday, he went straight to the Grand Mosque. He was overwhelmed by this holy place, not because of its size—he had seen larger mosques—but rather by its unique design. He entered through a heavy wooden door covered with burnished brass. He would later learn that it was called the Gate of Forgiveness. He passed through the court of orange trees, relishing the scent of the blossoms.

Upon entering the mosque, he imagined that he was in a grove of palm trees. The aisles were separated by an assortment of columns made of jasper, onyx, marble, granite, and porphyry. From the tops of the columns, double-tiered arches of alternating red and white voussoirs spanned across the aisles. The lower arches were horseshoe shaped, the upper ones half circles, the whole creating the effect of palms branching out from the trunks of date trees.

Hakeem was early for midday prayer. An attendant was just then unrolling carpets upon which the faithful, who were just starting to wander in, would pray. Hakeem stopped the attendant to ask about the unique design of the mosque's interior.

"There are so many different styles of columns," the attendant said, "because most of them came from ancient Roman temples all around the entire country."

"And the two-tiered arches?" Hakeem asked.

"Ahhh. That's a most interesting story. It is said that when the Umayyad emir Abd al-Rahman arrived here almost two hundred years ago, he saw a single date palm that reminded him of his home in Syria. He identified with the palm tree, both of them strangers in a strange land. He ordered the interior design of his Grand Mosque to mimic a grove of date palms."

"And can you please tell me, kind sir, which door is the Door of Saint Vincent?"

"It is that one closest to the east corner of the prayer hall."

"Why is it called the Door of Saint Vincent? That is a Christian reference, no?"

"Yes, it is. This was originally a church. When the emir arrived here, the Muslims shared space with Christians here in the church. It worked out quite well. Muslims held Friday prayer here at midday, and Christians attended mass on Sunday. When the Muslim population exceeded what could worship in the space, the emir offered to buy the church and convert it into a mosque. The original mosque was smaller than what you see. As the population grew even larger, the mosque was expanded by Emir Abd al-Rahman II to what you see today."

By now, the mosque was filling rather quickly. The faithful, including Hakeem, sat on the carpeted floor to hear the Friday sermon. They then went through the various positions for two *raka*s of prayer, invoking, at the appropriate moment, the name of the reigning caliph, Abd al-Rahman III. After offering the traditional gesture of peace at the end of the prayers, most of the people filed out. Those who remained were students who gathered around their respective teachers, who occupied distinguished chairs at this prominent mosque-university.

Hakeem approached the group that gathered near the Door of Saint Vincent. It was common enough for visiting students to listen in on the lectures of distinguished ulema. Hakeem immediately recognized the man who went by the name of Mokhtar Ibn Abd al-Karim. He was sitting on the floor directly across the circle from Hakeem, legs crossed, attention fully focused on the sheikh's lecture. He was wearing a black tunic and a matching black robe opened in the front, with gold piping trimming the cuffs of the sleeves. His head was covered with a *taqiya*, a tight-fitting cap, the same gold color as the trim on his coat, with a black sash around the outer edges of the cap. And yes, there was the black triangular patch over his left eye.

Sheikh Abu Ja'far spoke for about thirty minutes. His topic for the day was based on Quran 4:49: *O you who believe, obey God, and obey the messenger, and those in charge among you.*

When the teacher finished, a few of the students had questions. "Is this to say that we should follow the laws of the Umayyad caliph?" one of them asked.

"When one chooses to live in a certain place, he or she implicitly agrees to obey the laws of the land," was the sheikh's answer.

"And if one disagrees with the law?" asked another.

"Then he must choose. He could leave, or he could stay. If he chooses the latter, he must obey. If he does not, he must be prepared to bear the consequences."

As soon as the class was over and the students started to get up to leave, Hakeem approached his soon-to-be handler, who was still seated.

"Mokhtar, may I have a word with you?" Hakeem asked.

The man looked up, surprised at first, as if he was not expecting to hear someone call him by that name. But then rather quickly he said, "Yes, I am Mokhtar. How can I help you?"

"I have just arrived from Mahdiya," Hakeem said. "I have a letter for you."

Mokhtar took the letter, but he didn't have to read it to know that Hakeem was a newly arrived Fatimid *da'i* and that he was to help the recruit get settled in Córdoba.

As predicted, Mokhtar did not ask Hakeem's name. Rather, he said, "I will call you Abd al-Rashid. That is the name you will use here in Córdoba. Come with me."

The two of them left the mosque together.

"Where are we going?" Hakeem asked.

"I will tell you when we get there," Mokhtar answered. He said no more until they arrived at what Hakeem presumed to be the cell's safe house. "We can talk freely here," Mokhtar said. "This is where we can meet when it is necessary. I assume you know what your mission is. From time to time, you will report to me. You can contact me at Sheikh Abu Ja'far's class when you need to meet. Do you have any questions?"

Hakeem had only one. "Is it so dangerous that we need this degree of secrecy?"

"Yes," Mokhtar answered. "The Umayyad caliph is a direct challenger to the Fatimid caliph. Umayyad security forces would not take kindly to the kind of reconnaissance you will be conducting."

Hakeem wondered what he had gotten himself into.

"Come. I will take you to the flat where you will be staying here in Córdoba."

They left the safe house on foot. As they were walking, Hakeem said, "What can you tell me about this beautiful city?"

"It is unlike any other city in the world. There are perhaps as many as five hundred thousand people here. I have never counted them, of course," Mokhtar said with a slight chuckle.

Of course not. Hakeem rolled his eyes at this sorry excuse for a joke. "Is it true that there are seventy public libraries here?"

"I don't know how many there are," Mokhtar said. "I am not really a student here. But the most important library in the city, beyond a doubt, is the library associated with the university at the Grand Mosque."

Hakeem was tempted to ask what Mokhtar's profession was, but he knew he would not get an honest answer. So he said nothing.

Presently, they arrived at the place where Hakeem would reside. The door at street level opened into a hallway that took a ninety-degree turn into a large courtyard with an octagon-shaped basin in the center. At the second and third stories, a beautiful *masharabia* banister framed the balcony around the courtyard. His room, on the second floor, opened onto this courtyard. Friezes of carved stucco just below the ceiling and beautiful glazed tiles forming geometric patterns covered the lower third of the walls.

As he gazed around the courtyard, Hakeem said in a tone that betrayed his surprise, "This is a rather well-to-do house."

"This place was chosen by the agency," Mokhtar said.

The agency. Hakeem shuddered at the thought that he was now a spy.

Hakeem was based in Córdoba for a little more than a year. He was in enemy territory—the capital of the Umayyad caliphate—and wanted to do as detailed reconnaissance as possible. That was his rationale for staying here, but it was also an excuse to remain and read in the great library.

Among the works he sought, one he had not gotten around to reading in Baghdad was *Kitab al-Buldan*, the *Book of Countries*, written some three quarters of a century earlier by Ahmed Ibn Jafr al-Yaqubi. Although the title would not suggest it, the work was of the same genre as Ibn Khurdadhbih's *Kitab al-Masalik wa'l-Mamalik*—the genre of political geography of which Hakeem was becoming particularly fond.

Al-Yaqubi's work expanded the range of subjects. Most importantly, in Hakeem's view, it focused on the experience of the traveler, a feature Hakeem was becoming more and more adept at adding to his own descriptions of place. He was particularly interested in al-Yaqubi's description of two major routes across the great Sahara Desert, an eastern route passing through Zawila and a more western route passing through Sijilmasa. Hakeem knew the name Sijilmasa; it was on the very edge of Islamic territory, a place of refuge once sought by the Mahdi who founded the Fatimid movement for which he now worked.

As he read this work, Hakeem sensed a sympathy with the Shiite movement, a growing apprehension on the writer's part that all was not right in the *mamlakat'l-Islam* of the Abbasids. There were clear hints at economic and social tension, if not the outright ethnic and religious and dynastic opposition that was beginning to manifest at this very time. Had al-Yaqubi been still alive, Hakeem might have guessed that he too was a Fatimid *da'i*.

Everywhere he went, Hakeem took note of what he saw. Everything, absolutely everything, was potentially important data to incorporate into his report. Overall, he was most impressed by the city of Córdoba. He was told that it was the most important urban center in the entire Iberian Peninsula. Mokhtar had told him that there were a half million people in the city. Hakeem had his doubts that this was the case. Since it was physically separated from the large residential villas and suburbs, it looked smaller than it actually was. The streets were not straight or orthogonal, as they were back in Baghdad. They followed the contour of the land. But they did divide the city neatly into quarters. The streets were swept clean every day, and at night they were lit by numerous oil lamps.

Hakeem took his meals after evening prayer at various inns around town. He would usually linger to drink a cup or two of hot cider, wanting to engage in casual conversation with potential unsuspecting informants. Making it seem casual was the challenging part. He could not simply go up to someone and say, "Hello, my name is Hakeem Ibn al-Harith." That would be too forward. He found it better to open a conversation with a question, perhaps asking for directions to a particular place or a recommendation for a particular service. He found that Cordobans were generally quite friendly, anxious to help a stranger, but a little reticent to open themselves up to people they didn't know.

After spending just a few weeks in Cordoba, Hakeem decided, albeit reluctantly, to travel the five and a half miles due west to Madinat'z-Zahra—the "Shining City." This was where the Umayyad caliph resided, in a new palace built just some twenty or so years earlier, almost entirely faced with white marble and bright white stucco. It was much more than just a palace. There were also ceremonial reception halls, mosques, administrative and government offices, gardens, a mint, workshops, and military barracks. Soon, dwellings sprung up around the complex, constituting a small town of its own, residences of many of the caliph's loyal supporters as well as a population who provided services to the caliphal administration.

At first Hakeem was hesitant to go here, thinking that, being a Fatimid agent, he would be inside the lion's den itself, too close to the seat of power of the caliph who was rival to the true caliph, whom he served. It then occurred to him that for this very reason, it was crucial for him to take the risk.

He stuck to the practice he followed in Córdoba. After evening prayer, he went to one of the small inns near the southeast edge of town, closest to the road back to Córdoba. Not that it would make much difference if by chance he were suspected of being a spy, but it made him feel better to imagine that he could make a quick getaway if need be.

He sat at a small table for two not far from the entrance, hoping that a solo client would come in and, seeing the other tables occupied, would ask to join him. He felt safer in a one-on-one encounter, thinking that it would be easier to control the conversation and direct it to topics of interest to his ultimate objective.

After an hour or so—and several cups of hot cider—a slightly paunchy man, nicely dressed in a fine black mantle and contrasting white turban, sporting a full gray beard, approached his table. "Do you mind if I join you? There doesn't seem to be any other empty place in the inn."

Hakeem had learned that if he hoped to interact with a potential informant who would open up to him, it was important to be willing to talk about himself first, even if what he said about himself was not true. "Of course. Please join me. My name is Kareem." His first lie. It was a double alias: not his own name, nor the name given him by his handler. "And you?"

"Thank you. I am Isaac bin Yameen."

His full name, Hakeem thought. *Let's see how much more information I can get right from the start.* "Have you always lived here in Madinat'z-Zahra?"

"I am not originally from here. I moved here from Tyre in Syria."

"That's amazing!" Hakeem feigned surprise. "I am from Acco." His second lie. "Our families are almost neighbors."

"What brings you here?" Isaac asked.

Hakeem had already chosen a false occupation to go along with his alias identity in Córdoba. "I am an accountant by trade. I work for several merchants in Córdoba keeping their account books up-to-date. It is the perfect job for me. I am really an adventurer at heart." This part was actually true. "But I am good with numbers. And since I have won the trust of my employers, I often travel to other markets here in Iberia on their behalf." Hakeem thought that it was very clever, first, to suggest that he was such a trustworthy person and, second, to reveal that his work allowed him to travel around. "What about you, Isaac, why did you come here all the way from Tyre?"

"I work at the mint. You might have guessed by my name that I am Jewish. It is well known that Jews of Tyre are among the best glassmakers in the world. I would not say that I am among the best, but my job is to craft the glass weights that are used to maintain standards of weight both for the mint and for the marketplace."

"But you don't produce the coins themselves?"

"I'm afraid not. But my job is perhaps more important. I am the only one who cuts the mold for the weights. There are many craftsmen who strike the coins. Many are needed because of the large quantity of coins produced each year."

"Really? I am curious, how many…approximately?"

"Believe it or not, some 200,000 gold dinars a year. At an exchange rate of seventeen to one, that's 3,400,000 silver dirhems."

"Unbelievable!" Hakeem congratulated himself on acquiring a useful piece of information on the operation of the royal mint—information that was indicative of a fiscally healthy regime.

The two continued to enjoy each other's company for another hour or so.

"I typically come to Madinat'z-Zahra on business once a week," said Hakeem, "usually on Thursdays. Would you like to meet again next Thursday?"

"Of course. Why not?"

The two men put their hands on each other's shoulders and touched cheeks, first on the right and then on the left, and departed as friends.

Hakeem and Isaac met several more times, almost every Thursday afternoon. Most of the time, they talked about mundane sorts of things. They talked about each other's families—although what Hakeem said of his family was completely made up. Hakeem also described his work as an accountant.

That information was not made up. He really did some accounting work for actual businessmen in Córdoba, although under a different name than the one he used in Madinat'z-Zahra. From time to time, Hakeem gleaned real gems of information, like the day Isaac talked about taxes.

"Government revenues include property taxes, customs duties on a vast variety of merchandise imported or exported by sailing vessels from all over the Mediterranean, taxes collected on sales in the taverns—"

Hakeem interrupted, "So, it's permitted to drink alcohol in these taverns as long as one pays the tax?"

"Well, Jews and Christians are not forbidden to drink alcohol, and some Muslims will drink in spite of the prohibition. Why should the government not profit from this profane activity?" Isaac continued where he left off. "The revenue collected from these sources totaled twenty million dinars from the beginning of the reign of Abd al-Rahman III up to this year."

Hakeem thought this figure was somewhat inflated or exaggerated, but he nonetheless took note that the Umayyad government was far more than solvent.

Over the next several months, Hakeem took a number of "business" trips around Andalusia. Between each important point of interest, every major city, he was careful to note both the direction he traveled in relation to the rising and falling of the sun as well as the length of time he traveled at a normal speed on horseback. All of this information was potentially very useful for planning communications, be they commercial or military.

Each time he returned to Córdoba, he went to the Grand Mosque to make contact with Mokhtar. From there they went to the safe house, where Hakeem could relay his report to his handler.

"What do you think of the security of the borders of the Umayyad realm?" Mokhtar asked one day.

"Basically, Andalusia has two frontiers," Hakeem said. "The first borders the ocean to our south and east. All of the coastal cities I have described are indeed large metropolises, heavily populated, with abundant resources. The northern frontier borders the land inhabited by the Christians. The most numerous are the Franks. That borderland is not heavily populated, and the military defense along that frontier seems relatively weak."

"Why do you say that?" Mokhtar asked.

"I did not see large contingents of heavily armed soldiers along the eastern half of the northern border. Perhaps the inhabitants on both sides have no reason to be hostile. I was told that it is not uncommon for Andalusians to seek spouses for their children among the Franks rather than among the Galicians, who are much more, shall we say, aggressive."

"Hmm," Mokhtar said softly. "There is something more pressing to discuss. This will be your last report for a while. I have received word from Mahdiya to send you on to a new assignment."

Hakeem's face betrayed his disappointment. He really liked it in Andalusia, especially in Córdoba. Not only was it such a beautiful city, but he relished the intellectual life, the openness among people of different faiths. He was able to avail himself of all this when he was not...well, being a spy. "Where will I be going?"

"To Sijilmasa."

"I have heard of it. Is that not on the very edge of the world of Islam, the oasis where our Mahdi sought refuge decades ago, before he established his base in Mahdiya?"

"Exactly," Mokhtar said. "It is a desert town on the edge of the great Sahara."

Hakeem was not excited about going to what sounded like a remote outpost.

Mokhtar seemed to sense Hakeem's unease. He was quick to follow up. "It's not what you might think. Sijilmasa is a rich town, and it is crucial to the well-being of the Fatimids. You, yourself, have reported on the enormous quantity of gold coins being minted and circulated here in Andalusia. Where do you think that gold comes from?"

Hakeem didn't know. He waited for an answer.

"From across the great desert. It is mined along the banks of the rivers in the Sudan—the 'Land of the Blacks.' But it passes through Sijilmasa."

"What else can you tell me about Sijilmasa?"

"Not much, I'm afraid. Only rumors that we hear from travelers coming from there. We do not have an agent posted there. That's why we are sending you. Your assignment, bluntly stated, is to spy on the regime of the local governor. He has been ruling in alliance with the Fatimid caliph in Mahdiya. But it seems that he has taken steps to assert his independent sovereignty. Beyond that, our caliph wants a report on the lay of the land."

"I suppose that with no agents, there will be no safe house. How shall I report my findings?"

"You will be on your own. You will have to figure out for yourself how best to communicate with Mahdiya."

"And what is to be my cover?"

You will join a merchant caravan as a bookseller. Books are relatively inexpensive here in Córdoba but are very much in demand in Sijilmasa and points south. We will supply you with a modest selection of books: some Qurans, a few books on *tafsir*, some collections of hadith. I am told that Sijilmasa is developing a vibrant intellectual community. There will be interest in your books."

This idea appealed to Hakeem very much. What could be better? He would be posing as someone who dealt with objects that he loved. "When do I leave?"

"As soon as possible. Certainly within a few days."

As Hakeem was about to leave, Mokhtar added, "Oh, one other thing. Over the last few days, an official from the Office of the Marketplace Supervisor was inquiring about the activities of a so-called accountant who goes by the name of Kareem. No one in the market had heard of an accountant by that name. You wouldn't know who that might be, would you?"

Hakeem had not shared his second alias with his handler. The only person who knew him by the name of Kareem was his Jewish friend, Isaac, in Madinat'z-Zahra. Maybe he wasn't such a friend after all. Maybe it was good that he would be leaving soon. *I had best be careful until I am out of Andalusia,* he thought.

CHAPTER TEN

Algeciras, 951

It was early morning at the beginning of spring. The wind was blowing, and it was cold. When Hakeem arrived at the port of Algeciras, there was a long queue of passengers waiting to board the vessel to Sebta. The line hardly moved at all.

Hakeem arranged with a porter to have his two crates of books loaded onto the ship and then joined the line of passengers. "What is causing the delay?" Hakeem asked a man at the tail end of the line.

"It seems that inspectors are verifying the identity of each passenger who wishes to board," the man said. "They are apparently looking for someone."

Hakeem had an inkling as to whom they were looking for. *Isaac must have become suspicious of me and informed the authorities in Madinat'z-Zahra.* When they could not find an accountant by the name of Kareem, the authorities must have concluded that "Kareem" was a spy.

If indeed they were looking for him, he would never make it onto the ship. He decided to get out of line, at least until he could better assess what was going on. He stood behind some barrels stacked high in front of a storehouse on the dock, hidden from the officers screening the passengers. He waited.

It seemed like an eternity, but finally almost everyone had boarded except for a few latecomers who ran up to the gangplank just as the sailors were getting ready to raise it. It started to rain. Hakeem pulled his hood over his head, almost completely covering his face. He hurried to join the last-minute stragglers, hoping that the two officers were just as anxious to leave as he was to board. He carried only a bag with his personal belongings.

"Your name and profession, sir?" barked one of the inspectors.

"I am Hakeem Ibn al-Harith." He decided to use his real name rather than an alias. *If they begin to interrogate me, the closer I can remain to the truth, the better.* He pointed to the two crates of books, which had already been loaded and were sitting on the deck, waiting to be taken below. "My books that I hope to sell in Sijilmasa. I am a bookseller from Baghdad."

The inspectors were clearly anxious to get out of the rain. They waved him on.

The passage through the Strait of Gibraltar was rough, with heavy winds and choppy waves. At first Hakeem thought he was going to be seasick, but his stomach settled down after a short while.

On board the vessel, Hakeem found himself standing by the rail next to a well-dressed man who wore a heavy wool *burnus* to protect himself from the wind and the mist from the sea. Hakeem could tell that the *burnus* was very finely woven. *He is probably a well-to-do merchant,* Hakeem thought. He decided to initiate a conversation. "Have you ever made this voyage across the straits before?"

"Many times," the man said.

"Are the waves always this choppy?"

"It is a bit rough, isn't it? It is usually calmer. But not to worry, it is a short journey. Let's sit before we fall over."

Hakeem and the man found two places near the rear of the boat.

Hakeem introduced himself with his real name. "I am a seller of books," he said. Since his work was to be predominantly reconnaissance rather than clandestine spying, he decided that it was not so important to remain undercover. And even though he was not a professional bookseller, he did have books for sale.

"I am Aziz al-Sijilmasi," said his new friend.

"Oh, are you actually from Sijilmasa, as your name suggests?"

"There are many Sijilmasis all around the Mediterranean, but yes, I am from Sijilmasa. I am on my way home."

"What a coincidence! I too am going to Sijilmasa. I hear there is a growing community of scholars there. Hopefully, they will be interested in some of my books. In any case, I think I will be staying for a while." A short pause. "What kind of business are you in?" *Might as well begin my reconnaissance work right away.*

"I export dates from the Sijilmasa oasis," said Aziz.

"Dates!" Hakeem was surprised. "Why dates?"

"Well, first of all, dates are perhaps the second most abundant cash crop in the whole oasis. Second, our *madjhoul* dates are the very best in the whole world."

"I have been told that the best and most abundant dates are from the town of Basra in Syria."

"Are you by chance from Syria?" Aziz asked jokingly.

"No, but I lived in Baghdad for three years."

"Ah. Well, I'm sure that the Sijilmasa dates are much better than your Basra ones. All jesting aside, we actually ship ours the world over. I don't usually travel to export my goods; I just ship them to a foreign agent. But in this particular case, I brought some samples of our best dates to the chief steward of the palace in Madinat'z-Zahra. I succeeded in convincing him to serve only our best *majdhouls* at their banquets. That variety yields the largest, sweetest, and, I guarantee, the most succulent of all dates."

Hakeem's mouth started to water. "You are making me hungry. I don't suppose you have any with you now?"

"I'm afraid not. The caliph's household insisted that I leave all that I had with them. You will just have to come to my home in Sijilmasa, and I will give you some of the best dates you have ever tasted."

"I look forward to that, and to meeting your family."

By the time the ship was more than halfway across the strait, the weather had cleared up considerably. The sea was calm enough that the passengers could stand up without being tossed around. The two new friends stood at the rail at the stern of the vessel. As they looked back at the coast of Andalusia, they could barely see the steep cliffs of Jebel Tariq.

"It's calm enough to walk toward the bow," suggested Aziz.

Even though the sea was much calmer, Hakeem steadied himself with his hand on the rail. It was now just after dusk. They could see lanterns lighting the coastline of the port of Sebta.

"We will be there before the fall of darkness," said Aziz. "How do you plan to get to Sijilmasa?"

"Honestly, I haven't given it much thought." He'd been so anxious to get out of Andalusia before getting arrested that he hadn't considered what his next move would be.

"Well, in any case, it will be too late to head out tonight," said Aziz. "I am staying in the central *funduq* for the night and heading out with a small caravan of merchants at first light. Why don't you join me. I know the caravan master. I'm sure it will be alright."

The entire journey was slated to take eighteen days. The first part of the journey was easy enough, traveling on a clearly marked road connecting several towns and villages, including the university city of Fez. Hakeem remarked, "My teacher told me that Fez has one of the greatest universities in the entire Muslim world."

"It may well be the best," said Aziz. "That's a subjective judgment. But it is definitely the oldest. It was founded over a hundred and fifty years ago."

The two men continued to ride side by side. Hakeem had chosen to ride a mule rather than a horse. He was told that the mule would be much more sure-footed on the steep, rocky slopes that lay ahead of them. Aziz also insisted that he purchase a warm *burnus*, much heavier than the cloak he had been wearing. "The weather will be colder than you can imagine," he said. Tethered to Hakeem's mule was a sturdy little donkey carrying his personal belongings and his two crates of books.

Hakeem would have been tempted to stay in Fez to peruse the famous Qarawayeen Library, but he was a man on a mission, so much so that he asked question after question of his companion. "Tell me, what are the people of Sijilmasa like?"

Proud of his Sijilmasan origins but trying not to exaggerate, Aziz said, "They are kind and virtuous; generous and at ease; elegant, yet modest; they have a great love of learning. Never have I seen anywhere in the Maghrib so many ulama with such deep knowledge as in Sijilmasa. They sit in the great hall of the Friday Mosque debating the pressing issues of the day from the perspective of all the major schools of law."

"I'm sure I will like that very much." Hakeem remarked.

Ten days into the trip, the caravan found itself climbing the steep slopes into the Middle Atlas Mountains. When they reached an altitude of about 4,000 feet, they found themselves in the thick of a cedar forest, giant evergreens reaching up to 130 feet. "Oh my God!" exclaimed Hakeem. "They are so tall!" He was reacting to the height of the trees, not the mountains. "I was told there are giant cedars in the mountains of Lebanon, but I have not seen them. It is hard to believe that they are as tall as these."

When the sun was at its highest point and it was time to pray, the caravan stopped. After prayer, the travelers took food from their saddlebags to have their midday meal. They were quickly surrounded by a large troop of macaque monkeys. *There must be at least twenty*, Hakeem thought. *No, they just keep coming; there are at least fifty!* And they were aggressive…to the point of trying to get close enough to snatch the food that was not already in the hands of the consumer.

"Don't feed the monkeys," warned the head caravan guide. "That will only make them even more threatening."

"You should also warn folks of the lions," said one of the other guides.

Hakeem turned to Aziz. "He jests?"

"No, not at all. In this part of the forest, lions loom just out of sight of people passing through. But we are safe as long as we are more numerous than the lions…and as long as the lions are not too hungry." Aziz added the last comment with a smile on his face.

The sun had been pleasant most of the day, but by late afternoon, the trees cast a shadow of darkness. With the vanishing light went whatever heat the sun provided. What Hakeem had been told about the possible inclement weather, if anything, had been understated. The snow began to fall, gently at first, but within an hour it turned into a blizzard the likes of which Hakeem had never seen. The wind blew so fiercely that the horses, mules, and donkeys could not see the road ahead of them. Riders dismounted and dragged the animals forward. Of course, the humans could hardly see any better. Fortunately, they came upon a large rock overhang, under which men and beasts huddled together for the night.

It was still snowing when they prepared to leave at first light the next day, but the wind had died down. The lead guide insisted that they press on in spite of the weather. "It is likely to snow the rest of today and through the night again, perhaps even longer. That is not unusual for this time of year. If we wait until it stops, we could find ourselves having to stay put for several days or marching through more than two feet of snow. But if we leave now, we could be out of these mountains before the end of the day."

And so it came to pass as the guide had predicted. By nightfall, they were out of the snow and marching through the foothills on the south side of the Middle Atlas. Three days later, they reached the first upswing of the High Atlas Mountains, so different from those they had crossed a few days earlier. The ascent was so much steeper and higher. Forward progress required enormous effort. The only vegetation was scrub grass and thorny bushes here and there. Otherwise, the trail was flanked by the rocky face of the mountains. Occasionally, they passed a tiny village of ten or so houses nestled on the side of a slope, with a small herd of goats grazing on the terraces. Guides often depended on these villagers for goats' milk and meat for their clients and their animals.

"Now I know why you described Sijilmasa as remote," exclaimed Hakeem.

The descent out of the High Atlas was just as sharp. And the climate changes were dramatic. As the elevation declined, the temperature rose proportionally. When the caravan reached the bottom of the ravine, it began to follow the blue waters of the Ziz River as it flowed through the narrow but lush oasis of date palms below, in which farmers grew a vast variety of grains and fruits and vegetables. The travelers enjoyed cool temperatures during the evenings and through the nights but experienced high temperatures during the day.

"Within three days, we will be in Sijilmasa—home!" said Aziz.

It was almost dusk on the third day when the walls of Sijilmasa were finally in sight. The leader of the caravan ordered them to pick up the pace. If they hurried, they might make it to the city gate before it closed for the night.

Despite the effort, it was well after dusk when they arrived at the Bab Fez, and the heavy wooden doors were shut. "Will we be able to get in?" Hakeem asked.

"I'm sure we will," the caravan leader answered, "but the security guards might ask to inspect all of our goods very closely. That's just a ploy they use in hopes of getting a little backsheesh in lieu of a lengthy inspection."

The caravan passed through the Bab Fez, just as the caravan leader had predicted, after paying a modest contribution to the welfare of the guards. A single road beyond the gate meandered past a few private villas and open arable fields.

"This is the *gamaman*," said Aziz, "the agricultural zone that surrounds the city. It is protected by the outer wall that is now behind us. Just ahead is an inner wall that encircles the city center. That is where I live."

"And this road that veers to the right and crosses over the river?" Hakeem asked.

"That road goes to Suq Ben Aqla. There is a large caravanserai there and a small settlement that supports the long-distance caravan trade across the desert. Several of the people who traveled with us will leave us at this point to seek shelter for the night at the caravanserai. You, on the other hand, should come with me to my home. You can stay with my family until you get settled in a place of your own."

Hakeem had been the recipient of enough hospitality since he left home that he perfectly understood that it was just as important to be a gracious recipient as it was to be a generous host. "That's very kind of you, Aziz. I accept your offer."

As was the case almost everywhere Hakeem had been, the exterior of Aziz's house gave no indication as to what his home was like. Was it large or small? Did it open into a central courtyard? Was it decorated with exquisite glazed tiles and carved stucco? Were the floors covered in colorful wool, or maybe even silk, carpets?

The mystery vanished as soon as they stepped inside. It was immediately evident that Aziz was not the average merchant. He was *really* rich! The answer to most of Hakeem's questions was "yes."

Aziz disappeared into one of the rooms off the courtyard for a brief moment. When he returned, he said, "It's rather late, but I'm sure that Amina will at least have some hot soup and bread for us."

"Amina is your wife?"

"No, sadly, my wife died a few years ago. Amina is my twenty-year-old daughter."

"I'm sorry," Hakim said, and his sentiment was genuine.

When Amina came into the room, Hakeem took one look at her. His eyes opened wide. He was left speechless. *She is the most beautiful woman I have ever seen!* he thought. Then again, other than his sisters, he had not seen many women, except in passing on the street or in the marketplace—and most of them had their heads covered, if not their faces veiled as well. Amina's face was not veiled. Her complexion was light, with a slightly olive glow. Her eyes were dark—and intriguing. Nor was her long, black, wavy hair covered. She was wearing a full-length silk caftan, tied at the waist so that her figure was well defined.

Hakeem's reaction to Amina did not slip by Aziz. He was quick to say, "We are not Arab. We are Amazigh. It is not the custom of Berbers to cover their faces. When they are seen in public or in the presence of strangers, they do wrap their bodies in a long shawl embroidered with the markings of their tribe."

"Am I not a stranger in your house?" asked Hakeem.

"You are a friend; I mean a *real* friend, more than someone I just met on the boat coming over from Algeciras. And I told Amina that, when I checked on her as soon as we arrived." Aziz was sincere when he said this. Ironically, there was something about Hakeem that led Aziz to trust him implicitly.

They sat on cushions around the low, round table in the center of the room. Hamdi, the head servant, brought in a large decanter of *harira*, a thick soup made of lentils and vegetables, not steaming hot, but rather still warm from the supper that had been served to the household staff a little earlier. The two round loaves of bread were also still warm. The travelers were hungry and exhausted. They ate heartily with very little conversation.

Amina had already eaten. Still, she joined the men at the table. *This too is quite unusual*, Hakeem thought. He felt a strange, warm feeling—quite apart from the warmth provided by the victuals—as he sat across from her, staring into her beautiful brown eyes. It was a feeling that was totally new to him. He liked it.

Hakeem went to sleep that night fantasizing about what it would be like to have a woman by his side.

Hakeem's first order of business the next day was to find a place to live. That turned out to be quite easy with Aziz's help. He rented a room in a large house not far from the central marketplace. It was just three blocks from where Aziz lived—*and of course, Amina*, he thought. The room was completely empty, but furnishings were easily acquired in the market. He bought a large, plain, off-white Berber rug, the natural color of the sheep that provided the wool. He commissioned a carpenter to build three single-width sofa beds, upon which he placed matching red woolen mattress covers tightly stuffed with goose feathers. The beds lined three of the four walls. He ordered the carpenter to install bookshelves along the fourth wall around the door, end to end and floor to ceiling. The centerpiece of his room was a beautiful, round cedarwood table. The tabletop was black fossil stone cut from the nearby mountains. Like most well-built houses in desert towns, this one had very thick adobe walls providing excellent insulation and an almost constant temperature from midday to the middle of the night across all seasons. Hakeem felt proud of his cozy little nest. Deep down, he had to admit, he was especially pleased that it was near the home where Amina lived.

Hakeem went to the Grand Mosque every day, always for midday prayer and often for morning prayer. He went to pray, of course, but he was also anxious to engage with the scholars and students who gathered there every day. His intelligence gathering included, among many other subjects, what madhab was followed, what school of law was imposed, and how that impacted the daily lives of the people. His own studies focused more on science and mathematics, so in this environment, he mostly just listened and asked an occasional question.

Since the Fatimids ruled Sijilmasa through a local governor, Hakeem expected that Shiite Islam would be the law of the land. He was wrong.

The alim who seemed to be in charge explained, "Yes, the Fatimids imposed Shiite Islam, but recently our emir, Mohammed Ibn al-Fath, replaced it with a version of Sunni Islam known as Malikism."

Hakeem nodded; he was somewhat familiar with Malikism, the madhab that had been in force in Andalusia when he was there. "Why the sudden change?"

"That's a question we are all asking," the alim replied. "It would have made more sense simply to return to Kharijite Islam, the sect practiced here before the Fatimids came. But they did not."

Another alim stood and jumped into the conversation. "Some say that it was a move to recognize the Sunni authority of the caliph in Baghdad."

"That makes no sense," said the head alim. "The Abbasids adopted Hanifi Islam, a different Sunni sect."

Hakeem's eyes were moving back and forth, first to one scholar, then to the other, and back to the first. By now he was confused. In the end, he could not care less what madhab the new regime practiced. When he compiled his report, he would simply list what school of law was the official one and leave it at that. The important point to note was that it was *not* the one his employers had chosen.

As often as he could, Hakeem walked the few blocks to Aziz's house, ostensibly to visit his friend but in reality in hopes of seeing his friend's daughter. Whether he was there for a meal or simply for a visit over some hot cider or rose petal tea, Amina would pass through the room and remain long enough for a brief exchange.

One day, Hakeem came by unannounced. Aziz was not at home. It was Amina who greeted him. She invited him in and asked Hamdi to bring them some lemonade. Hakeem thought that it was highly unusual for her to invite him in during her father's absence. "I should leave," he said, not wanting to do something inappropriate.

"No, please stay," she said. "We are not really here alone. Hamdi is here. He will be just in the next room. You should know by now that my father is not as strict as most fathers. Don't be so nervous; we'll be just fine." She was carrying a small, leather-bound book. "Come and sit next to me on the sofa. I would like to show you this book that Abi brought from one of his trips to Andalusia. He says that it originally came from Baghdad."

Hakeem was quite interested in the book, but he was even more excited about sitting next to Amina as they looked at the book together; they sat close, but not as close as most fathers would object.

"It is a story from what Abi tells me is a collection called *The Book of the Tale of a Thousand Nights*. This particular story is about a genie and a fisherman."

Hakeem leaned over to get a better look at the picture of the genie. "Can you tell me the story?"

"Of course. The fisherman cast his net into the water. When he tried to pull it up, he could not. It was too heavy. He dove down to see what the problem was. Would you believe, there was a dead donkey in the net. The next time he threw his net, he pulled up a pitcher full of dirt. On his third try, there were only some shards of pottery and glass. Finally, on the fourth try, there was a beautiful copper lamp with a cover sealed with the seal of Solomon. When the fisherman finally succeeded in prying off the cap, lo and behold, a malevolent genie emerged in a puff of smoke."

"How do you know the genie was malevolent?" Hakeem moved a little closer to Amina.

"You'll see," she said. "Having been imprisoned in the lamp for centuries, the genie vowed to grant the person who liberated him the choice of his own mode of death. The fisherman was terrified, but he thought of a ruse. He asked the genie how he was able to squeeze himself into the lamp. 'Could you show me?' the fisherman asked. Anxious to show off, the genie reentered the lamp, and the fisherman quickly resealed the cap. The genie pleaded with his new captor, and…" There was a long pause.

"Yes…yes…and then what?" Hakeem pretended to be overcome with suspense. What was real, though, was the feeling that overtook his whole being from sitting next to this beautiful woman.

"That's as far as I have gotten in the story," she said, laughing.

Hakeem leaned back against the wall. Turning toward Amina, he was tempted to put his arms around her—until he realized what he was about to do. He simply said, "I have never met a woman…who…who knew how to read. Do you have other books?"

"I have a book of *jahili* poems of love and…" a long pause, "and a book that *you* might be interested in, a book of travels by a man named al-Yaqubi."

Hakeem was a bit taken aback. *Why would she think that my interests are so narrow?* "I am interested in all books," he said. "But yes, you are right. I am very interested in the work of al-Yaqubi."

"So you have read it?"

"Most of it," he said. "Perhaps we can meet again soon and compare what we have read."

"Why not?" Amina answered.

Hakeem wasted no time. He called on Amina the very next day. Once again, Aziz was not at home. "Are you sure your father will not mind if we are here together, just the two of us?"

"He trusts me."

"Fine. But does he trust me?"

"You are his friend. He told me so more than once." Hakeem suspected
that in truth, Amina was not so sure her father would not object to the two
of them being alone in the house. But she seemed as anxious to spend time
with Hakeem as he was with her. They were both willing to take the chance.
"Besides," she added, "you are here as my teacher." She was holding her copy
of al-Yaqubi's book. "Unlike most fathers, he encourages me to read and to
learn, even though my studies are confined to the four walls of this beautiful
house. Come, sit beside me on the sofa."

Amina opened the book to the page where she had placed a ribbon as
a marker. "Look here," she said, pointing to a line on the page. "Al-Yaqubi
describes two major routes across the great Sahara Desert—an eastern route
passing through Zawila and a more western route passing right here through
Sijilmasa. See, he confirms what all of us here in town believe. We are a vital
link between the greater world of Islam and the Sudan, that mysterious land
south of the great desert."

Hakeem leaned back against a cushion, raised his eyebrows, and wrinkled
his forehead in surprise. Not to be outdone, he was quick to point out what
he knew from his reading of al-Yaqubi in Córdoba, what now seemed so long
ago. "I remember that he expressed a growing apprehension that all was not
right in the *mamlakat'l-Islam* of the Abbasids."

"Oh, what were his concerns?"

"He saw clear indications of economic and social tension, of the caliph
losing control of the periphery of the empire. As I read it, I wondered if al-
Yaqubi suspected outright opposition to the Abbasid regime already back in
his time. Remember, he wrote almost a hundred years ago."

"You don't suppose that he was in sympathy with the Shiite movement, do
you?"

Had al-Yaqubi still been alive, Hakeem might have guessed that he was a
Fatimid *da'i* like himself. He did not say that to Amina. He simply answered,
"I don't know."

Just then, the servant Hamdi came into the room. "Your father will be
home shortly, Miss Amina." He said no more than that.

Amina's father was not as strict as most, but she understood that it was
perhaps best if Hakeem left at this time. She turned to him and said, "We can
pick up where we left off the next time you come, yes?" She closed the book
and escorted Hakeem to the door. "When will you come again?"

"As soon as I can," he answered.

CHAPTER ELEVEN

From where Hakeem lived, it was only a five-minute walk to the central market of Sijilmasa. He enjoyed watching the market come to life in the early morning as he sat having his breakfast at the small diner just inside the gate of the enclosed space. On most days, he would have some hot porridge, bread, a handful of dates, and a bowl of hot goat's milk. People were already showing up to begin the day's commerce. What began as a trickle soon became an unbroken chain of buyers and sellers coming from every direction on every mode of transportation available, many on foot, some on donkeyback, only a few on camels.

The market was organized such that merchants of a certain type of goods set up their stands close to each other. There was an area for textiles, another for shoes and other leather goods, and still another for spices. Hakeem loved to walk among the spice merchants. The strong scent of the cinnamon and cloves from Zanzibar overpowered the milder scents of sugar produced in the Sus and saffron and ginger roots from Andalusia. Bright sunlight accentuated the browns, reds, and yellows of the spices mounded on cloth sacks, as much a stimulus to his eyes as to his nostrils. The local spice merchants doubled as medicine men and thus sold a variety of medicinal herbs and drugs and, of course, dried animal skins, skulls, and bones used as magical fetishes. Hakeem was confident of the medicinal properties of the herbs and spices. His mother had used them often as he was growing up. He was skeptical of the fetishes.

At first, Hakeem thought he would rent a small space to set up a display of his books. He quickly gave up on that idea when he discovered that there was already a bookseller in the market, an elderly man who spent his day sitting on a stool in his small shop, reading. He did not seem to have any customers. One day, Hakeem asked him why.

"There is a vibrant intellectual community here," the man explained, "but the scholars are few in number, and they already have the basic theological works. I have nothing new to sell them."

Hakeem had gotten to know the scholars in town, and he did have a few things to interest them. He had a few books of *tafsir*, commentaries on Maliki law, that no one else had. He was able to sell a few of his rare books directly out of his own home. What's more, the scarcity of them brought a high price. Still, he knew that sooner rather than later, he would have to supplement his income if he planned to remain in Sijilmasa for any length of time. He decided he would resume his other undercover occupation and offer his services as an accountant to some of the merchants in town. Of course, he would have to spend more time in the market. That was fine. He liked the hustle and bustle of the place, especially on the triweekly market days, Tuesdays, Thursdays, and Sundays.

With Aziz's help, Hakeem managed to sell his services to an importer of fine manufactured goods from all parts of the world. The man's name was Saad al-Zenary. He was originally from Egypt but had been living in Sijilmasa for almost thirty years. He was a short, stubby little man with a bald head and a belly that seemed to bounce when he laughed; and he laughed loud and often, presumably because he loved his work. Even more, he loved interacting with his customers. Whether he made a sale or not, he was always willing to spend an hour or more with a prospective buyer, haggling over price.

Hakeem had traveled enough to know by now that bargaining in the marketplace was deeply ingrained in the culture. Still, one day, he tried to give Saad a piece of advice. "If you spent a little less time haggling with customers and more time actually selling your merchandise, you would make a lot more money."

"Perhaps, my friend, but there is much more to this job than just making money. A customer is much more than a customer. He or she is a client, someone with whom we establish a relationship, someone we get to know and who gets to know us. There is a whole ritual involved."

Hakeem nodded. "Now that you point that out, I have to agree. I have listened to you time and time again. You don't only talk price. You ask your customer—or rather, client—'How are you doing?'"

"Exactly. And, 'How is your family? Is your sick child getting better? Yes? Thanks be to God.' You have to show interest in their lives. And it is equally important for them to get to know me. If we agree on a price, so much the better. The buyer will tap my palm with his purse to indicate our mutual satisfaction with the deal. You see, a merchant is really a master at public relations."

Hakeem's job as Saad's accountant was to keep accurate records of his cash flow as well as a detailed inventory of items that came in and items that were sold.

"You have such an array of goods in your shop, dear friend," Hakeem said, "such that can be found nowhere else in Sijilmasa. Your shop is truly unique." Having said that, Hakeem showed Saad his account book and added, "But your account book is a mess!"

"That's why I have hired you, dear friend," replied Saad, referring to Hakeem with the same term and with the slightest tone of sarcasm to drive home the point. "Your job includes making sure that I pay whatever taxes I owe and not one fils more." Saad pounded his fist on the counter as he made this last point, revealing some degree of anger as he spoke of taxes.

Having picked up on that, Hakeem said, "It's quite normal for people to complain about taxes. That's a universal phenomenon, is it not? But you seem *really* upset about it."

Saad was no longer joking now. "Only three forms of tax are permitted under Islamic law: *zakat*, paid by all Muslims based on their assets, *kharaj*, paid by non-Muslims based on the value of their land, and *jizya*, a poll tax paid by non-Muslim People of the Book." As he spoke, Saad got even angrier. "When the Fatimids came not so long ago, they imposed more taxes, non-Quranic taxes, taxes on what was bought and sold, such as camels, sheep, cattle, and other merchandise going out and coming in from Ifriqiya, Fez, Andalusia, the Sus, and Aghmat."

Hakeem was far from pleased to hear that but said nothing to his friend.

Saad continued, "The new governor from the Bani Khazrun tribe continues to collect all of these taxes and, we suspect, at a higher rate than is actually due. We think he skims off the top of what he sends to Mahdiya for his own pocket."

This was information Hakeem would add to his growing report. Sooner or later, and the sooner the better, he would have to establish communication with officials in Mahdiya.

The real hub for the global economy of western Islam was Suq Ben Aqla. It was located about two miles west of town, outside the main city wall and outside the *gamaman*.

It was not unusual for there to be two or three large merchant caravans there at the same time. Each of the merchants could have seventy, eighty, up to a hundred camels, so that in all, there were thousands of these beasts, each capable of carrying two hundred and fifty to three hundred pounds of merchandise.

Several of the Sijilmasa merchants went to Suq Ben Aqla every time a large merchant caravan arrived. They wanted to get the first shot at the exotic merchandise from all parts of the world as it was unloaded.

Saad, too, made the two-mile trip. Being from Egypt, he was especially anxious to buy Egyptian wares that he remembered from his childhood: ornate brass Coptic lamps, etched glass plates and bowls, precious fabrics, smooth silks and brocades woven with gold and silver thread. He bought unique items from other parts of the world as well: beautifully carved pieces of ivory and ebony wood, ostrich feathers, shields made from the skin of the *lampt*, all from the Bilad al-Sudan, the "Land of the Blacks." He had a discerning eye for pearls and coral and amber and other semiprecious materials, items that local Sijilmasan artisans could transform into exquisite jewelry.

Hakeem was there too, watching as the seemingly endless chain of pack animals gathered in the huge open space on the west side of the market. The curiosity, if not the anxiety, of the crowd of spectators built as the cargo was unloaded. It was heavily guarded. Like most of the caravans arriving from the south, this one carried gold.

Some of the gold was transported in the form of dust. But most of it came as refined gold, melted down and poured into bricks, bars, or blank coins that were more convenient to carry.

Almost as precious as the gold, a cargo that attracted even more attention was the cargo in humankind—the slaves. A large caravan could have six hundred slaves or more. Some were sold locally to work in the fields or to shepherd livestock. Some would work as domestic servants, and others became concubines or prostitutes.

As Hakeem passed through the slave market, he would hear a slave trader shout, "Look at these pretty girls. They have light complexions, sculpted figures, slim waists, round buttocks, wide shoulders, and sexual organs so narrow that each of them can be enjoyed indefinitely as though she were a virgin." These women were sometimes called *funduqiya* because they tended to frequent the *funduq*s, where their services were offered to the transient merchants as well as to local residents of Sijilmasa. Hakeem recalled what his stepmother had said about *funduqiya*.

The caravanserai of Sijilmasa consisted of a large square enclosure. Along the inside wall of each of the four sides were stalls, most of them two stories high, faced by a colonnade of rough brick pillars. At street level they had stables for the pack animals, while the floors above had guest rooms. The stalls were also used as warehouses for products brought from afar or purchased in the local market for export across the great desert to the south.

Next to the caravanserai was a much smaller *funduq*, more like a small hotel than a caravanserai. It was here that the *funduqiya* entertained their clients. On a whim, Hakeem decided to check out the establishment. His feelings for Amina had awakened an urge to be with a woman. He had to admit that he was physically attracted to his friend's daughter. But because of the social restrictions of his culture and his close friendship with her father, he knew that his relationship with Amina had to remain platonic.

It would be different with Dalia. She was standing on the corner in front of the small *funduq*. She wore a white caftan, the edges of which were highlighted with silver thread. A black cord cinched close to her waist revealed her curvaceous figure. Hakeem could almost discern the shape of her nose and cheeks through the black lace veil that only partially covered her hair and face. He found that to be quite teasing. He started to walk past her but stopped as soon as they made eye contact for the briefest moment.

She said in a low, alluring voice, "I can tell that you are a searching soul."

Not sure how to respond, Hakeem hesitated for a moment. "And you… are you not a searching soul as well?"

Now it was her turn. She paused, then said, "Yes, I am. Can you help me find my way?"

She led Hakeem into the *funduq* and up the stairs to the second floor. She removed a lit candle from its holder just outside the door of a small room and used it to light a lantern inside. There was no furniture in the room other than a mattress on the floor covered with a blanket made of soft, white lamb's wool. A few embroidered pillows added color to the room.

She motioned Hakeem to sit on the mattress. Standing in front of him, she removed her veil, then unbuttoned the top of her caftan and let it fall to the floor.

Hakeem could now see that she was very dark complexioned, even for someone from the Land of the Blacks. The curves of her body were slightly accented by clear, sweet-scented oil. His eyes moved from the strong, angular features of her face, down to her firm breasts and the taut muscles of her abdomen, to the curly triangle between her legs, and finally to her long, muscular legs. He was aroused, but not as much as he had imagined he would be. He had been with prostitutes a few times before, but somehow this was different. "Can we just talk?" he said softly.

"I have never been asked that before," she answered. "But I…I suppose so."

Hakeem stood up, picked up her caftan from the floor, and handed it to her. She put it on, and the two of them sat side by side on the mattress.

"Since you are paying me for conversation," the young woman began, "we should at least know each other's name. My name is Dalia. In Ghana, where I am from, it means flower."

Rarely was Hakeem at a loss for words, but that was how he found himself now. "A beautiful flower, indeed," he finally mustered.

"And your name?" she pressed on.

"Oh yes…ah…I am Hakeem. Hakeem Ibn al-Harith." Then, for some reason that he did not understand, he threw all caution aside. After many months of saying little or nothing about himself and his true identity, he started to tell Dalia almost everything. "I am from Greater Syria, a very long way from here. My father is an imam. He would have liked me to follow in his footsteps, but I preferred to study science. With my father's permission and God's blessing, I was admitted to the great House of Wisdom in Baghdad."

"That's quite impressive." Dalia probably had no idea what the House of Wisdom was, but she knew it sounded important. "How did you end up here in Sijilmasa?"

"That's a long story. Let's just say that my work has brought me here."

"You are a merchant, then?"

"Well, sort of. But not a very successful one. I have some books for sale."

"I see. I would guess there is limited demand for books around here."

Hakeem caught himself. He realized that he was giving out more information about his true self than he should—certainly more than he had told anyone else. He turned the conversation back to Dalia. "What brought you to Sijilmasa?"

"Slave traders," she answered curtly, as if that should have been obvious. "I will never forget it. It was late at night when a band of heavily armed men charged into our village on horseback. They killed men indiscriminately, including my father and my brothers. But they were careful not to injure us women. Each of the riders hoisted one of us behind him on the back of his mount. They were clearly 'recruiting' prostitutes to sell in the 'port' cities north of the great desert—cities like this one."

Again, Hakeem was not quite sure what to say. "I'm sorry," he finally managed, lowering his head as if partly to blame for her present situation.

"Don't be," she said. "That was almost ten years ago. I have learned to accept what I am. Frankly, my life here is not all that bad."

I wonder about that, Hakeem thought, but he said nothing.

"God has blessed me with a beautiful body. I have many clients, and they treat me well—at least most of them do."

"What does that mean—that they treat you 'well'?"

"Well…they are not like you," she said bluntly. "They come for sex, and I am good at what I do. They pay me quite generously. Well enough that I was able to buy my freedom. What I earn now, I keep for myself." As an afterthought she added, "They pay me for sex, but you would be surprised how much they talk after they have gotten what they want. They tell me things they would not even tell their wives."

Again, Hakeem could only wonder. "What sort of things?"

"My clients tend to be rather wealthy—some of Sijilmasa's prominent leaders and businessmen. Others are merchants in the long-distance trade. Once they have spilled their seed, they are ready to spill absolutely everything that's on their mind. They reveal their dealings in trade and in politics. They tell me their…secrets. Sometimes they even seek my advice."

"It sounds like you have your hand on the very pulse of Sijilmasa."

"Yes, I suppose so," Dalia agreed.

Hakeem quickly came to the conclusion that Dalia could be a very useful informant. "I would like to see you again. Can I be one of your regular clients—I mean, just to talk?"

"Anytime."

Hakeem spent a little over a year in Sijilmasa, dividing his time among his friends and clients in the Sijilmasa market, and with the ulema at the Grand Mosque.

He spent as much time as he could with Amina. At first, he visited Aziz for one reason or another, hardly ever a serious reason, just as an excuse to see his friend's daughter. It did not take long for Aziz to figure out Hakeem's motive. Finally, one day, he said, "Listen Hakeem, you are a good friend. I trust you, and I trust you with my daughter. You know that I have always wanted her to have a good education, but that is just not possible for a young girl here in Sijilmasa, or for that matter, almost anywhere else in the Muslim world. There are educated women, of course, but they have private tutors, or they are self-taught. I have done what I could. I bring her books and help her to learn to read. But you can open up a whole new world to her."

Hakeem did not deny what Aziz said. He had already told her all about Ptolemy, al-Khwarizmi, and Ibn Khurdadhbih. What's more, he cherished his time with her. The sight of her, the scent of her body—mild, like rosewater— the sound of her sweet voice, sweet like the song of her caged canary as she quoted an early Arab poem of the desert:

> She married me
> > In spite of the tribe,
> And she traveled with me
> > In spite of the tribe,
> And she gave me Zainab and Omar,
> > In spite of the tribe,
> And when I asked her why,
> She took me, like a child, against her breast...
> > Because *you* are my tribe.

Hakeem knew that Amina was untouchable—unless he were to marry her. But given his professions of itinerant scholar, would-be bookseller, and intelligence agent, marriage was unthinkable.

Almost as often as he saw Amina, Hakeem traveled the two miles to Suq Ben Aqla—to see Dalia. His relationship with her was different than with Amina. Yes, he was sexually attracted to this exceptionally sensuous woman. But to satisfy his carnal desire with a prostitute would not be as useful as meeting with her regularly just to talk. She turned out to be a gold mine of information.

Somehow, Dalia was able to get advance notice of what caravans were coming from where and what products they were carrying. Hakeem was not especially interested in that information. Yet he did find it useful to pass the information on and ingratiate himself with those merchants in Sijilmasa with whom he had established a relationship.

More important to Hakeem were the insights Dalia could shed on the increasing complexity of the political situation. One day, she blurted out, "The emir's days are numbered!"

"You mean Emir Mohammed Ibn al-Fath?"

"None other than," affirmed Dalia.

"I thought he was a Midrarid tribal leader appointed governor by the Fatimid caliph himself."

"But the Fatimids are Shiites. The Midrarids, on the other hand, are not committed to Shiite ideology; they never were. If they are committed to anything at all, it is Kharijism, especially that aspect of it that insists on equality of all humans in the eyes of God."

An interesting observation coming from a former slave, Hakeem thought. "That seems to be a rather progressive position, worthy of support, don't you think?"

Dalia didn't answer that question.

Hakeem asked another. "Why do you suppose Ibn al-Fath choose Malikite orthodoxy rather than the Kharijism of Sijilmasa's founders?"

"Ibn al-Fath is not one of my clients, but some of the men close to him are. It would be very bad for me if anyone knew that I told you this…"

"You know you can trust me, Dalia."

"Ibn al-Fath is vying to win the favor of the Umayyad caliph in Córdoba in order to break away from the yoke of the Fatimids. Malikism is the school of law that governs the Umayyad caliphate. It's as simple as that."

That could be a problem, Hakeem thought. He found himself conflicted in his attitude toward Sijilmasa's governor. He liked what he saw happening here on the one hand, but he was sworn to the service of the Fatimid caliph. He hoped that Dalia was wrong about this. He would just have to wait and see.

As much as he loved Sijilmasa, Hakeem eventually decided that he needed to put his work there on hold. It was time that he made the trip back home, among other things, to visit his family, whom he had not seen now for ten years.

He dreaded telling Aziz and Amina that he was leaving. Aziz understood that it was motivated by much more than a desire to travel. He really had to go.

With Amina, it was not as easy. Aziz left the two of them alone. As they normally did, they sat together on the sofa in the reception room. "I'm not sure how long I will be gone, my sweet darling, but I promise I will be back."

"That's what you say now." She had never embraced him before, but she was now holding him close, both arms wrapped around his neck, pressing her body against his. She was trying very hard to hold back her tears. But she couldn't. All of a sudden, they poured forth like a raging river. She could barely get her sentence out through her sobs. "I…know that…you are a… traveler…above all else…I will never… see you again."

He liked feeling her body so close to him, but finally he had to pry her hands from behind his neck. "Amina, you have to trust me. I said I will return—and I will."

It was easier with Dalia. Men passed through her life quickly and often. Hakeem was different, though. Still, she knew what he was about better than anyone. She knew that he had to go. When he left her, she said nothing. She just looked at him—and smiled with a glint in her eye. She knew he would be back.

PART III

CHAPTER TWELVE

Aurillac, France

Albertus of Belliac, a colonus, and his wife, Ermentrude, were tenants of the Abbey of Saint Gerauld d'Aurillac. As *coloni*, they were legally free, not bound to the land, as were serfs. At the death of his father, Albertus inherited use of portions of the land owned by the abbey, along with certain specific manorial privileges attached to the holding, in exchange for clearly specified obligations. Since Albertus could not read, shortly after his father died, he was summoned to meet with the abbot to ensure that all of the terms were clearly understood.

"At the winter sowing," the abbot explained, "you may plow four perches in the common field, and half that much at the spring sowing. You will pay two hogsheads of wine for the right to graze your sheep in the common pasture. You have use of the windmill to grind your grain; for that you will pay two silver shillings a year."

"How can I possibly pay two silver shillings, Lord Abbot?"

"If you sell some of your produce in the market, you can pay in currency. Otherwise, you pay in goods. Do you understand, Albertus?"

"Yes, Lord Abbot.

"In addition, you will supply the abbey with three fowl and fifteen eggs monthly. Every week, you will perform two labor services toward the maintenance of the manor."

"Is that all, Lord Abbot?" Albertus, feeling a bit overwhelmed, took in a deep breath and slowly let it out.

"No. Every third year, you will provide one hundred planks and three posts for fences."

The young colonus knew that his father had managed just fine under these same terms. Yet, hearing all of them spelled out at once made the terms sound onerous.

The couple had two sons, Thomas and Gerbert. The younger of the two, Gerbert—Mother's favorite, in Thomas's mind—was a happy little ten-year-old boy. He had light blond hair and bright blue eyes, like his mother, whom most villagers described as beautiful. He was a bit overweight for a boy his age, perhaps because of his mother's overindulgent treats. Thomas, on the other hand, had very dark hair. He was almost as tall as his father and was already beginning to develop the muscular body of a hardened yeoman farmer.

Most days, Gerbert went out early in the morning to take the sheep to pasture. He was far more curious than the average lad, so curious that he unceasingly tried his parents' patience with questions about everything under the sun—and even about the sun itself.

"Why does the sun always rise on the far side of the pasture?" he asked one day. "Why does it always set on the near side? Why does it sometimes not rise at all?"

There was nothing that resembled a school in the hamlet of Belliac. There was a monastic school at the Abbey of Saint Gerauld in nearby Aurillac, but that was strictly for the novices of the abbey. Thus, it fell to his parents to try to answer the lad's questions.

On Sunday mornings, the family would make the one-hour trek to Aurillac to attend mass at the abbey church. Aurillac was a small town in the Haut-Auvergne in south-central France. It consisted of some fifty households. Most of the houses were modest structures made of wood with thatched roofs. On the rise above the village was the castle of the count, and just below it, the abbey. The church, like the castle, had walls of stone, very thick walls strong enough to support the wooden ceiling beams and the heavy round vaults, topped by a peaked roof covered with orange clay tiles. Like most stone churches, there were few windows. Hence, the interior space was dark, almost eerie.

It was the only church for miles around. Folks came from several surrounding hamlets to attend Sunday mass. The church formed the northwest corner of the enclosure of the monastery. One entrance at the west portal and another at the north transept were open to the public. There was a third entrance at the south transept through which the monks passed directly from within the compound into the choir.

Albertus and his family usually entered through the door at the north transept. It was closer to the front, where Gerbert insisted on sitting. The young lad was moved in a way that he did not really understand by the dark, seemingly vast interior space, lit only by a few candles. It seemed like a dark starry night, even in midmorning.

It seemed like most of the children tended to be fidgety during the service, especially the sermon, which was usually based on a story taken from the Bible. But Gerbert was captivated by it all, the beautiful vestments that the priest wore, the cross and the candlesticks that the servers carried, the prayers in Latin. That he could not understand the Latin words intrigued him even more. The priest preached in the common language of the people. Gerbert, even at his young age, could understand the sermon and was riveted by every word.

After the church service, the family would enjoy a simple picnic meal that they carried from home: hard cheese, fresh bread prepared the night before, and dried fruit. Then the children were off to play in the field adjacent to the abbey. A favorite game was club ball. With a stick about two feet long, the "batter" swung at a rag ball covered with leather that was tossed in his direction. If he hit it, he ran to the other side of the field before anyone could retrieve the ball. If he made it, he scored one point.

Thomas was the first at bat. On his very first try, he hit the ball well over the heads of all the children. No one was surprised. Thomas was by far the most athletic young lad of the manor. When it was finally Gerbert's turn, he swung and missed. "Strike one!" the other children shouted. He swung and missed a second time, and a third.

"You're out!" someone shouted. The words stung in his ear. Some of the children booed.

Gerbert was relieved when they finally moved on to a different game.

These children, not being descendants of nobility, had no aspirations toward becoming knights and ladies themselves. But that did not prevent them from pretending to be such on Sunday afternoon. The boys would stage pitched battles, wielding wooden swords and protecting themselves with round barrel covers as shields. Being a knight, even among the peasant class, was strictly a male thing. The little girls, restricted to pretending to be noble ladies, screamed and waved their scarves and cheered the knights on.

The boys took turns riding the wooden horse on wheels made by the village cooper. Three other boys pulled it as fast as they could run. The rider, armed with a wooden pole as a lance, charged the makeshift quintain. Gerbert tried it only once. He fell hard to the ground and started to cry. Again, the other children teased him mercilessly.

Even though Thomas sometimes envied Gerbert at home, he defended his little brother here among the other children. "Leave him alone. He's younger than us."

The adults spent the afternoon visiting with friends outdoors on the green in front of the abbey church. Lately, the men, after downing a pint or two of ale, would sit and complain about the poor harvest that had befallen the manor for a second year in a row.

One Sunday afternoon, rather than visiting with his friends, Albertus came to the gate of the monastic enclosure to see the abbot.

"Reverend Father, you know the harvest has been sparse again this year. I have been able to feed my family. But this is the year that my payment of planks and posts is due. Also, I am not sure I will have two silver shillings or its equivalent for my use of the mill. I came to place myself at God's mercy— and yours as well, Reverend Father. Is there any way you could defer these payments three months hence?"

The abbot was a compassionate man. But he was not just the abbot of the monastery. He was also the lord of the manor, and as such, he had to ensure that his tenants fulfilled all of their obligations if the manor was to prosper.

"Deferring the rent would be, at best, a short-term solution to this year's poor harvest, my friend." The abbot paused, and Albertus braced himself for a negative answer. "But there is another issue that should be of much greater concern to you—the future of your son Gerbert. I have been observing him when your family attends weekly mass at the abbey church. He seems quite pious in prayer and unusually attentive during the readings of Holy Scripture and during the sermon. Have you considered allowing him to enter the monastery? His presence here would be good for him—and for both of us, as well. Grooming young Gerbert for God's service, and the monastery's service, would more than compensate for your debt that God and the abbey could see fit to absolve."

Albertus's face fell. He perfectly understood what the abbot was saying. He was faced with the most difficult choice he would ever make. "Reverend Father, I need a few days to think about this."

That evening, he began to discuss it with his wife, but she would hear none of it, even when he tried to assure her that it was an honor to enter the monastery and that the boy would be very well cared for. Ermentrude cried uncontrollably. Finally, through her sobs, she managed to say, "I will never agree to send our baby away to the monastery."

True, Gerbert would only by an hour's travel away. But monks and novices lived within the cloister. They attended Sunday mass in the abbey church, as did the villagers, but they sat in the choir, away from the congregation. The family would be able to see Gerbert only at a distance. They would be able to visit with their son only on special feast days.

In the end, it was Albertus's decision to make. He loved his son no less than did his wife. But he knew that even with the help of his older son to fulfill his obligations to the monastery, the family was having great difficulty making ends meet. Gerbert would soon be old enough to be more useful with some of the vigorous chores required to support the family, more than just watching the sheep, feeding the chickens, and collecting the eggs.

On the other hand, it was common enough for the second son of a family to become a monk. It would be good to have a son in the monastery who would pray for the salvation of his family. He might eventually distinguish himself in study and rise to a prominent position in the Church.

After procrastinating for two days, Albertus called his younger son to his side. The joyful look with which he usually greeted his son was gone. It was replaced with sadness and perhaps even a sense of guilt. "You know, Gerbert, the abbey has such a fine reputation for teaching its novices to read and write."

"Yes, father. I thought that must be true. I watch and listen to the monks reading from the huge book in the choir of the abbey church when we attend Sunday mass. I cannot help but wonder what those beautiful words mean."

"Abbot Gerauld and I spoke two days ago. He offered to take you into the monastery, where you too can learn to read."

The boy suddenly recognized the dilemma. He hungered for the chance to attend the abbey school, but he would have to leave his family behind.

"Father, I am very happy living here with Mother and you and with my brother." Tears began to form in the corners of his beautiful blue eyes. "But I would also like to learn to read." The tears were now rolling down his chubby cheeks. "If it is your wish, I will go to Aurillac."

On a Sunday morning in the year 960, the family's usual trek to Aurillac was different from any of their previous trips. This was the last time that Gerbert would make the trip with his parents and brother. After the mass, the family went to the gate of the abbey enclosure, where they were met by Abbot Gerauld. Gerbert's father symbolically placed his son's hand into the hand of the abbot, as if to say, *Gerbert now belongs to you—and to God. I trust*

that you will take good care of him. Ermentrude was without emotion. She had already said everything she had to say about her husband's decision, and she had already shed all of the tears she would shed. She was resigned to her son being dedicated to the service of the Lord. It was Gerbert's brother, Thomas, who was teary-eyed.

"I will miss you, little brother. If anyone picks on you in there, you just call me, and I will come."

"Rest assured, Thomas," the abbot said, intending to comfort the whole family, "we will take good care of your little brother."

With that, the abbot closed the gate behind him and his new protégé. The sound of the gate's lock snapping shut seemed much louder than it actually was. It marked the end of Gerbert's childhood as he knew it, and the beginning of a life he could not even imagine. As he turned away from the gate and faced the open courtyard, he was struck by the orderliness of it all, a continuous row of buildings on the far side of the courtyard and all along the right side, forming the eastern and southern borders of the cloister. All of the buildings were modest, made of wood in contrast to the stone church that bordered the entire north side of the compound.

"This building to the right is the hostel," the abbot said. "Our holy rule obligates us to offer hospitality to pilgrims who travel in the service of God."

"Your holy rule?"

The abbot explained that the abbey had been founded almost fifty years earlier by Count Gerauld of Aurillac, who, just returning from a pilgrimage to Rome, was inspired to do this pious act. From that time on, the count lived in the monastery and served as its first abbot. "Thanks to Count Gerauld, today it is the Abbey of Aurillac, rather than the castle, for which our town is known. As his successor, I too took the name Gerauld when I became a monk."

"But the holy rule?" Gerbert repeated.

"The abbey is not subject to the control of any local lord or bishop; it remains under the direct control of the pope. Still, it is affiliated with the reform movement spearheaded by the Abbey of Cluny. We follow the holy rule of Saint Benedict."

This was more information than Gerbert, as young and precocious as he was, could absorb. He asked, "And these other buildings?"

"Next to the hostel is the kitchen and refectory. Our meals are modest but quite adequate. Then the dormitory. You will sleep on the upper floor with the other novice monks. The large building in the corner of the cloister contains a number of workshops, including the scriptorium, where duplicate copies of our precious books are copied word for word, letter by letter. Finally, directly in front of us is the school and the library. That is where you will learn to read and write under the supervision of Brother Raymond."

Gerbert felt a thrill of excitement. *This is why I came to the abbey*, he thought.

Within a few months, Gerbert felt somewhat at home in the monastery and comfortable with the daily routine. He began to appreciate the "holy rule" that had sounded so mysterious to him when Abbot Gerauld first mentioned it. He now understood how the "rule" determined every aspect of monastery life.

Since the abbey's tenants did the work in the surrounding fields and vineyards, the monks ate, slept, prayed, hosted pilgrims, cared for the sick, and studied, all within the confines of the monastery, without ever having to leave the enclosure.

The primary role of the monks was to pray and to sing the Psalms from the daily office: *lauds* in the middle of the night, *prime* at first light, *terce* at midmorning, *sext* at high noon, *none* at midafternoon, *vespers* at dusk, *compline* at the fall of darkness, and *matins* at the very beginning of the new day. These rigorously followed times for prayer established a predictable rhythm for the daily life of the monastery. The monks were never far in mind or heart from a connection with God. It was their assigned and accepted duty to pray for the well-being of the town, for all of its inhabitants, but especially for the abbey's benefactors.

In order to fulfill this obligation to recite the common prayers and to sing the Psalms, the monks needed to learn the very rudiments of music and reading, or at the very least, to recite from memory the Latin texts of the Book of Hours. That was the main purpose for the abbey school under the direction of the very able Brother Raymond de Lavaur.

Brother Raymond was younger than most of the other monks. He, like Gerbert, came to the monastery as a young boy. Also like Gerbert, he was exceptionally bright. He had learned well from the teaching of the elderly Brother Philip over a period of almost twenty years. When Philip died, Raymond was the obvious successor to the post of schoolmaster.

Brother Raymond sat at his desk in front of the class. His pupils filled the rest of the room, sitting on small wooden stools. Each pupil had a wooden tablet coated with wax and a stylus with which to write. Brother Raymond tried to teach all of the novices the letters. But in reality, he was quite satisfied if they only learned to pronounce the words of the Holy Office. Latin was new to novices. Most spoke a local dialect of this region of southern France known as *langue d'oc*, so called because of the way they said the word for the Latin *sic*. Novices that came to Saint Gerauld from further north pronounced that word *oil*. Their dialect was called *langue d'oil*.

For the most part, monks spent their days in silence. When they spoke, which they were allowed to do only in cases of absolute necessity, they were obliged to speak in Latin. To get around that restriction, the monks developed an elaborate system of sign language. In the refectory, for example, if a monk wanted someone to pass the bread, he waved his open hand in a chopping motion. When he wanted milk, he touched his lips with the tips of his four fingers. To ask for wine, he bent his index finger and touched his lips. If he wanted to spice his food with mustard seed or vinegar, he shook his closed fist up and down. For honey, he licked his fingers. Forming one's hand in the shape of a cup asked for water. There were signs for books and clothes, for blessings and bedding. To request a pillow, the monk combined the sign for sleep, placing a hand against one's jaw, with the sign for "alleluia," fluttering one's fingers as if to fly.

The rule of Saint Benedict required the monks to live a simple life— simple, but actually more comfortable and more secure than the life of a peasant. In the monastery, Gerbert had a bed of his own, on a mattress of straw "at least a half-inch thick," as stipulated by the holy rule. At home, he had shared a bed with his brother. Here, he had a thick wool habit to wear in winter and a much lighter one for summer. He had at least one hot meal a day of beans and vegetables, often with a side of fish; two hot meals a day during the season when days were very long.

The monks and the novices ate their meals together in the refectory, sitting around a common table on long wooden benches. They ate in silence as they listened to the words of Holy Scripture read to them by one of the monks, each of them in turn being assigned the reading for a day. For many of the monks, it was difficult to read the Latin texts with fluidity and correct pronunciation. Not so for Gerbert. When it was his turn to read, he spent hours preparing, practicing the pronunciation of every single word. It provided him access to the book and the opportunity to devour the words on the handwritten page.

The monastery, small by comparison to many Cluniac monasteries, did not have a library as such. Other than the teaching materials that brother Raymond prepared himself, the monastery owned perhaps as many as several dozen books—books of the Bible, psalters, a book of hymns—but also books that were not specifically religious in nature: history books written by Bede and Eusebius and Josephus and Livy, saints' lives written by Jerome and Gregory the Great, a book on mathematics written by Boethius, Priscian's *Institutes of Grammar*, a book on Carolingian law, a book on medicine. Two monks spent their working hours making copies of the books. As much as Brother Raymond would have liked to expand the library with additional titles, the monastery simply could not afford it. A single book could cost as much as one-third the monthly salary of a skilled craftsman. An especially rare book, or a highly decorated one, could cost three or four times as much.

Brother Raymond, amazed at Gerbert's eagerness and voracious appetite for learning, spent extra time and effort in instructing the young novice in the subjects of the trivium—grammar, rhetoric, and logic. Before the end of his first year in the monastery, Gerbert was able to read the texts on his own without the help of his teacher.

"Brother Raymond," Gerbert said one day, "I would like to read at mealtime more often."

"Do you not think that the other novices need as much practice reading as you?" Brother Raymond asked.

"What is the purpose of reading God's holy word aloud during meals? Is it so the novices can practice their reading, or is it for the spiritual enlightenment of our brothers?" Gerbert was confident that he was putting forth a valid argument. "If it is the latter, forgive me, Brother Raymond, but should not the reading be as clear and precise as possible? In all humility, brother, you know how much I prepare my reading ahead of time. You know that our brothers like it when I read."

Brother Raymond knew that what Gerbert said was true. He agreed to the precocious novice's request to read as often as he could, so long as it did not raise the ire of the abbot.

Gerbert spent the next seven years, wonderful years in his estimation, doing what he loved most. He worshiped the Lord in prayer and song. He read almost as much as he wanted from the books the monastery treasured in its tiny library. He was such an accomplished student that he became Brother Raymond's assistant in teaching the other pupils. He even developed a method of teaching them to count using different positions of the fingers and hands in combinations as signs to indicate numbers all the way up into the thousands. Calculations were done on a decimal system. The numbers in the "ones" place were represented on the pinkie, ring, and middle fingers of the left hand. The positions of the thumb and index finger gave the value of the "tens" place. The "hundreds" place was the same as the "ones" place, but on the right hand. The "thousands" place was the same as the "tens" place, also on the right hand.

Gerbert could not have been happier. But all of this was about to change with the arrival of a special guest at the monastery.

CHAPTER THIRTEEN

Suq Ben Aqla, 957

As he followed the Oued Ziz into the oasis, Hakeem could hardly contain his excitement. He recalled the first time he had approached this enchanting place with his friend Aziz. He replayed in his mind the first time he set eyes on Aziz's beautiful daughter. When he reached the fork in the road to Sijilmasa, with the right turn that diverted to Suq Ben Aqla, Hakeem surprised himself when he suddenly decided that he should see Dalia first. *I have been gone for three whole years. So much could have changed since I was here last. I have to be aware of the oasis before I settle into a routine once again. I need to see Dalia.*

"When we first met," he asked her, "you said that your clients often ask your advice. If you were to give me advice, what would it be?"

"Well, let's see…" Dalia paused. "You told me you are a bookseller, but you have sold very few books. My dearest Hakeem…" She reached out and touched his hand. "Don't think for a moment that you can fool me. It was perfectly clear the first time we met that you are not a bookseller. I know you are interested in books for the knowledge they hold, not for the price they can bring in the market. Here is my advice. If you are really interested in learning what you came here to learn, you must cross the desert and go to Ghana, where I am from, where Islam is just beginning to take hold. There is a greater demand for religious texts there, assuming you want to continue to pretend that you are a bookseller. More important, it is much closer to the source of wealth that feeds much of the known world with that precious yellow metal called gold. My guess is that is what your employer wants to know."

Hakeem joined the very next caravan that left Suq Ben Aqla, heading south across the great desert toward Ghana. On Dalia's advice, he purchased his own camel rather than renting one from the caravan master.

"In the long run, it will be cheaper," Dalia said. "You can sell it at your destination. If it is healthy, you will get as much as you paid for it. Abd al-Selam can help you pick out the right one in the camel market."

"Who is this Abd al-Selam?" Hakeem asked.

"One of my clients," she said with a sly look on her face.

"I should have known."

Within less than an hour after leaving the caravanserai, the caravan was well into the desert. It was very early in the morning, still dark enough to see the stars in the sky. They would travel until midmorning, when the temperature would be much too hot to continue on. Humans sought a spot in the shade, however small, created by a camel lying on its stomach with its four legs folded beneath it. Alternately, one could make a small lean-to by draping a blanket over a single pole or walking stick. Hakeem chose the latter.

The journey would resume in late afternoon. The sun would still be above the horizon but low enough for the coolness of the night to begin to set in. They would advance until dark. Traveling these two stages, they could expect to cover about twenty miles in a single day. At this pace, they would reach their destination, some eleven hundred miles away, in two months.

Hakeem's first night was an experience unlike any he had ever had. The temperature dropped considerably—he was *so* cold. He had been cold before, but the contrast between day and night in the deep Sahara was until now unimaginable. Something else he could not have imagined was the vast openness of the dark sky filled with stars that seemed brighter here than any he had seen before. Likewise, the stillness of the night was extraordinary—no wind and no sound other than the soft grunting of the camels.

As much as Hakeem had traveled since he first left home—first to Baghdad, then to Egypt via Damascus and Palestine, on to Ifriqiya, and from there to Andalusia by sea—traveling across the Sahra al-Kubra, the Great Desert, was a whole new experience. When he sailed in the Mediterranean, his ship was often within sight of the coast, the latter being a steady and reliable landmark. He watched mariners determine their position using an astrolabe.

Now, his caravan was in the midst of a vast sea of sand. The undulating dunes and rocks were like the waves in the sea, extending as far as the eye could see in every direction. Hakeem was overwhelmed by its vast emptiness. Yet the caravan's camels, steadfast "ships" of the desert that they were, cut through the choppy dunes with relative ease. And the guide used no instruments at all.

Hakeem remembered the stories he had heard in Suq Ben Aqla. A blind guide would ride at the head of the caravan. From time to time, he would dismount, scoop up a handful of sand, and smell it. On that basis, only occasionally would he find it necessary to correct his course. Of course, Hakeem knew that it was just a story. Still, he now marveled at the skill of the guide whose task was to keep the entire caravan on its proper course toward Ghana.

One day, Hakeem pitched his lean-to next to the guide. He wanted to quiz him on how he "navigated" the desert—a decidedly nautical term, he now realized.

"Khemidou," Hakeem addressed him. "That is your name, is it not? My name is Hakeem. Listen, this may sound strange to you, but I am curious to know how you know where to go."

The guide seemed amused by the question. "Why? Are you afraid that we are going to get lost?"

"Not at all. Just curious, that's all. Well…that's not exactly true. I'm actually a student of geography—you know, the science of knowing where things are in this world of ours."

"Science? I don't know much about science, but I do know where we are going—and I know how to get there."

"That's what I mean," Hakeem said. "*How* do you know?"

"I'm not sure I can explain it. I just know."

"Please try."

"Alright. First of all, you notice that it is still dark when we begin the first leg of the day's march, and when we stop at the end of the day, it is dark again. At those times, I can see our position in relation to the bright star in the north sky."

"That only works in the dark. What about during daylight, when most of our travel takes place?"

"There are many other signs. The rising sun in the morning and the setting sun in the afternoon tell me the direction we are traveling. And there are landmarks, features on the horizon that you would not recognize until you have made many trips. Landmarks on a very grand scale. Let me show you." Khemidou stood and motioned Hakeem to do the same. He pointed to a spot on the southern horizon. "Can you see that tiny point of a pyramid-like mountain?"

Hakeem squinted. "I see no such thing."

"Keep looking," insisted Khemidou. "Focus."

"Oh, yes!" Hakeem exclaimed, feeling as if he had made a marvelous discovery. "It is but the slightest bump on the horizon, barely visible to the naked eye."

"Enough of a bump, if you know what you are looking for. The next watering hole is between here and there. Now, can you see the canyon in line with another rock formation that looks like two doors carved into a sheer cliff?"

Again, Hakeem strained his eyes. Finally, what Khemidou described came into focus.

Khemidou continued, "As long as the pyramid is centered between the 'two doors,' we are following the correct heading."

"I am impressed. It is much more sophisticated than a blind guide sniffing a handful of sand."

"So, you have heard that story. It would be difficult for a blind guide, but look." Khemidou picked up two handfuls of sand, one from each side of a slightly elevated stone ridge. "The stone ridge forms a barrier," he explained. "Look carefully. The sand I pick up on this side is more reddish than the sand I pick up on the other. That's because these particles are heavier than those. The prevailing winds blow the lighter particles to the far side of the ridge. I know that the prevailing wind comes from the east. The heavier sand particles are on the east side."

"Have no fear, Khemidou. I will not challenge you for your job."

"Nor I yours, my friend. We had best get some rest for the next leg of our day's march."

Two months to the day after leaving Suq Ben Aqla, the caravan arrived in Awdaghost. After such harsh travel, the desert city was indeed a welcomed sight. Their arrival sparked the same sort of excitement among this urban population that Hakeem observed in Suq Ben Aqla whenever a large caravan appeared. The city was full of eager consumers for the vast variety of craft items from the north side of the Sahara and even beyond, from all over the wider Muslim world: brass lamps and candlesticks, steel swords from Toledo, etched glass from Egypt, ceramics, textiles, leather goods—items such as those Hakeem had so admired in Saad al-Zenary's shop in Sijilmasa, but in much larger quantities and greater variety.

Hakeem was new at the business of long-distance trade. He had a sense of the value of things in the famous markets of the great Muslim cities in the North and East. What he did not have a grasp of was how much the monumental task of transporting the goods across the desert affected the cost. He sought the advice of Abd al-Rafi, the caravan master.

"Whatever the cost would be in Sijilmasa, it will be at least triple the cost here in Awdaghost," the caravan master said. "It will be four times as much once we arrive in Ghana; that requires another ten days of travel."

"I imagine that the value is calculated in dinars?" observed Hakeem.

"Prices are stated in dinars, but it is not quite as simple as that. They are calculated in solidi. Let me explain," said Abd al-Rafi. "Here in the Sudan, the basic unit of gold is one solidus, a unit that goes back to ancient Roman times. A solidus is slightly heavier than a dinar. So, already, one dinar is worth a little less than the solidus. Merchandise that is valued at, say, ten solidi, would actually cost eleven dinars—or its equivalent in kind."

Hakeem nodded, trying to understand this unexpectedly complex system.

"That said, the Awdaghost market is quite different from the Sijilmasa market," Abd al-Rafi continued, "especially for certain commodities, like salt, which is in such high demand here. In Awlil or Teghaza, where salt is mined, it costs almost nothing. But it is heavy and expensive to transport. Here, it is said to exchange for gold on a weight-for-weight basis. So, for a certain weight in salt, an equal weight in gold." Abd al-Rafi tapped his hand against his purse. "That's why I will buy salt when the salt caravan arrives here tomorrow. I will purchase enough camels, perhaps as many as 140 of them, to transport it to Ghana, our next stop."

Hakeem scratched his forehead as he processed a calculation. Then he knelt on one knee and started to write some numerals in the sand. "Let's see now. A pound of salt would cost about 107 dinars. The camels that we saw coming in from Awlil carried two large slabs of salt, one on either side of their hump. I'm told that each slab weighs about 200 pounds. So each camel load of salt would be worth—"

Abd al-Rafi interjected, "What, may I ask, are you doing?" It seemed that he had never seen anyone do a mathematical calculation using symbols as numbers.

"The symbols come from India," Hakeem explained. "A different symbol for each number, one through nine. This dot we call *sifr*, literally 'nothing.' I place it here, where no number appears, in the place of tens and ones in my calculation. It serves the purpose of keeping the row."

"Hmmm. Very interesting," said Abd al-Rafi, shaking his head in what might have been bewilderment or amazement. "Anyway, when we say that salt is traded on a weight-for-weight basis, clearly, it's a myth, or at least an exaggeration. It's just what people say. Still, it suggests that salt here is very expensive. It all depends on the market, on the law of supply and demand.

"Listen," he said. "Let me give you an example in real time. I am holding a promissory note worth 42,000 dinars." He showed Hakeem a sheet of paper. The amount was written out in Arabic letters: *forty-two thousand dinars.* "I will collect that amount in Ghana. That is about 300 dinars for the salt carried by each of my 140 camels."

"My God!" exclaimed Hakeem. "I like my calculation much better. Each camel load would be worth 42,000 dinars."

Abd al-Rafi continued, "After all my expenses are paid, including the cost of the merchandise I brought here, I will take the balance in raw gold. I will take that north to Sijilmasa, where I will sell it to the Fatimid mints north of the desert. After a few months rest, I will reinvest some of my profit to buy more trade goods in the Sijilmasa market and start the cycle over again."

"What about my books?" Hakeem asked.

"I would hold onto them, if I were you. There are not many Muslim residents here in Awdaghost. There is, on the other hand, a growing Muslim community in Ghana. Your books will be much more in demand and valuable there, and the cost of transporting them is not so much for your two crates of books."

Ghana was not just the name of the kingdom; it was the name of its capital city as well. The capital was actually two cities. The first was the royal city, where the king lived.

The king must be the richest man in the world! was Hakeem's first thought. Everywhere he looked he saw ornaments of gold. Even the guard dogs at the entrance to the palace wore collars studded in gold.

Except for a few of the king's bureaucrats, some of whom were Jews and Muslims, most of the population was pagan. They were all clean-shaven; even the women shaved their heads. Hakeem was shocked to see so many women with a bright, colorful cloth wrapped around their lower body, but appearing bare-breasted in public.

Six miles separated the royal city from the city where the Muslims lived. This was a sizable metropolis with several mosques. As Hakeem walked along the main avenue, he was comforted to hear the resonant sound of the muezzin chanting the call to prayer, first one, then another, and yet another, each one sounding like an echo of the one before it.

When he reached the central market, Hakeem asked the *muhtasib*, the supervisor of the marketplace, "Where are the gold mines? Judging by the amount of gold that is visible everywhere, the source must not be far away."

The man looked up, somewhat surprised by the question, and apparently reluctant to give an answer. Finally, shaking his head, he said, "Dear sir, only the king and his officials know."

"That's hard to believe," exclaimed Hakeem. "How could that ever work? The volume of gold is so great. How could its source be kept secret?"

The *muhtasib* said, "Somewhere along the river south of here, merchants go and lay their merchandise along the banks. The Blacks from farther south then come and place a quantity of gold that they are willing to pay for the merchandise. Then they, in turn, walk away. When the owners of the merchandise return, if they are satisfied with the amount of gold, they take it and leave. If not, they retreat to allow the Blacks to increase the quantity until both sides are satisfied and the transaction is completed."

Hakeem shook his head incredulously. "I have heard this story before. Or, rather, I read it in the book of the ancient Greek writer Herodotus. What you say is a myth."

"You might be right. No one here has actually seen this silent trade. But the reality is this: no one here knows exactly where the gold mines are located. It is a tightly guarded secret. The mines are so far to the south, even outside of the territory controlled by the king. But the king controls every single load of merchandise, especially gold, that comes into or goes out of the kingdom, *every single load*. And he imposes a tax on everything that comes in and everything that goes out. It is as simple as that."

Hakeem decided that he would remain in Ghana for a while. There was much he could learn here. He felt at home in the Muslim town. Since Islamic law was enforced here, he knew what the "rules" were; he could live here comfortably. But outside the Muslim town was a world apart from anything he had ever seen in all his previous travels. Remaining here was outside of the scope of his assignment. But he was, after all, on his own, according to the exact words of his former handler in Córdoba. It was easy enough to convince himself that knowing more about this crucial link in the growing global economy would be useful to his Fatimid patrons. It would be good for his own pocketbook as well.

Hakeem managed to sell all of his books for a grand total of 372 dinars. With part of his profit, he bought a few gifts for his friends back home, including two beautiful, exotic boxes made of ebony and inlaid with ivory, one for Amina and one for Dalia. After all the expenses for his travel to and from Ghana were covered, and after he paid for his lodging for the months that he stayed there, he still had well over 200 dinars left, enough to support himself quite well for some time, when he returned to Sijilmasa.

CHAPTER FOURTEEN

When he returned to Sijilmasa the next year, Hakeem found that the city was different. There were fewer people in the marketplace than before. And those who were there were buying essential provisions to stockpile in their homes. Streets were almost completely empty. People kept their doors shut and barred. Those whose houses had windows opening onto the street pulled their wooden shutters closed tight, even during the daytime. Ibn al-Fath's soldiers patrolled the streets night and day.

Hakeem's first thought was to go to Dalia. She, more than anyone, would be able to give him an accurate reading of what was happening.

"Sijilmasa is on the verge of open rebellion," Dalia said, trying to sound flippant, as if she really didn't care. But her lips began to quiver, and she looked away from Hakeem. He could tell that she really did care—she was afraid.

Hakeem placed his hands on her shoulders and sat her down on the bed. He sat next to her. "You are not succeeding in hiding what you feel, Dalia. Tell me what is going on."

"Not much, really," she said, trying to maintain her feigned indifference. "Just that Ibn al-Fath has claimed the title *amir al-mu'minin*. He has claimed the title of caliph and declared his independence."

"But which caliph is he rejecting, the one in Mahdiya or the one in Baghdad? Do any of your clients share that kind of information?"

"I'm afraid they do. The answer is both. I am told that his sympathies lie with the caliph in Córdoba. The tension between Córdoba and the Fatimids has never been higher. The Umayyad fleet has been harassing the western coastline for months. They say that it is in retaliation for the attack on their port of Almería. The Fatimids, on the other hand, claim that the Umayyads struck first by seizing a Fatimid ship. It all sounds like excuses to me."

Hakeem shrugged his shoulders, shook his head, and threw his hands up. "I think you are exactly right. The Umayyads and the Fatimids are both trying to gain exclusive control over the gold trade with the Land of the Blacks. And here we are, on the northern end of the gold route, caught right in the middle of that struggle."

"Since Ibn al-Fath has declared his independence," Dalia said, "people will have to choose. Will they be loyal to him? Or will they support the Fatimid caliph? Either way, they risk making enemies, placing themselves in grave danger. No one will be able to remain neutral. Sijilmasa could find itself in the midst of a civil war."

Now she was crying. Hakeem put his arms around her. "So, you *do* care," he said.

"I've been having flashbacks, nightmares really, about the civil war in my native land and the raid that ripped me away and destined my fate. I fear the same thing could happen again right here."

Hakeem wished he could do more to comfort her, but he also needed a clearer picture of what was going on. He pressed her further. "Are there any open acts of defiance against the Fatimid regime?"

After a few moments, Dalia's sobbing abated enough for her to speak. "The clearest indication that al-Fath has defied both the Fatimids *and* the Abbasids is his coinage. He is issuing dinars in his own name. Right on the coins he stamps the epithet *al-shakir lillah*"—"the grateful toward God," another title exclusively claimed by the caliph.

"Are these coins accepted at full face value in the marketplace?" Hakeem knew that acceptance of currency was the true test of its legitimacy.

Dalia stood and walked to the corner of the room, her back toward him. "Hmmph! I'm afraid *any* dinar is far more than I have ever been paid, but *I* would surely accept one." She sounded indignant now. She turned to face him. "My clients tell me that they command the same high rate of exchange as the Fatimid dinars."

Hakeem was not at all surprised by that. It was common knowledge among the merchants he met on his trek across the desert that "*any* dinar minted in Sijilmasa was struck *with the purest gold in all the world.*" His mind raced as he paced back and forth across the room.

What did surprise Hakeem, on the other hand, was how much a woman of Dalia's background seemed to grasp about the emerging political crisis.

Then again, he had never really talked to her about her background, about her life in Ghana.

"Dalia, how do you know all of this? Surely, you are not a spy."

"My dear Hakeem, spies are not paid nearly enough for me to take that kind of risk. No, I am not a spy, but I work for spies," she said, looking Hakeem straight in the eye.

Her last remark stung a bit.

"What were you before you became a…before you came to Sijilmasa?"

"Before I became a *prostitute*, you mean?" Her voice held not the slightest hint of shame or embarrassment. "I was a princess." She paused for a moment to see his reaction.

He was startled at first. Then, knowing something about how the slave trade worked, that slaves were often victims of intertribal warfare, he realized that slaves must come from every social and economic class. Still, he was quite impressed.

Dalia continued, "My father was chief of our tribe. I became sensitive to the workings of statecraft growing up in the household of that great man."

This now made perfect sense to Hakeem. "Tell me then, why do you think the merchants who tell you all these things seem to favor the Fatimid regime?"

"It's quite simple, really. They profit from the extensive economic network that the Fatimids have managed to create and protect. Ibn al-Fath's declaration of independence threatens all that."

If what Dalia said was true, the disruption would vibrate east all the way to Mahdiya by way of the merchant caravans. Hakeem concluded that the threat to the Fatimid regime in Sijilmasa was real, and it was imminent. It was time to contact his patron in Mahdiya. He decided to confide to Dalia the full scope of his role as a Fatimid *da'i* and to ask for her help.

"Dalia, what is the quickest way I can get a message to Mahdiya?"

"There is a man who lives in a small villa on the far side of the Seguia Midrariya," said Dalia. "He raises pigeons. If you were to visit him, you would see that he has three sets of coops for his birds. One is for those destined to end up in our culinary specialty, pigeon pie. Another is for his sporting pigeons, homers. They are a special breed who find their way home when released from any far-off place. That is a sport for him. Then there is a third coop for the most special of all, the carrier pigeons. They were brought here from Mahdiya. When released, they head straight for the caliph's palace, where they arrive in less than three days' time.

"Can you take me to him?"

"Listen, Hakeem, the caliph in Mahdiya already knows the situation here. An army has already been dispatched and will be here in a matter of weeks. Why do you think people are boarding up their homes and stockpiling supplies?"

"What should I do then?"

"My best advice is to go about your daily business as best you can and keep your ear to the ground. When the Fatimid army arrives, they will need as much insider information as they can get."

In spite of the tension, Hakeem kept busy working in his small room at home. He spent most of his time reviewing his notes from his voyage to Awdaghost and Ghana. He recorded his impressions of everything he had seen of note. He wrote:

> The king of Awdaghost maintains relations with the ruler of Ghana, who is the wealthiest king on the face of the earth because of his treasures and stocks of gold. He sends gifts to the ruler of Khuga, who sends gifts in return. Khuga's wealth does not approach that of the king of Ghana. Both kings stand in pressing need of the goodwill of the king of Awdaghost because of the salt that comes to them from the lands of Islam. They cannot do without this salt, of which one load, in the interior and more remote parts of the land of the Sudan, may fetch between 200 and 300 dinars.

Hakeem also reviewed the time traveled between recognizable landmarks, noting the directions he traveled as they were defined by other landmarks on the horizon. He was mentally triangulating, and he began to visualize in his mind's eye the positions of these places on a map that he hoped someday to draw.

He went to the mosque daily. After prayer, he remained to sit with the ten or so ulama who gathered to discuss the weighty issues of the day. These days, the talk among the sheikhs was far more about politics than about theology. The banter back and forth around the circle of scholars often became quite heated.

"The Fatimids brought Shiite Islam to our country," said one alim.

"Sacrilege!" shouted another.

The conversation went back to the first. "But then Ibn al-Fath restored Sunni Islam."

"But a different school of law, as he favors the Umayyad ruler in Córdoba, who follows Malikism," interjected a third voice.

A calmer voice was heard. "What is the difference between one foreign ruler and another?"

"An excellent point," said still another. "For that matter, what is the difference between one Islamic sect and another? Here, we have been quite fortunate. The sect of the ruler has had little impact on us in Sijilmasa. We have enjoyed a considerable degree of intellectual and religious freedom."

Hakeem sat and listened—and took mental note of those who seemed to favor the Fatimids and those who remained loyal to the local emir.

And, of course, he went to see Amina as often as he could.

"I want to hear all about your voyage to places that I know about only through my reading," she pleaded. "Places I have only been able to dream about but you have seen firsthand. Please, my dear Hakeem, tell me everything you know."

As they had always done before, they sat in the reception room of Aziz's house. As was always the case when they were together, Hamdi was in the adjacent room. They sat close to each other on the same sofa, close but not touching. Hakeem sensed that Amina craved more intimacy than was allowed, a degree of intimacy that he too would have wanted in different circumstances. His relationship with her was so different from his relationship with Dalia. He was physically attracted to both women. His relationship with Dalia was…well, professional. Her sensual body aroused him, but it was what he could learn from her about the heartbeat of Sijilmasa that attracted him most. He presumed that she was similarly drawn to him. If she were not, she would not have trusted him to the point of being his informant. He feared that romance between them could jeopardize that relationship.

As for Amina, Hakeem thought he might be falling in love with her. When they were together, he thought she was perhaps the most beautiful woman he had ever seen. He loved Amina not so much for her bright eyes and lovely body as for her brilliance and curiosity to know everything he could teach her. Again, he felt that intimacy might jeopardize the relationship that allowed him to be Amina's teacher. And it could ruin the bond of trust he had with her father, his friend Aziz.

"You remember, Amina, what we read about Ghana in al-Yaqubi's wonderful book?"

"Of course. He said it was one of the two most powerful kingdoms in all of the Land of the Blacks—that Ghana's king had other kings under him."

Hakeem was pleased that she remembered what they had read together with such detail. "When I was in Awdaghost," he said, "I bought this book for you."

"I thought you went there to sell books, not buy books."

"You are right, and I did sell my books. I made enough profit to buy this one by Ibn al-Faqih. It is readily accessible in the East, but not so much here in the West. I was lucky to see it, so I bought it regardless of the price. Look, he mentions still a different route to Ghana than the one you pointed out to me in al-Yaqubi's book many months ago, a route that directly links Egypt to Ghana."

"You were in Egypt, were you not? Why did you not go directly from there to the Land of the Blacks?"

"Well, that's a long story, Amina." He was not about to share the secrets of his professional life with her, as he had with Dalia. "But even had I wanted to, it would not have been possible. That route was abandoned long ago—some say because so many caravans were attacked by bandits, while others were overwhelmed by wind-blown sand.

"And when did he write that?"

"Over fifty years ago."

"See! Our city has been important for a long time."

A courier loyal to Ibn al-Fath arrived early one morning on a lathered horse. He had ridden almost nonstop for several days, changing mounts along the way. He rode his horse all the way to the door of the *dar al-imara*, the House of Government. "The Fatimid caliph has dispatched an army to retake Sijilmasa," the courier shouted. "It is under the command of the notorious Jawhar. They are advancing at lightning speed; it is like a storm of locusts. They are less than two weeks away."

Within an hour after his arrival, news of the impending attack had spread throughout Sijilmasa. As soon as Ibn al-Fath heard that the Fatimid caliph was sending an army under the command of Jawhar, he fled with his family and entire household and principal officers. He took refuge with them and all his treasures in a stone fortress named Tasagdalt some twelve miles west of Sijilmasa. It sat atop a high, circular, stony mountain that locals called Jebel Mudawar, "Round Mountain." There was a single break in the face of the mountain with a narrow path leading to the flat summit. A solid stone wall surrounded the rim of the plate. With just a small defending force, the emir believed he would be safe.

Hakeem knew the location; he had been there once on one of his reconnaissance outings. *If only I could get word to Jawhar's army, they could divert their approach directly toward Jebel Mudawar in a surprise attack.*

He decided to see if Dalia could help.

"Dalia, does the pigeon man have any pigeons that would fly home to Fez?"

"Hmmm, why do you ask?"

"Dalia, you know what I am all about. I work for the Fatimid regime. I must get a message to the army that is about to head this way. They have regained control of the palace in Fez. If a pigeon were to arrive there with a message, it would reach Jawhar, the army's commander."

Dalia agreed to take him to the pigeon man.

"You will write your message on two small strips of parchment," the man said. "I will wrap one around each of the legs of the pigeon."

The man was clearly used to sending messages—for a price. He provided Hakeem with the two strips, plus pen and ink.

Hakeem thought for a moment, composing his messages. On the first strip he wrote, *Enemy fled to Jebel Mudawar – HH*. On the second, he wrote, *Twelve miles due west of Sijilmasa – HH*.

The double "H" was the signature he was instructed to use on any intelligence communications. He hoped that the agents traveling with Jawhar's army had been informed of his monogram.

The pigeon man removed one homer from a small cage that contained four others, an indication that he sent messages to Fez on a regular basis. Hakeem watched the man tie his two-part message securely to the bird's legs with thin leather thongs. He then tossed the bird into the air as Hakeem and Dalia marveled at how the creature rose quickly, flew in a wide circle three times, then veered due north—on its way to Fez.

There were two of them, burly men, both dressed in heavy woolen djellabas, hoods drawn well over their heads so that their faces were not visible. It was no surprise that Hakeem was not the only spy in Sijilmasa. Nor was it surprising that there were still those in town who supported the local emir, now a refugee in the fortress of Tasagdalt—notables who had the influence and resources to mount a resistance against Fatimid authority, a movement that included anonymous enforcers.

Hakeem was not the target of their surveillance on this day; the pigeon man was. He was not the only one whose sport was raising homing pigeons, but his collection of birds was different. Normally, someone who raised homers took them to some far-off place and set them free. Typically, the birds beat their owners home. In this case, the pigeon man had several small cages for his flock. In fact, they were not a single flock, but different ones, apparently from different places. Rather than carry them away, only to have them return, he set them free from his own home and watched them fly away in different directions, obviously to *their* homes. This pigeon man had caught their attention, and now Hakeem had as well.

The two enforcers followed Hakeem and Dalia back to Suq Ben Aqla. Hakeem had the hood of his djellaba pulled up to cover his head, so the enforcers couldn't yet be certain of his identity. They decided to continue following him back to Sijilmasa. They were surprised when they followed him to Aziz's home. They knew Aziz, at least by reputation. He was among the wealthiest merchants in Sijilmasa. He was also known to be a strong advocate for the independent sovereignty of the oasis—to be free of domination from any caliphate, be it Baghdad, Córdoba, or Mahdiya.

There was nothing unusual about Hakeem's visit with his friend, just a typical visit, getting caught up on each other's activities over the months that Hakeem had been away on his trip across the desert. Aziz knew very little about the Land of the Blacks. His own business was focused entirely in the opposite direction. And Hakeem was not about to share anything with Aziz that could place him in danger.

The two men, whose dark djellabas blended almost seamlessly with the darkness of the night, waited discreetly at the corner of the passageway that led to the main door of Aziz's house. It was not a busy street, and Aziz's home was at the very end of it. Rarely did anyone pass unless they were coming to see Aziz. They waited almost three hours before Hakeem came out.

Rather than continuing to follow Hakeem, they decided to interrogate Aziz. They knocked loudly, or rather pounded, at Aziz's door. There was no longer anything discreet about their demeanor.

"Who was that who just left your premises?" The question sounded more like a command. The man wasn't shouting exactly, but his voice was sharp and stern. He was clearly the one in charge of the pair. He had pushed back his hood to reveal a face that looked as if it had never smiled; its wrinkles formed a permanent frown, hardened by years of covert intelligence work. He was a towering man, head and shoulders above his partner. His hair was long and straggly and the color of ash. His eyes were a cold steel gray. And he had a jagged scar on his face. The other man, diminutive in stature, his face hidden in the shadow of his hood, remained at the door after closing it behind him.

Aziz's first impulse was to resist. "Who are *you*, and what do you want?" He stared at the spot just above the large man's nose where vertical folds crossed the horizontal wrinkles.

"Never mind who we are. We already said what we wanted—information about the man who just left here." The man's voice became more threatening. "I am not going to ask again."

The smaller man not only pushed back the hood of his djellaba, he removed the heavy robe altogether and put on a pair of smooth leather gloves as the larger man circled around behind Aziz.

As the inquisitors' insistence intensified, Aziz's resistance also stiffened. He refused to cower in fear. "The man who left is my friend, and that is all I have to say about him."

The two men looked at each other. They had enough experience in interrogating subjects to know that a man who shows braveness rather than fear is often telling the truth. They decided that they would not learn anything more by roughing up a prominent man in the community. It would actually be counterproductive. The small man removed his gloves, put his djellaba back on, and the two of them left without saying another word.

During this ordeal, Amina had been in the other room. She overheard the brief but frightening exchange. She realized that her father was in grave danger, and she was terrified. She knew that Hakeem was in danger as well. She came running in to her father.

"Abi, are you alright?" she said, crying and wrapping her arms around him.

"Yes, yes, Amina. I'm fine. Those ruffians should have known better than to try to get the better of me. But, tell me, why were they asking me about Hakeem? Do you know something about him that I don't know?"

Speaking through her sobs, she said, "I know that…he is a kind and gentle man…I know that…he respects you… and…he respects me. I know…that he is my teacher, and that is all I *need* to know."

The marks were barely perceptible, but Hakeem noticed that her attempt to camouflage the bruises on her face, neck, and arms had been for naught. "Tell me who did this to you, Dalia." Hakeem clenched his fists, seething with need for revenge. "I thought you were more careful in vetting your clients."

"They were not my clients, Hakeem. I never saw them before. One of them was very tall and burly. He had a long, jagged scar on the left side of his face." She started to cry again. "One of the men started to rape me, but the leader, the one with the scar, stopped him."

Her description of the scar raised an alarm in Hakeem. *Could it be...?* "What did they want?"

"They were here seeking information about *you*."

It could well have been Haytham al-Khariji, he thought. *If I ever get my hands on him... At least the man had shown some decency.*

Trying to downplay her hurt, Dalia turned her back to him. "Don't worry, they did not hurt me badly. It's an occupational hazard. I suffered much worse early in my...career."

She continued, "I can guess why they questioned me, but I assure you, I told them nothing." She turned and faced him again. "Let me give you one more piece of advice. You must leave Sijilmasa as soon as possible. There is a caravan leaving today going north to Fez. You should join it. If I were you, I would not even go home to get my belongings."

Hakeem was overcome with emotion. There were people here whom he cared for as much as anyone since he left home what seemed almost an eternity ago. "Dalia, how can I thank you for all your..." He was searching for a word.

"Love," she said, completing his sentence.

"I hope and pray that I will see you again." Nevertheless, Hakeem knew it was unlikely. He turned to leave.

"In shah Allah"—God willing—were her parting words to him as he walked out the door. She had not converted to Islam, but she had heard this Muslim phrase so often that it had become almost rote. When she used it this time, she meant it from the deepest reaches of her soul.

Hakeem wasted no time. Despite Dalia's advice, he needed to go home to get his most important possessions. Before he entered his residence, he paused and surveyed the street. When he was sure that no one threatening or suspicious was in the vicinity, he entered. He spent no more than a few minutes there packing a few books—including his copy of the Quran that had been a gift from his father—a small bag of personal items, his purse containing almost all of the two hundred dinars he had carried from Ghana, and, of course, the many pages of notes he had accumulated. He knew from his own experience as an intelligence agent that if two men had been tailing him earlier in the day, it would be only a matter of time before they were pounding on his own door. He moved quickly but cautiously. Within less than an hour, he was headed north to Fez. He did not wait to join the caravan that would leave later that afternoon. He would make the journey on his own.

CHAPTER FIFTEEN

As he approached Fez, Hakeem was intercepted by a band of soldiers on horseback. The standard-bearer carried a white flag, the color of the Fatimids, in stark contrast to the black flags of the Abbasid caliph in Baghdad. Hakeem was both shocked and confused. "I thought Jawhar had led the army to take Sijilmasa," he stammered.

"Never mind. Just who might you be?" asked the soldier who appeared to be in charge.

"My name is Hakeem Ibn al-Harith," he answered, with as much confidence as he could muster. He steadied his mount and reached into the leather bag that hung from his left shoulder across to his right side. He produced the authorization document bearing the caliph's own seal that identified him as a Fatimid *da'i*.

The soldier looked over the document, then looked up at Hakeem. Finally, he said, "You have a reputation. We have been told to keep an eye out for you. You're the agent who sent the message informing us that Ibn al-Fath had fled to Round Mountain. That was a crucial piece of information."

Hakeem relaxed a bit. He was relieved to be seen as an ally.

The soldier continued, "Jawhar's army has retaken Sijilmasa. Since the usurper had fled, Sijilmasa surrendered to Jawhar with virtually no resistance. They captured the traitor almost immediately thereafter."

Hakeem had left Sijilmasa only a few days earlier, before any of this happened. "How did you learn all that so quickly?" he asked.

"The same man who sent the pigeon with your message," the soldier answered.

Hakeem was pleased but no less confused. "Then what is going on here in Fez?" he asked.

"Yet another rebellion," the soldier answered. "The local governor, Ahmed Ibn Abu Bakr, has defected. Worse than that, he ordered the cursing of Shiite imams from every pulpit in Fez. This army is under the command of Ziri Ibn Bullugin, a staunch ally of the Fatimids." He drew a wide circle with his left arm and declared, "We have completely encircled the city and are prepared to enforce a blockade for as long as it takes to starve the city into submission. In the meantime, Jawhar is marching back to Fez as we speak."

The inhabitants of the city, loyal to Ahmed Ibn Abu Bakr, had rejected a guarantee of safe-conduct offered by the Fatimids. Ziri's army laid siege to the city, which was amply supplied with provisions, allowing the defenders to survive through the winter, spring, summer, and fall, up to the onset of the next winter.

During that time, while Ziri remained in charge of the siege, Jawhar dedicated himself to the task of subjugating the rest of the Maghrib.

Hakeem received a new set of orders from the office of the caliph in Mahdiya. He was to return to Andalusia to gather intelligence regarding the strength of the Umayyad forces.

What he learned there was alarming. The Umayyads had amassed a large army near the port city of Almería. They were perched in perfect position to launch a naval assault against the Fatimids.

Realizing that the Umayyad army could cross the straits at any time, Jawhar chose not to lay siege to the major coastal cities in North Africa. He did, on the other hand, dispatch his soldiers to secure all the rest of the northern Maghrib for the Fatimids. He understood perfectly well that to control vast amounts of territory, his army had to occupy the principal urban areas. His forces laid siege to one city after another, surrounding each one, cutting communications, and limiting the flow of goods in or out. Most cities did not have enough supplies to hold against a tight siege for very long, so this strategy turned out to be quite effective.

The last city to fall to his command was Fez. The besiegers stormed the double walls using ladders constructed from the trunks of giant cedars from the forest south of the city. The defenders had no choice but to surrender or perish. They chose to surrender.

Once the dust had settled, Jawhar entered the city in triumph. He looked rather stately, riding tall in the saddle atop his black stallion. Behind him marched his elite corps of foot soldiers, somewhat battle weary but still marching proudly, holding their lances straight up on their right side. Toward the rear of the victory march, a small cart pulled by a donkey carried an iron cage. It was heavily guarded. In it, bound in chains, was none other than Ibn al-Fath, the caliphal pretender of Sijilmasa, now caged like an animal of prey.

In the meantime, the rebellious ruler of Fez, Ahmed Ibn Abu Bakr, had gone into hiding somewhere deep in the dark alleys of the city. Jawhar's soldiers were relentless in tracking him down. They systematically searched up one lane and down the next, pounding on doors, crashing them in if no one answered. They interrogated residents. If they met with resistance of one kind or another, the soldiers used force, verbal at first but physical when necessary. The search continued for two days until the traitor was finally found in the root cellar of a small house just two blocks from the Qarawayeen Mosque. Who would have thought that he would try to hide in such a central part of the city?

As Jawhar prepared for his return to Mahdiya, he now had two notorious prisoners to contend with: the captured rebel rulers of both Fez and Sijilmasa. The distinguished Fatimid commander followed the specific instructions he received in a letter from the caliph himself:

> You will build for each of the royal pretenders a special vehicle, a platform on four wheels. Upon it will be a chamber inside of which a man can turn a mast-like axle with a platform at the top. Upon the platform you will place a chair. Each prisoner will occupy his own special throne. The chairs are to be rotated by turning the axle from within the chamber. In this way, all who look upon the two rebel leaders will see a traitor's face.

Before leaving Fez, Jawhar summoned Hakeem to his quarters. Hakeem stood at the commander's door and paused before he knocked. He hoped that since Fez was now securely in the hands of the Fatimids, he would be released from his duties. He had planned to spend some time pursuing his own interests in this university town that had attracted some of the brightest scholars from all around the Islamic world. Now, he was fairly sure that would not be the case. The most powerful commander in the entire Fatimid army had summoned him. This would be the first time he met Jawhar face to face.

He knocked.

"Come in." The two words caused Hakeem's heart to beat hard and fast.

Jawhar was seated behind a table, with several rolled parchments in front of him. *Orders to be handed to various officers?* Hakeem wondered. *Is one of them for me?*

Jawhar stood to greet him. Up close, he looked even more impressive, more stately than he had a few days earlier when he rode into the city in triumph. He was not a tall man. It must have been the power of his command that made him seem larger than he was.

Hakeem's suspicion was confirmed when the commander presented him with a new assignment. This time, it was not written out in a letter. Jawhar delivered it from his own mouth.

"The caliph is weighing," he explained, "whether to focus our military might westward to counter the Umayyads and secure the gold routes across the Sahara, or..." There was a long pause as Jawhar seemed to be searching for the best way to phrase what he was about to say. "Or to march east," another pause, "to *conquer* Egypt as a stepping stone to challenge the Abbasids in Baghdad."

Hakeem remembered what Musa had told him, that the Fatimids' goal was to spread their own view of the rule of law to the whole of Islamdom.

Jawhar, speaking softly now, continued, "Your mission is to continue gathering intelligence—all around the entire Roman Sea. You will assess the resources everywhere you go. Your report will provide input to the caliph as he decides where most to focus his efforts. Do you understand, Hakeem Ibn al-Harith?"

Hakeem lowered his eyes. There was not even a hint of enthusiasm in his voice. "Yes, my lord. I am to advise the caliph as to what will be more... *profitable*...aggression toward the West...or conquest of the East."

"I think you do understand the caliph's ambition. But let me be clear. It is not a question of acquisition of wealth. An expedition in Egypt will be extremely costly. As we secured our holdings here in the Maghrib, I managed to collect in taxes a half-million dinars that will help finance a military campaign—wherever that may be. I have heard that the caliph has at his disposal some twenty-four million dinars for that purpose. No, it is not about wealth. The caliph's ambition is all about power." With that, Jawhar dismissed him with the following advice: "You must be ever vigilant—and always discreet."

In the fall of 960, Hakeem departed Fez, traveling at first with Jawhar's victory march. His plan was to accompany the army as far as Mahdiya. Then he would continue on, all the way around the Middle Sea. He had a general sense from his earlier studies, especially his readings of ancient Greek geographers like Ptolemy, as well as earlier Persian and Arab writers, of the approximate scope and shape of this Middle Sea. His intent was to draw out on paper the path of his journey, however long that journey might take. Of course, as he went he would also be gathering and recording the intelligence data that were requested of him. Little did he know, it would take him the better part of a decade.

The line of march headed north to the Mediterranean coast, then turned east along the coast toward Ifriqiya. Hakeem carefully recorded as best he could, using the path of the sun across the sky, the length of time it took to travel between each major city. He also noted, again as best he could, using the shadows cast by the sun, the direction he traveled, taking into account the time of day. Time and direction, each day, every day: the two key components to envisioning how he would graphically sketch out his itinerary.

Realizing that his recordings were not as accurate as he would like, not to mention that variables beyond his control affected his pace and direction—obstacles like mountains to cross or circumvent and rivers to ford—Hakeem collected additional data by quizzing professional travelers: navigators on merchant ships, caravan masters, and guides, many of whom kept careful logs of their travels. "How long did it take you to get there from…" He would name the point of origin. "What direction did you follow?"

All of these data he wrote down on sheets of paper and collected the sheets in a leather portfolio that became one of his most guarded possessions. Each night before he retired, he added to his narrative:

> I pray that God will lend me his assistance to accomplish what conforms to the truth. God's help suffices. What an excellent collaborator!
>
> I will draw the sea in the center of the map. I begin with the place-names along the southern shore, starting from Mahdiya, the center of the coastline, the capital of the Fatimid caliphate, the very spot where I began this journey…
>
> On this, my first voyage around the sea, I sailed east, first to the port city of Sfax, then Gabes, Tripoli, Surt, Ajdabiya, and Barqa, with large outcroppings of land separating each of them. In the interior, traveling due south, are Djazirat Wadddan and Djazirat Audjilia.

Continuing eastward, we arrived in Alexandria and then the delta of the River Nile. Following the river upstream, we arrived in Fustat on the right bank, where I last saw my beloved teacher, and then, on the left bank, Giza, site of the Great Pyramids.

What came to mind as he wrote these last phrases was his visit with Sheikh Abu'l-Hasan al-Mas'udi, his former teacher, now deceased. His stay in Egypt this time was filled with an emptiness he had not expected. He missed his dear friend and mentor. With a heavy heart, he moved on and wrote:

Next in my journey were Antalya and the Peloponnese. Between these flow the Bosphoros River, along which sits the glorious city of Constantinople, capital of the mighty Roman empire and seat of the patriarch of the Christian church.

From the Peloponnese traveling west-northwest, we arrived at Otranto and then Brindisi, a city literally at the heel of a peninsula, where people speak a language quite similar to Latin. A few days farther along this trajectory we enter the bay of Venice. Alternatively, if we travel west-southwest from Otranto, we arrive at Reggio Calabria. Off the coast is the island of Sicily. I confess that my journey along the entire northern shore of the Middle Sea I did in haste. Thus, it will lack the detail and accuracy of other parts of my map.

With this reluctant admission, Hakeem ended his narrative of the first half of his journey. Later, he wrote:

On my second journey, again setting out from Mahdiya, I traveled west, reaching successively Tunis, Bone, Algiers, Oran, Nakur, and Ceuta.

Hakeem paused at this point. He decided to add an aside to describe the voyage that brought him to Sijilmasa and then across the deep Sahara. He shed a quiet tear as he thought if his friends Aziz and Amina and, of course, Dalia. *What became of Dalia?* he wondered. But he could not bring himself to write about any of them. Holding back his emotions, he only wrote:

Over a decade ago, I traveled from Ceuta to arrive in Fez, then Sijilmasa, from where I made the long journey south to Awdaghost and Ghana.

Then he resumed where he had left off:

> Continuing west from Ceuta, one arrives at Tangiers, the south side
> of the Pillars of Hercules. The other pillar across the straits is the
> port of Algeciras, port of entry to Andalusia. From there, one travels
> easily north to Córdoba, which sits on the bank of the Wadi al-Kabir.
> Or one can follow the coast east to Málaga, Almería, Cartagena,
> Murcia, and finally Valencia. To go beyond that, we would enter
> the hostile territory of the *Nisrani*, the Christians with whom the
> Umayyad caliph has an uneasy alliance. I chose not to venture into
> that territory.

CHAPTER SIXTEEN

Aurillac

In the year of the Lord 967, Count Borrell II of Barcelona came to the Abbey of Saint Gerauld. He crossed the Pyrenees en route to wed the daughter of the Count of Toulouse. His journey took him some thirty miles beyond the land of his bride-to-be to the door of the abbey. He came, as did so many before him, as a pilgrim, attracted by the reputation of the miraculous bones of the saint whose name the abbey bore.

Abbot Gerauld greeted the count warmly and offered the hospitality worthy of a nobleman, well beyond what was required to offer pilgrims according to the monks' holy rule. The count thanked the abbot profusely and said, "If there is anything I can do for you, Reverend Father, please tell me."

The abbot waited several seconds before responding, as if assessing the sincerity of the count's offer. Finally, he said, "In truth, there is one thing. We have heard that there are men of great learning in Catalonia Vella, where you are from, scholars of science, medicine, and mathematics. Is this true?"

"Yes, Reverend Father. As you know, the lands that I hold as a vassal to the king of the Franks provide a buffer between the lands of Christendom and the house of Islam. There has been conflict as armies pass back and forth. The borders themselves have moved—sometimes in one direction and sometimes in the opposite. But the lands have not only been fraught with violence and warfare. There have been good exchanges as well."

"Such as?"

"Christian merchants have profited much from trade with the Muslims. And perhaps even more important, ideas have traveled along with the traders. So has learning. Scholars from the great university at Córdoba—Muslim, Jewish, and Christian scholars—have brought their learning to us. Why do you make such an inquiry?"

"We have with us in our community a young novice of exceptional talent. He has learned everything that we have to teach him. He has read every book in our possession. This young man is an asset to the monastery, a good candidate to be the next abbot. But it would be unfair to him, indeed unfair to the world of science, to keep him here at the monastery. He needs to go where his mind can flourish."

The count stroked his beard. "So you would like me to take him with me."

"Yes, my lord. I know it is not a small thing to ask. But if it is at all possible…"

"Reverend Father, I am forever grateful for your hospitality…" A long pause. "Of course, I will do as you ask."

The following day, Count Borrell left the monastery to return home. Gerbert went with him. His preparation was minimal. He had very few possessions to pack: a winter habit and a summer habit, wool socks and an extra pair of sandals, a woolen cap—and a head full of knowledge and dreams. As he traveled south from Aurillac with the noble cortège of the count and his bride, he was filled with gratitude toward the monks of Saint Gerauld for the home they had given him, thankful for all that Brother Raymond had taught him and for Abbot Gerauld's thoughtfulness to send him forth to seek an even greater treasure of the mind. But at the same time, his heart was heavy with nostalgia for the only world he knew and filled with anxiety for the world he knew not and could hardly imagine.

Gerbert had never been away from Aurillac. The world beyond his village and the monastery had much to teach him. On the second day of the journey, the cortège arrived at the small town of Conques nestled around the Abbey of Sainte-Foy. The group of travelers sought hospitality in the guesthouse of the monastery. The abbey had been in Conques for almost two hundred years. The monks who founded it had been refugees from the Muslim armies moving north from Andalusia. The abbey church was small, but Brother Albert, the guest master, informed the visitors that there were plans to build a new church. The number of pilgrims had dramatically increased in recent times, attracted by the holy relics, the bones of Sainte-Foy herself.

The inquisitive Gerbert was more interested in quizzing the guest master about the Saracens who forced the monks to flee.

"Brother Raymond told us the Muslims were great scholars, men of science. Yet they would persecute your monks?"

"That was long ago, in the early years, even before the great lord Charlemagne, when the Carolingians served as mayors of the palace," said Brother Albert. "The Muslims, both Arabs and Berbers, came from across the water, from Africa. Very quickly they moved like a swarm of locusts over most of the land of the Goths. They crossed the great mountains of the Pyrenees and invaded the kingdom of the Franks. They were eventually halted in their march in Poitiers by the powerful Frankish lord Charles, grandfather to Emperor Charlemagne. For his miraculous victory against tremendous odds, Charles became known as the 'Hammer.' The Lord only knows what might have become of all of us had it not been for Charles the Hammer—"

"How do you know all of this?" Gerbert interjected.

"Among the few books we have here is a copy of the *Vita Karoli Magni*, a biography of Charles the Great. The first part tells of the early Carolingians."

Gerbert then turned his attention to Sainte-Foy, for whom the abbey was named.

Since she was the patron saint of the monastery, Brother Albert knew her story well and was pleased to satisfy Gerbert's curiosity. "Back in the era of the Roman emperor Diocletian, she was burned at the stake in her native town of Agen, some 140 miles west of here. The story is that the flames of the fire were miraculously extinguished. So the determined executioners beheaded the young girl."

Gerbert shook his head and grimaced. "How did her relics end up here?"

"Initially, her bones were kept in a monastery in Agen. A monk, again, as the story goes, stole the bones and brought them here to Conques. Since then, many miracles have been attributed to the presence of those bones. The lame were made to walk. The blind were made to see." He paused. "Have you noticed the iron shackles just inside the door of the church?

"Yes, many shackles."

"They were left by the many prisoners who were set free."

Gerbert was beginning to yawn—from tiredness, certainly not boredom.

"It is getting late," Brother Albert said. "Count Borrell intends to leave at first light. Let me take you to the dormitory, where you can rest for the long journey that lies ahead."

It was late in the afternoon on the sixth day since they had left Conques.

As they rode over the crest of a hill, their destination revealed itself in the distance. The count picked up his pace. Gerbert, who had been daydreaming yet again as he rolled with the movement of his horse, was startled by the sudden acceleration. His eyes opened wide as he gazed across the valley to the river below and across the river to the forest.

"My God," he exclaimed, "they are huge!"

He was referring not to the trees but to the fortifications that towered above them, a crown of walls and towers circling the terrace that was Carcassonne.

"What a powerful city this must be!" Gerbert said, loud enough that the count heard him from several paces away. Up to now, Count Borrell had not engaged the boy in conversation. What would he, a man of politics and war, have to say to a young novice monk? But prompted by Gerbert's sudden excitement, the count reined his horse around to ride side by side with his new ward.

"Carcassonne is famous for its walls," he said. "Indeed, they look impenetrable. But perhaps there is a lesson to be learned here. Can you imagine *why* one would build walls such as these?"

"To be secure within them, my lord?"

"Precisely. One builds walls like these when one feels *insecure*."

As the cortège crossed the River Aude over the old Roman bridge, the count continued his lesson. "Architecturally, the bridge is a marvel of Roman engineering. The rounded arches make it possible to span wider distances with fewer supports."

Gerbert nodded in immediate understanding. "I have not seen a bridge such as this, but I read about these rounded arches in the work of Vitruvius."

"You have read Vitruvius?" the count asked in surprise.

"His *De Architectura* was among the books at our monastery."

They were now close enough to see that the blocks of stone at the base of the massive walls were larger than those above. Count Borrell, who knew the history of the walls, explained, "The oldest fortifications, still visible at the base, were built in the time of the caesars."

"Why only the base of the walls?" Gerbert asked.

The count, although weary from a long day's travel, had rarely encountered such an inquisitive ear as that of young Gerbert. "The Roman empire, like so many imperial regimes, eventually overextended its power. When it was no longer strong enough to hold this area, it ceded it to the Visigothic king Theodoric, who restored the fortifications."

"Are those the walls we see today?"

"For the most part. They served well warding off the Frankish king Clovis. They were not as successful in defending the city against the Saracens.

The Muslims held it until they were driven out by Pepin, the father of Charlemagne. The Carolingians ceded it to Count Bello, whose family still rules the city today."

Shortly after they entered the city, they passed the Basilica of Saints Nazaire and Celse. The count, now acting more like a tour guide, said, "The Visigoths also built this, the first church in Carcassonne. Originally, it was an Arian church, as were most of the churches in Visigothic lands."

"Brother Raymond taught us about the beliefs of the Arians. They believe that since Jesus was born almost a thousand years ago, he did not exist before that. On the surface, that seems logical enough, but the Church of Rome interpreted that claim to mean that Jesus was somehow less than God. The Church declared Arianism a heresy."

The count was impressed with the boy's knowledge. "And you, what do you believe?"

"I have not really thought about it before. I have never questioned that God is Father, Son, and Holy Ghost. But regardless of what the Arians believe, they built a beautiful church." Gerbert said this as he marveled at the arched doorways and windows. "They look like horseshoes resting on top of two parallel columns or pillars."

"They are in fact called horseshoe arches," the count said.

Gerbert was also impressed. *This man is more than just a politician and soldier*, he thought. He was pleased that the count had taken this interest in him.

Having left Carcassonne, Count Borrell and company followed the course of the River Aude for two days to reach the city of Narbonne. The contrast between this large, busy port city on the Mediterranean Sea and the small hamlet of Belliac, where Gerbert grew up as a peasant farmer's son, was almost more than the boy could absorb. Nor did his years in the monastery prepare him for all that he saw and heard—and smelled: crowds of people so thick that he had to push his way along as he walked through the market; a cacophony of languages, some of which sounded remotely like the *langue d'oc*, *langue d'oil*, and Latin that he knew, but other languages he had never heard before; aromas of exotic spices he did not recognize, as well as foul smells of things he did recognize but preferred not to think about. There were people from every part of the Mediterranean world, a lot of them. And, of course, the balmy sea, which he now saw for the first time.

Count Borrell had a number of affairs to attend to in Narbonne before moving on. He invited Gerbert to accompany him. As they passed a large stone building with a Star of David on the pediment above the door, the count described it to Gerbert as a center for studying Biblical exegesis. "It was recently founded by a group of Jews who came to Narbonne from the caliphate of Baghdad."

"Are there many Jews here in Narbonne?" asked Gerbert.

"Yes, many. Most of them are salt merchants. Salt is a much-needed commodity—and expensive. It is a very lucrative trade. By charter from the count, the Jews have a monopoly on it."

"Do Jews get along without prejudice here?" Gerbert asked.

"For the most part. There are incidents from time to time, squabbles of one kind or another. Some jealousy over the control of the salt trade. But rarely do people of different religions argue over matters of *faith*. There is enough of that kind of arguing *within* each faith."

As they continued to walk through the market, Gerbert saw many things he had never before imagined: iron tools much more sophisticated than the crude hand tools used by farmers in Aurillac, glazed pottery with both floral and geometric designs, manufactured textiles of silk and fine wool dyed in the most brilliant colors, oil lamps, furniture inlaid with shells and ivory, finely woven carpets—and coins, stacks of coins.

They were now standing in front of a *banca*, a bench, where a well-dressed, heavyset man was exchanging coins from foreign places for a local currency. Gerbert had never seen so many coins all in one place. In Aurillac, objects were traded for objects: eggs for oil, chickens for a goat. His father had difficulty in acquiring two silver shillings a month to make his payment to his lord, the abbot; so he paid in kind.

"Here, most purchases are paid with currency," the count explained as he stepped up to the *banca* to exchange money of his own. He had been there many times before and knew the banker, who greeted him warmly. Gerbert stepped up to the bench with him, close enough to see a few silver coins stamped with strange but beautiful writing.

"Arabic," the money changer said, noticing the expression of confusion and delight on Gerbert's face. "This coin bears the name of the caliph al-Hakam II." He handed the coin to Gerbert. "Only to look at, not to keep," he said jokingly, then added, "More and more, Arabic is becoming the language of international commerce here and all around the Mediterranean Sea."

Gerbert felt a sudden desire to learn to read those letters stamped on the coins. It seemed that each new day presented him with new and exciting knowledge, but along with that, so many more new challenges.

Three more travel days brought Count Borrell's party deep into the Pyrenees. As they crested a peak, they could see the Abbey of Saint-Michel-de-Cuxa below. From their vantage point, they could look right down into the enclosure. The cloister was just to the far side of center, and the abbey church just beyond that. The stone face of the mountain rose sharply on the west side and descended just as steeply to the east. Traveling through these rugged mountains was slow and arduous to say the least. The travelers were relieved when they passed through the gate.

The guesthouse was empty, and the guest master invited the count and his entourage to stay two nights, with a day of rest in between. Gerbert was pleased. He spent much of his free day walking around the abbey church, which was undergoing renovation. He was fascinated to compare the construction techniques here to those in Aurillac. During his years at Saint Gerauld, their church had also been under construction. Being the precocious learner that he was, he had learned much about measuring angles, cutting, and laying stone just by watching.

Abbot Garin happened to be inspecting the construction as Gerbert entered the church.

"I see you are making use of the horseshoe arch," Gerbert remarked, feeling quite pleased to be able to make that observation.

The rule of silence did not apply to guests, and the abbot was quite proud to describe some of the architectural features to his young visitor. "Good observation, son," said the abbot with a surprised look on his face. "How is it you know about horseshoe arches?"

"I must confess, Reverend Abbot, I just learned about them. Count Borrell was kind enough to point them out to me at the basilica in Carcassonne. He told me that the style was introduced by the Visigoths."

"Were you to go into Muslim territory to the south, you would see many more of these arches in the mosques in Andalusia. Apparently, the Saracens liked the design as well. And in return, they gave us these keyhole arches." The abbot pointed to the transverse arches in the choir and the niche to the right of the altar. "As you see, they are similar to the horseshoe arch but gracefully pointed at the top rather than perfectly round."

"So would you say that it was a fair trade?" asked Gerbert.

"I would." The abbot was impressed by the shrewdness of the boy's question. "You know, there is much to be gained from interaction with the

Muslims. We can learn from them without accepting their religious beliefs."

"Are they not seeking to expand their faith by the sword?" asked Gerbert.

"Muslim rulers are like rulers anywhere," the abbot replied. "They sometimes go to war seeking to expand their territory. But extend their faith? That is rare. The Muslims of Andalusia are quite tolerant of Christians and Jews. They call them 'People of the Book,' people who believe in the God of the Bible."

"Do Muslims believe in the Bible?" Gerbert asked incredulously.

"They believe that the same God who revealed the Quran also revealed the Bible. Many prophets that are in the Bible are also in the Quran. Jesus is mentioned many times in the Muslim Holy Book."

Even more surprised at this statement, Gerbert asked, "Have you read the Quran, Reverend Abbot?"

"I have not. I do not read Arabic, and as of yet there are no translations of it."

Another reason for me to learn Arabic, Gerbert thought.

Gerbert thanked the abbot for sharing his knowledge, as well as for his gracious hospitality. Although he knew that hospitality toward travelers was required of monasteries, it was not always as gracious as that offered by Abbot Garin. But more importantly, Gerbert felt that he had made a friend.

Gerbert retired to the cell where he was to sleep through the night. He was tired and knew he still had several days of travel before he reached his destination. But he could not sleep. His mind was racing. Silently, he prayed, *God help me, there is so much to learn.*

Count Borrell and company had been traveling almost an entire month when they finally arrived in Ripoll, where they would be the guests of the abbot of the Monastery of Santa Maria. They were less than a day's ride from the city of Vic, where the count intended to deposit young Gerbert into the care of Atto, bishop of Vic. But Borrell was anxious for the budding scholar to see this monastery. It was the most important monastery in the diocese and was especially famous for its library, which had sixty-seven manuscripts and counting. The abbey was working very hard to add new acquisitions to the collection. Monk copyists laboriously made copies of manuscripts they already had. With great difficulty, they managed to borrow from elsewhere, some of them from the great library in Córdoba, far to the south in Muslim territory.

With the abbot's permission, Count Borrell took Gerbert to visit the library. Six monks sat stooped over their desks, quills in hand, copying manuscripts. Gerbert eagerly approached close enough to peek over the shoulder of a monk who seemed a little older than the others. His head was not tonsured in the style of monks; it seemed naturally bald. But his beard was long, wiry, and gray. He squinted at the text he copied as if struggling to decipher what it said. But his hand was steady. Gerbert asked him what the text was about.

"Algebra." The monk's answer was brief.

The vow of silence, Gerbert reminded himself. *He is not being rude, only complying with the rule.* Gerbert looked as closely as he could at what the monk was writing. He thought he could recognize the word "al." He pressed the monk for more information. "Is that a name? Al-Khwarizmi?"

"This section describes his *Kitab al-Jabar*, the 'Book of Algebra.' 'Algebra' means 'restoration.' One adds a number to both sides of an equation to consolidate or cancel terms."

"I'm not sure I understand," said Gerbert.

"Well, I'm sorry, young man," the monk responded. "I am not the person to explain it to you. I am only a copyist."

Gerbert suspected that the monk was not saying as much as he knew, but he decided to respect the man's preference for silence.

Count Borrell said, "Worry not, my son. You will be back here to read and learn. We are only a few hours from Vic, where you will study with Bishop Atto."

"The bishop...will oversee my studies? Is that not a bit unusual?" exclaimed Gerbert.

"Yes, a bit unusual. Atto is a churchman and, I must say, one of the most powerful political leaders in the diocese. But he is also a scholar. He studied mathematics from the books of Arab scholars. When Abbot Gerauld asked me to find you a teacher, Bishop Atto was the man who came immediately to mind. You will find him a formidable teacher—exacting but kind. And I expect that he will send you, from time to time, to study in the Monastery of Santa Maria."

A warm feeling rushed through Gerbert as he heard Count Borrell reveal the plan for his future. He rode the rest of the way to Vic without saying a word—very happy indeed.

CHAPTER SEVENTEEN

"So, Brother Gerbert, you have come to the Hispanic Marches to study mathematics and astronomy."

"Yes, Your Excellency." Gerbert had never spoken to a bishop before. Thanks be to God, Brother Raymond had instructed him in how to address people at various levels in both the religious and the secular hierarchies.

Bishop Atto was not a tall man. In fact, he was a man of rather slight build, much to Gerbert's surprise. Gerbert had imagined bishops to be heavyset, with round, fat faces. At least that was what he was often told, perhaps by people who had not seen bishops before either, but rather imagined them to be rich and very well fed.

Still, Bishop Atto looked impressive. He was impeccably dressed in a long, black cassock made of expensive, tightly woven wool of the finest quality, with bright amaranth-red piping and thirty-three buttons down the front— thirty-three to represent the number of years of the life of our Lord Jesus Christ. Over the cassock the bishop wore a black shoulder cape, also with red piping, and around his waist, a satin sash with silk fringe at the ends that hung down almost to the floor, also amaranth-red. His silver-gray hair was tonsured in the style of monks, forming a crown around his head. His neatly trimmed, silver-gray beard framed his narrow face.

It was Atto's eyes more than anything else that sealed Gerbert's initial impression of the bishop. They were exceptionally bright, wide open, and seemed to never blink. It felt as if the bishop could see right into the deepest reaches of Gerbert's soul.

In addition to overseeing the churches and monasteries in the borderlands, Atto held the demesne of Vic as a fief from Count Borrell. As the count's vassal, he presided over the judicial courts of Vic, hearing complaints of tenants, resolving disputes, sentencing criminals, and keeping all fines for himself. He collected the tolls on roads and bridges and taxes from the town markets. He even minted his own coins. Second only to Count Borrell, Atto was the most powerful man in the entire region.

Gerbert was not aware of Bishop Atto's political status at this first meeting. But as he learned of it over the days to come, it confirmed his first impression of the bishop as a man of considerable intelligence and authority.

"Brother Gerbert, you will stay here in Vic for the rest of the week to rest from your journey. You will then return to Ripoll, to the Monastery of Santa Maria. Among the monks there are some excellent scholars who can teach you the subjects of the quadrivium: mathematics, geometry, music, and astronomy. I have heard that you come already well introduced to arithmetic. You will soon learn that there is much more to mathematics than adding, subtracting, multiplying, and dividing. You read Latin, I presume?"

"Yes, Your Excellency." Gerbert said no more on this point, though he had already decided that he wanted to learn Arabic as well.

Bishop Atto dismissed him, saying, "You will return to Vic the last week each month to attend the cathedral school. At that time, you will report to me on your progress."

"Yes, Your Excellency."

Although Gerbert had spent only one night there, returning to the Monastery of Santa Maria in Ripoll almost felt like he was coming home. The guest master assigned him to a tiny cell of his own with barely enough room for his bed, a wooden frame supporting tightly strung ropes that in turn supported his mattress of straw. Gerbert remembered reading the details in the holy rule of Saint Benedict: "Let a straw mattress, a blanket, a coverlet, and a pillow be sufficient." It was adequate but simple, all in accordance with the Benedictine rule of moderate asceticism. A small table in the corner supported one candle, the light by which he hoped he would be able to read at night. All of the rest of his belongings, his one alternate habit, his string of rosary beads, two feather pens and an inkwell—departing gifts from Brother Raymond—he stored under his bed in a small wooden box.

Since he had been sent to the monastery on the directive of Bishop Atto specifically to study in the library, Gerbert was not assigned to any manual labor. But he was a monk and would be expected to participate in the abbey's prayer schedule, singing or praying the Psalms at the designated hours each day. These were moments he relished in his daily routine.

Weary from his journey from Vic the previous day, Gerbert was excused from attending the chanting of *lauds* during the middle of the night. Come the hour of *prime* at first light, Gerbert was anxious to begin this next chapter in his life. He was the first person to appear in the abbey church. He had been there just a little over a week earlier as he passed through with Count Borrell, but now he felt that this was *his* church. He was awed by the spaciousness of the Romanesque interior: four aisles, each roofed by a vast barrel vault. Gerbert was deeply moved to piety in this sacred space.

After all of the monks had filed into the beautifully carved wooden choir stalls, the choir master opened the huge book of Psalms perched on the pedestal so that all the monks could see the large square notes inked on the page. They began to chant the simple melody of *prime*:

> O God, come to our aid.
> O Lord, make haste to help us.
> Glory be to the Father and to the Son and to the Holy Spirit,
> As it was in the beginning, is now, and ever shall be,
> World without end.
> Amen. Alleluia.
> Father, we praise you, now the night is over,
> Active and watchful, stand we all before you;
> Singing we offer prayer and meditation:
> Thus we adore you.

Following *prime*, the monks left the church and filed into the refectory. Gerbert enjoyed his breakfast of hot porridge, dried fruit, and a cup of warm cider. This was exactly what he was used to at the monastery of Saint Gerauld in Aurillac. He enjoyed the peace and quiet of taking his meal in silence, as was also the custom there.

He was anxious to get to the library. His first impulse as soon as breakfast was over was to find the monk whom he had met a week earlier, the one who was working on copying a text allegedly by the famous Muslim mathematician and astronomer al-Khwarizmi. Again, he was the first to enter this space.

Six monks worked as copyists in the library. Copying was a task that required not only skill in penmanship—the ability to draw letters clearly and even elegantly—but also careful attention to detail, without making errors that could, in some cases, completely change the meaning of the text. Any error at all was serious.

The monk who had been copying the book of al-Khwarizmi during Gerbert's first visit was the last to arrive for his morning's work. Gerbert walked over to the table where the copyist, whose name was Brother Matthew, was readying to resume his work. "Are you still working on the book by al-Khwarizmi?"

"Yes, and I'm afraid I will be working on it for quite a while. Copying any book is a long, slow task. But this one will take an especially long time." The monk was more talkative than the previous time Gerbert had been there. "First, you should know that it is not a book *by* al-Khwarizmi. It is actually a book about mathematics in general. This section describes the use of the astrolabe. It was translated by a scholar whose name we do not know. It refers to al-Khwarizmi, perhaps quoting his actual words describing how the astrolabe is made and used. And it must be a very rough draft at that. Look…" Brother Matthew pointed to the page he was working on, and Gerbert looked closely over his shoulder. "It has so many cross-outs, additions, and corrections," Brother Matthew complained. "That is what makes this one so difficult to copy."

"So, it is not a book describing al-Khwarizmi's mathematical concepts?"

"I'm afraid not."

"Well, then, can you tell me what he says about the astrolabe?"

"I really need to be getting back to work. Besides, we are supposed to be silent here…" Nevertheless, perhaps not wanting to put off the newest member of the community, Brother Matthew proceeded to explain, "I can tell you generally—and briefly. The astrolabe has many uses. It can show how the sky looks from a particular place on earth and at a given time."

"You mean it can provide a map of the sky?"

"Well, yes…I guess so," Brother Matthew said. "It can also tell the time of both day and night. It can tell when the sun will rise and set, and it allows us to reference celestial positions."

"How does it work?"

"All of this is done by adjusting the movable components. That is really all that I have been able to figure out. You must understand that I am a copyist, not a scholar. You really have to speak with Friar Miro Bonfill."

"Where does he work?"

"He is not a member of our community, but he comes here as often as he can to use the library."

As it happened, Miro Bonfill became Gerbert's closest friend at the monastery. He was the third son of Count Miro II of Cerdanya, hence a nobleman of high rank. Being a *third* son, it was thought that his best chance for social advancement would be in the Church. And so it was that he became a monk at an early age. Before he reached his thirty-fifth year, he was archdeacon to the bishop of Girona. His official duty as archdeacon was to serve the bishop. When his older brother Sunifred II died, he inherited the title of count. But Miro much preferred academic pursuits to politics. Thus, he spent as much time as possible at the Monastery of Santa Maria and its library full of books.

Gerbert had been at Santa Maria less than two weeks when Miro Bonfill showed up. In appearance, he was not at all what Gerbert imagined a scholar to look like. He was an older man. That much Gerbert had expected. His hair, wavy and silky white, hung down to his shoulders. His beard, also long and wavy, was divided in the middle, each half tied with a thin ribbon. He wore a long white linen tunic and a long matching cape. In stark contrast was the coal-black, full-brimmed hat on his head and black leather boots on his feet. A long ornamental dagger hung over his right shoulder in a silver scabbard suspended on a black sash. A large black leather bag hung over his opposite shoulder. He was clearly a man of means.

Bonfill had already heard that a new monk had arrived at the monastery, sent there by the bishop to study mathematics and astronomy. He was excited by the prospect of having a colleague, a bright mind with whom he could discuss subjects so dear to him. Immediately upon his arrival, he asked to be introduced.

"I have come here specifically to meet you," said Bonfill. "Your reputation as a scholar of great potential has preceded you."

"I too have heard a lot about you, my lord," said Gerbert.

"Oh no, please don't address me that way. I am just like you, a traveling scholar in search of knowledge. Please, just call me Miro."

"But you are the son of a count, an archdeacon in the Church."

"Yes, my heritage has condemned me to that. I hold those titles and, yes, to some degree fulfill the obligations that come with them out of loyalty to my family and the Church. But my interests lie in the same place as yours."

Gerbert imagined that Bonfill carried his manuscripts and writing tools in the leather bag. He was impatient to find out. "Your bag looks a bit heavy, my lo—or rather, Miro. Are you working on a treatise?"

"Yes, I have some pages that I have just penned. I am struggling to write a short piece on astrology. I say struggling. Reading the works of another with comprehension is hard enough, but producing a written page that comes out of one's own mind, taking a vague idea of one's own and making it clear enough to articulate in writing, is a different matter, a challenge at best and a slow process to say the least."

As Bonfill spoke, he sat down at one of the study tables in the library. He took the pages from his bag and showed them to Gerbert.

The young monk read aloud from the top page, "'What follows now has been translated by the wisest scholar among the Arabs, as he was instructing me.' So these are not entirely your own ideas?" Gerbert asked.

"That is correct. I imagine that you have already experienced that yourself. What you hear from a great master, you must absorb, process in your own mind. You then combine an assortment of ideas with your own and thus move knowledge slowly forward."

"Who is this 'wisest scholar' you mention?"

"His name is Maslama al-Majriti. He is a Muslim from Madrid. But I met him in Córdoba, where he now lives. He is quite young, probably not much older than yourself. He is exceptionally bright and has had the benefit of living in what is perhaps the most stimulating intellectual environment known to mankind."

"And that is…?"

"The mosque-university of Córdoba, the school supported by the caliph al-Hakam. As an institution of higher learning, it has no equal."

"Tell me more."

"There are sixty-seven books here in this monastery," Miro explained. "In Córdoba, books and manuscripts are counted not even in the hundreds, but in the thousands. And there is an instrument that can measure time and distance and map the position of celestial objects."

"That wouldn't by chance be an astrolabe, would it?"

"Exactly! You know about the astrolabe?"

"Only what Brother Matthew told me. He said you know much more."

"Brother Matthew exaggerates, I'm afraid," Miro said modestly as he stroked his beard. "It will take some time for you to read all of the books here at Santa Maria. But if it is at all possible, you really must go to Córdoba."

The next year was an important formative period in Gerbert's education at Santa Maria. He read voraciously. Of course, most of the books in the library were religious books, commentaries on Holy Scripture and the writings of the Church fathers, sermons of Saint Ambrose, *Confessions* of Saint Augustine, *The City of God*. The Latin classics like the *Aeneid* were a welcome change of pace. Most of all, he relished the relatively few books on science. As Bishop Atto had instructed, he focused on the subjects of the quadrivium. He practiced his skills in arithmetic, always trying to find ways to do calculations more quickly. Einhard's *Vita Karoli Magni* and the *Vita Hludovici Imperatoris*, written by someone known simply as "the astronomer," filled him with pride and nostalgia for the glory days of the Carolingians. He regretted seeing the power and prestige of the dynasty in decline.

His new friend Miro Bonfill introduced him to the few manuscripts available on astrology. "Have you read Boethius yet?" he asked one day.

"Back home in Aurillac, but I am revisiting parts of it now. I am relieved to learn that Boethius did not believe that everything was controlled by fate."

"Exactly," Miro agreed. "Quite to the contrary, he believed that divine Providence imposed no fatal necessity on the human will. We are always free to choose. Nature, on the other hand, is constrained by the planets—hence the science of astrology."

As instructed, Gerbert went to Vic at the end of each month to report to Bishop Atto. Occasionally during his monthly visit, the bishop invited him to sit in and listen when he met with his council of advisors. He also attended the bishop's court, which heard a wide range of cases: religious cases, such as the legitimacy of a marriage and rights of inheritance; civil cases, such as conflicts in property claims; criminal cases, such as theft and, God forbid, murder.

Gerbert concluded that Bishop Atto administered "justice" harshly. One day, he attended the trial of a serf accused of stealing a gold-plated monstrance. It was a beautiful glass receptacle in which the consecrated Eucharistic host would be exposed for veneration. The glass was framed in a gold-plated silver sunburst.

Two witnesses testified against the alleged thief. The first was a priest from the parish church of Manlieu. "Yes, Your Excellency, that is the monstrance belonging to my church," he declared.

The other witness was a manorial lord. The bishop asked him, "Do you know this man?"

"Yes, Your Excellency. He is one of my serfs who has run away."

The bishop then asked the accused, "How is it that the monstrance came into your possession?"

"I found it in a ditch by the side of the road, Your Excellency. I was just about to bring it to the church."

"So, you deny that you stole it?"

"Yes, I am innocent," the man pleaded. But he could offer no witnesses in his own defense.

The bishop gave him the option of confessing his guilt or facing trial by ordeal: he could choose to remove a large stone from a pot of boiling oil. If his hands were not injured, or were minimally injured, he would be found innocent. On the other hand, if his hands were scalded and blistered, he would be found guilty. The man confessed. The bishop condemned him to be hung from the gallows.

There was something about the case that bothered Gerbert. Back in the bishop's study, he discussed it with Bishop Atto. The bishop explained, "It was a very serious crime. In the first place, the item stolen was of very high value. Secondly, it was stolen from a church. It was a crime against the Church."

Gerbert understood the seriousness of the crime, but he was not convinced that the serf was guilty. "What on earth would a serf be able to do with a stolen monstrance? It would be of no use to him. He would not be able to sell it, since anyone would know that he could not have obtained a monstrance except by stealing it."

The bishop listened carefully to what Gerbert said. He was sitting in his wide, high-backed wooden chair behind an oversized desk positioned on an elevated platform. If there was an irony here, it was that the furnishings made the bishop's diminutive anatomy look even smaller. Gerbert was sitting on a stool on the opposite side of the desk, looking up at his mentor. He too was listening intently.

By way of explanation, Bishop Atto rationalized, "Listen, my son, harsh punishments publicly executed are the best deterrent to crime. Had the crime been petty—stealing a sack of flour from the mill, perhaps—a sentence of a few days in the stocks might have been a sufficient deterrent. The thief's family would have to come to feed him and bring him drink. It would have been humiliating for them as well, so even more of a deterrent."

"And if the accused had been a nobleman?" Gerbert asked, still with an expression of concern on his face.

"If the criminal were a person of means, a stiff fine could be substituted for corporal punishment. That, too, would be a deterrent—and would benefit the diocesan coffers as well."

With that, the bishop dropped the discussion of the trial and turned to the subject of Gerbert's education. The reports he had received from the abbot at Santa Maria confirmed all expectations of Gerbert's ability and desire to learn. There were two paths to a high position in the Church hierarchy: noble birth and exceptional intellectual ability. Bishop Atto knew that Gerbert did not meet the first criterion, but he firmly believed that the alternative was a real possibility. Without being overly laudatory of the young student's work, Bishop Atto said, "I know that you have been somewhat frustrated in your studies at Santa Maria. You have read many of the books in the library about mathematics and astronomy—or rather, more aptly, astrology. At the same time, our mutual friend Miro Bonfill has planted this idea in your mind that the best work in these fields is being done to the south of the Christian-Muslim March—in the city of Córdoba."

Lowering his head slightly and looking down at the floor, Gerbert said, "Yes, I admit that is so, Your Excellency."

Wrinkling his brow, as he had a habit of doing when he was in deep thought, the bishop said, "Well, Count Borrell visited just a few days ago. It appears that the relationship between the county of Barcelona and the caliphate in Córdoba has reached an impasse. He has asked me to accompany a delegation to confer with the caliph. I have reluctantly agreed to go. I have decided that you too should accompany that delegation."

What Gerbert had just heard was so far removed from anything he had ever thought possible that he remained silent with eyes and mouth wide open. Finally, he said, "Reverend Bishop, why were *you* reluctant to accept?" He could not understand why anyone would hesitate to go to Córdoba, the very epicenter of higher learning in the western world. Before the bishop could respond to that question, Gerbert blurted out, "Of course I will go," and then quickly added in a more subdued tone, "if that is your will, Your Excellency."

By then, the bishop was ready to respond to Gerbert's question. "A better question would be why the count is sending a delegation to begin with. The count feels that we—that is, the Christian counties immediately to the north of the Christian-Muslim border—will soon suffer a major defeat from Muslim invaders."

"What are the signs?" Gerbert asked.

"There have been confrontations in this march area of late, occasionally even violent ones. The previous caliph of Córdoba, Abd al-Rahman III, was ambitious. It was he who took the title 'caliph,' establishing a rival caliphate to the caliph in Baghdad. As a symbol of his regal ambitions, he built an enormous and beautifully decorated royal complex eight miles outside of the capital city. He also began an aggressive military campaign against the Christian states of Aragon and Castile."

"But not against Barcelona?"

"What saved Barcelona was a treaty signed by the previous caliph and Count Borrell's father, Count Sunyer. It was at a time when twelve Cordoban warships blockaded the harbor of Barcelona. That treaty, signed some thirty years ago, recognized the caliph's supremacy in exchange for peace and mutual support."

Gerbert cocked his head to one side and, looking quizzically, observed, "It seems that the Christians negotiated from a position of weakness."

"We did. Still, the treaty procured neutrality for us, at least officially. In the best of times, it provided much more: periodic manifestations of actual friendship, a window into the Islamic world, a position of a privileged intermediary between Christendom and Islam. And, not the least important, material benefits: trade, especially in cloth, priceless manuscripts, and, of course, gold."

"And now?" Gerbert leaned forward in his chair, intent on grasping every word the bishop spoke.

The bishop also leaned forward. "Right after Abd al-Rahman died, there was a Muslim raid. When the new caliph, the current one, was still trying to establish his authority over the realm, a band of Moorish renegades launched an attack against the towns and villages along the southern edge of Barcelona's territory. These raids were conducted by small bands of armed brigands. Their goal was not conquest. It was simply looting and plunder. That's why the border is not a fixed one. It moves forward and back like the tides of the sea."

Bishop Atto stood, walked to the window of his study, and looked out at the horizon to the south. He turned back to Gerbert. "Now, Count Borrell feels a bit…" He hesitated, searching for the word. "A bit *nervous* about our relationship with our Muslim neighbors. He has had to renew our treaty with Córdoba not once but twice—first almost twenty years ago, and then more recently only four years ago. Apparently, he feels that it is necessary for him to travel to Córdoba yet again to renew the treaty and guarantee our…'neutral' relationship." He stressed the word "neutral" with a touch of sarcasm.

"You speak as though you are not in full agreement with the count," said Gerbert.

Bishop Atto smiled. "Very observant of you. For the most part, I believe that our relationship has been peaceful—beneficial even, especially in matters of learning. My own vision of a delegation would not consider it to be a defensive mission on the part of a state facing defeat, but rather an extension of friendship to our neighbors, an offer of cooperation and exchange. That is where you come in, Brother Gerbert."

"Me?" Gerbert was dumbfounded. "What would I have to contribute, Reverend Bishop?"

"Your open and brilliant mind, Brother Gerbert. Who knows how far you can take the knowledge Córdoba has to offer to a higher level."

Before they parted, Gerbert had one more question. "Reverend Bishop?"

"Yes, my son?"

"I understand the importance of appearances before the court, but…do you really believe the serf stole the monstrance from the church?"

There was a long pause before the bishop answered. "What would you have done, young man?"

"I would have discreetly let him go—and let God be the judge."

"Hmm…and let God be the judge." The slightest of smiles appeared on the bishop's face. He was pleased. "Be ready to leave in a few days, Brother Gerbert."

CHAPTER EIGHTEEN

Count Borrell's delegation left Barcelona three days after Christmas. Leaving his wife, Letgarda, at home to manage his estates, the count was accompanied by his personal chamberlain, Bishop Atto, and a bright but humble monk, Gerbert d'Aurillac. The cortège was guarded by a small troop of twelve soldiers. Signs predicted a mild winter, so the count hoped that it would not be too cold. Clearly, he felt that the matter of affirming his relationship with the caliph was pressing. The party pushed on steadily, stopping only to sleep and eat. The count estimated that it would take a month of travel before the delegation would arrive at its destination.

A couple of days before predicted, the delegation reached Córdoba. They reached a fork in the road just north of the city. Much to Gerbert's surprise, and somewhat to his dismay, the party rode past the sign pointing south toward the city gate. It took the other road and circled around to the northwest. They stopped at a small hamlet called El Tablero. There, they freshened up for their reception at the court of the Umayyad caliph at his royal residence in Madinat'z-Zahra. They were met by a small welcoming party that included none other than Maslama al-Majriti, the very young man whom Gerbert's friend Miro Bonfill had described as one of the brightest men he had ever met.

Maslama had recently come to Córdoba to study astrology. He very quickly came to the attention of the caliph, who saw in the young man great promise as a scholar. Maslama had no official status among the caliph's bureaucratic personnel; yet, from time to time, he was asked to perform some task for the court. On this occasion, he was asked to greet Count Borrell's delegation, to escort them on the final leg of their long journey, and to assist them in getting settled.

It was as if fate had played right into Gerbert's destiny once again. It had not been announced that a brilliant young monk would be part of the Christian delegation. Gerbert had come simply on the whim of Bishop Atto, who instinctively hoped that an opportunity would open for Gerbert to feed his now insatiable hunger for advanced learning. Gerbert did not consider it fate. He believed that it was the grace of God.

An hour later, Count Borrell's delegation, escorted by Maslama and two officers of Caliph al-Hakam's royal guard, arrived at the entrance of Madinat'z-Zahra. Fifteen arches stretched out along the entrance portico on the east side of what was clearly more than simply a royal palace. The central arch was in the shape of a horseshoe, similar to the shape of the doors of the early Visigothic churches Gerbert had seen as he traveled in northern Spain. The horseshoe arch here was on a much grander scale. And it was flanked on each side by seven segmented arches only slightly lower in height. The rounded part of the arches was accentuated with alternating voussoirs of white stone and red brick, creating sort of a sunburst effect, fifteen sunbursts all in a row across the horizon.

The portico opened up to what amounted to a small city itself, a royal city where Caliph al-Hakam lived and worked, where he governed his kingdom insulated from the pressures of the hustle and bustle of densely urbanized Córdoba. Immediately in front of the party was a large rectangular-shaped garden, divided into four segments by two intersecting paved walking paths that crossed in the center. To the right of the garden were two structures. The smaller of the two was a guesthouse where special guests of the caliph could be housed. This was where Count Borrell and Bishop Atto would be lodged. They were taken there to prepare for their audience with the caliph. The larger building was the *dar al-jund*, the "House of the Army," where the caliph's royal guard was housed. Borrell's soldiers would be quartered there. The caliph's staff had not been apprised that Gerbert, an ordinary monk, would accompany the delegation; lodging for him had not been assigned. Speaking in Latin, the written language of the western Christian world, Maslama said, "You can freshen up in the *dar al-jund*. After I escort your lord bishop and Count Borrell to the audience hall of the caliph, my duties are completed. I will be returning to Córdoba. Since you were not announced in advance, you will not attend the audience with the caliph. You can come with me and stay with me in my home. It is very modest, but I do have an extra cot where you can sleep."

Gerbert was pleased to be shown this kindness. "If my bishop gives me leave, I will be honored and most happy to go with you."

"Freshen up. Then I will take you to the guesthouse to see your bishop."

Bishop Atto had changed from his riding clothes to something much more appropriate to meet the caliph: his long black woolen cassock, a purple biretta on his head, and a matching purple silk sash around his waist.

"Yes, my son, of course you can go on to Córdoba. That is the reason I brought you here. You will not be missing much here today. Our first session with Caliph al-Hakam will be brief, only introductory formalities. Real negotiations will begin tomorrow and may continue for several days." The bishop began to walk toward the door.

"Can you predict how the negotiations will go?" Gerbert asked with more than perfunctory curiosity.

The bishop turned toward Gerbert, shook his head slightly, and said, "I sincerely wish I could, but I cannot. I know that Count Borrell will be seeking my counsel as he enters these negotiations. I am not sure what advice I can give that will be helpful to him. Tell me, Brother Gerbert—how would *you* advise our lord the count?"

Gerbert looked up in disbelief. He could not imagine why his bishop, a brilliant scholar in his own right, would ask him, a humble monk. "With all due respect, Reverend Bishop, why do you ask *me* such a question?"

"Because you are intelligent; because I know that you have begun— albeit *just* begun—to gain some insight into Muslim culture, a culture most Christians see as so different from our own; because *you* do not think like a politician. Would you help me with my cloak, Gerbert?"

The young monk picked up the long fox-fur cape, stepped behind the bishop, and held it as the bishop took hold of it and fastened the silver clasp across his chest.

"You must not underestimate my interest in politics, Reverend Bishop." Gerbert was reluctant to contradict his bishop, but he continued anyway. "It is true that I have not yet had opportunities to be politically involved. Nonetheless, I feel very strongly that we must get along with our Muslim neighbors to the south if we hope to move forward in our understanding of *all* of God's children."

The bishop smiled in approval. "That is precisely why I am asking you,

Brother Gerbert."

"I am both flattered and humbled by the confidence you place in me, Reverend Bishop. This is what I would say to Count Borrell. He must remain firm in his commitment to reach agreement with the Umayyad caliphate without compromising the security of his own domain of Catalonia. At the same time, he must in every way be respectful and maintain an air of humility."

"Hmm. Humility." That was a term the bishop rarely associated with negotiation.

Gerbert quickly picked up on the bishop's quizzical reaction. "By 'humility,' I mean the opposite of arrogance. If the negotiation is to succeed, neither side can assume a posture of superiority over the other. They must come to the table as equals."

Just then, two horse-drawn carriages stopped in front of the guesthouse. Count Borrell emerged from his quarters to join Bishop Atto, and the two were escorted to the first of the two carriages. The other carriage was for the bishop's secretary, for their guide Maslama, and, much to Gerbert's surprise, for him. Maslama had explained that Gerbert would not be attending the audience, but he could ride along as far as the Great Hall, where the audience would take place. Maslama, too, would not attend the audience. Gerbert and he would continue on to Córdoba, a little less than an hour's ride away.

When the carriages stopped in front of the Great Hall, Gerbert was again surprised when at the last minute he was invited to go in. He would be greeted by the caliph himself, if only for a brief moment, before he was excused to take leave with Maslama.

Upon entering the throne room, Gerbert was overcome with amazement. He had never seen anything quite so beautiful. He was struck by a balance between decorative ornamentation and simplicity. There was a central aisle flanked by an aisle on either side. Simple columns with capitals of carved, stylized floral designs separated the aisles. The columns supported horseshoe arches of alternating red brick and white stone voussoirs, similar to those of the portico through which they had entered the complex two hours earlier. The walls were decorated with marble panels, each with a stylized tree of life carved in relief. Gerbert could not help but look at each panel one by one as he noticed that each of the many renditions of the tree of life was unique. It was as if the artist was reproducing, albeit in a stylized way, the individuality of each tree in a natural forest of towering cedars. The scent of the cedarwood ceiling permeated the air.

The caliph was seated on a slightly raised platform at the far end of the central aisle. He motioned the visitors to approach. He greeted each one by name. Gerbert could hardly believe that the caliph of western Islam would acknowledge him, a lowly monk from the land of the Franks. After that brief but celebrated moment, the caliph dismissed both Gerbert and Maslama.

When the two emerged from the Great Hall, Maslama pointed to the southeast, toward Córdoba. It was an unusually clear, crisp day. It was actually possible to see, way off in the distance, smoke in the air emitted from the many hearths of Córdoba some five miles away. Standing there on the terrace overlooking the residences of the service attendants on the downslope of the hill, what stood out was the *jamaa*, the Friday Mosque. Gerbert was struck by the fact that both the settlement below and the royal complex on the upper level were set on a parallel orthogonal grid, on a north-south and east-west axis. Only the mosque was offset by at least twenty degrees. He could not help but ask Maslama why this was the case.

"As you may or may not know," Maslama said as he pointed toward the mosque, "when Muslims pray, they face the Great Mosque in Mecca. Imagine, when Muslims pray, five times a day, wherever they pray, they all face a common point on the face of the earth."

"That is truly amazing!" said Gerbert. "When Muslims are praying their midday prayer here, Muslims in…say…Jerusalem…are also praying, perhaps their evening prayer, but facing a common center." Gerbert paused, looking toward the sky, palms extended upward. "My God! The power of group prayer…" Another long pause. "Even if it is to Allah."

Maslama interjected, "Allah is just the Arabic name for God. He is my God—and yours too."

A slight, contented smile came over Gerbert's face. "That makes it even more powerful," he said. "I like that."

"I like it too." Maslama patted Gerbert on the back. "But back to your original question. The mihrab, or prayer niche, inside the mosque points toward Mecca—here in Córdoba, to the southeast. That is why the mosque is aligned differently than any other building in this entire complex. But in truth, this mosque is perhaps the only one in all of Andalusia that is oriented correctly. Most others are actually facing south, like the orthogonal plan of Madinat'z-Zahra."

Gerbert looked puzzled again. "Why is that?"

"I wish I knew," said Maslama. "What I can say is that it is not a mathematical or astronomical error. Muslim scholars are much too accomplished in both mathematics and astronomy to make a mistake on such a large scale."

Gerbert nodded in agreement. "I am well aware of the reputation of Muslim scholars in these sciences. I am bursting with impatience to learn from them."

"You are a student, then?"

"Yes, I suppose you could say that. I am a monk from the Abbey of Saint Gerauld in Aurillac. I spent several years there studying under the instruction of Brother Raymond." Gerbert raised both arms in the air, then let them drop, as if to admit his frustration. "I must have exhausted Brother Raymond's patience. Upon his suggestion, my abbot decided to send me to Catalonia to study with Bishop Atto."

"So you are the bright young student of Bishope Atto. Our mutual friend, Miro Bonfill, has told me about you."

At that, Gerbert's face turned red, but continued, "When the reverend bishop was asked to accompany this diplomatic mission, he decided to take me with him, thinking I could benefit from exposure to this great center of learning that is Córdoba."

The carriage circled around to the south side of the city. It crossed the Wadi al-Kabir over the bridge that led directly to the Grand Mosque. Córdoba! Gerbert stepped out from the carriage into the city that until now he had known by reputation only. His friend Miro Bonfill had told him wondrous things about this city of merchants and scholars, things that seemed too good to be true. His first reaction was everything he had imagined and so much more. It was the largest, most beautiful city he had ever seen.

Maslama, now serving as a tour guide, began to brag, "Córdoba is the largest city in all the world. Its population is said to be five hundred thousand strong. I am not convinced that there are quite so many, but it is perhaps the most populous city in the west."

Gerbert would later learn that Constantinople was larger still.

Maslama explained that one indication of the size of a city's population was the number of public baths. "Here in Córdoba, there are more than can even be counted."

Although Gerbert believed in the benefits of personal hygiene and bathed as often as was practical, he knew that bathing weekly, let alone daily, was not part of the culture he had left behind in Aurillac.

Maslama was every bit as excited as Gerbert. Here he was, a young scholar, having the opportunity and the privilege to host another young scholar with boundless zeal and an open mind, in so many ways like himself, yet from a world apart.

"Is it true that there are seventy public libraries here in Córdoba?" Gerbert asked his host.

"That number, too, is surely exaggerated," Maslama responded with a laugh. "I have heard that more than once. On the other hand, there are many private libraries, since many scholars have managed to procure a few books and manuscripts of their own. But the most important library in the city, beyond a doubt, is the library of Caliph al-Hakam. It is open to scholars and students at the University of Córdoba. It is housed in the Alcázar next to the Grand Mosque. The number of books that the caliph al-Hakam has managed to assemble is, I would guess, many thousands of volumes."

"I can hardly wait to see it."

"I will take you there tomorrow. But in the meantime, let us go to my home on the edge of the *Judería*, the Jewish quarter north of the Grand Mosque. We will have some supper and get to know one another."

Gerbert had not realized how hungry he was until he finished his second bowl of hot soup and some bread fresh from the bakery next to Maslama's house. They sat across the table face to face, probing each other's minds. Gerbert was anxious to know about this scholar who was so young but whose reputation far exceeded his years and who was working in the service of the caliph.

"Tell me, if you please, Maslama, what brought you to the court of al-Hakam?"

"I have been a stargazer for as long as I can remember—which, as you can see by my age, was not so long ago. I think my father grew impatient with me, and with his good wishes and the support of his financial fortune, he agreed to send me here to Córdoba."

Maslama paused long enough for Gerbert, who was listening intently to Maslama's every word, to say, "To study at the university?"

"Yes, I studied mathematics and astronomy with some of the best scholars found anywhere in the world who are specializing in these subjects. My interests and, praise be to God, natural aptitude for these subjects came to the attention of the caliph himself, who commissioned me to work on special projects. I am working on verifying and updating the tables of coordinates of both Ptolemy and al-Khwarizmi. Are these names that you know?"

"Yes, of course. Brother Raymond told me about Ptolemy, and I read a little about al-Khwarizmi when I was at the Monastery of Santa Maria. In fact, in the monastery library, I watched a monk copy a Latin translation of a manuscript that described some of al-Khwarizmi's work."

"Ahh…I know that book," Maslama was quick to interject. He scratched his head as if trying to pull out some details about the book. "It contains, among other things, a brief description of the astrolabe—a topic for another day."

He hadn't told anyone of the special project the caliph had assigned him to develop an astrolabe. His superiors did not want him to publicize his work. He was tempted to say more about this marvelous instrument but decided to let that wait until another time.

"It's getting late, my friend. We had better get some sleep. We have another big day ahead of us tomorrow if you want to see the Grand Mosque, the library, and begin to meet some of the scholars here."

Maslama led Gerbert to the other room in his modest two-room flat and pointed to a straw-filled mat on the floor. "You can sleep here. Take this warm blanket and pillow. I hope you will be comfortable enough." He patted Gerbert on the shoulder and said, "I'll see you in the morning."

It was several days before Gerbert returned to Madinat'z-Zahra to link up with Bishop Atto. He arrived with a very special favor to ask. Maslama had invited him to remain in Córdoba for an extended period of study.

"How will you support yourself, my son?"

Gerbert offered an answer that he was sure the bishop would have to accept. "God will provide, Your Excellency."

With Bishop Atto's permission and blessing, and with the promise of a very modest monthly stipend from his friend Miro Bonfill, Gerbert began what would turn out to be nearly a full year's stay in Córdoba.

Right at the start, he said to his new friend Maslama, "As long as I am here, I have to learn to speak and read the language of the land. I want to study Arabic." His demeanor betrayed a level of determination the likes of which Maslama had not seen before.

The Arab scholar could only say, "I will help you. From now on, we will speak only Arabic when we are together. For you it will be swim or sink. For me, it will be…amusing."

What surprised Maslama was how quickly the determined Frankish monk learned not only to understand and make himself understood in most situations but to read and write the beautiful language of the Quran.

The two young friends met at least weekly to discuss what Gerbert was reading, sometimes in the library but most often in Maslama's home, which had also become Gerbert's home.

Gerbert was overwhelmed by Maslama's generosity. He vowed to apply himself in his studies with every bit of energy he could muster. He would not disappoint his new teacher, who, surprisingly, was only slightly older than himself.

"A good place to begin your study of mathematics," Maslama said one day, "is al-Khwarizmi's *Zīj al-Sindhind*."

Obedient student that he was, Gerbert went to the library every day to read the book until he finished. He followed the Arabic word for word and relished both the mathematical content and the expression of the language. He quickly learned the Hindu numerals. At the same time, he loved the musical rhythm of this language that was so foreign to him at first but with which he was beginning to feel a little more at home.

Then came the day for his first test. Sitting at the table in Maslama's flat, the Muslim mathematician presented Gerbert with a multiplication problem. "Tell me, then, what is the quickest way to multiply 123 by 11?"

"Well, the quickest way is to do it on one's fingers, like this."

Gerbert flashed his fingers in various positions for several seconds and said, "The answer is 1,353." Back in Brother Raymond's class at the monastery in Aurillac, Gerbert had perfected the art of calculating on his fingers further and faster than anyone had ever seen. He confessed, "This system takes a lot of practice and a very good memory. Where I am from, mathematicians would solve it using Roman numerals. They would write…"

Using a slate and white chalk, Gerbert began calculating, from left to right, a lengthy series of Roman numerals. "As you can see, this is quite clumsy," he said. "Al-Khwarizmi has made it much simpler for us with his numbers. Now we can simply write…" He penned the Hindu numerals and multiplied them in a simple calculation.

"Bravo!" Maslama exclaimed as he patted Gerbert on the back. "Now that you can manage the numbers, we can begin to talk about al-Khwarizmi's *Kitab al-Mukhtasar fi Hisab al-Jabr*." Excitement and enthusiasm was all over his face. "Today, we are going to talk about algebra."

"I am ready, teacher."

"We'll start with simple equations. Think of two sides of a scale." He raised both hands and alternately lifted and lowered each one. "For the scale to be perfectly balanced, you need the same mass of items on each side of the scale."

"That seems obvious enough," said Gerbert. "I imagine that's why it's called an 'equation,' yes?

"Exactly." Maslama nodded in agreement. "If one adds or subtracts anything on one side of the equation, one must do the same on the other side, if the balance is to be maintained."

Gerbert did not seem particularly impressed. He closed his eyes, shook his head, raised both his hands, and then let them drop. "Why is this something to get excited over?"

"Well, let's see how this plays out in a real-life situation. You know that we pay six fulus per week in rent for this apartment. When you moved in, our landlord could have raised the rent. He didn't, but he could have. Typically, in this situation, a landlord would raise the rent by one fourth. Had that happened, what would our monthly payment be?"

Once again, Gerbert flashed his fingers on both hands and said, "Thirty fulus per month."

"Okay, Mister Know-It-All. But there are advantages to algebra over counting on your fingers. Let me illustrate its broader application. Let's do the math to solve the problem that I presented. We multiply the amount of our rent by one fourth; then we add that to what we are paying. Using the Hindu numerals, we would write that this way."

Maslama wrote on the slate: $6 + (6 * .25) = 7.5$. "Now, I will multiply the seven and one half per week by four weeks." He wrote: $7.5 * 4 = 30$. "We could write the entire equation this way." He wrote: $(6 * 1.25) * 4 = 30$.

"Now, here is where it starts to get interesting. Suppose our landlord gets really greedy and decides to raise our rent every few months, but by different amounts. Can we write a formula that can account for any such situation?"

"I'll wager you are about to show me how."

"And you guess correctly. Look. Our Hindu numerals are symbols for a specific value. What if we use letters to represent a category rather than a specific value? Let's say that the letter *alif* stands for what we pay in rent per week, whatever that amount might be. *Ba* stands for the percentage of increase. And *dal* stands for what we will pay each month after a rent hike. We would write this out as follows." He wrote: $(a * 1.b) * 4 = d$.

"Hmm. This works for any situation our landlord might impose?" Gerbert sat staring at the slate for several seconds. His mind was working. Then it came to him in a flash. "These letters could serve as symbols for *anything* quantifiable: for trade items, prices, price discounts. And not just for economics, but also for agriculture, for politics, for—"

"For anything!" Maslama quickly interjected. "If we step away from the specific application that we have assigned to the formula, it becomes a quantifiable abstraction. It's like—"

"A language of its own." Gerbert completed Maslama's thought. "A language that transcends your Arabic and my *langue d'oc*."

"Yes, a universal language that is understood by all who know algebra, regardless of what language they speak."

Over the next several weeks, Gerbert's mind kept coming back to the astrolabe. Finally, one day, he said to Maslama, "The first day I came to your home, you started to say something about the astrolabe. But then you brushed it aside, saying we would come back to it someday. Could that someday be today?"

"In all honesty, my friend, I have been just as anxious as you to talk about it. The astrolabe has been my special project since I entered the service of the caliph."

"Please, Maslama, tell me all about it."

"Well, we know that astrolabes have existed since the time of the ancient Greeks. During their golden age, astronomers envisioned the earth as a ball inside a much larger ball that is the cosmos. On the inside surface of that larger ball are arranged all of the stars and planets that can be seen from the earth." As he said this, Maslama extended both arms upward as far as he could, and with his palms and fingers fully extended, he spread his arms farther apart to emphasize the vastness of the sky overhead. He paused to let the magnitude penetrate the attentive mind of his guest.

Then he continued, "There is a tale that is told of Ptolemy having created a celestial orb—that is, that ball representing the dome of the sky on which he pictured the pattern of the stars and planets as he could see them. One day, he was riding on his donkey, carrying his celestial orb. He dropped the orb, and before he could retrieve it, the donkey trampled it with his hoof. The pattern of stars and planets was no longer an orb but rather a flat, two-dimensional map of the cosmos as we know it—the very first astrolabe. Ptolemy must have used one to verify the coordinates in his tables. Al-Khwarizmi, too, must have used the astrolabe."

"Miro Bonfill told me that there is an astrolabe here at the university. Have you seen it?"

"Of course. What Miro referred to is a very simple planispheric astrolabe. It was made about forty years ago; we know not where. But a man's name, 'Nastulus,' is written in fine Kufic letters on the back of the base."

"Will I get a chance to see it?" Gerbert asked impatiently.

"I might be able to show it to you when we go to the library…but…in the meantime…" He raised his right hand, index figure extended, and injected a tone of mystery into his voice. "Right now…I can show you the one I have made myself." He walked over to the trunk on the far side of the room. He opened it and proudly took out a flat, circular object made of wood. It looked like a pancake. "Most astrolabes are made of brass. But for my own purposes, wood is more accessible and easier to work with.

He proceeded to explain how it was made and how it worked. He began by disassembling his instrument to better describe each component. "As I begin, I must beg your indulgence for summarizing a lot of information."

Don't worry, Maslama," Gerbert said. "I have been waiting with utmost patience for this moment."

Maslama said, "The base of the astrolabe is called the *mater*, which means 'mother.' The rim around the *mater*'s edge is called the limb. Around the limb is a scale measuring the twenty-four hours in the day. The circular plate inside the rim, actually inside the mother's womb, has a series of curved intersecting lines that form a sort of web. These are the celestial coordinates of latitude and longitude. Most astrolabes have a series of these plates, each one to represent the specific latitude where the instrument is likely to be used. Lines of latitude run parallel to the equator at the center of the earth, and lines of longitude run parallel to each other from the north pole to the south pole. The celestial sphere has similar lines that we call altitude and azimuth, but let's not confuse matters with that right now."

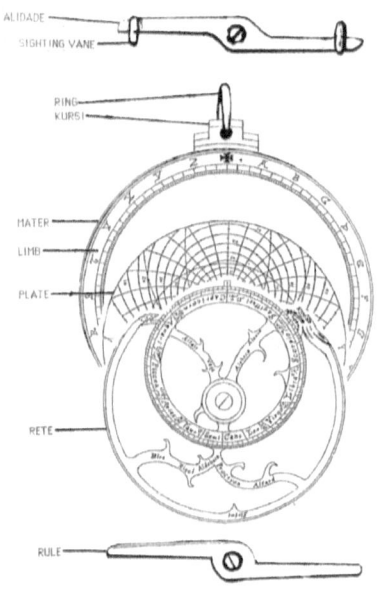

"Thanks for that, Maslama. Now, what about this other disc?"

"You mean this one that is mostly cut away and has these sharp points? You can almost envision it to look like your savior's crown of thorns."

At this comment, Gerbert wondered if Maslama was being somewhat sarcastic. "You know about Jesus's crown of thorns?" he asked sharply.

"Not really. Only enough to imagine. I meant no disrespect. The disc is called a *rete*. Each of those points represents one of the principal stars in the sky."

"And that off-centered circle?"

"That is a zodiac calendar. Before we learn how to use that, let's look at the back side of the instrument." He turned the *mater* over. "Here we see two adjacent scales that we use to convert our *hijra* calendar to the zodiac calendar. The scale on the outside edge marks the degrees through 90 in each of the four quadrants, completing the circle of 360 degrees."

Gerbert remembered Brother Raymond talking about constellations, the zodiac calendar, and 360 degrees around a circle. He was comfortable with all of that, but…"How did the makers of the first astrolabes know where to place the stars we see on the *rete?*"

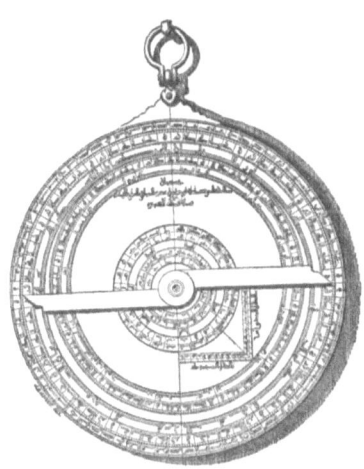

"Excellent question, my friend. By a mathematical technique called stereographic projection. That means the mapping of the points, in this case the stars, of the celestial sphere onto the equator-plane by joining each by a line to the south pole and taking the intersection of this line and the equator-plane as the image."

Maslama could tell by the look on Gerbert's face that this was not registering on the young mind of the monk sitting across the table from him. It was a very difficult concept to explain. He looked around the room, searching not for an object but rather a way to describe this rather technical process. And there it was right before his eyes, the two bowls he and Gerbert used daily to eat their supper. He placed one bowl on the table in front of Gerbert. He then fetched a serving plate and placed it on top of the bowl. Finally, he placed the other bowl upside down on top of the plate.

"Imagine that these bowls are the celestial sphere. The plate is the equator that passes through the center. We can only map one half of the orb at a time, so we'll do the top half."

With his left hand, Maslama opened his imaginary celestial sphere. With the index finger of his right hand, he traced a line from the center of the lower bowl, passing through the plate, to a spot on the inside of the upper bowl. "That's how we know where to mark the star onto the flat disk in the middle of the sphere. We would do that for each of the

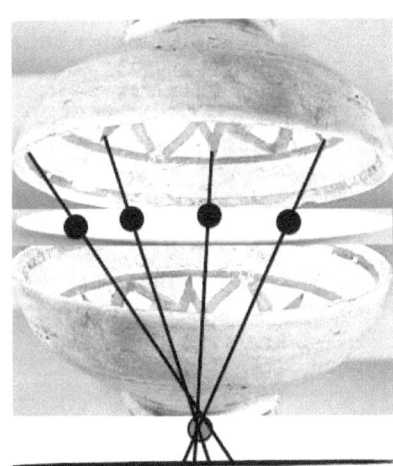

stars we want to map."

Maslama pursed his lips and shook his head. He could tell that Gerbert still didn't quite get it. "You have a question. I can tell."

"I can see how it works here on the bowls, but I don't understand how it works on the grand scale of the universe."

"Let's go up to the roof. I'll show you. We'll take the astrolabe." Maslama proceeded to put it back together.

The two men went to the roof. It was a perfectly clear night, and the sky was filled with thousands of stars. "Do you recognize any of them?" Maslama asked.

It had been a long time since Gerbert had contemplated the stars—not since he was at the monastery in Aurillac. He remembered standing under the starry sky as Brother Raymond pointed out some of the constellations. His mentor had also told him a story from Genesis, the one where God invited Abraham to gaze at the stars above, too numerous to count, and promised that his offspring would be just as numerous.

"They are not exactly in the same place," Gerbert admitted. "But, yes, I do recognize the brightest ones."

"Excellent! Go ahead and pick one."

Gerbert gazed across the sky and then pointed to a bright star he recognized. "How about that one? I think it is called Prokyon."

"Yes, it is. Now we have to measure its altitude with the *alidade* on the back side of our instrument." Maslama raised it to his eye level and adjusted the *alidade* until it pointed at the star. "Now, you do it." He handed the astrolabe to Gerbert.

Almost giddy with excitement, Gerbert raised the astrolabe and adjusted it.

"Now look at the number indicated on the rim by the *alidade*."

"Thirty-five degrees," Gerbert said.

"From here, it's a matter of mathematics. We have to maintain that angle through a series of calculations in what we call spherical trigonometry. We have to do the same with the arcs of latitude and longitude. Remember that we must portray a three-dimensional sphere onto a single flat surface."

Gerbert was intrigued. *A single flat plane that reflects three dimensions*, he thought. For a brief moment, his mind drifted elsewhere.

Maslama brought him back to the subject at hand. "I'm afraid I cannot teach you trigonometry in the next few minutes," he said apologetically. "Honestly, that will take you months to learn."

"Months! Surely not. I assure you, I will work at it very hard. I will do it in less time."

"If you are really serious about studying mathematics at the highest level…" Maslama walked to the edge of the roof, facing south, and looked out to the horizon. "You must go to Fez."

"Why Fez?" Gerbert asked.

"The Qarawayeen University in Fez is the oldest university in the world. It was founded well over a hundred years ago, just about the time that al-Khwarizmi was developing his mathematical theories. The scholars in Fez have devoted themselves not only to theology but also to mathematical sciences. If it is math that has captured your passion, then it is to Fez you must go."

Somewhat embarrassed, Gerbert had to ask, "And where exactly is Fez?"

Withholding his temptation to laugh, Maslama said, "I should not have assumed that you knew. It's across the straits of Jebel Tariq south of here, in the land known as Jazirat al-Maghrib, the 'Island of the West.'"

"I'll think about that. But in the meantime, I want to know more about the astrolabe. Miro told me that the astrolabe has many uses. Is that so?"

"It is. In fact, a Persian astronomer, Abd al-Rahman al-Sufi, wrote a treatise on the astrolabe in which he lists over one thousand uses in such wide-ranging fields as astronomy, astrology, horoscopes, navigation, surveying, timekeeping, and indicating the direction and time for prayer."

"Can you tell me what time it is right now with your astrolabe?"

"Yes, of course—more precisely than with any other instrument we have to tell time. First, we have to set the instrument to today's zodiac date. To do that, we measure the altitude of a particular star. We have already done that for Prokyon. What was it?"

Gerbert scratched his head. "Ah…thirty-five degrees."

"Good. Now turn the instrument over and rotate the *rete* until the point that represents Prokyon aligns with the curved line on the plate that represents the latitude of thirty-five degrees."

"Done."

"Fine. Now the instrument is set for today. Next, align the rule with Prokyon." He waited until Gerbert completed the task. "What time does the rule point to on the rim?"

"Just a little after nine hours past noon."

"There you have it. We can also tell what time the sun will rise tomorrow morning and what time it will set tomorrow evening—or any other day of the year, for that matter."

"Really?" Gerbert exclaimed.

"For that we have to know the zodiac date. Look on the back side. There's a conversion scale to convert today's date to the zodiac date." He reached toward the instrument in Gerbert's hand and pointed to the scale. "What does it say?"

"Ten Pices."

"Now, rotate the *rete* so that the mark for Ten Pices aligns with the horizon on the left side of the plate. The rule will point to the time of sunrise tomorrow."

Gerbert did exactly as Maslama instructed. "Seven hours before noon. Amazing!"

Maslama pointed to the upper half of the *rete* and plate. "Notice here above the horizon line, we have the coordinates of all the other stars on the *rete* that are visible to us tonight."

Gerbert looked down at the astrolabe, then gazed up at the sky. "Someday, I will have an astrolabe of my own." Then, in spite of himself, he yawned.

"You look so tired, my friend."

"Tired, yes, but overjoyed at what you have shown me tonight. I know it's getting chilly and the astrolabe has told us that it is after nine o'clock. But I have one more question—for tonight."

"And that is?"

"Can we tell how far away the stars are from us?"

"That we will probably never know. We can only know what we see from where we are." Maslama's thoughts veered off on a mystical trajectory. "At the same time, who knows who or what is out there looking down at us?"

Gerbert picked up on the shift in Maslama's thoughts and said, "God is out there looking down at us."

Before the end of the week, Gerbert was on his way to Fez.

PART IV

CHAPTER NINETEEN

One day gave way to the next, and before Hakeem realized it, nearly a decade had passed. In the summer of 968, Hakeem's mission was all but accomplished. He had circumnavigated the perimeter of the great Middle Sea and finally returned to Fez, where he had begun this project over nine years earlier. He was a bit heavier than a decade ago, and he had grown a beard that was now gray, as was the hair on top of his head.

Weary of travel, he found a room to rent in a house in the Qarawayeen section of Fez. The house was owned by one of the scholars at the university. There was nothing of note to distinguish it. It looked just as plain on the inside as it did on the outside. A small central courtyard had separate doors leading to four apartments, one on each of the courtyard's four sides. His was the smallest apartment of the four. He had decided to stay here for a while; how long, he had no idea. His intent was to produce a draft of his picture of the world, what his teacher al-Mas`udi called a "map."

Hakeem understood that Ptolemy's coordinates of latitude and longitude could form a template for the map, a web or a skeleton upon which he could put the flesh and bones of cities, rivers, and mountains. As to those details, he would rely on his own notes on time traveled from point to point and the direction he took, determined by the angle between his line of travel and fixed landmarks visible on the horizon. Then, he had the data he collected from travelers, hundreds of interviews and multiple descriptions of the same itinerary. When he found one or more that contradicted others, he would tweak his map, taking those discrepancies into account.

Hakeem unrolled two new parchment scrolls and glued them together to form one large template. He stretched it horizontally across his table and began to draw. Using a quill with a relatively broad tip, he inked a square just below the center of his parchment.

With a finer quill, he wrote the word "Mahdiya" to identify the square as the capital of the Fatimid realm. Using the width of his index finger as the

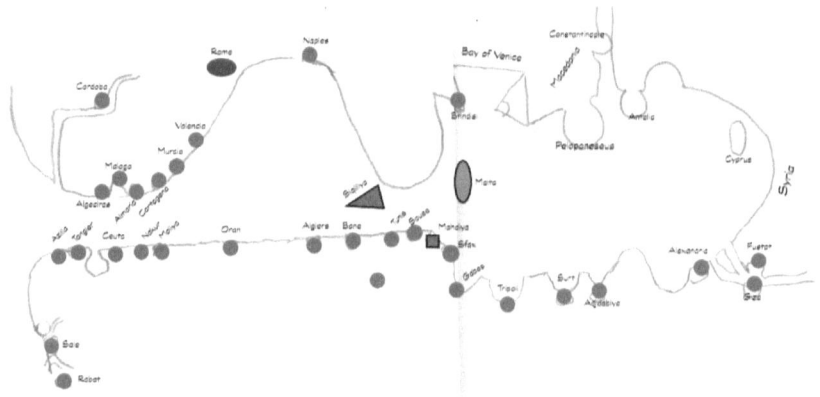

scale to equal the distance of a single day's travel, he then added each city listed in his narrative, approximating the direction he had traveled and the distance, as represented by his finger's-width scale. He realized that this would be, at best, a crude approximation of what his world would look like if he viewed it from the sky. But it would be a start.

Hakeem did most of his work at home. Back when he was at the House of Wisdom, he had spent hours upon hours alone with his books. As he remembered it, he relished that time being deeply ensconced in his studies. But from his last few weeks in Baghdad, through his journey to Egypt, Andalusia, deep into Black Africa, and all around the Middle Sea, his life had been nothing short of a whirlwind of action—and, too often it seemed, of intrigue. He was no longer used to sitting quietly without something to investigate or someone to interrogate.

Hakeem went to the Grand Mosque almost every day to pray, but he did not linger to converse with the sheikhs, as he had in Córdoba and Sijilmasa.

Perhaps four or five times a month, Hakeem walked to the Qarawayeen Library. It was only a few blocks from where he lived. He was not actively engaged in gathering intelligence anymore. Still, he enjoyed the interaction he had with the scholars he met there.

And then it came. By special messenger from the Fatimid caliph himself—a demand for the results of his reconnaissance of the Mediterranean world, along with his advice. He read the letter:

> We are prepared to make a military move to strengthen our mission as the one true caliph.

Hakeem fully endorsed this rather idealistic objective. In fact, that was why he agreed to work for the Fatimids to begin with. It was becoming clearer, though, that there was more to it than that. The caliph had other ambitions. Hakeem continued to read:

> We have considered two different scenarios. The first, to march west and confront, in a definitive way, the Umayyad pretender who rules from Córdoba. He has made significant inroads into North Africa and has apparently secured almost exclusive control of the gold routes across the desert.
>
> The second scenario is to send our armies east under the capable command of Jawhar, whom you have come to know. That would be a move against the Abbasid caliph in Baghdad.
>
> We cannot engage on both of these fronts. We must choose one plan or the other. God will surely guide us in the right direction. Still, we seek your opinion. Based on your extensive travels around the great sea and the careful observations you have made, what is your best advice?
>
> Of course, you must understand that this correspondence, as well as your response, must remain strictly confidential.
>
> As always, in God's service, I remain Commander of the Faithful.

Below the caliph's seal, written in his own hand, was the caliph's signature:

Abū Tamīm Ma'ad al-Mu'izz li-Dīn Allāh.

Hakeem answered without hesitation or delay, as he was instructed, using the same courier who brought the caliph's message to him. He wrote,

> Go east, my lord. Were you to go west, you would find that the
> Umayyads are well entrenched in the western half of the Middle Sea.
> But you must separate trade from politics. You can continue to reap
> the benefits of the gold trade without controlling the routes, as long
> as the routes are secure. It matters not so much who secures them.
> Merchants will trade with whomever offers a good exchange. Besides,
> the Umayyad caliph's only son and heir is but an infant. I predict that
> Umayyad power will begin to wane after al-Hakam's death.
>
> If you go east, on the other hand, you will be moving into a
> power vacuum, into an area where the true caliphate will prosper.
>
> Your loyal servant,
>
> Hakeem Ibn al-Harith

The next day, Hakeem slept late. He was confident that the message he sent to the caliph contained sound advice. At the same time, though, he was no longer convinced that the caliph's goal was an honorable one.

On this day, he was not inclined to work at home on his journal or his map. He went to the library instead.

The attendant at the entrance to the library greeted him warmly. "Good day to you, Sidi Hakeem." The library was not open to just anyone. One had to be an established scholar or a student approved by the ulama of the Grand Mosque. Hakeem did not come on a regular basis; yet he was well known and accepted as the outstanding alim that he was.

"And a good day to you as well, my friend." Hakeem shook the man's hand and touched his hand to his heart, as was the custom when one greeted a friend. He entered the reading room. Alone in the room, two men sat together at one of the long reading tables. Hakeem recognized one of them as his friend Mohammed. A younger version of Hakeem, Mohammed was a self-proclaimed traveler from Jerusalem. A generation separated Mohammed and Hakeem, yet they enjoyed each other's company immensely, as they had much in common, comparing notes on many of the same places they visited.

Hakeem did not recognize the other man, also quite young. There was something about him that made him look different. Hakeem relied heavily on first impressions in his line of work. From the start, he was suspicious of this stranger. The man was dressed like an Arab but did not look like an Arab.

Hakeem decided not to approach the two men. They were deeply ensconced in conversation, and Hakeem was content to eavesdrop.

Mohammed was explaining the basics of trigonometry. "The three primary functions of trig are *jaib*, *kotijaib*, and *utkramajaib* as they relate to the angles of a right triangle."

Apparently confused, the stranger interrupted, "What language are you speaking?"

"Those are the Indian terms for those functions. If you like, we could use terms more familiar to us. The most important thing is to memorize the formulas for each of those functions." Mohammed iterated the formulas as he wrote on a slate. "Sine equals opposite over hypotenuse. Cosine equals adjacent over hypotenuse. Tangent equals opposite over adjacent."

The student was quick to say, "I recognize those terms: opposite, adjacent, and, hypotenuse. They are the sides of a right triangle."

"Excellent!" exclaimed Mohammed. "If we know at least two of any of the angles or sides of a right triangle, using these trigonometric functions, we can determine the remaining angles and sides."

When Mohammed paused to reflect on his next step, Hakeem decided to interrupt. He walked over to the table where they were sitting.

Mohammed stood to greet his friend. "Good morning, Master Hakeem."

Hakeem shook Mohammed's hand and again touched his hand to his heart. "And a good morning to you as well, my dear friend. And whom may I have the pleasure to meet?" He looked at the other young man.

"This is Gerbert d'Aurillac," said Mohammed. "He has come to us by way of Córdoba."

Hakeem did not wait for Mohammed to introduce him. "I am Hakeem Ibn al-Harith." He added, "Aurillac. That is in the land of the Franks, is it not?" There was a condescending tone in his voice.

"It is indeed," answered Gerbert with some pride, perhaps sensing Hakeem's haughtiness. "I'm surprised you have heard of it."

"I haven't," Hakeem replied rather abruptly. "I guessed that it was in the land of the Franks only by the sound of its name."

"It is several days ride due north of the port city of Narbonne."

Hakeem had been all around the western Mediterranean. He knew the city of Narbonne quite well, but he had not been inland anywhere in the land of the Franks, which had somewhat of a reputation of being barely civilized. He prided himself on being a fine judge of character, even at first sight of someone. His profession demanded as much. But as he scrutinized the young man from head to foot, he found that Gerbert did not fit any of the types that he was familiar with. His clothes were neat but quite plain; the young man was certainly not a person of means. His Arabic was poor at best. He was clearly not a Muslim, yet here he was in what was becoming the premier university in western Islam.

Hakeem took a step closer to Gerbert and extended his hand. Gerbert stood up and likewise extended his hand to accept the greeting. And then, in a movement that took Hakeem by surprise, the young monk touched his hand to his heart.

That was when Hakeem noticed it—a leather thong around Gerbert's neck supporting an object under his robe. The object could not be anything but a cross.

"You are a Christian," Hakeem declared.

Gerbert took the object out and let it hang openly on his chest. "Yes. Not only am I a Christian, I am a monk of the order of Benedict of Nursia. I am not ashamed of who or what I am. The cross is a part of our monastic habit that I decided to keep—if only discreetly."

"Don't worry, my friend. I doubt that most people would notice. For me, it's part of my job to notice things that others don't." Hakeem said this jokingly, even though it was the truth. He added, "Christians are tolerated here in Fez, just as they are in Córdoba."

"I know tolerance, and I am thankful for it," said Gerbert. "But is that good enough? Is tolerance the same as acceptance?"

Hakeem appreciated the young man's directness. "I can't speak for all of Islam," he replied. "I can only speak for myself. I try to assess each individual not by his religion or where he was born, but rather by his character. So, whether or not I accept you remains to be seen." Hakeem sat and motioned to the other two men to do the same. "But, frankly, if you are a friend of Mohammed's, I expect we will get along just fine. A piece of friendly advice, though: I would put the cross back under my robe if I were you. As you said, tolerance is not exactly acceptance, and discretion is a good thing." Hakeem then fell into his role as an interrogator. "May I ask, what brought you to Fez?"

Gerbert answered with a single word: "Mathematics."

Mohammed quickly interceded on Gerbert's behalf. "He is an amazing mathematician, advanced well beyond his years. He says he has come here to learn, but he is also teaching us a great deal."

Hakeem nodded and softened his tone a bit. "Then I guess you know that in our world we use Hindu symbols to represent numbers, making calculations much easier."

"Yes. I learned about them as I read the work of al-Khwarizmi in Córdoba. I even learned about algebra."

"And of course you must know that al-Khwarizmi introduced the various functions of trigonometry."

"Trigonometry—derived from *trigonon*, the Greek word for triangle, the science of triangles."

"Young Gerbert, I am impressed!" Hakeem's tone was no longer condescending. Quite the opposite. He nodded his head in approval. It seemed that as soon as he began to explain something, this precocious young man had already grasped what he was about to say next.

Gerbert continued, "I must confess, Master Hakeem, I am just beginning to learn the basics of trigonometry. That is why I am here."

"May I know why that is so important to you?" Hakeem asked.

"Of course, Master Hakeem." Gerbert, it seemed, was excited about what he had learned in Córdoba and was more than anxious to talk about it. "When I was in Córdoba, I met a remarkable young man named Maslama, barely older than myself, who introduced me to the marvelous instrument called an astrolabe. He even showed me how it worked and let me try it with my own hands. That was not so difficult. It's when he tried to explain to me the process of drawing a spherical celestial globe, that mystical dome that forms the sky, onto a flat surface that he completely lost me."

"Ahhh!" Hakeem drew out a sigh. "That age-old problem among mapmakers—to draw a three-dimensional object such as a ball onto a single flat piece of paper or parchment. I have been struggling with exactly that same problem, only on a different scale. I am trying to draw a picture of our very own earth onto a flat surface. You are hoping to draw the sky, while I am trying to map the lay of the land right here on earth. Same problem, different target."

"Maslama said that it involved measuring certain angles and curves using the astrolabe, then reproducing those same angles and curves on a much smaller scale through a branch of mathematics called spherical trigonometry."

Hakeem, who felt his initial haughtiness slipping away, lowered his head a bit. "I must confess that I have not been able to master this advanced level of trigonometry." Feeling a desire to rationalize this deficiency, he added, "My work drew me away from my formal studies earlier than I would have liked." Of course, he did not go on to say what his real line of work was. "I further confess that I have done very little of this in my own attempts to draw my map."

"How did you do it, then—draw your map?"

"I started with a template derived from Ptolemy's coordinates of latitude and longitude, later corrected by al-Khwarizmi," Hakeem said. "I then drew a rough draft based on the template, relying on the extensive notes I made on my journey around the entire Mediterranean, making minor adjustments based on how long it took me to travel from one particular point to another and the direction of the line of travel. I make further adjustments as I compare my own traveling experiences to those of professional travelers—merchants, mariners, and the like—who carefully recorded their itineraries."

"I would love to hear more about your travels, sir," said Gerbert eagerly.

As Hakeem would discover, Gerbert was content to listen to him talk all day about his travels. In less than two years, Gerbert had journeyed from southern France to North Africa. As he later admitted to Hakeem, at first thought, it had seemed to him that he had traversed half the world; but listening to this man sitting across the table from him made him realize that he still had so much to see, so much to learn.

"When I have time," said Hakeem, "I would be more than happy to spend some time with you."

There was something about the lad that Hakeem really liked. Perhaps it was his almost insatiable desire to learn, or perhaps his complete openness and honesty. *This is someone I should get to know better*, he thought. *Not because of my work as an intelligence agent but because I think he can somehow enlighten me as a person.*

At that moment, a library attendant entered the room and handed Hakeem a leather-bound manuscript.

Hakeem accepted the manuscript and thanked the attendant. He then turned back to Gerbert. "I will let you know. I will get word to you through my friend Mohammed here."

With that, Hakeem found a place at the opposite end of the room and sat down to work.

Over the next several days, Gerbert racked his brain trying to apply what he knew of trigonometry to solving his problem of drawing the stars in the correct place on a flat surface. *This is not going to be easy*, he thought. *Clearly, I do not understand this right now. I'm just going to have to be patient and work my way through it.*

Sitting in the reading room of the library, recalling Maslama's demonstration with the two bowls and the plate, he envisioned himself standing in the center of the plate that represented the sphere's equator. As he imagined looking into the upper bowl—the upper half of the terrestial sphere—a process began to form in his mind.

Okay. I imagine that I am standing on the equator. He actually stood up at his place and closed his eyes.

There are two dimensions of this plate, left to right and front to back. The third dimension of the sphere is—how shall I define it?—up and down? Yes, that's it—an axis from the center of the lower bowl to the center of the upper bowl.

Now, from where I stand, I'll measure the angle formed by my line of sight to the star I'm trying to plot and the equator. He remembered doing exactly that when Maslama was showing him how to use the astrolabe.

Next, I draw a line perpendicular from the star to the point of intersection with the equator. Finally, I draw another line from where I stand to the point of intersection, closing the right triangle. My line of sight to the star becomes the hypotenuse for the triangle. I see that the hypotenuse is equal to the radius of the sphere.

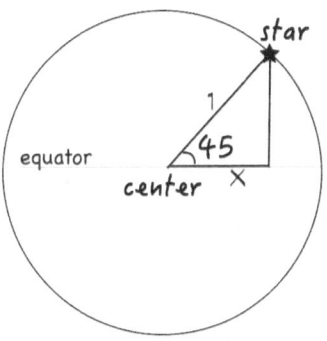

Of course, I don't know the distance to the star, so I will simply define that as one. What I need to learn is the distance between the point of intersection and my position in the center of the plate.

Aha! This is where I can use the functions of trigonometry that Mohammed taught me. Let's see now…there are two elements that I know: the angle that I measured at forty-five degrees and the length of the hypotenuse, which I defined as one. The element that I want to learn is the length of the adjacent line. I'll call it x.

Hmmm. I can use the formula cosine equals the adjacent side divided by the hypotenuse. Using the table of sines, cosines, and tangents that Mohammed gave me, from here it is simple algebra.

After doing the math, he knew that the length of the adjacent line was just over seven-tenths the length of the radius of the sphere.

But wait. I am only taking into account two dimensions. How can I measure the third?

Hmmm…Don't give up, Gerbert. Keep working on it. Slow down and think this through one step at a time. You'll figure it out.

Gerbert struggled with this issue for several minutes. Then it came to him.

First, I have to identify where north is by virtue of identifying the North Star. Then I will turn my instrument away from my first measurement and establish a line of sight from where I stand to the North Star. I will then measure the number of degrees I have turned my instrument. If I were actually doing this with an instrument on the ground, I would probably put it on a pole to hold it steady as I rotated it from one sighting to the next, making it easier to measure the number of degrees that I turned.

As these thoughts raced through his head, he actually stood, and, holding his right hand in front of him, he pivoted his entire body, imitating a wind vane.

At that moment, Hakeem happened to walk into the room. "What on earth are you doing?" he asked.

"I'm not exactly sure," Gerbert answered. "I'm trying to figure out how to draw a picture of the layout of the stars and the planets as we see them up in the sky. What we were talking about the other day—projecting three dimensions onto a flat plane."

"Ah, yes. You were telling me about that young man in Córdoba... Maslama?"

"Maslama al-Majriti."

"Yes, that's it," Hakeem said. "You were telling me what he was saying about stereographic projection. You realize, of course, that no matter how exact your measurements are, there will be some distortion in your image as you go from three dimensions to a flat surface. You just have to take that into account and live with it." He gestured for Gerbert to join him at the table.

"It seemed so straightforward when Maslama placed a soup bowl upside down on top of another one with a flat plate between the two." Gerbert made an attempt at mimicking Maslama's model, forming a large ball with his two hands extended up, then narrowing the shape with his two closed fists, one on top of the other at waist level.

At that point, Gerbert fondly remembered the thought that had flashed through his mind back in Córdoba—the thought of shifting from three dimensions to one, and the reverse, from one to three. He also remembered his lapse into a more spiritual realm of thought. "Explaining that," he said, "was about as *clear* as trying to explain the Christian mystery of the Holy Trinity."

Hakeem was not averse to this change in subject. "You use the term 'mystery' to describe your three gods in one," he said. "That's exactly why we Muslims cannot accept the idea of the Trinity. God should not be a mystery. Three in one is completely illogical. You are a mathematician. You should know as well as anyone that one plus one plus one equals three—not one. The very thought of Father, Son, and Holy Spirit as God is nothing short of tri-theism."

Gerbert had never thought of it quite that way. But his brilliant mathematical mind was quick to come back with, "Yes, but one times one times one equals what?" Even before Hakeem could answer, Gerbert said emphatically, "One!" Then he added with maybe just a touch of sarcasm, "Maybe it's like stereographic projection. When you go from three to one, there is a bit of...distortion. We just have to take that into account and—what was it you said?—and 'just live with it.'"

"Hmmm," said Hakeem, shrugging his shoulders. He had no response to that other than to assert categorically, "Monotheism in Islam is absolute."

"As it is in Christianity," Gerbert said. "Christians are emphatic in believing that God is *One*—tri-*unity* rather than tri-theism. But our God manifests himself in at least three different ways. Perhaps it would be better to replace the term 'Trinity' with 'Tri-unity.'"

Hakeem chewed on the thumb of his left hand for just a moment, then commented, "Our God manifests Himself in different ways as well. We have a different name for each manifestation—ninety-nine of them, in fact. The name 'Allah' that you might translate as 'God' contains the meaning of all ninety-nine names. But we would not consider these names as separate persons."

"Maybe 'persons' is not the best word to use. Clearly the Father, Son, and Holy Spirit are not persons in the same sense that you and I are."

Neither the senior scholar nor the apprentice had ever argued this point before. Each, within his own community, had never had to. The oneness of God was never contested within Islam. The relationship among the three 'persons' of God in Christianity, on the other hand, was so hotly debated in some of the Church councils that it threatened the unity of Christianity itself. That threat was only somewhat abated at a council of bishops in Nicaea. Gerbert knew something of the history of that struggle, but he had never experienced the impact of it himself. The doctrine of the Trinity was never questioned in Gerbert's own education in the monasteries of Saint Gerauld or Santa Maria.

Gerbert then changed the direction of the conversation. "When you say 'our God,' do you mean the God of Muslims—or the God of us all?"

"The Quran identifies 'our God' as the God of Abraham, Ishmael, Isaac, and Jacob."

"Interesting," said Gerbert. "So is ours. So they are the same."

Here in the great Qarawayeen Library in Fez, neither Hakeem nor Gerbert found himself the least bit inclined to alter his own understanding or feeling about the concept of three...*whatevers*...in one God. The discussion did cause each of them to pause and think about it—at least for this briefest of moments. But they were inclined to accept that they worshiped the same God.

As soon as the library attendant brought Hakeem the manuscript he had requested, the "mapmaker"—as Hakeem was beginning to be called by the learned community in Fez—was ready to get on with his own work. Gerbert, for his part, scratched his head and continued searching in his mind's eye for how he could map the sky.

Before they were both completely lost in their own work, Gerbert looked up at Hakeem sitting across the table and reminded him, "You said you would tell me more about your travels around the world."

"Yes, I did," Hakeem said, sounding just a bit annoyed at the interruption. "I did, and I will. But not today. Let's have dinner together sometime soon, and we can talk about the world."

CHAPTER TWENTY

Within just a few days, Hakeem sent a message to Gerbert, written in Arabic. It was as much a test of the young monk's knowledge of the local language as it was a genuine invitation to have dinner at Hakeem's home.

Gerbert read the note with only a little difficulty.

> Let us break bread together at my home on the morrow. We should meet at the mosque after evening prayer, and we will purchase our dinner at one of the vendors en route to my house. It was signed, The Mapmaker.

Gerbert was so excited that he completely forgot about stereographic projection for a while and started to make a list of questions to ask this man who, as far as he knew, had traveled to the ends of the earth.

The two of them, the "mapmaker" and the "monk"—as Hakeem now referred to his new young friend—walked the few blocks from the mosque to Hakeem's home. The aroma of roasting meat drew them to the stall of the *harraas* to purchase some *harissa*, ground meat on a skewer, cooked to perfection over hot coals. Hakeem purchased ten skewers. "Five for each of us," he said to the monk.

Gerbert was not used to eating much meat. All the more reason that his digestive system was already starting to anticipate a wonderful feast.

Next, they picked up some roasted vegetables: onions and aubergines, also cooked over coals, still crisp but just beginning to turn brown. Finally, Hakeem directed them to his favorite baker, where he picked up two large rounds of piping-hot bread as they were taken out of the oven.

Once settled in Hakeem's flat, the host placed the rounds of bread on the table to serve as trenchers for the meat and vegetables and poured two mugs of slightly fermented cider. He then motioned Gerbert to sit and eat—and to talk.

There was so much that Gerbert wanted to ask, he didn't know quite where to start. "Tell me, Master Hakeem, in your travels around the great Middle Sea, what was the most exciting place you saw?"

Hakeem had been asked this question many times before. He had a pat answer. "You know, Monk, that's like asking a father of many children, which one is his favorite."

Gerbert could somewhat relate to that. Thinking back to his childhood, he knew that his father had loved him as much as his older brother, maybe even more. But he loved the two of them in different ways.

"Okay then, the most...*unusual*."

Hakeem paused for a few moments, which seemed like such a long time to Gerbert, who put the last piece of his trencher in his mouth, washed it down with a draft of cider, and waited impatiently for an answer.

Finally, Hakeem said, "Constantinople."

After they finished eating and cleared the table, Hakeem took the rough draft of his map from the chest in the corner of the room and rolled it out on the table. This was the first time he had shown the map to anyone. He pointed to a spot near the top right-hand corner.

"Right here, do you see this peninsula that juts out into the sea at the mouth of the river? That is Constantinople. Not only is it the capital of the Roman empire just to the east of that..." Hakeem slowed his speech to emphasize the rest of his sentence, "but it is the border between your world and mine."

"Believe it or not," Gerbert said, "in my limited knowledge of the world, I have heard about Constantinople. I heard Bishop Atto talking about it one day with his council of advisors."

"Really?"

"He was describing how Pope John—you know that the pope is the head of our church?"

Hakeem nodded.

Gerbert continued, "How the pope sent a letter to the emperor Nicephoras, trying to arrange a marriage between a Byzantine princess and the son of *our* emperor of the Romans."

Hakeem, shaking his head in disagreement, said, "Listen, Monk, I was actually in Constantinople when the pope's delegation arrived. The letter that you mention was hand delivered by Bishop—what was his name?—Bishop Liutprand, I believe. As I recall, the bishop insulted Emperor Nicephorus by addressing him as Emperor of the Greeks. He further insulted the emperor, calling him a monstrosity of a man, a fat-headed, foul-smelling pygmy. Not only did the bishop request the hand of the princess in marriage, he demanded, as the price of the dowry, the rich territories of Longobardia and Calabria in southern Italy. The emperor rejected that demand, of course."

"And the marriage?"

"As you can guess, the emperor rejected that as well."

"How do you know all this? These were high-level negotiations behind closed doors, were they not?"

"Of course they were. But it was the talk of the town. As we went about our daily business, we would catch glimpses of the delegation's cortège passing through the main roadways. Apparently, there was animosity between the emperor and the pope's envoy even before the delegation arrived in Constantinople. They were housed in the Blachernae Palace in the northwest corner of the city, barely inside the city walls. They had to travel some thirty minutes from their lodging to the Great Palace.

"Daily we watched the cortège make its way along the Mese, the main ceremonial road of the city. A detachment of soldiers cleared the way in advance. Spectators lined the pavement. Others watched from the balconies and windows above, hoping to catch a glimpse of the pope's special envoy.

"Shortly before they reached the Great Palace, they entered into the stately Forum of Constantine." Hakeem made a grand gesture, holding both arms out and spreading them wide. "That was a large open space surrounded by a peristyle of white marble columns. It was here that the pope's delegation was met by members of the imperial family adorned in their richest finery. Embroidered on their cloaks was the double-headed eagle signifying the empire—East and West—united there in the new Rome. Noticeably absent was the patriach of Constantinople, the head of the Orthodox Church.

"From there, they crossed from one end of the forum to the other and continued along the Mese for another ten minutes before they entered the Great Palace through the Chalke Gate.

"It was perhaps the most impressive ceremony I have ever seen. I was lucky enough to see the parade again and again over the next several days, although with diminishing fanfare at each successive venture.

"For the duration of the entire state visit and for weeks following, rumors abounded in all of the taverns and inns. Everyone seemed to speculate about what was being discussed. I would have given anything to have witnessed the verbal jousting between the emperor and the papal legate. I could only rely on the rumors."

Looking somewhat skeptical, Gerbert asked, "How did you know which rumors to believe?"

"That was my job, Monk."

Gerbert was not sure what to make of that comment, so he let it pass. "What a fascinating story."

But Hakeem was intent on pursuing the same line. "Yes, it is, and quite important in maintaining some semblance of balance of power in the Mediterranean."

"I'm afraid I don't know very much about politics, Master Hakeem. Can you explain that?"

"It's quite simple," said the mapmaker. "The Byzantines, as they are sometimes called, dealt a major blow to the forces of Sayf al-Dawla, the emir of the Hamdanid rulers of Syria. Since he is the real political and military force supporting the Abbasid caliph of Baghdad, the Abbasid position in the world of Islam is considerably weakened."

Gerbert was confused. "The Abbasid caliph of Baghdad? I met the caliph in Córdoba," he exclaimed.

Hakeem pointed to his map. "Well, let this be your first lesson in political geography. Different caliph. Look." He indicated the right-hand side of his drawing. "The Abbasid caliph controls close to a third of this territory, which includes Syria." He pointed to the extreme right edge. He indicated the toponym Antalya and said, "Here is Cilicia, which the Byzantines just succeeded in reclaiming from Sayf al-Dawla. The caliph that you say you met is here…" He pointed to the extreme left edge. "As you said, in Córdoba, which lies here on the shore of the Wadi al-Kabir. And there is a third caliph—the one I serve."

"The one you serve?"

"I have not told you anything about the work I do, Monk. For all you know, I am just a mapmaker."

Gerbert interrupted his speech. "I wouldn't say just a mapmaker."

"Fine," Hakeem said. "You're right. There are not many people who draw maps. What you don't know is why I do it. It is part of my work as an intelligence agent. I gather intelligence for the Fatimid caliph in Mahdiya."

Gerbert looked at him incredulously. "You mean…like a spy?"

"I mean exactly that."

At first, Hakeem didn't even realize he was admitting to being a Fatimid agent, essentially a spy. But he chose to continue. His intuition told him there was no reason to hide that from Gerbert. There was something about this lad that seemed to pose no threat whatsoever. Hakeem felt completely at ease opening up to him. He was willing to teach him what he knew.

Shaking his head, Gerbert said, "Why are you telling me this now?"

"That's a good question. I certainly had no intention to. Maybe it's because I trust you. Maybe because I want to caution you, a person with an insatiable appetite for knowledge, from falling into the same trap that I did."

"Trap?"

"Listen, Monk—"

Gerbert cut him off again. "Why do you keep calling me that?"

"I hope you don't think that I intend it to be demeaning. I mean it as a term of…of endearment. I have grown very fond of you. You are more than a mentee…and more than a friend."

"Frankly, I feel the same about you. Shall I call you 'Mapmaker,' then?"

"I would prefer that to being called 'Spy.'"

Gerbert backtracked a bit. "You said you fell into a trap. Can you explain?"

"It's complicated. I work for the Fatimid caliph, whose seat of power is in Mahdiya." Hakeem pointed to the city on his rough draft. "Right here, almost exactly halfway across the southern coast of the great Middle Sea. You see, I have marked it with a square rather than a circle because of its importance as the legitimate capital of the Islamic world—at least, in my own humble opinion."

"What makes your caliph more legitimate than the others?" Gerbert asked

"That's a fair question, Monk. I support him as the direct descendant of our Prophet Mohammed, and I also support the Fatimid concept of governance that allows freedom of thought and religious practice of all subjects under Fatimid rule. Take Sicily for example…" Hakeem pointed to the triangle almost exactly in the middle of the sea. "This island has been hotly contested by Byzantium and Baghdad. For more than a century now, it has been under Muslim rule, initially under the Aghlabids, who were loyal to the Abbasids, but more recently under the rule of the Fatimids. More often than not, the Fatimids, theologically Shiites, ruled the island through diplomacy, appointing a semiautonomous emir over a mostly Sunni Muslim population. The Fatimids kept the Byzantines at bay by negotiation, being content to collect tribute from the emperor and to collect the jizya tax from the Christians who were concentrated mostly in the northeast corner of the island."

Gerbert's exposure to the Islamic world had been minimal. Still, based on what he knew, he could not help but remark, "How is that different from Muslim-Christian relations in Andalusia? My mentor, the bishop of Vic, was on a diplomatic mission along with the Count of Barcelona. That was the very occasion that brought me to Córdoba. In that amazingly cosmopolitan city, I witnessed with my own eyes scholars and students of all three Abrahamic faiths intermingling on a daily basis."

That gave Hakeem cause to pause for a moment. *Why am I so devoted to the Fatimid cause?* he asked himself. He had spent a lot of time in Andalusia, so of course he knew that what Gerbert described was completely true. The Umayyad caliphate was at least as tolerant as the Fatimids. Yet they were intense competitors, one against the other.

He said, "The truth of the matter is that I was drawn into service of the Fatimid caliphate slowly and gradually by a tightly connected chain of events—the influence of close friends and, yes, in a very subtle way, the mentoring of my first teacher at the House of Wisdom in Baghdad."

Hakeem turned his attention back to politics. "Quite recently, the balance of power in the Mediterranean began to change. The emperor decided to make a bid to retake Sicily, probably because he was encouraged by his victory in Cilicia."

"So the Byzantines regained control of Sicily?"

"No. On the contrary. They lost a fierce naval battle in the straits between Sicily and Calabria. In fact, it was called the 'Battle of the Straits.'"

Hakeem's chest puffed with pride as he began to describe the battle. "We resorted to a ruse that the Byzantine navy had never seen before." He clearly identified with the victors as he described the strategy as if it were his own. "Arab divers swam from their own ships to those of their enemy. They tied ropes to the rudders of the enemy vessels, then swam back to their own ships. They then slid clay pots containing Greek fire down those ropes from their own ships, shattering the pots on the sternposts of the enemy ships, setting them on fire, and causing them to sink. It was such a resounding defeat for the Byzantines that they agreed to a new round of negotiations. They abandoned all hopes of regaining control of Sicily and agreed to a truce *and* to renew tribute for Calabria."

"Why is Sicily so important?" Gerbert asked.

Hakeem shrugged his shoulders and responded as if the answer should be obvious. "Just look at the map. It sits almost exactly in the middle of the Mediterranean Sea, perfectly positioned to benefit from, if not to completely control, communications of all sorts from east to west. The Fatimid caliph is based across the sea on the south. The emperor controls the territory on the opposite shore. It is a precarious balance of power.

"When I was in Sicily, I could hardly believe how well-fortified it appeared—castles and fortresses on every mountaintop, the main city of Palermo suurounded by an immense wall of stone, higher than any other I have seen. And rich! Most of the countryside is inhabited and under the plow.

"I attended Friday prayer at the Grand Mosque. I counted thirty-six rows, with some two hundred men standing shoulder to shoulder in each row. There must have been over seven thousand men praying at the same time."

Gerbert sat on the edge of his seat during the entire narrative. He was completely enthralled by this story of war and diplomacy. "Master Hakeem, you describe all of this as if you were personally involved."

"I was," Hakeem finally admitted. "I was actually in Mahdiya when the Byzantine delegation arrived."

"You mean you actually participated in the negotiations?"

"No, not hardly. I will be honest with you. As a special agent for the Fatimids, sometimes I am sent on a specific assignment. Most of the time, though, I am basically on my own, taking note of everything I see and reporting to the authorities whatever I deem important for them to know. My job is to keep my ear to the ground, to gauge the popular reaction on the street. I can tell you this: the Fatimid caliph is not insensitive to what the populace thinks. That's why the Fatimids have propagandists throughout their sphere of influence and beyond, not only to feel the pulse of the street but to shape it to fit their own agenda."

"And that agenda is…?"

"Another good question, Monk. I am no longer sure. I was once convinced that it was to restore the legitimate spiritual head of the Islamic faith. I'm sure that's what it was at one time. What started as a movement has now become an institution that not only is bent on its own self-preservation but is moving more and more toward expanding its hegemony."

"What makes you say that?"

"Not so long ago, I was asked to assess the relative merits of conducting a military campaign westward to challenge the Umayyads against an effort to move into Egypt. Dutifully, I conveyed my honest opinion to march on Egypt.

"That brings me back to the negotiations between the emperor's envoy, a man named Nicolas, and my caliph. The rumor, well-substantiated by people I know and trust who were present, is that the caliph remarked to Nicolas, 'I expect to receive you soon as an ambassador in Egypt.'"

"As I sit here and listen to you talk, Master Hakeem, it seems clear to me that these alternating waves of war and peace are not determined by Muslims being Muslim and Christians being Christian."

"What exactly are you trying to say, Monk?"

"Well, when wars break out, is one side trying to convince the other to change their religious beliefs?"

"Some say that Muslim expansion in the early decades of Islam was an attempt at conversion by the sword. I have never believed that."

"What was it, then?" Gerbert persisted.

"I think the early caliphs were determined to make the world…ah… *safe* for Islam. But more and more, I begin to think that they are driven rather by a desire to protect, and perhaps even to expand, political and economic interests. There is no economic benefit to trying to convert Christians to Islam. In fact, since Christians and Jews are liable to pay jizya, a special tax for non-Muslims, it is more economically beneficial if they do *not* convert."

"Master Hakeem, it has been my experience, as limited as it is, that Muslims and Christians…and Jews as well…can get along rather well—on a personal level. You have traveled so much more than I have. What has been your experience?"

"Well, on a purely personal level, of course you are right. We—you and I—have already proved that we can even discuss our religious beliefs and still remain friends."

Gerbert smiled. He was rather pleased that this man, with so much learning and experience, considered him a *friend*.

Hakeem continued, "Why, just the other day, we talked about what is perhaps the single most divisive issue between our two religions—the very nature of God, one or three. I know, I know—you convinced me that Christians, too, believe in *one* God. And I somehow want to believe you, even though the idea of 'trinity' doesn't make a lot of sense to me. But then you catch me off guard and make me recall that we Muslims think about God in at least ninety-nine different ways. But let's not return to that issue right now. There are many 'truths'—if we can call them that—that we actually share in common. Let me tell you a story about my journey to Bethlehem."

"You mean the birthplace of our Lord? You have actually been there?"

"Yes, the birthplace of the prophet Jesus, may peace be upon him. I was just passing through when I first left Baghdad to seek out my teacher, who had moved to Egypt. What struck me most was observing lines of worshipers, both Muslim and Christian, merging to file into this tiny church that contained a relic, a palm branch that allegedly fed the Virgin Mary, mother of Jesus, may peace be upon him, as the holy family fled to Egypt to escape the wrath of King Herod."

Gerbert was astonished. This short narrative gave rise to so many questions that he had trouble deciding which one to ask first. "Muslims believe that

Jesus was born of a virgin?"

"Yes, of course. No Muslim would ever doubt that. Our Holy Quran is very explicit about it." Hakeem had not memorized the entire Quran, as his father had, but he remembered these key verses:

> We sent to Mary Our spirit, and He appeared to her as an immaculate human. She said, "I take refuge from you in the Most Merciful, should you be righteous." He said, "I am only the messenger of your Lord, to give you the gift of a pure son." She said, "How can I have a son, when no man has touched me, and I was never unchaste?" He said, "Thus said your Lord, 'It is easy for Me, and We will make him a sign for humanity, and a mercy from Us. It is a matter already decided.'" So she carried him, and secluded herself with him in a remote place.

"Your scripture mentions Mary and Jesus?" was Gerbert's next question.

"Mentions them!" exclaimed Hakeem. "It does much more than mention. There is an entire chapter about the mother of Jesus. It is called the 'Chapter of Mary.' Jesus himself appears more than thirty times in the Quran."

"Tell me about this relic, this branch of a palm tree. Brother Raymond taught us about relics, but I have never heard about this one."

Hakeem told him the story of how the relic came to be and how the infant Jesus spoke. It is the infant Jesus who ordered the tree to lower its branch.

"That's truly amazing!" exclaimed Gerbert. "Jesus was but a newborn infant, yet he was able to speak thus?"

"I do not find it hard to believe," Hakeem said. "There is a story in our Holy Book where Jesus spoke shortly after his birth when his mother presented him to visitors for the first time. He said, 'Peace is on me the day I was born, the day that I die, and the day that I shall be raised up to life again.'"

Gerbert felt warmed by this shared experience of knowledge. He had learned something new about his own faith from a man of a different faith—from a Muslim. Hakeem, for his part, was becoming more and more impressed with this young monk, so bright yet so open and eager to learn.

CHAPTER TWENTY-ONE

Shortly after the day's last call to prayer, Hakeem thought he heard a knock at the outer door of the house, the door that gave access to the courtyard. His room was along the back side of the courtyard, farthest from the outer door, and he was not certain that what he heard was actually a knock. It sounded more like a woodpecker doing his work. But it was too late in the evening for a woodpecker. *I suppose it could be the monk. He knows that I often go to evening prayer and that afterward is a good time to stop by for a visit.* He waited to see if the sound would occur again. It did. Why was the *bawab* not opening the door to see who it was? Then he heard the sound a third time.

I guess I had better answer the door myself, Hakeem concluded. He was a little annoyed that he had to get up from the cozy cushion beneath the lantern on the wall of his reception room, where he sat comfortably, rereading a recent entry in his journal. Hakeem left his flat, walked across the courtyard, and, without giving it any thought, slid the bolt out of its locked position and began to open the door. Suddenly, the door crashed wide open and three burley men pushed their way into the courtyard. It was immediately clear why the *bawab* had not answered the door. He was lying, apparently unconscious, or maybe even dead, on the ground outside the door.

Hakeem saw the jagged scar on the cheek of the first man who came through the door. Even after so many years, he knew who the man must be. *Haytham al-Khariji*, he thought. *I can't believe it!* His first impulse was to attack Haytham and beat him to a pulp in retaliation for what he had done to his dear friend and confidant Dalia, back in Sijilmasa some ten years earlier.

That, of course, was out of the question since there were three of them and only one of him, and Haytham appeared at least twice his size.

"Surprised to see me, Master Hakeem?" Haytham sneered. His two cohorts rushed in, circled around Hakeem, and seized him by his arms so that he could barely move.

This was the first time Hakeem had gotten a good look at Haytham. He recognized the jagged scar from the descriptions Musa and Dalia had provided. "So you are Haytham al-Khariji."

"I am. We have been trying to track you down for quite some time now. We were almost certain you were the second man who fled the mosque the night Suhrab gave his treacherous discourse in Baghdad. You were much too quick. You eluded us that time. But don't think too highly of yourself. You did not really become a target of interest until we saw you seek out the pigeon man in Sijilmasa. We had been watching him for some time. The only folks who sought his services were agents of the Fatimid usurper to the caliphate."

"You did not have to hurt Dalia the way you did."

"Oh, but we did," said one of Haytham's ruffians with a grin. "Once it became clear that you were sending messages to the caliph—or at least to someone close to the caliph—we had to find out just what you knew and with whom you were sharing it. We were prepared to do whatever it took. Unfortunately, in spite of all of our…*efforts*…we were not able to get anything out of her—information-wise, at least." Another grin.

Hakeem wanted to kill him, but he couldn't budge from the vicelike grip of his two assailants. He stopped squirming and decided to save whatever energy he had for whatever might come next.

"You are a slippery devil, I must admit," Haytham said. "When we arrived at your house back in Sijilmasa, you were already gone. We could not get any information out of your landlord either. Too bad for him as well."

"You hurt him too, I suppose."

"He was able to recover," was all Haytham said.

"How did you track me down here?"

Hakeem did not really expect an answer to this question. No intelligence agent worthy of his profession would divulge that kind of information. But Haytham was obviously not a professional intelligence agent. He was a thug, as were his two accomplices.

Haytham proceeded to answer Hakeem's question. "When Jawhar's army left Sijilmasa to return to Fez, we pretty much gave up on you. It was too late to worry about whatever intelligence information you had amassed. My job was basically over. I decided to go to Fez as well and took up residence in the Qarawayeen section of the city, just as you did. In fact, my flat is less than two blocks from here."

"Why Fez?" Hakeem asked.

"I could ask you that same question. What I can say is that it had nothing at all to do with you. We had given up on you. Whatever you knew or whatever you were up to no longer had any value to us."

"That still does not answer my question," said Hakeem.

"Don't be so naïve, Hakeem. You know that the Qarawayeen quarter here was settled by religious refugees from Qayrawan; almost all of them to a person were of the Kharijite sect. There are still many descendants of the original settlers in this part of town. It's as simple as that. I feel rather comfortable here."

Hakeem had not thought of that. He rarely thought of sectarian divisions in Islam. His father had taught him to downplay sectarian differences many years earlier, and that was still a fundamental cornerstone of his own worldview.

"That still does not explain what you are doing here today in my home."

"My friend here overheard you talking to that young foreigner, foolishly telling him about your 'work' in Sijilmasa. I knew it had to be you."

"But why now? Of what interest am I to you now?"

"Vengeance! You once supported Emir Ibn al-Fath in Sijilmasa, and then you turned on him. You diverted Jawhar's troops right to him at Jebel Mudawar, leading to his capture and disgraceful public display as they carried him off first to Fez and then to Qayrawan."

"How do you know that?"

"The pigeon man. We went back to pay him a visit after you fled. He was not as able to withstand our *persuasion* as your sweet Dalia was. When we last saw him, he was grovelling in the dirt beside the roosting house of his *special* birds."

Hakeem was now seething with anger. But still he could do nothing in retaliation toward his oppressors.

"Let's just slit his throat here and now and be done with it," said the same man who had admitted to *questioning* Dalia.

"No! We cannot do that," insisted Haytham. "This man is an important informant for the Fatimids. If they find his murdered body here, they will not rest until they track down his assailants."

"What shall we do then?" asked the other brute. The two thugs were now struggling to contain Hakeem, who squirmed all the more as he listened to what they plannned to do with him.

"We will do as we discussed," said Haytham. "We will take him to the river. We will hold his head underwater in the nearby fountain until he drowns.

Then we will throw his body over the bridge, making his demise look like an accident."

"He is getting more difficult to handle. We should tie his hands behind him."

"No! You fool," Haytham said. "The rope would leave marks on his wrists—an accident, remember? Let's go to the river."

As soon as Gerbert turned the corner and approached the outer door of the house where Hakeem lived, he saw the *bawab* trying to get to his feet. He rushed to give the injured man a hand. Before Gerbert could say anything, the *bawab* motioned him to keep silent. He whispered, "There were three of them, and they are still in there. I believe they mean to do harm to Master Hakeem."

Gerbert put his ear to the door and overheard the exchange between Haytham and his esteemed friend. His first impulse was to charge in and rescue Hakeem, but he immediately realized that since there were three of them, it would be futile. As soon as he was sure that the *bawab* was no longer in immediate danger, Gerbert left to seek help. There were always a few armed soldiers in the area of the Grand Mosque when people were leaving after evening prayer. That was where he decided to go.

Meanwhile, Haytham and his two henchmen left, pushing Hakeem, who resisted as much as he could, along in front of them. To minimize the chance of meeting passersby, they proceeded toward the bridge through narrow, dark alleyways rather than on the main street. They had stuffed a cloth in Hakeem's mouth to prevent him from shouting out cries for help.

They passed a couple of drunks along the way. "That's it," observed Haytham. "If anyone stops us or says anything, we will just say that our friend is drunk and we are seeing that he gets home safely."

"Good idea," said one of Haythan's accomplices. "I have a flask of wine. We can pour some over his clothing. When his body is recovered, the authorities will think that he was drunk and fell into the river when he crossed the bridge on his way home."

When Gerbert arrived at the mosque, there were no soldiers there.

My God, what am I going to do? He was not thinking clearly now, only reacting. He set off toward the bridge, not having any idea what he would do when he got there. He had already decided that it would be hopeless to try to rescue his friend on his own. He ran toward the bridge anyway. When he arrived, he could hardly believe what he saw. The two largest brutes were restraining Hakeem as the third held his head underwater in the public fountain.

Gerbert had to think quickly. *It would be futile for me to try to overpower these three huge attackers. I need to come up with some kind of diversion.*

He was suddenly inspired by an idea.

The incident unfolding before his eyes was not in the back alleys but in a rather public place, a square with a public fountain, even though no one was usually out at this time of night. Gerbert took his leather bag off his shoulder and held it open in front of him. He then boldly walked into the square, saying in a loud voice, "Alms for the poor…a donation to the poor is a donation to God himself."

The three assailants looked up as if they had no idea what to do next. Likewise, Gerbert had no idea what to do next.

All of a sudden, a handful of soldiers appeared seamingly from nowhere. There was not much of a scuffle. The number of soldiers simply overwhelmed the ruffians who were trying to kill the mapmaker. One of the soldiers pulled Hakeem's head from under the water. The poor man coughed out multiple mouthfuls that he had swallowed and gasped for air.

"Uhh—aah! Thank…uhh—aah…God! Another…few…seconds and…I would have been…dead…" Hakeem continued to gasp for air. "It had to have been God…who brought you here…to rescue me."

The officer in charge responded, "You can credit God if you like, but this Kharijite agent has been under surveillance for some time. We knew that he had tracked down where you live. When our agent saw him push his way into your house, he sent word for us to come immediately. As it turned out, immediately was none too soon."

"You know where I live? Have I been under surveillance as well?"

"Not under surveillance. Under our protection, as per the caliph's own orders. You must be rather important in the eyes of the Fatimid administration."

Hakeem had nothing to say to that.

The soldiers put iron cuffs on the three attackers' wrists and chained them together. As they started to lead them away, the officer informed Hakeem, "The two accomplices will be imprisoned for a long time." He put extra emphasis on the word "long." "But this one"—he pointed to Haytham— "will be executed by beheading."

"Do with the accomplices what you will," Hakeem said, "but I want you to let their leader go."

"What? You can't be serious. Let him go?"

"Yes, you heard me correctly. You must let him go."

"May I ask why?" the commander asked.

"At first I wanted to kill him. But I now realize that he is an ideologue—just as I am," said Hakeem, "a Kharijite, and an extreme one at that, not so unlike me in my support of the Fatimids. At least not so unlike what I used to be. He is a man with strong convictions that what Kharijites teach must be carried out to the letter. At his core, he is not an evil person. I want you to set him free. Since you know that I am a ranking Fatimid agent, you must do as I say."

Reluctantly, the officer in charge removed Haytham's restraints. Haytham fled the instant he was released, almost bumping into Gerbert as he left the square. He paused briefly, looked back at Hakeem, and looking straight into his eyes said, "This is not over, *da'i*."

The soldiers left with their prisoners, and Hakeem and Gerbert stood alone in front of the fountain, lit only by a sliver of moonlight, which had managed to find its way past the tops of the buildings that almost completely hid the sky from sight. Hakeem was still breathing hard, and Gerbert's heart was still pounding as he balanced the emotions of fear and relief.

Hakeem asked, "What on earth brought you here at this time of night?"

"Ah…collecting alms for the poor?" Gerbert answered unconvincingly.

"Somehow you learned that I was in trouble and you came to help. Is that not true? You saved my life."

"No, the soldiers saved your life. I only delayed your demise a few seconds, allowing the soldiers to get here on time."

Gerbert could see that his friend was alright, so he did not ask. Rather, his opening words sought to clarify the course of events he had witnessed in the short while since he first saw the *bawab* lying in the street outside Hakeem's door.

"That man, the one with the scar on his face…he called you *da'i*. What does that mean?"

"It means that I am his enemy. It's complicated. I will explain later. Right now, walk with me back to my house."

As difficult as it was, Gerbert refrained from asking any more questions. The two men, bonded deeper in friendship in spite of the generation of years that separated them, walked silently back to Hakeem's home.

The silence opened space in Gerbert's mind that quickly filled with more questions, questions he could no longer contain when they arrived where Hakeem lived. Once Hakeem was certain that the *bawab* was not irreparably harmed, he allowed Gerbert's interrogation.

"Who was that man you allowed to go free?"

"His name is Haytham; he is called 'al-Khariji,' the Kharijite, a sect notorious for its opposition to the very idea of caliphate. Like me, they lament the deplorable state to which the Abbasid caliphate has fallen. Not only do they oppose the caliph of Baghdad, they oppose the two rival caliphs in Córdoba and Mahdiya as well."

"Why does he want you dead?"

"Humph! How much time do you have? A few minutes ago, you asked why he called me a *da'i*. That is a special agent of the Fatimid caliph. No, more than just an agent, and more than a spy. It is an ideological supporter of the caliph and a promoter of the Fatimid cause. That is what I am—or at least, what I was. Just like Haytham, although not quite as…loyal to the cause as he…and to a different cause. Now, I am not so sure what I am beyond a gatherer of intelligence and a mapmaker."

"Why did you tell the soldiers to let him go?"

"I am not so sure about that either."

"Could it have something to do with forgiveness? In my religion, Jesus teaches that when someone harms us, we should turn the other cheek."

"Sure, but how often does that ever happen? It is the same in our religion. God is merciful. We are reminded of that with the opening words of every chapter of the Quran. 'In the name of God the Compassionate, the Merciful.' Ironically, we appreciate God being merciful toward us, but more often than not, we seek vengeance when someone offends us, retribution for harm like Haytham has done to people who are dear to me and for what he tried to do to me as well tonight."

"To be perfectly honest," Gerbert said, "it is the same in the Frankish kingdom where I am from. The Bible tells us that we should love God with all our heart, with all our soul, and all our mind, and all our strength, and we should love our neighbor as ourselves. But in truth, if anyone harms a single person among our kin, the offense must be repaid with a comparable attack. The integrity and honor of families depend on it."

"We are not so different, then, are we, Monk?"

CHAPTER TWENTY-TWO

Hakeem and Gerbert had only two more months together in Fez. They met every few days in the library. They chatted briefly about what each was doing, curious to learn what the other was up to.

Gerbert spent most of his time studying geometry and trigonometry. Hakeem found it quite odd that Gerbert, a monk, a man of God, was so interested in mathematics. One day, Gerbert explained it this way.

"Really, I love numbers for their own sake. There is nothing contradictory between mathematics and God. It's quite the opposite. Numbers actually bring me closer to God. I see God in numbers."

"How so?" asked Hakeem.

"Well, we could say that God was quite mathematical in how he created… how he created everything. It says that right in the Bible."

"Sure. 'The Bible says it's so,'" said Hakeem with a touch of sarcasm. "That's just like the Quran. People often say, 'The Quran says this' and 'The Quran says that.' Then you look it up in the Holy Book, and nowhere does the Quran say any such thing."

"Well, it's different with mathematics," insisted Gerbert. It's in the book of Wisdom, chapter eleven, verse twenty. 'Thou hast ordered all things by number, measure, and weight.' Take the days of the week, for example. How many days in the week are there?"

"Seven," answered Hakeem.

"In Islam or in Christianity?"

"Uh…"

"In both." Gerbert did not wait for Hakeem to answer. "But it is God who divided the week into seven days."

"Come to think of it, seven is an important number in Islam," said Hakeem. "When Prophet Mohammed journeyed to Jerusalem, he ascended through seven phases of heaven to reach God. Likewise, there are seven gates to hell. When a pilgrim makes the pilgrimage to Mecca, he circles around the Qaaba seven times. There are seven verses in the first chapter of the Quran."

"There, you see," Gerbert said emphatically. "There is nothing natural about seven. God just determined it to be so."

One day, Hakeem entered the reading room and found Gerbert sitting at his usual place at the long table. The young monk had cut up a parchment into several small squares. He was placing the squares over a drawing of a triangle.

"What on earth are you doing?" asked Hakeem.

Gerbert did not even look up for an instant. He continued to place the squares over the triangle. "I am trying to figure out the area of this triangle."

"Hmmm," said Hakeem. "Would you care to explain?"

"This is an isosceles triangle. All sides are—"

"Yes, I know, all sides are equal."

"Exactly. Each side of this triangle is seven units long. I have cut these little squares each to equal one unit by one unit. It takes twenty-eight of these squares to cover the entire triangle."

"So the area of the triangle is twenty-eight square units?"

"That's exactly what the philosopher Boethius said…but he was wrong! Look, the squares all along the two sides extend beyond the edge of the triangle. Those portions of squares that hang over the limits of the figure have to be subtracted. They are equivalent to seven squares. So the true area of the triangle is twenty-one squares.

This was almost more than Hakeem wanted to know, but Gerbert's enthusiasm, it seemed, was limitless. "The triangle," he said, "is the basis of all other figures. It is the mother of all figures."

From time to time, they met at Hakeem's home. Gerbert was a little reluctant to go there for some time. It brought flashbacks of that dreadful night when

Hakeem came so close to being killed. But he got over it. It was only when he went there that Gerbert could see the progress Hakeem was making on the final version of his map of all the regions around the Mediterranean Sea. Typically, he would ask Hakeem about some famous, far-off city he had read about. Hakeem would point it out on his map, and Gerbert's mind would travel there.

"Can you show me where Jerusalem is?" Gerbert asked one day. "Brother Raymond told us many times that it was at the very center of the world."

"Central in importance, perhaps, but geographically? That's hard to say—unless you happen to be in Jerusalem, that is. In a sense, wherever a person is on the face of this earth, that is his center—or hers," Hakeem added. "I imagine it is the same as you gaze up at your celestial sphere. From wherever you are, the celestial sphere is equidistant all around you."

"That's very interesting. I am not disputing what you say, but you did not really answer the question I intended to ask. Where is Jerusalem on your map? Where is it in relation to where we are right now?"

"Yes, that is a different question. And I'm afraid I can only give you an approximate answer. I went to Jerusalem shortly after I left Baghdad as a student. I have not been back since. When I circumnavigated the Middle Sea, I did not stop anywhere along the eastern coastline, rationalizing that I had already been there. Nor have I yet questioned any travelers as to their itineraries that might have included Jerusalem."

Hakeem unrolled his scroll, which was large enough to cover his entire table—so large that he did not have a single parchment large enough for the entire map. He used three separate sheets that he had glued together.

"All I can tell you is that it is somewhere near the middle of what I have labeled here on my map as 'Syria.' It is here, number 48. " Hakeem pointed

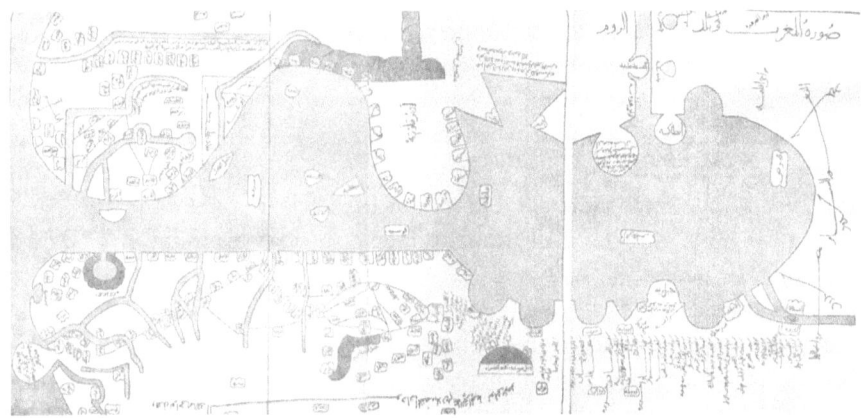

to the area at the far right-hand side of his map. "Clearly, this is a deficiency I will have to amend at some point."

"I have heard so much about Jerusalem. But you are the first person I have met who has actually been there. What is it like? Is it a huge city like Córdoba?"

"No, not nearly so large as that. And frankly, not as important politically. Right now, it is under the rule of the caliph in Baghdad. But I think all that is about to change."

"About to change? More of your spy work?"

Hakeem nodded. "Listen, there is something I need to tell you. This will perhaps be the last time we are together. I am leaving Fez in a few days."

"Leaving Fez?"

"Yes, I will accompany the Fatimid army under Jawhar's command. Their mission is to conquer Egypt. You already know what I think about that. But I feel that I should follow through, at least that far, in what the Fatimids have asked me to do. I will link up with Jawhar's army in Raqqada, just outside of the caliph's capital of Mahdiya. I will accompany the army only as far as Egypt. My hope, then, is to continue to follow my own dream of seeing the rest of the world. We both know there are so many more places to map, far to the east of what I have mapped already. That is where my heart is calling me to go."

It was several seconds before Gerbert spoke. Then, his throat choking with emotion, he said, "Master Hakeem, perhaps I should have told you this earlier, but I am leaving Fez as well."

"But why? There is so much more for you to learn here."

"Yes, I know. But my monastic vows demand that I obey my superiors. A few days ago, my dear friend Miro Bonfill forwarded a message to me from Bishop Atto. Count Borell has been asked to be a special envoy to Rome. The bishop has decided that I should accompany him." Trying to lighten the mood just a bit, Gerbert asked, "Can you show me Rome on your map?"

"I can," Hakeem said in a low voice. At this moment, as he thought of the two of them leaving, each to his own world, each to his own destiny that did not include the other, somehow his map did not seem so important. Still, he pointed to the upper right-hand corner of the left parchment and said, "It is here, inside this triangle." The thought flashed through his mind, *My God, the lad might be right about triangles.*

The mapmaker swallowed hard and said, "Within this triangle is an area I have not mapped. Rome is here next to the land of the Franks, your homeland. I have never been there. That said, I have learned from a close associate of an outpost of mujahideen, holy warriors of Islam, in the foothills of the Alps. They have established a ribat, a fortress from which they can wage jihad against the Christians. It is called Fraxshineet. I believe you Franks call it Fraxinetum. If you travel to Rome overland, surely you will pass through the territory of these warriors. They are seen by the Christians all around them as brigands who prey on all who travel through those mountains. But I am told that they can ensure safe passage through the narrow passes—for a price. Crossing the Alps is difficult under the best of conditions. It is perhaps impossible without the assistance of dependable guides. Maybe you can suggest to your patrons that they employ these holy warriors."

Gerbert shook his head. "Thank you, Master Hakeem. My mentors have in fact renewed their alliance with the caliph in Córdoba. But I doubt that either Bishop Atto or Count Borrell would be inclined to trust Muslims whom they would likely see as renegades. Nonetheless, thank you for the suggestion. Can you show me the route we will take?"

"I'm afraid that part of my map is not to scale, so I cannot tell you how far away it is. It is part of your world. I doubt that I will ever get there. I will just have to depend on you to tell me about it when you send news of yourself."

"I should indeed like to write to you, Master Hakeem. Tell me how I will be able to get messages to you."

"Good question. The informal mail service around the entire Mediterranean functions rather well. Find a person you can trust who is heading in the direction of your intended recipient and entrust that individual with your letter. It may take a while, but sooner or later, your letter will arrive."

"But how will I know where you are?"

"Address your letter to me and send it to the caliphal palace in Egypt. The new capital city will be called Cairo, the 'City of the Conqueror.' Officials at the palace will know how to get the message to me. But how will I find you?"

"I have no idea what God has in store for me. I am going to Rome. After that, only God knows."

"There is a tradition of Prophet Mohammed in which he taught us to say this prayer: 'Our Lord God who art in heaven, hallowed be Thy name. Thy kingdom is in heaven and on earth, and even as Thy mercy is in heaven, so may Thy mercy be on earth. Forgive us our debts and sins. Send down mercy from Thy mercy, and healing from Thy healing for those suffering, that they may begin to heal. For Thou art Lord of all that is good.'"

"Mohammed taught this prayer?"

"Yes. It is a tradition told by the hadith narrator Abu Dawoud. Is that so strange?"

"Strange? No—more like a miracle. It is almost exactly the same prayer that Jesus taught his disciples when they asked him how to pray."

"Well, ultimately, it comes from the same source. Shall we say it together before we part?"

"They are almost the same," Gerbert said, "but not exactly. I am a guest in a Muslim land, and a guest should not come in and start to rearrange the furniture. Let's say your version. Please write it down for me."

Hakeem did as Gerbert asked. Then they prayed together.

At that, the two men, both of them stangers in a strange land who had discovered in each other a kindred spirit, said goodbye. They embraced in a way that was practiced among the closest friends. As they hugged each other, they touched cheeks three times, first right cheek to right cheek, then left, then right again. Moisture welled up in Hakeem's eyes to the point of almost forming tears. Gerbert was far less sucessful in holding his tears back.

This was the last time the two would ever see one another face to face.

CHAPTER TWENTY-THREE

It was December in the year of our Lord 970. Bishop Atto, Count Borrell, and Brother Gerbert d'Aurillac crossed the Alps in the dead of winter. The crossing, difficult at any time of year, was particularly hazardous in winter. But the gravity of the mission was such that Bishop Atto felt they could not wait until spring. No one told Gerbert the reason for the journey. Nor did he ask. He was simply ecstatic over the prospect of seeing the epicenter of his faith.

The cortège had barely reached the foothills of the Alps when Bishiop Atto conceded that conditions were far worse than he had anticipated. The snow and sleet, pushed by bitter cold wind, was blinding. One of the pack horses lost its footing and slid off the edge of a narrow cliff. One of the handlers was quick enough to cut it loose from the train before it dragged other horses down with it. The unfortunate horse was not seen again.

Reluctantly, Gerbert offered the suggestion made by his friend Hakeem. "Your Excellency, I met a man in Fez who told me that there are capable guides who can lead us safely through the mountains. They are located in a place called Fraxinetum."

"Who is this man who told you that?"

Gerbert did not really want to get into the details of befriending a Muslim intelligence agent. He simply said, "He is a man who circumnavigated the entire Middle Sea. He draws maps. I met him at the university."

"And these men who serve as guides?"

Gerbert was even more reluctant to describe them as Muslim warriors of the faith. "They are Saracens. Some have described them as brigands."

"I think that Count Borrell's armed escort should be quite adequate to protect us against brigands."

"I am certain you are right, Your Excellency. But wouldn't it be better if the brigands were actually on our side? The mapmaker was quite certain of what he told me, that they serve as guides for travelers in these mountains—for a price."

Weighing whether to risk going forth across the mountains through the snow and ice or to trust traveling under the guidance of these Saracens, the bishop asked, "How will we find them?"

"Soon we will come to the town of Fraxinetum. The mapmaker said we should be able to see their fortress high on the hill above the town."

The snow was falling so hard as the cortège approached Fraxinetum that the fortress was barely visible. Count Borrell took the lead, and they started up the narrow pass with great caution. Quite suddenly, seemingly out of nowhere, at least twenty heavily armed men appeared on the ridges on either side of the line of march. A third band came forth to block their forward progress. Before the count's soldiers could react, they were completely surrounded.

What have I gotten us into? Gerbert thought. Not sure exactly what to do, he felt that he had to take the initiative, relying on his faith that God would see them through. He reined his horse slowly forward—alone. He approached the man who seemed to be in charge. It was Gerbert who spoke first, in the best Arabic he could.

"We have not come to fight. We are on a diplomatic mission to Rome." Gerbert doubted that their purpose would make much difference. He was quick to add, "We were informed by a reliable soul, a Muslim who holds you in high regard, that you would help us cross these treacherous mountains. We are prepared to pay."

With a sneer on his face, the commander cocked his head back, narrowed his gaze, and said, "We could just slaughter you all and take your money."

"Yes, you could do that, but our escort consists of battle-hardened soldiers. Before the last one falls, you will have lost several men of your own, perhaps even yourself. Would it not be better to see us through, have our money, and live?"

The Muslim commander was nothing less than startled at the sight of this man of diminutive stature, dressed as a humble monk, struggling with his Arabic, still coming forward with such confidence. Now it was his turn to decide on the next move.

"Very well. We will guide you through the mountains."

Thanks be to God, Gerbert thought. *And thank you for the recommendation of my dear friend Hakeem.*

The remainder of the journey through the Alps, although the weather continued to make it difficult, was without serious mishaps, thanks largely to the assistance of the guides Hakeem had recommended. Likewise, the journey on to Rome was without incident.

The cortège approached from the north, entering the Leonine City, an area surrounding the Basilica of Saint Peter. Around the basilica were numerous shops and food stalls, moneylenders, hostels for pilgrims, peddlers selling pilgrim badges, holy oil, candles, and religious trinkets of all kinds, edging up to the very doors of the huge church.

They exited the Leonine City on the southeast corner and crossed the River Tiber and continued on toward the Papal Palace.

Arriving in Rome was bittersweet for Gerbert. The hardships endured on the long journey through difficult terrain and violent storms only increased his impatient anticipation to see the famed holy city, the home of the Holy Father Pope John XIII, whom he, a humble monk of the order of Saint Benedict, was about to meet. What he saw as the cortège made its way into the city was not at all what his imagination had prepared him for. The city had been reduced to squalor. He recalled to mind what he had read of Alcuin's description of Rome, *caput mundi*, the head of the world: "Golden Rome, there remains to you now only a great mass of cruel ruins." Gerbert had somehow refused to believe what Charlemagne's teacher had written. He had expected to see the greatest city in the world. What he saw instead was a city that once had a population of a million people now reduced to about fifty thousand, most of whom were clustered in the bend of the Tiber River. Many of the structures from the time of the caesars were now hollow shells, quarries for stone to build churches and palaces for the diminishing number of rich merchants and powerful churchmen.

In contrast, the Lateran Palace was as stately as that of any temporal ruler. In one of the courtyards stood the Lupa Capitolina, the she-wolf suckling the mythical twins, Romulus and Remus. Gerbert fondly remembered the legend Brother Raymond had told of the founding of Rome, the story of the two brothers who were abandoned to die but were rescued and raised by the she-wolf. In another courtyard was a bronze statue, allegedly of Emperor

Constantine mounted on a stately steed. Gerbert wondered if the sculptor had known what the great Christian emperor really looked like.

Gerbert was not present when Bishop Atto had his audience with the pope. But the bishop shared the gist of it with his protégé after the fact.

"Our Holy Father has agreed to separate the churches of Catalonia from the archbishopric of Narbonne."

"What does that mean, Your Excellency?" asked Gerbert.

"It means that our diocese is being elevated to the status of an archbishopric. I am the first archbishop of Vic. The archbishop of Narbonne will not be happy. I will be returning home promptly."

"I too am anxious to return, Your Excellency."

"Perhaps you will not be returning, my son—at least not at this time. I mentioned to our Holy Father that you are a mathematician and a teacher of mathematics of extraordinary ability. He has recommended you to our emperor, Otto the Great, to serve as tutor to his young son and heir."

"But—but Reverend Bishop—I mean Archbishop—I have never served as a teacher."

"Don't be so modest, Brother Gerbert. I have heard reports of how you instructed fellow students and even taught a mathematical trick or two to some of your teachers. In any case, on our Holy Father's recommendation, the emperor wants to speak with you."

"So you are a stargazer as well," said the emperor as he leaned forward on his throne. "Do the stars tell you the future?"

"With all respect, Your Imperial Majesty, I have never asked them that. My interest is in describing the movement of heavenly bodies. I want to learn to accurately map the sky."

"Map the sky?" The emperor pulled back a bit. "To what end, may I ask?"

"To better understand the cosmos and our place in it, Your Imperial Majesty."

"Can you teach my son to understand our place in our own world?"

"I can try, Your Imperial Majesty."

Being the tutor of the future emperor should have been the dream post of a lifetime for anyone. But over the next two years, Gerbert felt as if he was not growing in his own pursuit of knowledge. He was intellectually bored.

This would change on Easter, 972, the wedding day of his young pupil to the even younger Byzantine princess Theophanu. Gerbert, of course, was in attendance at the wedding. So was Garamnus, archdeacon of Rheims, schoolmaster at the cathedral school in that city. The two were drawn to each other like filings to a lodestone.

"The cathedral school of Rheims is by far the premier center for higher learning in all of Europe," insisted Garamnus.

"Is that so?" responded Gerbert, sounding only a little haughty. "I have never heard of it. What do they teach there?"

"Logic! There are other subjects too, of course, but Rheims is most famous for logic. That is what I teach there." Garamnus was in fact the most noted of the logicians at the school, as Gerbert discovered as their conversation progressed.

Gerbert had always wanted to focus more on the study of logic. Of course, it would have been impossible to squeeze that in amidst the other subjects that consumed the time he had devoted to study, be it in Catalonia, Córdoba, or Fez. *Maybe, just maybe*, Gerbert thought, *I could accompany the archdeacon back to Rheims.*

At first, the very thought of it seemed nothing more than an impossible dream. But there was another factor at play. The archbishop of Rheims, Adalbero, was also in Rome in the spring of 972. He had come to seek the advice and support of Pope John XIII for his reform program in his archdiocese, a program that included a revival of spirituality and learning among his clergy.

The pope knew exactly what Adalbero needed: a *scholasticus*, a scholar, fired up with a zeal for reform. Garamnus was already the great master of the trivium at Rheims, the study of grammar, logic, and rhetoric. What the cathedral lacked to raise its status was a master of the quadrivium, a master of mathematics, geometry, music, and astronomy. The archbishop had heard tell of Gerbert's exceptional skills in these subjects.

Since young Otto was now with wife, he no longer needed a tutor—and Gerbert was in need of a new job. What an amazing coincidence—or was it? It was later said that Gerbert was directed to Rheims by God himself.

EPILOGUE

January 1, 1000, Rome

It was a holy day for the Church, a celebration of the circumcision of Our Lord, Jesus Christ. The pope had slept in after retiring later than usual, having celebrated midnight mass on the eve of the new year. Brother Anthony brought a light breakfast to the pope's room.

"Thank you, Brother Anthony. So, you see, the world has not come to an end. It is just as it was at this time yesterday, only one day later."

Anthony accepted this mild rebuke, but he quickly recalled the pope's promise. "You said you would tell me about your studies, about your time in the world of Islam, and especially about the mapmaker."

"Yes, yes, Brother Anthony. I have not forgotten. Let me start from the beginning. Stay and share my breakfast. There is always more than enough on the tray. This may take a while."

Over the next several hours, through breakfast, lunch, and well into the evening, the two of them sat side by side in the pope's study. The pope held nothing back, starting from the very beginning of the mapmaker's life—or what he knew of it—as well as his own. At dinnertime, the pope proposed that they take a break and share a quick meal together there in his studio.

After he took his last bite and his last sip of wine, the pope was ready to resume his story. "Let's see, where was I? Oh yes, the cathedral school of Rheims.

"Shortly after I arrived, the headmaster Garamnus died unexpectedly. For better or not, Archbishop Adalbero appointed me to take his place. In all humility, I knew in the deepest reaches of my soul that whatever trust Archbishop Adalbero placed in me to head the cathedral school—more than that, to raise it to the next level, to the status of one of the most prestigious centers of learning in all of Europe—I was ready. But I never thought of myself as a scholar. I was first and foremost a teacher. My dear friend the mapmaker told me many times that learning was the pathway to God. If that was indeed the case, then no profession could be more noble than teaching.

"To that end, I did everything I could to help my students learn, orienting them to reading the great literature of the classics. I made every effort to procure the most important works in our library. I developed a crude form of an abacus, an instrument that would assist the students in making challenging mathematical calculations using the decimal system and the new Arabic numerals.

"Why, I even constructed a celestial orb to illustrate the movement of the planets in their precise orbits around the earth. I suppose one could compare that to the mapmaker drawing his maps to illustrate the physical relationship among places that most of us only hear about."

The pope stood and walked over to a square box in the corner of his room and removed his celestial orb.

"I have not shown this to anyone in a long time, but here it is. You see this ball in the center? That is the earth. That is where we are. Now, I warned the students, as I must warn you now, that as we look at this model, we are looking at the universe, as if we were completely outside of it; we are looking at it as God sees it."

Only occasionally did the secretary interrupt with a question. "Excuse me, Holy Father…the road from Rheims to Rome…what brought you to the position where you are today?"

"Well…" The pope hesitated. He was not sure just how far he wanted to go down this road. "It is quite complicated," he began. "Ironically, it was my relationship with Archbishop Adalbero, the same man who was responsible for me becoming a teacher.

"I served the archbishop as his secretary. No, more than that—I was his personal assistant. As you are becoming more and more aware, Brother Anthony, the higher one is in the hierarchy of the Church, the more one becomes embroiled in politics. The archbishop dragged me down that road.

Don't get me wrong—I was not disinterested in politics. In fact, the challenge at times was quite exciting…" The pope paused. "As long as I felt that I was working for the common good. But that is precisely the problem—knowing what is for the common good. My dear friend the mapmaker warned me of the trap of mistaking the human quest for power for the common good. He worked hard to facilitate the shift of power from one ruling dynasty that he felt had become corrupt to another that, at least for a time, was less so. And so did I."

"How so, Holy Father?" the secretary asked.

By now, the pope had already told so many of his secrets—why not tell all?

"It goes back to when Lothair was our king—I mean my king, king of France. Hugh Capet, the duke of France, was his main opponent. A third party in the conflict was the Holy Roman emperor. Keep in mind our relationship—that is, Archbishop Adalbero's and my relationship—with the emperor. Remember that at archbishop Atto's behest, I became the tutor for the young Otto II. When Otto died, Lothair made a bid to seize the region of Lorraine from the new emperor, Otto III. The archbishop Adalbero opposed that move, as did Hugh Capet. The archbishop sent letters reflecting that opposition, letters that *I* wrote."

The pope stood, walked over to the chest where his correspondence was archived, and pulled out a scroll.

"Let me read to you just a few phrases: 'We are completing this secret and anonymous letter in a few words: Lothair is king of France in name only; Hugh Capet not in name, it is true, but in fact and in deed.'"

"Well, I must say, Holy Father," Brother Anthony said, "it is easy to see why you raised the ire of the king."

"His ire? It was worse than that. The king planned to put Archbishop Adalbero and me on trial for high treason. If tried and convicted, surely we would have been executed. I wrote to Empress Theophanu to intercede on our behalf. She did not reply to me. But if it was not she who intervened, then it was God himself.

"In the interim, the king went hunting, fell off his horse, damaged his liver, and died—without an heir. The assembly that was to decide my fate along with that of the archbishop now had a different task—to decide who would be the next king of France. The archbishop compiled a very strong case against the election of Charles. He rejected the idea that the throne is bestowed solely by noble heredity. In a speech long remembered and often cited for its eloquence, the archbishop said, 'We should elevate to the throne one who distinguishes himself by the nobleness of his person and the wisdom of his spirit.' Of course, it was none other than Hugh Capet whom he had in mind."

"Did you perchance write that speech as well, Holy Father?"

"Why, Brother Anthony, you overestimate my persuasiveness." The pope smiled. "Nonetheless, the assembly of nobles did choose Hugh, who then successfully claimed the throne. It gave rise to yet another rumor: Gerbert was one who deposed kings and elevated others.

"From that point on, Brother Anthony, I'm afraid that my involvement in politics was irreversible. That is the trap that my dear friend the mapmaker warned me about. I convinced myself that what I was doing was important, that it would benefit the emperor, that it would benefit our Mother Church and our faith."

"Holy Father, what became of the mapmaker after you parted ways? Did you not hear from him? Did you try to contact him, as he asked?"

"Ah, yes…" The pope closed his eyes and rubbed his chin. "I wrote to him soon after I arrived in Rheims, and as he had instructed me, I sent the letter with a private courier to the caliphal palace in Cairo. I wanted to inform him of where I was. Remember that when I left Fez, I was headed for Rome, but beyond that, I had no idea what path God had in mind for me.

"But, more important than that, I was eager to receive news from him. When we parted, he was leaving for Egypt with the forces of the caliph in Ifriqiya. They were on a mission of conquest. I was…*curious*…to learn the results."

"And…did he answer?"

Once again, looking away from his secretary and nodding his head, the pope said, "Yes…yes he did."

There was a long pause as the pope considered whether or not he would show Hakeem's letter to his secretary. Finally, he said, "As I previously explained to you, my correspondence with the mapmaker has not become part of the papal archive—for reasons I imagine you can appreciate. The rumors, remember? The pope consorts with the Saracens. He is the anti-Christ. But I have kept the letter with my personal belongings. I will read you my translation."

The pope went to his dresser. He took out a folded paper and began to read:

> Monk, my dear friend,
>
> Once I arrived in Mahdiya, I remained several weeks, waiting for my caliph to order the march to Egypt. It finally came in the dead of winter, during the month you call February. The expedition assembled in Raqqada, just beside the caliphal capital of Mahdiya. I remember it as if it were yesterday. Jawhar's tents were already

struck. The caliph, the Commander of the Faithful, mounted on a magnificent stallion, came out to meet his faithful commander Jawhar. It was something to behold. Jawhar appeared before the caliph, also mounted on horseback. He took his position at the caliph's left side. He dismounted, kissed the hand and foot of his sovereign.

The caliph commanded him to mount again. Jawhar obeyed and steadied his horse at the side of the caliph's mount. The caliph spoke at a level that only Jawhar could hear, apparently giving him detailed instructions for the campaign. Finally, in a commanding voice that could be heard by all present, he said, "Be off!" The expedition to conquer Egypt had begun. Jawhar's army marched into the delta of the great River Nile four months later.

You will be pleased to hear that there is much talk that Jawhar will establish an institution of higher learning. It will be called al-Azhar, the Most Luminous. At first, I thought I would remain in Egypt to be a part of that institution. But my desire to travel to those parts of the Islamic world that I had not yet seen, to continue gathering information and to add it to my "map of the world," was so strong that I decided I must leave. As I sign and seal this letter, my dear friend, I prepare to leave for the East. Continue to write to me here in Egypt. I will be back, God willing!

Hakeem Ibn al-Harith

"Was that the last time you heard from him?" Brother Anthony asked.

"*From* him, yes…but *about* him, no. He traveled to the end of the world and back, recording everything he saw, just as he did before we met. The scope of his work is almost unimaginable. I know this because of his book. At the end of his journey, he must have returned to Baghdad, where he compiled all that he learned in his travels in a book called *The Book of Routes and Kingdoms*. He finished his map of the Mediterranean. He drew other regional maps. And he drew a map of the world, not as he imagined it but as he actually saw it with his own eyes."

"Have you seen it, Holy Father, the map of the whole world?"

Again, the pope went to his dresser and pulled out a scroll. "I have never shown this to anyone. But yes. Not only have I seen it. He arranged for someone to send me a copy. Look."

He unrolled the scroll and spread it out on the table.

Brother Anthony was dumbfounded. He had no idea even how to phrase a question.

The pope continued, "If we look at the world as Hakeem drew it and divide it into four more or less equal quadrants, what we Christians know about is at best one-fourth of the world, the lower right-hand corner of the map."

Brother Anthony's mouth dropped open.

"Yes, Brother Anthony, the world is vast—larger than we can imagine. That Hakeem Ibn al-Harith knew it firsthand is even more remarkable."

"Do you think of him often, Holy Father?"

"I did for some time. But now, it must be twenty years or so since he has died. I believe he spent his last years in Cairo, at al-Azhar University. That was his dream."

The pope stood. He folded Hakeem's letter and rolled up his copy of the world map. Then he carefully put them both back into his dresser.

"Please, Brother Anthony, let's have another cup of tisane... One more thing—about the millennium. I don't think we have to worry about it for another thousand years."

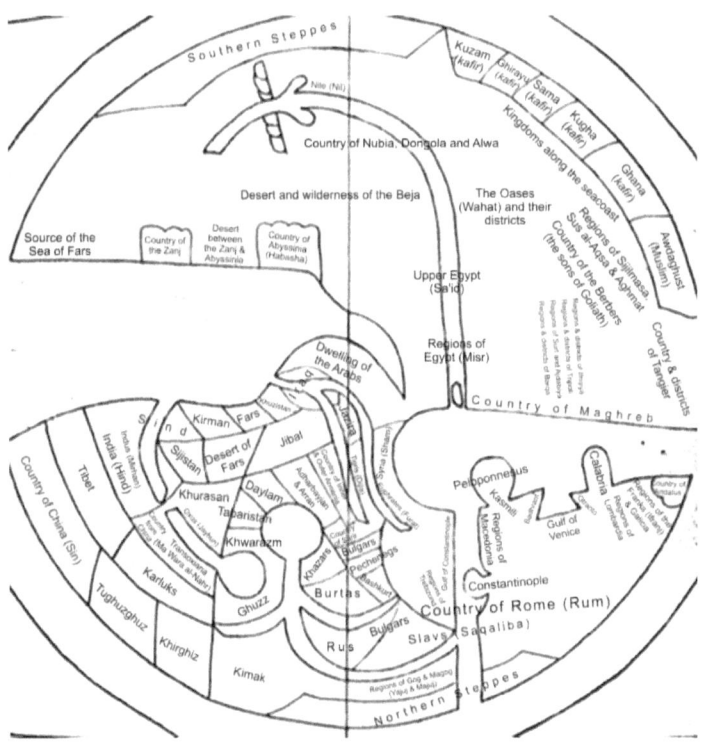

ACKNOWLEDGEMENTS

My interest in Islamic Studies began in my senior year at the University of Rhode Island largely due to the influence of a dedicated instructor, Richard Roughton. Not only were his lectures inspiring, but well beyond his classroom instruction, he agreed to tutor me in Arabic to better prepare me for graduate work at the University of Michigan. My major professor and mentor at Michigan was Professor Andrew Ehrenkreutz whose red pencil was literally and metaphorically as sharp as could be. He used it often, but always constructively and in friendship. To both of these men, I will always be grateful. There were several other great professors along the way, too many to mention here, who inspired me in my attempt to better understand the history and culture of the Islamic Middle East and North Africa.

Thanks to a Fulbright Fellowship in 1969-70, I spent nearly a year evenly divided between Morocco, Tunisia, and Egypt. It was in Cairo that I first met Ibn Hawqal, the medieval mapmaker on whom my mapmaker, Hakeem Ibn al-Harith, is based. A grant from the American Institute for Maghreb studies allowed me to spend the summer of 1985 in Morocco, much of it in Fez where I met Gerbert d'Aurillac; he was the future Pope Sylvester II who, according to local tradition, studied at the Qarawayeen University, allegedly the oldest university in the world. I am profoundly grateful for both of those grants.

Several of my professional colleagues provided invaluable service by reading all or parts of my manuscript. I mention especially Dr. June Hall McCash, Dr. David Rowe, Dr. Reuben Kyle, and Dr. Kenneth Perkins.

Thank you for your many helpful comments.

I thank members of the Murfreesboro Writers Group, dedicated writers of fiction who meet faithfully every Wednesday evening to share and critique each other's work. They patiently read along with me most of the manuscript at the rate of five pages a week for many, many weeks. From them I learned so much about writing fiction.

I am indebted to my editor Abby Webber and book designer Art Growden. Both have helped me present this story in the best possible light. Thank you. In the end, any errors are clearly my own.

Finally, I thank my wife Emily who was willing to share me with the mapmaker and the pope for many months.

Thank you, my readers, for choosing my book;
and thank you for any review you are able to post on Amazon.

For Further Reading
(a selective list)

Zayde Antrim,
Routes & Realms: The Power of Place in the Early Islamic World

J. Lennart Berggren and Alexander Jones,
Ptolemy's Geography

Nancy Marie Brown,
The Abacus and the Cross

Glen Van Brummelen,
Heavenly Mathematics

Richard Erdoes,
A.D. 1000, A World on the Brink of Apocalypse

Michael H. Harris,
History of Libraries of the Western World

Jonathan Lyons,
The House of Wisdom: How the Arabs Transformed Western Civilization

André Miquel,
La géographie humaine du monde musulman jusqu'au milieu du 11e siècle

Karen C. Pinto,
Medieval Islamic Maps, an Exploration

Edmond Pognon,
La vie quotidienne en l'an mille

Pierre Riché,
Gerbert d'Aurillac, le pape de l'an mil arris

About the Author

Ronald A. Messier is professor Emeritus in History at Middle Tennessee State University (MTSU) where he taught Islamic history and historical archaeology from 1972 to 2004 and was director of the Honors Program from 1982 to 1992. From 1992 to 2004, he was also adjunct professor at Vanderbilt University, and full time Senior Lecturer from 2004 to 2008. He received his MA and Ph.D. degrees from the University of Michigan. He is president of the advisory board for the Atlantic Institute of Tennessee. His teaching and research focus on Islam and the history and archaeology of the Middle East and North Africa. From 1987 to 1998, he directed the excavation of the ancient city of Sijilmasa in Morocco, famous for its gold trade and its contacts with Timbuktu. In recognition of that work, he received MTSU's prestigious Outstanding Research Award in 1997. He is currently directing an archaeology project at Aghmat, near Marrakech, Morocco. He has published over two dozen articles, co-edited with Hadia Dajani-Shakeel a book entitled *Jihad and its Times*. His recent publications include, *The Almoravids and the Meanings of Jihad*; *Jesus, One Man Two Faiths: a Dialogue between Christians and Muslims*; and *The Last Civilized Place: Sijilmasa and it's Saharan Destiny*, co-authored with James A. Miller, which won the the L. Carl Brown AIMS Book Prize in North African Studies for 2016. He has won several teaching awards including the CASE Tennessee Professor of the Year Award for 1993. Since 1992, he has been the lecturer for over forty study tours including twelve tours to Morocco, five to Israel, five to Spain, three to Syria and Jordan, three to Egypt, three to Tunisia, three to Turkey, one to Oman in the Persian Gulf, and two to Mali and Timbuktu.